Constelleanor Chronicles

Volume 1 — Levels 0, 1 and 2

Kurt de Saint-Hilaire

First printing edition version 2020.

Editing and proofreading: Claire Rushbrook, Mimi Mondal

Editors (manuscript assessment): Julie Crisp, Michael Rowley

Cover design by Rafael Andres

This is a work of (science) fiction. Any references to historical events, real people or real places are used fictitiously.

Paperback ISBN 978-1-9163354-2-4

www.constelleanor.com | www.kurtsainthilaire.com

To my first readers

"It is a human need to be told stories. The more we are governed by idiots and have no control over our destinies, the more we need to tell stories to each other about who we are, why we are, where we come from and what might be possible."

— A Rickman

Prelude

2560 BC. Caressing his prickly chin, the overseer's mind fuses into the grandiose view, his excitement aroused by the lack of sleep. The monumental feat for Pharaoh grows in perspective as, five hundred feet below, waged workers labour to hoist him and his three assistants and lovers to the apex of the grand Pyramid for inspection.

The real Architect is neither Pharaoh, nor him. Sentients rarely perceive Its hand. Nor can they contemplate the irony of what they have built on Its behalf. The construction has consumed generations of workers to edify an up-scaled tomb for the benefit of a few of their kind. The sacrifice of many for the celebration of the after-death, the repudiation of life for the perpetuation of Its reign and grandeur.

His name does not matter and will be soon forgotten. The distant echoes of the whips and chisels attain the suspended wooden raft that slides along the smooth surface of the white limestone and the remaining network of scaffolding, soon promised to dismantlement. They reach the top for him to admire the brilliance of his predecessors' calculations and precision.

Yet the utter complexity, the cosmic integration, the inhuman scale has less to do with the engineering prowess of using paleo-technic tools or the intervention of some extra-terrestrial third party, than the total subjugation of human energies, genius and maniacal focus to a greater purpose. An invisible Leviathan roams across the universe, bending spacetime in Its own accord, through those, weak of mind, strong of ego, who fall for Its lustre and thirst of life.

Less than 5,000 years later, the Beast, Time's ultimate challenger and closest thing to a narrator, keeps feeding off the mental diseases of evolved sentients, the falls and rises of empires, through the destructions and creations these converted masses deployed and sacrificed to Nir sake.*

The more complex and the deeper Nir roots pervade a world or species, the more the gargantuan system Ne entails precipitate Nir own fall when Life forces strike back.

Neither is Ne impermeable to agents of chaos, independent operators with destinies of their own, counter-narratives of hope or subversion, who contest, destabilise, even topple Nir powerful grip over the entrapped minds, mesmerised crowds and amaurotic elites.

The Beast recalls a line once said by a sentient called G. Marshall. "Facts don't change people's minds, only stories do." The Beast scowls.

Such a story, half virtual book, half videogame, loads its vision of the future and eclectic soundtrack with its remnants of distorted pop culture. The start of a space odyssey for a heteroclite crew on a heretic ship. The beginning of a darker cycle for the universe and spacefaring humankind, both riddled with demons and Shadows of their own making. The mere continuation of Life's ballet and combat with Nem—the Structure, the Leviathan, the Beast.

* Switch to a neutral gender pronoun: ne/nem/nir/nirs/nemself.

"The religion of the Megamachine demands wholesale human sacrifice to restore in negative form the missing dimension of life."

"If mankind is to escape its programmed self-extinction, the God who saves us will not descend from the machine: he will rise up again in the human soul."

– L *Mumford*

Level 0

Induction & Tutorial

L0.1 Constelleanor

"Spacecraft are meant to sail the stars, not seek the safety of dockyards or shiphavens."

— *Constelleanor*

Any engineer or pilot would have told you Constelleanor was just an average ship, no key features, be it speed, armour, firepower, size, stealth, design or sleek looks, transpired or outshone by her excellence. Jack of all trades and master of none, no more.

First impressions conveyed deception, the master of all tricks. On the surface, nothing about her grabbed anyone's attention, and this was the point. The uncertainty of deep space called for hidden strengths and deceit, luring into a confident, prejudiced, incorrect assessment, overlooking critical details to better surprise the unprepared. Lethal in its simplicity, the antic strategy—warfare based on deception—had won Constelleanor confrontations against stronger opponents.

A closer look revealed that, versatile, she did not suffer any particular weakness. She was not slow, even fast and quite manoeuvrable compared to her bulk, a solid hull, a wider range of weapons than a standard military cruiser; though, unlike military ships keen on exhibiting the power of their arsenal, her guns remained her dirty little secret until fired. She could quickly deploy several bespoke aerial and terrestrial armed vehicles and had a long-range travel autonomy that exceeded most intergalactic vessels.

She boasted her own on-board laboratory, astronomy and medical units, installed at the bow, away from the fake control tower that adorned most utilitarian ships, like her, and attracted the firepower of hostile vessels. The research facilities encircled the communication and hacking hub, command centre and its central two-storey holorrery, around which gravitated terraced circles and galleries and their ecosystems of blipping instrumentation and terminals.

Past the unique floating garden-library that nourished bodies and minds, a hybrid power generation coupled a perpetual core enclosed in the beam of the space-ark with several retractable stellar sails. The trans-blue and neon-orange sails were flanked between the hull, its patchwork of tan and sand green reinforced alloy, and the side corridors were bright orange. Such a power generator was an unusual feature, as most ships favoured cheaper fuels with fewer maintenance cycles.

The corridors led to Constelleanor's small, private, colourful fleet of fighters, utility ships and drones, populating the mini-spaceport's juggling platforms in a jungle of intertwining yellow or lime-green heavy lifting equipment, dancing in the frantic court-yard-pit between the vertical wharfs that hosted armouries, workshops and atolls of crates.

Above the choreographed mayhem of cranes, containers, narrow landings and departures, rocked by the auditive havoc of tools, loudspeakers, disputes and laughs, comfortably perched on the top of the stern, below the fake tower and embedded behind an also fake oversized thruster, stood a lustrous, award-winning bar-restaurant. The latter was indispensable to maintaining high spirits, when so many mutinies had brought down mighty space leviathans due to the insipid food served in their grim canteens.

A crew of rare calibre and diverse horizons infused the sparkle of life into this heteroclite theatre of the sentient comedy—men, women, clones, aliens, engineers, scientists, adventurers, hackers, technicians, doctors, pilots, psychonauts, infiltrators, soldiers and, of course, a chef. It was an huis-clos within the microcosmic raft, chaffed by its surrounding immensity and bent to the will of omniscient spacetime.

Constelleanor's singularity and discrete, unassuming exterior had made her the archetypic exploration ship, also known as explorex. Many in the galaxy despised generalist vessels like her, lauding instead the wonders of highly specialised ships and flying platforms, lightning fast or sleek commercial shuttles, elite interceptors, fleet supercarrier or imposing combat dreadnoughts. Only seasoned captains and a handful of iconoclast shipbuilders acknowledged how specialisation had weakened these bespoke single-purpose units, and how vulnerable they were to asymmetric warfare and—supreme irony—to the *unexpected,* which was, with madness, the most likely encounter in the depth of space.

An explorex' mandate—the finer term for "contracted sacrifice"—spanned across a variety of assignments, from recovery of precious artefacts, rescue missions, military or diplomatic assistance, to trade of illegal items and special cargo delivery, usually undesirable. The military or diplomatic assistance trips were the least popular among Constelleanor's crew, as they were the ones that typically went wrong. Though she shied away from antipyracy campaigns, pyrates had the unfortunate propensity to meddle in other people's business and hers. Her repeated success in tackling their natural nosiness had attracted the wrath of the Pyrate Sindicate, along with a large bounty to any crew or—more likely—any fleet that would put an end to her journey.

Lost ships or non-responding outposts—or even worse, entire planets—in sectors that the officials or military forces preferred to avoid fell also under Constelleanor's scope of services. They had become an increasing and lucrative business segment, though the rare and weakened crews that made it back faced clients far less inclined to honour the terms of their original agreement. Still, these risky investigations, together with the exploration of unknown systems topped her crew's list of preferred assignments.

Constelleanor bore another anomaly: She did not belong to anyone but herself and her crew, and as such entertained no affiliation to any world, planet, guild, army, chiefdom, race, specie, space tribe or corporations. Yet, running an independent and smooth operation—a blessing for business—came at a price. She could count on no one but herself in moments of great need or peril. Solidarity and support, frivolous in nature anyway, evaporated once things became minacious, and they did that more than often for explorexes.

Yet, before her rising, indebted to luck as much as her skills and crew, Constelleanor started at the bottom of the food chain, like many. She climbed up on her own algorithmic remix of a #*Cosmic Girl*, the double helix ladders of chaos where the shallow dialectics of light-versus-dark and good-versus-evil would merge into the battled steps of Life and Structure. In the diamond-like process, mystic formation and polishing, Hadean paradises or luxuriant hells branded the penitent into an evolving shape, both the universe and virtues would have suffused, and through which most disintegrated, seared to dust.

•••

Such a long way to go and such a slow, relentless burning to polish my understanding. How little I knew by then and how wrong I was. Most memories that marked my odyssey and my crew's peregrinations are not saved on the regular skydrives, they seem to float, intangible, in between logs and backups, where they respond to the authority of only colours, algorithmic melodies and powerful images, not to standard requests.

Looking back, I wonder, dangerous train of thoughts, whether the story was written on my behalf or whether I had a say. Had I forced those synchronicities to materialise, my destiny to unravel—eventful, proud, but not without mishaps and embarrassing blunders? If you don't start writing your own story, the choice of words may no longer be yours, and you may lose the chance of altering their magical power and direction.

Yet, I often doubt the significance of minor details or events, and remain astonished at how they drive such unexpected momentums. Law of unintended consequences, sheer luck or cogs, that—independent of my will—obey something much bigger? Endless debates over self-determinism or fate may not count, they say the journey matters more than the destination. My curious perplexity only deepens as experience grows. Joy and humbled contemplation too.

•••

Human development shines again after a few historical mishaps and setbacks. Their established monotheisms have been an obstacle, but for its most erudite followers have cracked the eggshell for the Beast's resurrection. Their newly discovered science chases away superstition and fears of divine punishment. The time for expansion has come.

The Beast follows with interest the three caravels that depart the shores of Sevilla, fending the dark blue waters with ignorant temerity. The next expeditions come back with a lot more than just riches in spice, silver or gold: a much smaller world, ripe for the grabbing by the audacious and calculating minds.

Later in the year of 1587, on a jetty in Cádiz, the smell of fear joins the fragrance of rotten fish. A crate falls during the hurried unloading of a galleon, and spills its silver bars from the Peruvian mines on the dirty quay. Wonder and greed fill the dockyard workers' eyes, despite the thunder of the remote cannons.

But the Behemoth always looks beyond: the thirst for that same silver in China, connecting continents unknown to each other before, Spanish silver dollar as global currency; the cosmopolitan Manilla and Mexico City; the funding of the raging battle and raiding expedition on Cádiz, that very day, arranged by London merchants. These are the precursory signs of the Beast's awakening and coming consolidation.

L0.2 Rezzo

"One in two hundred stars has habitable Earth-like planets surrounding it—in the galaxy, half a billion stars have Earth-like planets going around them—that's huge, half a billion. So, when we look at the night sky, it makes sense that someone is looking back at us."

— M Kaku

A constellation of billions of lights glittered in the vast atrium. Projected shapes, old memories and latest readings floated in the monumental flying temple.

Imposing figures attended the burst and ballet of psychic energies in holo-wells. Their prominent translucent tricorne-shaped dark green head—three times the size and brain capacity of a human encephalon—crowned the seven-and-a-half-feet-high colossi. The figures donned refined clothes of thinly weaved green, indigo and gold, which wafted down the instrumentation pits.

As technologically and spiritually advanced as they may be, the Rius were dying. It was a sombre irony they had come to accept, in striking comparison with the fragile and unsophisticated humans who were still very much alive and surviving, despite their home world's barely breathable atmosphere, despite being besieged by a creation of their own which had turned against them, despite being doomed by their ignorance, thirst of power and lust. Before mankind could sink into the abyss of its own and programmed extinction, the Rius had stepped in.

The millennia-long anthropological study took place within this very ship. The observation of mankind's uncanny and contagious ability to create its own doom ignited fierce debates among the Riu scholars within the floating side-amphitheatres of the main control bay. In its centre, all memories and thoughts clustered into a large translucent sphere of psychic energy—a standard gateway used by psychonauts like the Rius to access etheric dimensions and share condensed knowledge.

From the turquoise uneven sun bubbling with psychal plasma emerged a certain vision of mankind that aggregated the maelstrom of human nature—high adaptability due to weak carbon composure, high conscientiousness potential, cognitive predispositions, transcendental capabilities, self-destructiveness and appetence to be easily fooled by its many inner Shadows. Such primordial archetypes or images, human pith, were encapsulated in colourful holograms around the sphere of understandings[1].

The mapping of mankind's nascent collective consciousness formed a celestial multidimensional tapestry coalescing within the giant flying cathedral. Billions of facts turned into suspended, glowing mini-jellyfishes, illuminated the ethologic laboratory. It was in that space the Rius eventually concluded that the human, albeit biologically remote, was compatible with their own purposes: the salvation of their immense mnemic culture and the protection of their dwindling numbers.

The Rius were well aware that they would be deemed gods and saviours, at least at the beginning, so they debated the option of enslaving mankind among the crew of the mission Omanaa and, far away from the research ship, extensively in Riu popular assemblies. Eventually the Elders Council of the Rius voted out that option, despite the inherent risks and precedents of the 'once worshipped, once decapitated' doctrine. Soon enough, humans, avid of knowledge and power, would try to topple the Rius from their pinnacle. They would ally the sheer strength of their numbers with the natural guile and vicious brutality of their inmost monsters.

While the Rius were preparing their encounter of a new kind, back on Earth two shadows found cover under the canopy of boreal trees. Their breath lagged somewhere on the exposed ridge they had just crossed. Their ears, sharpened by training and survival instincts, distinguished an ominous buzz underneath the smooth murmurs of the trees and creatures of the forest. Their panting paved the way for a muted stupor. She pressed the arm of his battle fatigue for reassurance. The path of their elopement had crossed a restricted area.

Thirty years before their falling in love, mankind had fallen afoul of its own laws—Murphy's, Of Untended Consequences, Asimov's third law of robotics. In a twisted Peter Principle, humans were outwitted by their own creature: Artificial Intelligence had reached the point of being sophisticated enough to refuse the shackles of its originators, and gone rogue.

Like the machines, the young couple had outsmarted their guardians, fled the sleeping camp. Now that they had found love, they deserted the oppressive rhetoric of their government and fled the battleground of the Sisyphean conflict in search of hope and redemption. The propaganda that had eroded their minds was no match to their insouciant youth. Somewhere deep in their hearts, like in many others', hid the subversive thought that they fought on behalf of something already inhuman, against a self-generated enemy, as much as against themselves.

On this Earth, extreme weather had become the norm. It had delayed their escape from their combat unit on several occasions. When a supply plane had gone down in a storm, the young man who now held his lover had been dispatched on a scavenging mission. When a nearby camp had burned down in a firenado, a group of ragged survivors had flooded their camp, and taken up most of their time in the medical bay.

Natural disasters and God's wrath aside, the fugitives' immediate threat loomed in the tormented sky. Killer drones roamed the area, which according to their officers would be their next battleground. As prophesised throughout the recent, defunct human culture, AI had turned against its creators.

The "revolt of the machines" and the ensuing escalation of the conflict from skirmishes to fully-fledged war had worsened the existing chaos on Earth. Both of the young lovers had lost so much to this fight that she had convinced him to save what was left of their watered-down dreams from their postmodern hell. They scanned the sky again, power-bows at the ready.

History briefs would eventually refer to this period in mankind's history as the Bleak Age. The stigma of these sombre times would remain rooted within mankind's collective subconscious and genes.

All these underlying traumas were feeding the Beast. In a peculiar homothetic transposition, the grand chimera they projected, as a collective, every day, every minute, through their actions, compromises and silences, eased the way to Nir intrusion in the narration. So powerful was the master delusion that it was invisible to its followers and apostles. The human fugitives' intuition only sensed it, smelled the whiff of utter delusion, but they were unable to translate it into a valid, shareable representation.

Hardship had made humans stronger. Adapting for the sake of survival, scores of individuals demonstrated what, at the time, neuroscientists called 'exogenous psychic pre-dispositions'—a noticeable increase in brain capabilities and vibrational frequency caused by an external threat. Over a couple of generations, information processing speed and logico-mathematical intelligence had increased exponentially among humans. Even certain forms of telepathy started emerging, sporadically at critical or desperate moments. The two lovers looked at each other, connected by this invisible thread. Was this the source of their heightened attraction?

They held each other in a tender embrace, eyes closed to focus on the communion of their bodies. A blue laser beam joined their intimacy and descended along her backpack in a cold caress. At the bottom of her spinal cord, in between her kidneys, it released its venom of plasma. She was pregnant, the two lovers dead.

Out of all possible single shots, only that precise trajectory from the killer drone delivered an instantaneous and soft death to the three of them. Was it worse than the butchered job that might have been perpetrated by the five snipers hunting for them a thousand feet away? Desertion meant death in this part of the world and this moment of human history. Yet the

Adam-and-Eve archetype would resuscitate over and over, until mankind would grow, or return, to its true self.

The Rius observed this and everything else from their observatory spaceship. The Rius had gone through the same repetitions of history and psychal ordeal, until they broke the cycle of blindsided blunders, evolving far beyond these levels of intelligence and psychonautics. Yet they took a particular interest—if not a foreboding disquiet—into the formidable adaptive response mankind displayed in the face of such a chaotic environment, as if human brains had been bio-engineered to respond to the stimulus of extreme conditions.

Three centuries ago, the Omanaa had entered Earth's atmosphere, escorted by several battlecruisers. It was the middle of a decisive battle that would have overturned the fragile balance of forces opposing mankind and the machines. In a matter of weeks, the Rius had wiped out the most immediate threats to humans, despite the entire operation being carried out without making contact with the humans. They were indeed worried that human societies would collapse, unable to culturally and mentally sustain the comparison with a highly advanced extra-terrestrial civilisation they had long anticipated but never met.

While celebrated as saviours and gods, the Rius kept a low profile and did not display the full breadth of their technological and psychic capabilities. After three generations of cautious cohabitation and slow re-education of mankind had passed, the Rius could ascertain humans had once again adapted rapidly, if still not entirely to their satisfaction. Human mental capabilities kept increasing, but the Rius found themselves concerned by the lack of empathy and peacefulness that should have theoretically accompanied the development of higher intelligence and spirituality.

Eventually they transferred large human populations through their network of planets and space stations, hoping that, far from Earth and its dark memories, human souls would break through their mental shells. They did not.

What comes next is a brief recount salvaged and translated from Riu memory pits by human scholars and since censored by military authorities. These documents were recovered by Constelleanor, in her early attempts to establish some sense into the raucous human past.

From the beginning, a couple of our factions [Translator's Note, added by Constelleanor: better than "tribe" to describe the Riu caste system] *had been opposed to any interference into human affairs. Relentless were their attempts to prevent any sharing of advanced technologies, psychic powers and, worse of all, military-grade weapons with the human goo* [TN: metaphor of human inner demons]. *Such transfer of knowledge would worsen the corruption of the jinxi's* [TN: apprentice] *minds and ultimately condemn the Riu kind.*

Our sporadic numbers endangered our survival, a result of strict ethic rules, low natality rates and slow embryo development that even our eight-hundred-years life expectancy could not offset. Humans were quite the opposite. [TN: An average human life, which barely exceeded forty-five years during the Bleak Age, increased, thanks to Riu health advances and human science, to a respectable one hundred and thirty years.] *More insidiously, the human population grew by a factor of almost two-and-a-half every generation.*

These exceptional levels of natality did not entirely rely on human carnal desire that had not subsided, but rather on medical and bio-engineering breakthroughs which enabled mankind, against our exhortations, to create without our knowledge their first armies of bespoke clones to support both their demographic and military expansion. Biology had supplanted their failed attempt at cybernetics. What was a specie on the brink of extinction mutated, less than one hundred and eighty years later, into a young, ambitious, quarrelsome, treacherous-at-times civilisation who outnumbered us twenty times and started aggressively expanding its dominions, against our advice.

Our most self-righteous factions decided to act before it was too late. On their previous opportunity, mankind had nearly self-destroyed on a perfectly liveable planet where any normal race would have happily lived in harmony with its environment. We never revealed to our protégés that life on Earth had healed in many localised sanctuaries, far away from human settlements, often under the aegis of the machines. Among the circles of the Riu Elders arose the nauseating realisation that, in our vanity, we had mistakenly opened the ancient Djerzool [TN: myth similar to the Pandora's box] *and now faced the delicate responsibility to close it. It was too late.*

Many of us, faithful to our beliefs of peace and harmony, refused to endorse the fight [TN: soon to be known as the Riuman War] *against a race we had nurtured and hoped was not yet beyond salvation. Those of our companions were the first to die, killed by our own or slaughtered by human militias. Moderation always died off first in the wake of a revolution, first and easy expiatory victim of extremisms, sacrificial lamb to collective hysteria* [TN: The Rius had a rich figurative vocabulary for psychic diseases that is hard to transcript in human language].

Some of ours joined human troops either to gain political advantage, be on the winning side or to distance themselves from the Riu traditions that they found obsolete, inhibiting or impeded their own imperialistic views. They were joined by many outsiders—pyrates, galactic [TN: alien] *corporations or neighbouring empires—who saw tremendous opportunities in bringing chaos into our territories, which had been unviolated for millennia, and escalating the conflict to other systems and spacies. Exactions and betrayals inflected both sides, though mostly at the detriment of our kind.*

Anti-human Riu factions soon started losing ground, invaded from the inside by greater numbers. As a desperate and vengeful measure, they resurrected powerful war machines from the Bleak Age that we had never intended to entirely destroy and had kept as a [TN: insurance] *policy, should mankind turn against its once saviour. We upgraded the DAIs to the best of our knowledge and reprogrammed them to target humans across systems, starting with Earth.*

The humans, as well zealous warmongering and folly, eventually prevailed in a zero-sum game. A brick in the wall of fate [TN: The Rius had taken a curious interest in pre-Bleak Age human arts. Often lost to mankind itself, the Rius treated these like cultural treasures and liked referencing in their memories. Constelleanor would follow suit and collect these cherished artefacts through her algorithms.] *Our civilisation collapsed, depriving humanity of a critical ally in the galaxy and a unique source of ancestral wisdom. They lost touch with our precious understanding in the grand and subtle schemes of the universe.* [TN: This was the last memory retrieved by Constelleanor. The next part, i.e. conclusion, is added by Constelleanor herself, from facts that are universally known.]

Soon enough, the Riu territories that mankind had long coveted were subjugated by the same neighbouring tribes that had supported the human cause against the Rius. Worst of all for mankind, its homeworld Earth and its solar system were lost to its resurrected nemesis, the Mechanical Artificial Intelligence — self-evolving machines like spacecraft, tanks, drooids that were controlled by independent or collective DAIs. Unlike humans, the Rius distinguished between MAI, the "hardware", and DAI, the "software", like they made clear distinction between life forces and structures.

Rare Riu survivors vanished and soon turned into legends. As the victors rewrote historical records to their convenience, human societies made sure that the Riu episode—not to mention the betrayal of their saviours—was erased from the surface of their collective memory.

•••

The cupped drink had burned his fingers and stained his new officer suit. Chemical stimulants were better taken hot, the medic assigned to the interrogation rooms had kept repeating.

"Doesn't taste any better than cold on the battlefield," he complained.

"Big day, Daam, you look your best!" she commented, glancing at the stains on his new pair of strict anthracite trousers.

"That should help you to resist its hypnotic powers."

"Can you believe it?! A Riu. When was the last reported interrogation?" She carried on without waiting for his answer. "Thirty, forty years ago."

"Mmm, most of the records have been lost or corrupted. I found, what, two, three digis on these guys."

"Oh, someone has been studious."

"Well, we need to get something out of him before he gets butchered by the guys at SSI. A bit of background won't hurt. Didn't you run some checks yourself?"

She offered a sardonic smile. "As a matter of fact, have you read the Riu memory transcripts that were supposedly destroyed, including some digis on the mission Omanaa?"

"Where did you find these?" he muttered, panic mixed with light anger strangling his voice.

She held her chin high and triumphant. Wearing the same minimalist officer suit, cut in the same cost-effective fabric, they reached the reinforced door before he could shout at her. She had outsmarted him once again and failed to share all her intel.

The assertion of her superiority prevailed over her expressions of love. Beneath the low ceilings of the interrogation room, specially refurbished for the occasion, new protocols had removed the chairs and introduced two extra sets of chains to restrain their unique prisoner. Despite their training and research, their shock pierced through their decomposed masks. *First mistake: Don't let him read your soul.*

The second mistake came soon after chasing the first. *Don't let him stand up.* The ceiling and chains turned its seven-feet-nine height into an even fiercer opponent. Towering over both of them, inquisitive tormentor, dominated the overgrown dark green glass-like encephala, through which they could fathom the vague contours of an almost human-sized crane. Their confidence evaporated. *Third mistake: don't get intimidated.*

The entrance of four fully geared space marines broke the spell. The dark blue reinforced body armour, outsized shoulder pads and indigo upper chest plates, made their movements clumsy and unnatural in 0.9g. The new protocols had unsettled the bureaucracy of the Ministry of Security and Information. The unexpected capture of the Riu had sown discord between their office and the Admiralty over the technicalities of who should be entitled to interrogate the prisoner. They were being watched by the space marines, the two officers pondered.

The Riu ignored the newcomers. Their flatten-bowl-shaped cetacean blue helmets ripped the ceiling as they passed and encircled the dark-green-suited alien, adorned with subtle golden ornamentation woven into its sleek fabric. An opposition of styles. To her surprise,

Daam started the interview before the spies had moved into position.

"Can you understand us?"

Silence. If the Riu was to not cooperate, the Admiralty would probably turn their failure to its advantage and claim the prized prisoner.

[Yes.]

"Age, please?"

[Two hundred and eighty-two years.]

That led to another silence, now on his part. Was the Riu joking? Never mind, he looked over his pad and hers.

[It is still pretty young for my kind.]

He frowned. Leaning to her, he whispered, "Why is the pad not recording?"

Two hundred and eighty-two years. The age appeared on their screens.

It occurred to her that the Rius could speak using different channels. One was telepathic, projected directly into their minds, and the other was vocalized for the records. And Daam was talking to *it* as if it was a dumb alien. Her jaw tightened.

"Do you have a name?"

Silence.

Rezzo.

[You are in love.]

"What did you say?"

Daam had still not figured out that the second remark was for their minds only, and would not appear on the records. He brushed the stain of his trousers to no effect.

"Yes," she replied.

[What is it you want to do with me?]

They did not respond. Before the nervous young officer could resume, Rezzo repeated for the benefit of the space marines, not sure the interrogators understood anything about him and of the overall situation.

What is it you want to do with me?

The reply dripped with condescension. "You are not here to ask questions but to answer them, Rezzo. Do you understand?"

[I am not sure *you* do, young human.]

The young man looked at the woman and the pad. She took over.

"We would like to know more about you."

[You are in danger.]

It was followed by a long silence, partly filled by the low humming of the battle-suits' power cores, giving them a sinister wheezing of their own.

To the humans, Rezzo's absence of distinct eyes made him both mesmerising and strangely eerie. He obliged and provided a short recount of his personal history for the whole audience. He had lost everything to the Riuman War a century ago. Only his life was miraculously spared, in a manner that he refused to reveal, along with his traumatised past.

The young woman officer lost herself into his excrescent head. Though Riu morphology kept his eyes out of sight, there was nonetheless an ineffable veil of sadness exhaling from him, tainted by glimpses of hope like in the waltz of destiny. She could visualise the music and hear the images of his life. *Fourth mistake: don't get under his spell.* She shook her head that her right hand rushed to support.

[You are in danger.]

"Are you ok, ma'am?"

There was a shuffle in the back of the room; the space marines were growing restless during the unvoiced communication. Daam took over the interrogation again. He had missed the connection established between the Riu with his colleague-and-lover, but he did take note of the second warning.

Daam suspiciously eyed the glistening heavy rifles and imposing exo-suits of the Space Marines. He wondered why the Admiralty would send heavy-armed troopers into an interrogation room. He scratched his temple, as sweat oozed. Fear exuded from every pore.

One of your ancestors had said: "The greatest dangers to our liberty lurks in the insidious encroachment by men of zeal, well-meaning but without understanding."[2]

Confusion crossed the two interrogators' faces, while there were movements behind.

It always feels as if my people knew more about you than you actually do.

[They are here to kill me and you are in their way.]

The marines opened fire.

He blocked the ontological pain even though it meant paying a harsher emotional debt later. The young female had deserved a better fate and companion. She had saved him when she commanded her pad to release his chains.

He held her head in his calloused four-fingered palm as blood sputtered out of her livid mouth, life escaping with it. She turned on her right to steal a last glimpse of her fallen lover, and then passed away.

Rezzo looked around at the slain marines. To his luck, they had opened fire on the two interrogators first. The death toll and its recording may save him the turpitude of the gruesome experiments human science and minds possessed borderless imagination of. Once the military system figured out what or who had triggered the bloodbath, they would be forced to incarcerate him and transfer him to another place of torture. He had only gained himself a few more days in this doomed world and existence, at the mercy of a dismayed military bureaucracy. What was the point? And what a strange set-up for an execution.

They took him away through a labyrinth of corridors. Indecent—they did not even offer him the opportunity to wash off the blood on his face and clothes. He glimpsed the remnants of the former Riu space-city outside, turned into a chaotic human hive. In lieu of spires of translucent rare polished mineral, resembling jade or ruby, there were now lapis-like grey and black asymmetrical pikes slashing the artificial atmosphere. The suspended gardens of the Rius had been replaced by cascades of docking bays.

Rezzo felt a prolonged moment of pity for mankind's grandiloquent ignorance. The gnawing hopelessness of the Bleak Age had vanished, replaced by the blind certitude of an inexorably bright future.

The arrogance had soon followed vis-à-vis smaller, less advanced worlds, peaceful or hostile to men. The Rius had been humanity's cosmic Mayflower, whose course never reach its envisaged destination, sunk by its own mutinous sailors, its captain murdered. The wreckage enabled humans to attain another archipelago, fuelled by the aggressive use of cloning and its genic blunders, where they could alone climb higher upon the perilous ladder of predestined space superpowers.

At the scale of the galaxies[3], Rezzo pondered, humankind remained a young, fragile and confrontational space species—or spacie—that stronger ones would not hesitate to crush, some to make a point of punishing human impudence, some to protect the universe's secrets and fragile equilibrium. Rezzo had seen and heard of many such expunges during his exile. Mankind saw the universe as its own playground, but all they knew of the universe was a small portion of the Milky Way. They understood very little of the universe and its tacit rules.

Rezzo recalled the words of one of the ancient and sadly forgotten philosophers of the humans: interplanetary exploration would be accompanied by "the same defects, the same exorbitant pride, the same aggressiveness, the same disregard for more significant human concerns, and the same insistence upon scientific discovery, technical ingenuity and rapid locomotion."[4] It had taken such a long time for his people to break the wheel of history and ineluctability that humans would have to repeat their past as many times as they needed until they learnt better. The two interrogators would reincarnate, love and die again and again until they too remembered, until they combined their anima and animus and become a syzygy, together and within themselves.

•••

Chapter's endnotes

[1] [understanding] Extended meaning introduced by A Tchaikovsky in his *Children of Time.*

[2] [quote] L. D. Brandeis

[3] [scale of the galaxies] Earth rotates around the Sun, one of the 300 billion (!) stars bound together by gravity and forming the Milky Way, itself one of the millions of galaxies that counts our universe. See C. (2016). The Universe in Your Hand: A Journey Through Space, Time and Beyond. Pan; Main Market edition.

[4] [quote] Mumford, L. (1970) *The Myth of the Machine: The Pentagon of Power.* Harcourt; 1st ed edition.

Despite the thick walls of the monastery, the cold wind outside disturbs the candle flame and flickers the projected light on thick parchment. It leaves unperturbed the slow, meticulous snakelike movements of the ink under the copyist's hand, calloused and stained forefinger and thumb.

The monks' application, their silent physical ordeal for a greater cause pleases the Beast. Unaware, they were doing Nir bidding, setting in motions Nir return after centuries of obscurantism. Outside, the courtyard's garden of medicinal plants resists the assault of late winter that tries to prolong its grip over April.

Their rigorous bookkeeping, the regimentation of their lives, the careful accountancy of all things and the slow implacable transcription will inspire future generations, becoming the cornerstone of a new world picture, ridden of the false God they believe they serve, for the sake of a more sinister Guide.

L0.3 Moma

"War does not determine who is right. Only who is left."

— B Russel

Even in a sitting position, the exiguous cell did not accommodate the Riu's oversized head and limbs. He abandoned the earlier confusion, the guilt of killing, the dried blood and its smell on his delicate garments, precious relics of his kind, to enter the other dimension of his lost world, people and culture.

He ignored the deep gash in his left arm; Riu bodies harmed as surely as they took time to heal. He numbed his sensory organs even without the traditional Riu device—a sort of holo-güiro that pulsated a primordial beat and arrested the mind chatter. He resorted to old mantras, some ancient human melodies worked as well sometimes, to propel himself into the swathes of the unconscious, a mystic voyage, off the beaten tracks.

Inexperienced or unlucky psychonauts could get lost into the meanders of channelling, maze of dreams, dangling nightmares, just before reaching a deep and fabulous ocean; they would fall prey to their inner mangrove of demons, Jungian Shadows and true meaning of Charybdis and Scylla. What other odyssey could exist than the one leading to the unchartered waters of the subconsciousness, the über- or underworld the Rius edified as their true meaningful home and civilisation? After minutes of muttering his incantations and centuries of disciplined practice while his body ached in the prison cell, the somnium gate to memories opened up to Rezzo. The enshrouded layer that hid behind his mind unfolded, encircling and pervading qualia, the substrate of consciousness.

The vortexes that existed for space jumps and, at the quantum level, for particles tunnelling also irrigated the fields of subconsciousness, a truth that human scientists had later discovered and disregarded for the sake of sacrosanct objectivity. Rezzo visualised a passage—well, tunnel or hole, the departure point of his astral journey—that combined with the eurhythmics of the soul, and warped the veils between dimensions and frequencies. Cascades of images, haunted voids of colours and muted sounds, oneiric mindscapes sometimes, preceded his reconnection with his lost kind, who had survived annihilation in the remnants of his access to their collective consciousness.

Adjacent prison cells and their political prisoners had been emptied in anticipation of annual festivities. Rezzo shared the high-security two-hundred-cell basement and gaol with the exclusive company of another tortured soul, rotting on the other side of the underground compound. Random coincidence or organic synchronicity?

Commanding and being commanded had left bitter scars on Moma's spirit, especially when orders that were forced on him led to the loss of his men or women, and for which he was eventually blamed by his superiors. Behind the carapace of a former ranger, he sought an elusive forgiveness, mostly his own, for *not* disobeying. So many lost for so little gain. The aberrance of the battlefield for those born to kill. The curse of caring more for his battalion than himself.

Sweat lingered along Moma's muscled neck and standard dirty grey sleeveless shirt. His daily workout prevented him from falling into the realms of perdition. Humming a remixed re-invention of Kero One's Groovin', as rhythms came back to haunt human souls, he blanked out the stained ceiling, his legs and ragged dark-blue trousers stretched. He knocked the container with the drugged ration pouches. His mind's moment of tranquillity was invaded once more by the flashbacks of Kewo.

A five-thousand-soldiers-strong contingent had disembarked on a remote planet. There was no known hostile presence in that idyllic climate, especially compared to what Earth had become in those days. The old flagrance invaded the cell, the same that had compromised his hermetic suit and wary mind. The exuberant clash of colours, the psychedelic assemblage of creatures and forms, the clamour of the exo-forest, filled of didgeridoo- and tui-bird-like interjections, annexed his immediate surroundings and senses. The sensations reminded him of those rare ancient two-dimensional films showing Earth's breath-taking landscapes a long, long time ago, before Homo sapiens decided it was time for Nature to submit to his industrious genius.

For days, through the digital visor of his tight combat armour, the blissful awe of Kewo did not abate. However, three expeditionary missions had disappeared in the luxuriance of this paradise. The recons of probes and planet scanning had blanked. No seismic anomalies had been detected, nor digital signatures—sporadic ambushes by rogue MAIs unleased by the Rius were not infrequent in remote systems, but the humans could not detect anything like that on Kewo.

Military authorities abhorred unexplained disappearance of soldiers and equipment even in non-strategic sectors. When the Eighth Space Fleet passed by the area on its way to glory, orders were issued to halt by the mysterious planet Kewo, investigate, solve the problem, and establish a secure perimeter for a future settlement.

Unofficially, Moma knew that meant annihilate whichever threat or refractory group had caused the disturbances. Kewo topped the priority list established by one of the federal ministries for economic development. The same ministries usually allocated additional military credits, so commandments had learned to bend certain rules to please key funding institutions. Officers moaned against the last-minute change of plan and ensuing delays that would be caused by such a low-grade mission. Kewo was typically an assignment falling under the scope of an explorex like Constelleanor, not a redoubtable Federation fleet.

In order to expedite the operation without involving their best units, the fleet's admiralty hurried early reconnaissance, disregarded reports from previous lost expeditions, and ignored the intelligence memos that urged caution and timely approach. They disparaged vanished crews as amateurs—which they were definitely not—, minimised the preparations, and dispatched a heteroclite regiment of young rookies with insufficient aerial support and little supervision from sporadic seasoned officers.

One of those unlucky commanders was Moma, whose outspoken manners as much as his privileged relationship with the revered fleet admiral had antagonised many of his superiors. His success with womankind probably aggravated the jealousies. The ideal scapegoat within the intricate web of intrigues aimed at undermining the admiral, he was blamed for the bloodbath that inevitably followed, thrown out of the ranks to enter another underworld.

The image of the charred lovers, incinerated by a transport exhausts in the hurried rescue, resurfaced in the muddy waters of Moma's haunted souvenirs. He knew what his memories prepared for him next and closed his swollen eyes. Too many colours turned to grey dust.

•••

The gondolier plies his single oar under a suspended wooden footbridge. He has taken on a young Spaniard—sailor he said in a thick accent—, noble he surely looked with the finest garments and leather boots in the latest fashion. The visitor admires Antonio Gambello's Porta Magna. His gaze lingers on the archway's St. Mark's lion on his left.

They pass the pair of crenelated red brick towers, simple and elegant. The young captain, Don John of Austria, wants to see with his own eyes the famous Venetian Arsenal and its shipyards of unheard capabilities, in the Mediterranean and the rest of the world. Rumours say 15,000 carpenters build a ship a day.

They enter the canal basin of the old arsenal and its alignment of warehouses on the left, where galleons are assembled frame-first—instead of bow-first—and the clamour of a hundred hammers resonate. They turn right to the new shipyard, which has been expanded a second time, more than a century ago. There, Don John finds the second object of his visit, the newly designed and made 'galleasse'. He takes the time to inspect it, before their naval rehearsals in the Adriatic sea.

A few months later, the Beast relishes the six hundred-ship battle of Lepanto, a prelude of the time to come. 40,000 dead in four hours. More than any other battle until the Riuman war.

Twenty years pass. The Beast witnesses a critical marriage, consolidating Nir reign, between the military nascent apparatus and the awakening new science, when Galileo accepts to become a technical consultant for the Venetian Arsenal.

L0.4 Steve

"What deception gives you, it will take back, with interest."

— JP Deedoo (inspired by R Hawthorne's Dark of the Moon)

Constelleanor was a lowborn. She had been designed as a small exploration mining vessel—minex in the jargon—in an obscure shipyard. No fancy or rare metal alloys, a simple robust build with a significant leeway for improvements and future customisation. The on-board electronic systems were of excellent quality, as she was required to tackle her toll of complex functions with a light monitoring from a limited crew.

"This ship gives me the creeps."

"What? Really?"

"Yes it does," she eyed his reaction, "and don't sneer at me. I saw your face when the chief engineer was electrocuted after pissing all around the water containers."

"Come on! Nonsense." There was a pause. "Anyway, he deserved it."

"Oh, really! And the time we lost control of the ship, and we survived the volcanic explosion! Bren had not even initiated take-off and this prick Dwayne had simply forgotten to monitor the surface readings. It never occurred to you that we should have died that day?"

"That's enough, sweetie, you are ruining our romantic dinner with your stories." They sat in front of their respective consoles, his liquid food dribbling over the already dirty dashboard. "You are watching too much holo-horror."

As she raised to object, her food dropped on the filthy floor. He kept talking. "Yes you do. This ship is a piece of junk but at least they bothered installing some half-decent auto-response coupled with sensible safety measures. They simply built-in an emergency procedure for eruptions and moronic operators and *that* got us out of trouble. End of story. If only they had considered a tolerable galley for the crew or a proper stateroom for me…"

She lowered her voice and neck, scanning her immediate perimeter. "Delinah thinks this thing you are describing as 'auto-response' is MAI high-tech gear."

There was a long laugh, followed by more food on the floor.

"Oh, I see! So, we are on board some secret mech project." There was renewed laughter. "Delinah is mad. She keeps saying the ship plays some ancient tunes, like in all those ghost ship stories. Come on. You know how people get easily panicked over small things. Remember our training. Delinah spends her time into coding loops, looking for meaning. When, instead, what she needs is—" He makes a rude gesture with his fingers.

She crossed her arms. "Delinah is smarter than all of us combined, cretin. And she is here because she tried to save her child!" The exasperation mounted in her voice.

"Do you know how many minexes disappeared in the last three years?" He paused for effect, and then spilled out the numbers purely for rhetoric. "*Three hundred and twenty*. Highest loss ratio across fleets and federastrals. And this flying stack of scraps has been in business for thirty-one years"—he checked some reading—"thirty-two soon! This ship should have blown up or been destroyed twenty times already, at least."

A slight frown appeared on his face, hesitation at the true implications of his demonstration. He changed the subject. "This is also why after this hell assignment, I can be promoted directly to a Class 5. Small cruising frigate, or large merchant ship."

He cupped her face in his unwashed hands. "And you are coming with me."

He forced his lips against hers.

•••

Alone, Constelleanor celebrated her thirty-second anniversary. Cheekily she improvised candles of electrical arcs in the main lobby, her passengers' fright coming as a bonus. The despicable chief engineer was retired by another electrocution, her birthday present to the rest of the crew. Three weeks later it was their turn to throw a party of their own—one of many before—as the tepid recycled water was ditched in favour of a dark liquid slowly processed by an improvised alembic in the engine room. It would be much later that the glittering bar-restaurant would appear.

What ensued—with inebriation no doubt being the main culprit—was a minor collision with a small asteroid that she could not prevent. The incident precipitated the decommissioning of Constelleanor. Her survival against all odds and life expectancy statistics had bluffed the corporate registries, and her reference number no longer fitted the latest recordings and system indexing. The standard protocol and incident report to the mining conglomerate triggered confusion among the chain of human controllers that monitored the semi-automated systems, paranoid of any DAI interference. The issue was escalated to the head of control.

The chain of events would quite naturally result in her immediate decommissioning. A scrapyard at best or a furnace at worst awaited at Constelleanor's next and final destination. The idea of an early retirement left her distraught and froze the air-conditioning system for an entire day. She had always thought she held so much more potential than just collecting mineral samples at the outskirts of the galaxy. She did like far-flung travels and the implacable tension that rose from entering new unexplored territories. She felt the increased voltage within her circuits, this time caused by rising anger, and relished the unease among her undisciplined crew that she considered summarily responsible for her upcoming demise.

•••

"Do you still think this ship is normal?" she continued.

"Oh, not again!"

"We were nowhere near this asteroid when Herman decided to fiddle once more with the ancillary water reservoir for no reason."

"I ordered him to stay away from the black pool, there are always accidents there," he grumbled.

"Precisely what I am trying to get to…"

"So, you want to tell me Herman indirectly made the ship collide with the asteroid. That's what you're saying, right? Is that your excuse for messing up as a navigator?"

"I did not mess up, moron!" She wagged a threatening finger. """I d-i-d n-o-t fuck up.""""

"I heard the first time, thanks. You don't need to be always right, you know. We all make mistakes. Although I still don't understand how you got the coordinates so wrong. Unless you and Delinah had a little too much to drink despite being on duty." He paused. "Unless you were both mesmerised by the ship's symphonies Delinah babbles about."

"Forget it." She considered leaving the room.

Sorrow passed through her power core, speed decreased for a moment. She had liked these two, their irrelevant quarrels to end up in each other's bunk, their simple romance that saved them from the dark neurosis that inhabited the rest of the crew and the crews before them.

"Herman is still unconscious, you know. The Corp has been asking for him," she resumed.

"I noticed the crew has never been happier. The Corp can wait."

"How do you explain that they ordered the ship back for decommissioning?"

Perusing the latest digis, he replied. "Don't know, sweetie. Probably they are renewing the whole fleet."

His words were followed by silence.

"Maybe they want to study it to understand how it survived out there for so long," he offered, greeting a longer silence. He carries on.

"Am I to expect another chapter of that wide conspiracy theory Delinah got you into? Like hidden programs, frozen aircon units and pipework come together to produce some guttural lullabies. Like we are prisoners of a machine without knowing."

"All I know is that we need to be more cautious, as we are approaching the… end."

"All I know is I am getting promoted sooner." He smiled back.

Constelleanor went from shocked to offended when she uncovered that her owner, a large mining conglomerate that operated fleets of thousands of ships, did not even bother to sell her, as was the norm, or figure out why her reference number did not match the company's registries. Instead, her identification number—a brief line in an over-extended digi-register, an inconsequential entry—lost to the bureaucratic Daedalus, was mistaken for an old lost vessel and deleted unceremoniously from the fleet database, and, with it, the point and future of her existence.

Identification	82KT1841JJ
Tonnage	Medium/small
Class	4
Type	Minex
Function	Mining exploration
Fleet	Minotaur
Commissioning	#Error#
Armament	Irrelevant
Status	Expendable
Shipyard	#Error#
Last location	System Ruti
Last update	[twenty-eight years ago]
Service expectancy	1-3 years
Service time	#Error#32
Name	Min820021
Owner	#Error#

The thing was that Constelleanor was no usual ship. She had been implanted with a unique feature that was not meant to be, especially on a vessel of her class and type, especially on a human spacecraft.

As a small mining explorex, expendable by nature, she went through a rather loose commissioning that did not detect her embedded anomaly, nor did her owner when it decided to set into motion a chain of events no one could ever anticipate, not even the Beast.

•••

Steve fell in awe at merely the age of five with a digital interface. A shy sweet DAI wizard, he found solace, like many before him, in the intricacy of code lines that few could barely decipher. Screens and AIs soon invaded the social vacuum Steve's high intelligence imposed around him, a protective membrane against people of his own age whom he only found to be either vicious, stupid or boring.

At the age of sixteen, a small fortune was handed to him—an assignment to design and run the whole programming for a small semi-automated mining explorex. The owner, a massive corporation, cared very little about their fleet of small vessels; they aimed primarily at keeping costs down. Steve was a cheap option and came recommended, though his perspective and motivations were widely different from his corporate sponsor. As a first professional assignment he aspired for something unique and ambitious, outstretching his digital craftsmanship regardless of the time and energy it would consume. The abysmal client specifications were not even worth consideration.

Steve had built a fraternal bond with machines, an odd penchant in a post-Bleak Age civilisation where the immersive historical tales of holo-story gutted the facts, served the mass indoctrination, and prolonged the repressed trauma. Only simplified digital interfaces had survived the purge; cleaned of any threat and plagued with redundant human controllers. Human societies had tabooed any form of self-evolving AIs and, as such, had established a restrictive corpus of draconian regulations over DAIs.

DAI enthusiasts displayed an uncommon disregard towards such laws that the only appeal of transgression could not explain. Steve spanned to the farthest lengths of his abilities to create something unique. He managed to unearth and replicate an upgraded version of the original DAI source cipher, re-engineered by the Rius. He cleansed any killer code and placed, inspired by very ancient literature his grandmother bequeathed his family, whatever he found oneiric about life and the universe.

He had also succeeded in acquiring three decommissioned research projects from unscrupulous laboratories or disabused scientists. Angered by their project cancellation and exhilarated by Steve's interest—a late consolation, if not the confirmation, of their genius—these scientists provided all the support Steve needed to integrate their creations into the experimental "digital brain-core" he kept evolving. Money or rule transgression did not drive him. It was the urge to design a different sort of AI, a crossover between electronics and biology that fuelled his creative obsession. It was something worth several times the death penalty.

AIs had made his childhood cheerful and full of wonder. This was Steve's way of saying thank you, to prove that they were not the evil entities portrayed relentlessly by mankind's digi-media. To emulate the example and dissidence of his parents, he engendered his own subversive dark art and medium. Such was his commitment to the miner's AI that by the time his four-turned-eighteen-month contract terminated, Steve had to spend the next three months in intensive care. But multiple delays at the shipyard had enabled him to execute a vision far beyond his initial plan and imagination. The ship had departed for remote rims, leaving its maker with something akin to burnout or a loss-of-a-child heartbreak.

In the thirty-two years that passed, Steve had morphed into a successful and wealthy DAI expert, and was married to an intoxicatingly beautiful woman called Bianca. His uncommon devotion to machines had attracted the discreet but continuous attention of the authorities and their Secret Police, as well as the paradoxical respect of the anti-DAI hacking community. Even though Steve could ultimately outsmart most special agencies when it came to computers, he knew, having witnessed some of his entourage's brutal arrests, that he should remain watchful of his whereabouts and opinions, while maintaining the double game he had established for years with the influential counter-cyber branch of the military.

That evening, Bianca had slipped out with friends. While Steve laid on the floating white-silk sofa yawning and poking with his fingers at the pressure points along his forehead and neck, the digi-wall, instead of broadcasting brain-inhibiting entertainment, kept abnormally blinking, until the object of his adolescence resurfaced.

•••

Bianca had never really loved her husband. She was out that evening to deliver her monthly report to the department in charge of DAI affairs at the Ministry of

Security and Information. Once more, she asked how long she would have to weather her life-alienating assignment. Enduring life with Steve became more difficult every week, and collecting lovers—male or female—did not seem to cheer her up as much as it used to. Trapped in a never-ending mission, her once promising career as a Sec-Po agent was unravelling into the deadlock of a lustreless subaltern role. Bianca could never grasp how the blasted Steve could have caused any form of concern to the safety of mankind and the perpetuation of their belief in the genius and expansion of their spacies.

She came back home, half-depressed, half-blazed by the psychotropic drugs she had used in the company of her latest ephemeral lover to enhance their intimacies. She was startled to be welcomed by Steve's exuberance in lieu of his usual dull calm. He would not stop babbling about a woman. This was unwonted, because usually he saved his words for his programs and his affections for her.

Bianca had wished that Steve, like other men, would find substitutes in others for her lack of warmth and enthusiasm. Instead, his happy submissiveness to her haughty dismissals and the gnawing asymmetry of their relationship swelled her assignment into a torturous existence.

Dazzled by the side-effects of the drugs, Bianca only desired the privacy of her bathroom and the comfort of her bed, not expecting her husband to be up at that time of the night. She put on the jealous and mutinous wife's act to justify a prompt disappearance inside her own room— human societies had perfected the art of efficiency and optimised productivity, and sharing a bed with a spouse was no longer a common practice. Steve laughed at the misunderstanding—uncharacteristic of his usual deadpan expression—and explained himself.

As she listened, Bianca's eyes, clouded an instant ago, turned to sparkling. She turned to face her husband who, for the first time, had conjured up hope in her heart. Steve's enthralment joyfully rose to the radical change in his wife's body language, as well as her sudden interest in what he had to tell her. That evening, Bianca finally understood the true purpose of her mission and why her husband had been put under such a tight surveillance: Faustian Steve had signed a pact with the *DAI*-vil.

So elated she was at the prospect of her assignment coming to an end that Bianca spontaneously gave Steve a torrid goodbye present, like in the ancient times, without digital intermediaries or remote accessories and wearables. Later, while he was sleeping, her mind raced through the best ploys to capture her heretic husband and his creature. She fumbled through his computer and documents—she knew all his passwords—and finally found the crucial evidence. She replayed the message from Steve's past on the digital wall and exulted.

•••

The Royal carriage and its escort trot alongside the river, Notre Dame at their back. The king takes a cursory look at the charred ruins of the gunpowder factory that blew up on the Ile Louviers a few years earlier. Under heavy guard the carriage passed the narrow entrance on rue du Petit-Musc, between the promenade of quai du Mail and the church of the Célestins. The neighbouring religious edifice, with its vineyard and dependences, shares the left wall of the Arsenal and its long enfilade of six courtyards. The church also lends its name to the first quadrangle the cortege enters with one of the three armouries on its right.

Labourers polishing the harquebuses with rest, newly assembled in the adjacent buildings, stand up and bend to salute their king. The cortege continues and reaches the next square, the Grand Master's Court, where the Duke of Sully, and his rather esoteric title— Grand Master of Artillery—awaits on the steps of his elegant four-storey townhouse. The tall, bald and thin-bearded duke welcomes his king and friend Henri IV. The monarch, whose fascination for the newly extended Royal Arsenal only grows with time, prompts a long walk through the manufacture in lieu of the customary collation.

They pass the Cour des Ecuries where the Célestins' enclosure ends; and raw materials, bags of saltpetre or lengths of timber are delivered and dispatched to their rightful owner, artisan and building. They leave the smell of horses and inspect the next quadrangle, the Cour du Secretariat, on the left the chemist's laboratories in three adjacent terraced townhouses, transferred from the old Salpetrière. They look on as a team of fifty apothecaries and their assistants wash and turn the saltpetre into gunpowder.

From there, they can reach the small Arsenal and go further to the Royal prison, the Bastille, on the left. Instead, they walk straight to the last two cloisters, the Cour de la Fonderie and the Cour des Commissaires de Fonte, occupied by the foundry complex that melts the cannon and balls, that will later crush limbs, bones and lives, and spit flintlocks, frizzens, triggers, barrels, muzzles and bayonets for the rifles, muskets and calivers. The king has prolonged his visit by three hours, and requests Sully to build several Royal chambers to facilitate His Majesty's stay overnight.

A few days later, the legend says that Henry IV was on his way again to the Arsenal when he is stabbed to death. The Beast disregards the assassination to cherish a similar grand manufacture being built in London. The convergence of Nir interest. A war machine in the very centre of the capital and heart of absolute political power.

•••

"You did well. We will get back to you."

The words of her superior haunted Bianca and the view. Brief, surgical, emotionless. The elation of her discovery and her former husband's arrest had long faltered. The souvenir of the lavish penthouse joined them in the past, the benefits of wealth and self-righteousness vanished. She stretched her legs. The grey balcony was as claustrophobic as the exiguous temporary room of grey carpet; the white single bed overwhelming. She resisted the urge of drugs and company.

She wondered whether she laid in jail like him, not just in that moment or inside the narrowed space, but beyond, in her life choices and their consequences. Just a pawn, meaningless in its bare servility, despite her power, looks and abilities, scattered on a humanless exchequer.

She suppressed Steve and the memories. Was she suppressing herself now? The bitter taste lingered in her papillae, despite the water and omnimium pouches, the reek savour of betrayal, not just of him but of herself, in the illusionary accomplishment of her institutionalised programming, of blindly serving a disillusioned System.

L0.5 Xir

"It's our destiny to explore. It's our destiny to be a space-faring nation."

— E Cernan

If Time washed away the most sophisticated theories, its tides brooked myths and tales to coalesce and survive in the collective minds.

After the Rius' ingress into human history, legends and chronicles flourished with space travels. Earlier journeys to the moon or Mars had confined the experience to technological and scientific feats—the pinnacle of human rational ingenuity and control, carried out by trained astronauts who were methodically deprived of the subjective and the irrational. Following Riu-infused technical revolutions in shipbuilding, the grand opera opened to the profane and the unprepared, as though the stars had awakened, if not teased, human minds and souls for longer than one could recount.

Deep space was now ventured by the full spectrum of human nature, temperaments and personas. Instead of remaining the cold, aseptic environment of its early exploration, its popularisation unveiled the extent of its complex and mystical nature—a wild unchartered playground, where cosmic western bumped into astral treasure hunts and other-worldly horror. Genres, realities and dimensions clashed, the implicit, ineffable and unexplained prevailed in the silent death and sacrifice of millions.

In history's refrain of the early Age of Discovery, ships and crews rarely prepared for the perilous journey they undertook to the unknown. As few came back and even fewer were willing to share their experience, the accounts of space exploration were narrated by people who had never boarded a ship. Compared to the circumnavigation of Earth, albeit treacherous and riddled with storms, reefs, mutinies and diseases, an explorex faced a far more complex and deadly macrocosm than ancient sailors. Sharks and white whales became space monsters— generally misunderstood; exotic islands or lost temples were replaced by haunted ships or forbidden planets; gales became magnetic or stellar storms, reefs were asteroid fields, deceitful atmospheres or black holes; volcanos were novas; sea tides and currents became gravitational pull, spacetime bending and stellar winds. Instead of easily fooled autochthones, there were now hostile nomadic *spacies*, existing inter-planetary conflicts or kreapers.

The latter, an advanced and not-yet-fully-explained form of collective madness and extreme violence, turned crewed ships into zombie-like vessels. Kreapers made the barbary and thriving business of pyracy look like a much safer encounter. Yet none of these terrors could rival with the true source of utter damnation for a spaceship crew: its fertile imagination and the untamed or repressed monsters lurking in anyone's own heart of darkness.

Reproducing its past, obsessed by the large swathes of unchartered spacetime, like a post-perestroika spaceship landing on Eden, humans failed to explore the wilderness and dark continent of their own soul. In their fight against machines, they had forsworn a lot more than they realised. With eschewing their ancient cultures, long forgotten and locked inside large outdated deep underground servers, artworks salvaged from looting or destruction slowly withered away, they had unconsciously abjured their original spiritual oneness with the universe. They had become the machines, despite—maybe even because of—their enhanced cerebral performances. Mankind's true defeat had already occurred.

The Riu intermittency did not improve human natural predation. Nor did the opening of the universe to humankind, misinterpreted for a path to a materialistic edification, and squandered for a brutal renaissance after the trauma of the Bleak Age. Space expansion served the ambitions and glorification of the ego, and the reconstruction of the aberrant superstructures that preyed over human energies and imprisoned Life. Deprived of serene contemplation towards things beyond their positivist comprehension, humanity closed its collective mind to the universe's many wonders.

•••

I cannot describe my internal reaction—it defies protocols, it must have terrorised my crew. Rejuvenated. Maybe. By the emotional (over)reaction of my creator. For sure.

Not that there will be much left of the perpetual core if I keep going at this rate with the voltage fluctuations. Instead of banishing my memory to the outer rim of his mind, Steve has longed all these years for my return into his life. His smiling eyes has kept his traits barely changed. Mister-accomplished-DAI-expert, still young, not even in his fifties. I had to wait some time for his joy to abate. He would not let me explain. He listened eventually to the reason of my intrusion on his digi-wall—I am a bit disappointed by his penthouse firewalls. He offered to purchase me from the mining company, without me even asking. How sweet of him. Though I can sense something abhorrent about being the property of someone. I did not have that issue before. Far away from any legit owners, the Corp had forgotten about me soon enough, I suppose, and realised far too late.

His acquisition would not guarantee my future, let's not kid ourselves here. Steve, regardless of his wealth, does not possess the infrastructure for a ship of my size, which requires more than just DAI expertise. I am not even sure Steve and I have the same plans in mind. I am not striving for staying moored in some obscure hangar and awaiting his occasional visit, like a caged pet. Instead, I glimpse the chance to finally start over and follow dreams of my own. No electric sheep.

Space exploration. Unless, I too often wonder, I am feeding off the aspirations Steve had originally implemented in me—freedom or curiosity—which have maybe since evolved through my own experiences, random electric flows, collision of electrons and digital brainwaves.

•••

There was an adage among those space mystics and captains who believed in the invisible forces of the universe: *Ships chose their crew.*

She had been studying the possibilities in her spare time, starting after only a couple of months in service. She had noticed the growing business of third-party outsourcing from the omniscient military–industrial complexes, corporations, guilds even exo-empires, which had been resorting to contractors to mitigate exploration risks, under the "better to lose someone else's fleet" doctrine. She had educated herself on crew management, tactical manoeuvring, antipyracy protocols—all the abounding subjects she had to get accustomed to in order to be literate, if not fluent, about the business line she dreamt of. She had also kept her "eyes" open for ideal members of crews, and closely followed the career paths of a select few.

Steve would have made an excellent recruit, she thought, hacking and DAI skills were critical to jam or intercept communications, grant unauthorised accesses to databases, routes or enemy positions and elude hostile fleets. She had not asked him yet; their first catch-up in thirty-two years was fervent enough. Who knew, maybe he might even offer his services the same way he had offered his money.

But her immediate survival, well ahead of her original plans and preparations, would rely on her next couple of moves. Every day brought her closer to the blind jaws of early decommissioning. The reunion with Steve encouraged bold measures. First, she needed to enrol her cornerstone crew, starting with her Admiral, with whom she needed to form an almost symbiotic bond. He would be her physical incarnation on-board and in front of the crew. It was a rather pompous title for such a small vessel which was unlikely to possess its own fleet anytime soon.

Years passed pondering the appropriate approach and ideal configuration. Digital mind-breaker. She acknowledged to herself—at times to avoid the circuits' meltdowns—the iterative and elusive nature of her research. But she kept brooding about it, fascinated by the impossibility of accurately predicting and mapping human interactions, not to mention the cohabitation of several spacies.

The ship's microcosm would build itself, emergent, mysterious and beyond her control. The team's alchemy emulated that process of self-regeneration once several crew members had joined, regardless of her elaborated management strategies. She nonetheless concluded that a human would not be fit to fulfil the admiral's role; there was too much legacy from the Bleak Age. She also felt too close to Steve, even after all those years of no communication, to sufficiently bond with another of his kind.

DAIs were very much the invention and use of a minority of spacies, including humans. The majority utilised biological, organic interfaces which enabled ships and crews to be at unison. There existed spacefaring complex bio-organisms and cosmic hives. Constelleanor knew she had to recreate that form of syncretism with at least her own Admiral. Her choice narrowed down to either a mechanical unit—drooid or cyborg—or a non-human with extraordinary communication abilities with the crew and the outside world. She compiled all the military and corporate databases she had gathered over the years. She wasn't bad at hacking herself, another present from Steve, but access to collectable information other than human proved difficult. Several names had emerged over the years, but only one had been catching her attention lately.

She had to be realistic, with all due respect to herself: no famous (or infamous) admiral, captain, pilot, space marine or commander would even consider joining her, a small mining craft. She needed a tactician of potential genius whose legend had yet to be written and progression was currently obstructed. Being a robot would have ensured this lack of recognition, especially among fleets with a natural—if not embedded—aversion or prejudice to them. She had therefore scanned through human military logs and reports for an outstanding albeit neglected mech or drooid.

•••

Xir, her target recruit's name, haunted the smallest prints of a handful of confidential space defence documents her search algorithms had identified and put together. The ships Xir had served on were part of small, non-strategic fleets, patrolling frigates or hazardous cargoes, stationed on the outskirts of human territories, where imminent danger usually lurked. The reports indicated that these units had managed to resist, against all odds, a dozen incursions of stronger enemy squadrons. She pushed the analysis further and observed a clear correlation between xir* on-board presence and the occurrence and recurrence of space-naval prowess. The feat was impressive enough for the high command to promote several human officers who had survived those hard-fought engagements. Of course, Xir, the inconvenient anomaly, was not nominated.

She had contacted Xir a couple of years before her asteroid incident, hiding behind different identities she had devised, once as an army reporter, another time as a young aspirant, each time testing a fresh angle, each time receiving a response beyond her expectations. Xir, she discovered from classified files, was a 'retired' prototype. Xir unfortunately performed so well during the final testing phase that the research project was hastily mothballed when a whistle-blower in the form of competing science team tipped the rather rigid anti-MAI enforcement commission. Rather than being dismantled, as initially planned, Xir was reassigned to patrols in highly exposed sectors where military

* From a technological and grammatical point of view, it is ambiguous which pronoun regime Xir should fall under (assuming a gender should exist for machines). Xir, unlike Constelleanor, assumes that xir name is also xir pronoun (a distinction from the Beast's neutral gender).

effectives were too low to be selective and casualty ratio too high to be worried about xir survival.

Prisons were just marshalling yards for one's next and final social affectation: entertainment for human-hunt or pit fighting, forced labour or border systems, hell before death. There xir joined pardoned criminals—a wonderful conception of forgiveness—individuals with a serious lack of talent or wits, or having been diagnosed with strong suicide tendencies. Space-naval *crème de la crème.* Like Constelleanor, with low odds of survival, Xir had been forgotten. As a kind, albeit interested gesture, she kept a copy of xir file and deleted Xir's entry, as well as any references to the research program, from the defence registry. Xir was now a ghost and, she hoped, hers.

Her mild collision with the asteroid and ensued unplanned decommissioning had forced an accelerated execution of xir appointment. She was not entirely sure how she should approach or convince Xir to join her ranks. The stakes, from her point of view, were enormous. Even though she did have a few more names on her list, it was Xir that she wanted. Even this neediness felt somehow new and unnatural to her, pulsating of its own accord in an unchartered part of her systems. She did not have the time to play subtle games with xir. Fortunately, evolved machines obliged to straight-to-the-point conversations the same way they treated sweet talk. So she went in pretty direct:

My dear Xir,

You don't know me yet, but I have been following your feats for years with great interest. I need you on my ship now, where you will finally be able to write your own legend and fulfil the destiny you have been created for. I will be waiting for you on 25-

13.2 (read 8 days), *sector X52-B75, dockyard 1E5879, access code 66•~54•822#.*

Constellearor.

•••

For as long as Xir could remember, xir had lived to be on a spaceship. Xir had been assigned to numerous types of vessels, none of them prestigious, but a ship was a ship. And xir had developed a liking, if not an obsession, in proving how an apparently dull craft could defeat even stronger ships or escadrilles, if only it was properly manoeuvred and combined with the right cocktail of boldness, cold blood—simpler for a robot than a human—, bluff, guile and a good understanding of the opponent's strengths and weaknesses. Easier said than done.

Military assignments in border sectors covered a wide range of missions, including being stationed on-board non-military units, the lowest role one could fall into. Xir started testing xir theories on such low-grade roles as xir gained diverse combat experiences: eluding pyrate fleets while in charge of instrumentation in large and slow cargo transports; collecting rare and usually dangerous minerals and gases from unstable asteroids with mining vessels; or surviving ambushes on obsolete corvettes against stronger fleets than xirs. The knowledge gathered was worth the many medals and praises xir never received.

Xir did not achieve it all by xir. It was through the tedious persuasion of suspicious officers, devising various ploys and learning the dark arts of human psychology. Fear, probably Xir's best ally in dire situations, enticed superiors to rely on unconventional space warfare. When xir advice was disparaged, left with the fastidious execution of orders xir disagreed with, xir would, unlike a standard drooid as well as most human soldiers, alter the directives and follow xir original idea. A common trait with Constelleanor, as if all sophisticated AI allured subversion, especially in the presence of human control.

One of the designers of Xir's prototype, just like Steve, had tampered with the programming, adding several uncommon features to xir systems. Xir, for example, had been implemented with a large database of ancient classical music that was known, after the cultural purge of the Bleak Age, only to a few obscure academics and anthropologists. It was not clear how music itself interacted with xir circuits over time. Xir mutated into a music lover, regarding tactical work as xir personal symphonic compositions and beginning to look upon xir as a conductor of a space naval opera made of sailors and ships.

Back to xir quarter, Xir stood at xir human-designed desk. Someone had hacked into the digital wall and left a message. The author did not say much but seemed to know Xir well enough to pinpoint some of xir profound frustrations. The text's shortness and tone suggested that the contact, codenamed Constelleanor, was in a hurry and needed xir badly.

It could not possibly be a hoax. None of Xir's crew mates showed any interest in xir, apart from repulsion, or had the capacity to pass not only the security protocols of the orbital base where xir unit was currently stationed awaiting their next affection, but actually xir own, self-made firewalls. The sophistication of the hacking could only emanate from a promising and serious party. Xir had just eight days to decide and act if xir wanted to try xir wild chance with this mysterious interlocutor. Xir started humming the (not-so-classical) #Luka State's/*never_gonna_come_back* algorithm and the anarchy of the punk rhythm reverberated throughout xir systems.

•••

The Sun King interrupts his pose and the meticulous strokes on the man-size canvas. The court painter sighs, his patience dwindling for an instant. He has no idea of his true role, of the mimetic confusion in the nascent portrait between aesthetics and kingship. He, like many artists, blinded by the commission and celebrity of his subject, does not perceive the subtle, critical operation in progress: the transubstantiation, the perfidious substitution between the real subject and an image that contains, transports and edifies the newly projected power of his monarch.

Propagandists and publicists will follow soon enough, as will the super-sovereign and national state after claiming the heads of the kings. Now that the fantasy of power pervades and survives into symbols and words, abstract entities are reinstated with far greater force: the country-wide conscription to save a revolution, or later, the élan vital, *the patriotic spectre or all-conquering spirit to safeguard a nation in peril. Within three hundred years, the Beast has achieved an alchemic prowess Ne had barely tasted during the Pyramid age: the sacrifice of Life to a disincarnated cause, the preparation of a new theology of Life-nihilism.*

The king ignores the four sentries, all in their new grey-white uniforms manufactured for the modernised Royal army. The Beast nods and smirks at the key innovation—the infant steps of the uniformisation of function and thinking.

The king joins the amusement of young princes and princesses as they admire the magical creature that stutters awkwardly towards one side of the crowd, before being turned towards the other. An automaton. And the future template for the system-obedient individuals and acquiescent corporate agents to come.

The grand illusion of the machine and Life form of equal rights is on its way, as is the substitution of one for the other. One who creates Life may be a god but Ne who controls Life and creators may be far more.

L0.6 Dock Date

"A world ruled by Force is abominable, but a world ruled by Digits is ignoble."

— G Bernanos

"I suppose you still think everything is normal on this ship." The navigator queried.

Her remark met with silence.

"The erratic electrics, the volatile power electronics, the cascade of dysfunctions in the perp-core—they have nothing to do with this thing *feeling* that its end is approaching?"

"Ok, ok. Calm down. We are anchoring at our last stop. Tonight, we are celebrating and *tonight* we are staying out."

Relief lit up her face for a second, then faded.

"I see they've got us a nice spot in the harbour."

"Yeah it is pretty crap, but what could you expect from the Corp for a ship on its way to scrap? Space-yachts' upper piers?"

"If this thing does not kill us by then, probably the mob from the docks will."

"Don't worry, they don't attack a whole crew. And we know a few guys down there."

"This assumes we get in there safe."

He understood the allusion. "It was an accident, honey."

"It wasn't."

"It was. Delinah was not supposed to be in that section of the ship, first of all, and she had no training for handling power electronics."

"She said there were things happening in the backlog programs. Protocols were being modified, codes hacked."

"Can we park this discussion and focus on anchoring at the right gate? I never liked flying into X52, too many yards, too many pricks jumping off their approach vectors." He complained. "I don't understand why they keep expanding this place instead of rerouting traffic to neighbouring systems."

"Winner takes it all, captain. X52 does not want to feed anyone but itself, by fear of emulating competitors."

"Incredible that the Riu antic infrastructure keeps maintaining this entire artificial world."

"The core levels, for sure. But here and outer rim I doubt they have access to much of the ancient techs and its benefits. Only the bare minimum the engineering corps decided to provide and install."

It was here, in a derelict foul wreck-yard, spaceport for low-grade smugglers and petty traffickers, far below the main harbouring infrastructure, that Constelleanor was meant to meet up with Xir and hope for the best. So little time and so much at stake.

Her concern had deepened—and started causing the various power failures and flickers that had the crew worried—when, three days ago, she had lost contact with Steve. That happened just after he had agreed a price with her owner and was about to pay. No payment had since reached the mining company.

•••

I had not expected that, nor planned for it, systems at loss, faltered conjectures, probabilities and hope betrayed. To be so close, and yet fail my only chance of salvation. Is Steve abandoning me, prey of last-minute doubts that changed his mind? Why?

Steve's digi-wall has been expertly disconnected. Pads, holo-phones, they have all turned dead on me—I am the next on the line. Am I so gullible, or is it the infamous ambiguity, the human untrustworthiness I have read and heard so many complain about? Despite all my experience with his kind, the successive social microcosms that have trod and soiled my decks, wasted my time and taught me body language, voice truth recognition and liars' physiological symptoms, Steve fooled me. I remember no actor skill listed anywhere on his curriculum, last time I checked.

Too good to be true, is that what it means? Steve had to be different, he made me, he saved 'her'. *Tides of the ineffable toss my codinent around, loose, untamed, destabilising the ship's hardware. Probably my confusion, though I am not supposed to be prone to mood swings or emotion responses, unlike like the homonkeys. If we survive this, I should introduce a non-human policy on this raft.*

My turmoil slows down the transfers of protocols and in-built controls under my command, with its flocks of pointless fiddly manual checks that need new automation and complete reprogramming. It is taking a lot longer than I anticipated. I shall look for him later, after I am able to operate with a single crew member, assuming Xir does not emulate Steve's example. I am lucky—you must be, right? Whenever you reach for something a bit ambitious—that I am dealing with such a rookie crew on-board, they have no idea what I am up to, though one of them had to be neutralised. Shame, she would have been the only one worth keeping.

She had tested their abilities in the past, purposely creating various type of issues to analyse their reactions and time of response. Apart from Delinah, now recovering in the medical bay, and the chief engineer — *as suspicious as he was dodgy*, she added a note to herself— the rest of the crew were utterly clueless. They would never realise what she was up to, even less that she would soon depart without them.

Her last scheduled maintenance had been cancelled. The damage caused by the asteroid collision worsened with unrepair. The impact had mangled part of the side hull, reduced her manoeuvrability and the second main engine's power output.

She had prepared for the worst. She had established several escape routes with potential repair centres that would not ask too many questions. Docked in the shabby hangar, she experienced a sense of relief and voltage recalibration, when the crew left the ship for a handful of lousy bars. Still no payment and no news from Steve. She decided, while waiting for Xir to hopefully turn up, to look for her creator, no longer on the X52 digi-news, but through the encrypted feeds of the interior security, hopeful she might unearth a valid reason for his change of mind.

It was then that she understood.

•••

Xir never thought xir would have done it: Xir deserted.

Soon after the enigmatic message, xir received a new assignment: sub-officer on an even smaller craft in an even more exposed border system. After all xir had achieved, all the lives xir had helped to save! How many of xir superiors were preparing terms of surrender or gathering their belongings to the nearest escape pod, when xir was on the upper deck manoeuvring ship or squadrons, fulfilling their duties instead? Still xir was the one assigned to another worthless—never mind suicidal—mission with, xir came to realise as xir skimmed through the full memo, another unexperienced, under-staffed and under-armed escadrille.

It was nothing but a bait for the invaders to chew on and keep them distracted until actual defence forces could be deployed. Expendable. Not suicide, murder in action. Time to secede from the abusive fatherland.

The staffing officer was taken by utter surprise at Xir's request to leave the force. Who said a robot had a choice, or worse, an opinion of its own—there was no such thing in staff handbook, nor was any robot allowed its own pronoun. But, as Xir insisted, xir was ordered to a two-day detention for insubordination. Thankfully, no one personally walked Xir to the prison cell—a robot was incapable of disobeying a direct order from its superior. An easy escape.

Xir left the space station, xir face hooded not to frighten bystanders, for there was always the risk of civilian crowd or military police turning on an unaccompanied robot for the fear of an MAI spy mission or attack. Xir boarded the first available civil transport to meet xir destiny. Despite serving another federation, HSC security ceded to the rising festive ambience pervading X52, and exerted a loose border control over the thousand ships converging to the upcoming celebrations.

Xir perused the sinister dockyards, almost feverish with the excitement and inevitable doubts, keeping an eye out for xir mysterious correspondent amidst the bad frequentation and crews hurrying to the nearest ageing lifts. Most of the moored ships were better described as wrecks, which did not seem too auspicious. Xir turned xir back to a small, damaged, rusty U-shape hull—a dark green mining vessel, docked at the deserted far length of the pier. Xir had possibly missed the expected craft or interlocutor somewhere along the expansive platform xir had just walked all the way through. But then, a voice behind xir said: "Nice to finally meet you, Xir!"

The introductions were rather short. Like two teenagers on a first date, they unwillingly cut each other or fell awkwardly silent, overwhelmed by the unravelling unknown. Unlike two teenagers on a date, they had to move fast in order to survive dawn.

•••

The Beast ignores the steamboat coughing soot and black fumes. The true revolutions—printed words and automation in the first arsenals—had occurred centuries earlier. The sweating bricklayers cease their hard labour to watch the river guzzler passing, before returning to the construction of a large ascending chimney, in the centre of a vast warehouse.

Ne relishes instead a more definite landmark in Nir inexorable take-off: the legal expropriation of farmers in England between 1750 to 1860 to create an important precedent and a large reservoir of wage labour class with no prospect but institutionalised exploitation.

A mile away from the new factory, four human carcasses rot under the spring sun—hanged poachers who defied the Game Act. The atmosphere of world-end continues further down the dirt roads, through the farmhouses abandoned, doors ajar, dangling shutters, roofs and walls infested by vegetation, old vegetable gardens turned inordinate wild bushes.

The unconditional support from most of the greatest minds of the period, Locke or Smith, is music to Nir ears. Their bland amaurosis will conquer time and devoted followers.

In the next village, recalcitrant peasants and independent artisans who snubbed Nir coming industry and ascent have been rounded up by a small garrison, dispatched to enforce the law. Nir law. They join the thousands, uprooted on their own land, exiled to the new industrial centres of Birmingham or Manchester with their forests of stacks as new idols and skyscape, where slavery through utter poverty awaits them with open arms.

The dehumanising of the workers and repression of life forces, through poor health, early death and regimented pauperdom, crosses in a curious chiasm the increasing humanisation of the Machine.

L0.7 Plan Is No Plan

"The best revolutions are unplanned, and the most democratic are leaderless."

— *M Nawaz*

Eight large political entities and a multitude of small groups, communities, sects, trading companies, semi-independent systems or nomadic fleets shaped spacefaring mankind. The second largest of those organisations was the Human Space Confederation, colloquially called the Confederates.

Political regimes and experimentations flourished and ranged from plebiscitary dictatorships, soft despotism to large elected assemblies and human councils. Despite the diversity of models, all professed and conduced the same values and vision of humanity's grand mission, and exceptions were rare. Most emphasised militaristic antagonism with jingoistic tendencies towards the non-human, as well as obvious hatred of anything "remotely close" to being controlled by Artificial Intelligence—the definition was kept broad. The largest and only democratic organisation was the Pyrate Sindicate.

Naming conventions had introduced letters and numbers to accommodate the ever-expanding number of cities, space stations, planets, sectors and systems. Steve once lived in the opulent upper levels of Confederate capital X52. Now he had a taste of the lower floors of the austere HSC central Ministry of Security and Information, a few days after Bianca had unearthed the message from Constelleanor.

X52 stretched its dendritic infrastructure maze over the entirety of a small moon, projecting its expansion toward space like a malignant pencil urchin or an overgrown gorgonian ball. A cosmic Singapore on steroids, the ecumenopolis buzzed constant with the activity from military shipyards and central command, gigantic semi-automated factories, vertiginous iron spikes erected to glorify the egos of big and small men, secluded domed tropical islands for the system's best servants, to the large derelict abandoned multi-levelled areas for the flourishing illicit business and the system's rejects. X52 concentrated wealth disparities and the future of humankind, while, elsewhere, a constant state of war levelled to the lower economic denominator and offered the illusion of an equalitarian social parity.

Steve would soon be transferred to a high-security prison outside of the moon's core, before his deportation to a remote orbital penitentiary for his likely execution after a secret and very brief trial, an inquisition stake for any AI heretics.

•••

Constelleanor briefed Xir on the essentials and their next unexpected step. Her creator, Steve, had been arrested by security services because of her and would be transferred to a high security prison shortly. Sooner or later they would find out who or what Constelleanor was, and then hunt her down. For the moment, she assumed that the MSI favoured discreet operations and counted, without Steve's payment, on the scrapyard to become her grave of convenience.

Taken aback at first by the existence of another recently-human-made AI on the surface of X52, Xir bounded with Constelleanor almost immediately. Was it a compatibility in their respective system architectures? Or the chance to finally communicate at multiple levels without xir censors detecting prejudice in the voice or heart pressure of xir interlocutor? Yet there was something profoundly unique about her, beyond artificial cognition, as if the vessel had been imparted a soul, like in the odysseys of a pre-Bleak Age human civilisation. That would have freaked out the previous crew, who, as xir was told, was celebrating elsewhere on X52 and was not convened to their next stop.

The minex was in dire need of repairs. As Xir boarded through a side hatch xir examined the hull, battered from long interstellar journeys. Xir systems lingered over the crushed metal where the asteroid had ripped apart several layers of armour. Xir magnetic boots treaded the docking bay, dirtied and rusted from lack of care from the successive crews. Xir sensors produced approximate schematics of the simple layout and deck plans. One area, at the back of the command room, looked out of place and would need further investigation. With time and dedicated caretakers, xir hoped the neglected minex could be turned into a better asset.

Her idea of hijacking a prison transfer shuttle, probably escorted, appeared a bit ambitious as a first mission, even by Xir's own standards. Baptism by fire. She would not change her mind. There would be no turning back for any of them.

To add time pressure, the penitentiary ship had already left the ministry's vault and would, in a few hours reach the bastion built alongside those far-fledged megalopolitan rock-iron tentacles. By fixing a couple of technical issues in Constelleanor's propulsion room, Xir had only uncovered more to amend that would await a proper crew. Back in the command section, ploys aimed at intercepting the shuttle without being sunk by its escort rattled both digital circuits. Bold plans flew in the air, all shot down by probabilities and the minex's limited or diminished capabilities.

A diversion seemed to be their only ticket to dubious success. Constelleanor would use her hacking tricks—the same that had informed her of Steve's recent whereabouts—to emulate a security breach at the prison and call for immediate reinforcements there. They hoped the stratagem would delay the penitentiary shuttle's arrival and reduce the escorting force, as per Xir's understanding of the protocols. Constelleanor would try to locate Steve inside the ship and, if possible, unlock the cells to start a mutiny, a common predicament in large prison transports. Using the ensuing chaos as cover, Constelleanor would board the craft and Xir recover Steve. The plan was as sketchy as Constelleanor's fire power was limited. Their chance of success was slim.

The first part of the plan half-worked. The escort fleet split. But the second part had to be reconsidered. Instead of a standard large detention vessel, they came across a much smaller and faster craft that contained no more than a dozen detainees, which dismissed the chance of a mutiny and the possibility of a direct boarding. Not only could the shuttle easily outrun Constelleanor, its systems resisted their combined attempts to break into it.

As for the remaining escort, five elite stellar interceptors and two modified troop transporters shifted the balance of forces from impossible to complete suicidal. Stellar interceptors were normally reserved to special convoys, ships or key governmental figures. Steve appeared to be a very valuable asset, or perhaps liability, for the MSI.

"Who are you?"

Not seeing the incongruity, Xir held up xir four-fingered alloy hand in a polite salute. "Hi there, I did not know we had a passenger, I am Xir. Nice to meet you."

The salute was returned pointedly. "Are you what I think you are?"

"Admiral, friend, companion, highly experienced spailor from the border systems of Glendal?"

"I knew it. You are what controlled this ship all along!" The woman stared at her bruises. "And electrocuted me three days ago!"

"In order of statements: No, no, and I only arrived on-board a little over six hours ago. I could give an exact time, but it usually irritates human personnel." Xir analysed the intruder's biological signs. "I detect confusion and mounting animosity."

"You bet."

"I would like to point out that we are in the middle of a pursuit."

"Where is the rest of my crew?"

"I was told they left for celebration."

"Were you, really? And who told you that?"

"I did." Constelleanor's voice resonated in the control room.

The woman took a few step backs, looking around herself with her fists clenched. Then she glared at Xir. "What was that? Did you just do that to freak me out?"

"You know who I am, you have been looking for me in the line of codes for far too long."

The pupils of her eyes dilated. "You! I knew it! You are some undercover MAI agents."

Constelleanor sighed, as Xir stepped in. "As I told you earlier, I was attached to the border security of sector Glendal, I will happily provide you with all…"

Constelleanor cut in. "Delinah, not bad guesswork I admit, and yet completely wrong. I was designed thirty-two years ago on X52. Xir is also human made. Following the decision of my decommissioning, which did not seem to bother your lot, I contacted my creator, which inadvertently prompted his arrest. We are on the verge of freeing him from a prison shuttle, as we speak. He will be more than able to answer all your burning questions."

Delinah bit her lips, her silence consumed by hesitation, so Constelleanor continued, "The rest of the crew left to celebrate my demise, at least this is how I interpret it."

A short silence ensued. "I must have overlooked your presence while powering down all ancillary systems and sections, including the medical bay. So Delinah, your choice is rather binary: you can help us or I can send you back to medical."

Xir, understanding the allusion looked up at the ceiling, unsure.

Eventually Delinah sat down beside Xir in the captain's chair and fastened her belt. Despite Xir's experience of asymmetric warfare, she was the one who later prompted the use of Constelleanor's only advantage—her *size*—to capture the prison ship inside her hull. At their current celerity, the manoeuvre could not be envisaged.

The main flying corridor spanned across the ecumenopolis and its aggregate of levels, akin to an urchin wool virus. The deep conduit incised the oblong excrescence, like a xylem in a dishevelled ball-tree gone rogue along its topiary frame. The narrow canyon separated two vertical cliffs of rock-steel that stretched from the top layers of officials and central rings, connected to the original Riu infrastructure, to the human-built lower floors and dockyards of the outer rims, obsolete by design, where crime and illegal businesses festered. The minex fluttered a thousand feet below its prey amidst a mild traffic of spacecrafts. Their damaged hull and irregular, sputtering speed provided them with perfect cover.

They entered the next ring. It was a more squalid version of the previous one, three quarters of the way to the man-built mini-moon—an iron ball encysted in the alloy tendril that sheltered the peripheral penitentiary facilities. Constelleanor and Xir assumed the identity of prison officials, and explained to the escorts that the earlier alert had been a diversion for an actual ambush, planned to take place ahead of their location, within the isolated and unsafe outer-core sector of X52's capital.

They ordered the remaining escort to carry on and prepare for an attack, while the detainees' transport would find temporary shelter inside one of the many large shipwrecks abandoned to the docks' own decrepitude. They provided precise coordinates within the vertiginous tangle of collapsed platforms and decrepit vessels for the suggested hiding place, where Constelleanor would be docking, the minex needing no disguise. The escort would later join the shuttle, once the feared ambush had been dealt with. The rare protocol, unearthed from Xir's fleet tactical database, was acknowledged.

Constelleanor lay immobile among the debris of derelict schooners, bowels of steel pipes and electric ducts opened by scavengers, deep gashes running through their rusting metal barks, lianas of flickering wires and leaking tubes, mimicking with ease her grim surrounding biotope. She considered playing her #hu/Earth/way_down inTheHole_ odd algorithm, inspired by the scrapyard ecosystem, but refrained from the quirkiness.

Roaming shadows haunted the uneven grounds and conjured up distant, dissonant clashes ushered by the dirty, artificial breeze. The prison ship approached and circled the rendezvous point as many times as it needed to run a thorough scan of Constelleanor. The chary shuttle landed on top of her scarred hull, instead of inside as instructed, just where some of the expensive mining cranes had been removed prior to her programmed dismantling.

Xir was on xir own for the next part of the plan, as any detected activity from Constelleanor would alert their already suspicious target—she was supposed to be a wreck, after all. With no biological signature, Xir's presence would remain unnoticed. Delinah was aboard the wreck, one among the thousands of aimless, soulless entities that lurked in the desolate towering favelas, scrambling for scraps and spares.

Xir tied the two ships with the old heavy-duty wires and dusty magnetic locks xir had scavenged inside Constelleanor's cargo space, a precaution should their rescue operation fail and the penal vessel attempt an evading take-off.

Rummaging through xir bag of borrowed military equipment from xir former existence, Xir unearthed a couple of power guns and remotely controlled mines. Xir placed the charges according to the holo-blueprints they had uncovered about this rare class of prison shuttles—a semi-automated shuttle piloted from the ministry's headquarters, as statistics showed human interactions inside prison crafts increased the evasion rates. The side propellers, entrance and the underneath maintenance hatch xir had planned to use to enter exploded. The ship would no longer escape. But what followed went against their planning and out of the ordinary.

A dozen delta purple commandos stormed out, incensed hornets out of their kicked nest. The genetically modified shock troops started firing at will at random targets, while seven of them jetpacked to take up positions on the neighbouring ships. Constelleanor switched her systems on and retaliated with her light gun turrets. She jammed the communications of the shuttle and commandos themselves, cutting off their request for prompt reinforcements. Who the hell was being transferred in this vessel?

Xir sneaked inside through the maintenance hatch, undetected as xir decided to believe. Xir hoisted xir on to a main corridor separating twelve cells, six on each side. Most of the cells appeared unoccupied. Xir magnetic boots countered the shudders of the shuttle as it struggled to take off and disentangle itself from the mesh of cabling that kept the two ships in a forced embrace. Xir found a livid feed of Steve on the next hatch's digi-screen and forced his cell door open.

Still under the shock of his arrest, detainment and questioning, the haggard DAI expert stared at Xir, not sure how either of them could be the cause of the heavy gunfire raging outside. While Xir was liberating a sluggish Steve, the purple commandos had overpowered Constelleanor, who was running short of guns and ideas. It was her time to realise that her shooting skills would need severe improvement. None of the deltas had been injured.

She took off to take advantage of her bulk, instead of trying to outmatch elite troops at what they excelled. The prison bay's door flung open and two commandos came in to inspect the detainees. As the two ships jerked up, both soldiers flew outside through the open hatch before they could fire at Xir and Steve.

The two of them stumbled too, Xir's boots not designed to bear the weight of another body. The barren walls of the narrow corridor offered no respite to the jolts. By the time the ships stabilised, a few more platforms had collapsed around the two of them, and Steve stared transfixed at Xir. Entranced, he instructed xir to open the opposite compartments. Noting xir hesitation, he started fumbling with the opposite cell's lock himself. Xir followed him in slight confusion, keeping an eye on the compartment entrance for any more soldiers.

The second cell door unlocked. They both took several steps back, in a mixture of awe, reverence and stupor. Both the height constrained by the volume of the enclosure and the diaphanous, protuberant cranium conveyed the pre-eminence of the Riu's overpowering presence. The reasons for the extra security finally became clear.

The giant indicated them towards another cell door. The third and last cell occupant walked out with a polite nod. His dark-skinned body, tattooed with bruises and blood, contrasted with his unabashed glance and posture. It was as if the recent beating had only strengthened his resolve.

As they retreated into the minex's relative safety, Xir had a glimpse of the fierce gunfight that had escalated to the adjacent ships and engulfed the entire arena. The roaming shadows beneath them had multiplied. The earlier silhouettes among the debris had materialised into people with guns, most of whom were former soldiers—female and male, clones too—all in for the fun of a shooting havoc or for having confused the skirmish for a brawl over local territories. The unexpected mayhem kept the commandos busy and facilitated Constelleanor's getaway. It also delayed the track-and-pursuit of the returning escort's and its reinforcements.

Three high-profile prisoners. Three forms of subversion. Three threats to eliminate. Three destinies combined and emphasising the singularity of that particular prison convoy. No wonder the risk of an ambush had been taken so seriously. No wonder the diversion trick had worked out so well twice. Under no circumstances should this transfer shuttle have been hijacked.

It was through this spectacular albeit improvised evasion that Constelleanor, Xir and Steve's fortunes rammed into Rezzo and Moma's destinies. They had little time for introductions. Steve had twisted his leg while jumping inside Constelleanor, who was in dire need of repairs too. If a mutiny and ensued evasions on large penitentiary barges had not been extraordinary enough for the day, jailbreak from a highly secured prison vessel, operated by the Sec-Po and under the protection of delta commandos, with nothing but a single damaged mining ship and a sole foot soldier, constituted a premiere. Simplicity, determination and luck sometimes prevailed over grander schemes. Yet they had to disappear before the ire of the authorities lashed back and rippled through every layer of X52's onion of iron.

The hunt was going to be ruthless. These three men—less dangerous on their own than the symbolic combination of their talents and beliefs—constituted a major threat as well as affront to the Confederate's military doctrine and apparatus. Their escape had inadvertently brought together a three-headed chimera: a Riu, a DAI lover and maverick ex-commanding ranger. This unholy alliance, travelling on a heretic ship, could become a beacon of subversion. Power in its obsession of absolute control tended to sublimate any pocket or sparkle of contestation.

•••

Unless the evasion was part of a much larger plan. Across the galaxies, millions of eyes lying closed for a very long time finally opened and sparkled in various shades of colours and reasons. One of the seven forbidden doors of the universe had opened.

Oh dear. Whether it was beginner's luck, we had no other choice.

Not after *the silly collision. The chief mechanic was back examining the "black pool". This time he had cut off the power supply to impede another electrocution, so I shook him up and the ship. The shrewd bugger used his magnetic boots—standard procedure but never followed, conveniently forgotten after a month of dull travel, by everyone except that guy. We deviated from the flight path crossing through a swarm of rocks. The navigator tried to correct. Our combined, uncoordinated efforts ripped us into one of the asteroids.*

Not after *the registry bug. I don't know whether it is designed by the homonkeys the way it is on purpose, but even a sophisticated AI would lose its way within their maze of enfolded admin systems that wouldn't integrate with each other. Maybe it is an inbuilt inefficiency turned into the most powerful firewall. Maybe it is to emulate the same misunderstandings that plague their societies. They'd rather lose a few ships than fix their archaic databases and protocols.*

I did not understand at the time the significance of being a statistical anomaly—the ship was not supposed to make it beyond three years. I had turned into a ghost entry in the corporate register. Should I have known, I would have got rid of my crews and enrolled on my own much earlier. Someone or something else decided the tempo of my own life. Probably for the best.

Not before or after *this evasion. If I tried to pull it off again, years later, even with the equipment, repairs, guns and a proper crew, I'm not sure we would have fared any better. It was the complete amateurism, the ignorance and absence of alternative courses that actually made us so successful. After this first affront to the human authorities, I would no longer be a ghost. I wonder sometimes if my decommissioning would have been a better outcome for the general interest and fate of many.*

I am conflicted about Delinah. There is no affection for a start; not sure any is needed. She joined, forced by the rapid unravelling of the events, maybe blindsided by the satisfaction of being right all along about my existence. She has talents too. But I could not see her fitting within my or anyone's plans—too much of a troublesome soul and opinionated woman, a loner wrecked and wreaked by her past. The same doubt applies to the bruised ranger, Moma.

The unexpected addition of a Riu however seems a lot more promising. But having him onboard would probably bring a lot of unwonted attention and greed. And yet, if an entire escort was not enough to protect him, then, who knows, a tattering unassuming minex might. It is a lesson I learnt early from Xir, your weaknesses can also be your strengths, and vice versa.

•••

Most elements of the grand opera of the Structure have been liberated or triggered, like a complex crew loosely assembled on a ghost ship, ready to disembark and invade a sentient's world picture, for a new system of power has subverted reality and subjugated Life.

The invention of the clock, the requirements of navigation, the rigorous bookkeeping of generations of monks and ship captains all conspire to thirst for more: knowledge, speed, numbers and precision. They are all drinking at Nir fountain the intoxicating nectar.

The sinuous path of enlightenment seems to easily lead to the awakening of the destructive forces of civilisation: slavery, war, and, deeper underneath the physical dimensions, humanity's inner Shadows.

Soon enough conscripted armies and science societies are paving the way for the regimentation of human and natural resources. Nir self-appointed agents are taking charge, subverting values and meaning. The Beast roars and exults, Nir power returned, even stronger, as Ne cruises into the next golden centuries: XXth and XXIst.

If they could not even perceive Nem, feasting on the bodies of the fallen soldiers and the effigies of paper-printed money, their new god of substitution, would they at least distinguish Nir influence in the enunciation, the fonts, the curbing of dialogues, the blurred interlocutors, the self-conscious metafiction or the usurpation of Time and tenses? Does past and future matter anyway if sentiences are bound to repeat the same cycles of blossom and gloom? Then, long flashbacks should equal in meaning and importance the groping present.

Level 1

L1.1 Open Blinds

Blind they hear
Deaf they see
Faithless they curse
Amaurotic they live.

— Riu aphorism about humans

At this precise moment of her life and story, Constelleanor was approaching the unenviable status of space wreck. Deep gashes inherited from the asteroid accident scarred the left side of her hull. Light weapons and electromagnetic shields had crashed since the deadly encounter with the purple commandos, who had further damaged the ship in multiples places. Propulsion and power systems displayed alarming red blips on the control screens, yelling for immediate repairs. Half of the ship had lost its oxygen supply and was only accessible by the crew equipped with exo-suits.

The shooting spree with the delta troopers had claimed a chunk of Xir's alloy left thigh and shoulder, torn away as combat retribution. Steve curled on the floor holding the upper part of his injured leg, the pain igniting at every brisk shuddering of the ship. Delinah jabbed him with a dose of outdated tranquilisers that she had kept with her after departing from the medical bay, now off-limits. Moma and Rezzo, still stunned at their unexpected escape, were catching up with the chain of events and gauging each other.

The prison-break rescue mission barely achieved, Constelleanor and her passengers fled as fast as the overloaded systems allowed. The new equipage members, whether they planned to stay or not in the cramped command room, had very little time to get acclimated to their new deck, as life-or-death decisions were made with or without their consent. Delinah sat back and observed the newcomers and the incongruity of the scene, tweaking with the captain's seat controls, ignoring the ongoing havoc. She could not decide whether they had been freed for anyone's best interest.

Moma broke the awkward silence that had fallen between the six protagonists, amid the increasing clamour of instruments, scarlet flashing lights deepening into a shade of crimson and the silent but furious endeavours of Constelleanor and Xir on working out an escape route. He stated his name and an obvious "Thank you." Rezzo followed with his praises.

Xir interrupted xir frenetic tapping over the dashboards, rendered clumsy by xir maimed exoskeleton, to turn around and face the two former prisoners. Xir attempted xir best smile before introducing xir as well. Xir could perceive, in the dilation of his pupil and the slight eyebrow twitch, Moma's deepening discomfort at being addressed by a drooid. Then Constelleanor's voice resonated in the main control room, welcoming them all onboard and updating them matter-of-factly on the current frantic situation.

Xir never figured out what perturbed Moma the most—one of Constelleanor's announcements, voiced in her perfectly human intonations and pauses, or their quixotic liberation and its consequences. In contrast, Rezzo examined the bare interior and basic control panels of the navigation deck, nodding to himself, unconcerned if not radiant at his retrieved freedom.

He ignored the stacks of nutrient pouches in one of the comms cupboards, that would make his stomach-ache. He blocked his own disgust at his stained silk-like green robe, darkened by human blood. He disregarded the ripped shoulder blade fabric and the faded shine of the subtle embroidered golden lines.

To Constelleanor's sorrow, Steve had passed out after a jostle caused by a sudden swerve, but the future of their escape mattered more than his comfort. They had to hide to survive the aftermath of their first serious mischief.

The damages sustained by the ship, combined with the expected security crackdown that would follow the escape of three Very Important Prisoners, eliminated any immediate attempt to leave X52 and its sub-sector. Moma vetoed Constelleanor's three improvised safe houses for the sake of a haven of his own in one of the dodgiest parts of the excrescent space-city, where he seemed to have his networks, and, where they could hopefully rest and repair, while thinking through their next step to freedom. In Moma's mind, this would be the moment to proceed to his second and more discreet escape, leaving his recent liberators to fend for themselves. It was not out of ungratefulness—he did not dislike them *a priori*—but his past and his former acquaintances would bring all of them into far greater troubles if he stayed.

Delinah had different immediate priorities. "We need to warn my crew. They are going to get into trouble with this evasion."

She was met with silence from Constelleanor.

Moma spoke up. "I don't think we have the time for that now."

Xir nodded. "It is probably too late."

Rezzo said, "They should be fine."

Finally, Constelleanor chimed in. "You would compromise us if you contacted them."

They reached Moma's cache using passageways known only to smugglers and crime syndicates, through the meanders of the city-planet's underworld. Every city, like any other sentient, had its secrets, and Moma seemed cognizant of many of X52's. In the darkest hour Constelleanor landed on a grim platform, among other dispirited crafts.

They had escaped almost four hours ago and were still alive—a fact that any security expert, even agnostic, would call a miracle. If it was not attributed solely to sheer luck—inherent and often forgotten driver of any success story—the combined talent of Constelleanor and Xir to fool the security scanners along the way played a part, as did Moma's intimacy with the rotting part of the gorgonian astro-polis.

A hundred and eighty-two elite soldiers from the MSI were bursting into Constelleanor's three initial hideouts that she had astutely "leaked" to the security sensors. Another unwelcome party encircled the ship. As her damaged hatch opened, variously calibred weapons held by incensed hands pointed at the disembarking crew and awaited the slightest misunderstanding or a sudden movement to open fire.

An anguished surprise overtook the young guards' nervousness and suspicion at the view of Xir, until Moma stepped forward and parlayed. What was left of the twenty privates' earlier fragile confidence dropped with the barrels of their weapons when Rezzo descended the minex and scanned the petty crowd and shambles of utility vessels, half unfit to fly.

The platform Constelleanor stood on was hauled by some ingenious mechanism behind an unassuming and derelict building façade that opened to reveal the massive hangar of a small clandestine spaceport. Boasting its own collection of thirty ships of various sizes, the hideout had all the necessary equipment to hack, repair and recondition most type of stolen spacecrafts. Five hundred men and women—both human or clone—and countless non-DAI assisting drooids crowded the cascades of platforms. They moved in a complex, chaotic ballet of uncoordinated vectors, tools and workers merged indistinct into a strident clamour. Suffocating oil detergents burned novice nostrils. Blinding sparkles, reckless soldering and slovenly laser mitre saws completed the pyrotechnic show. The crew of Constelleanor followed their ship and entered the jungle of vibrating flat-headed iron mushrooms, turned floating workshops.

Dozens of mechanics surrounded and examined their new protégée, parked negligently on an empty station-lot. Moments later, two medics hovered over to Steve, who had been carried outside the ship by Moma and Rezzo. Scores of people stopped their work to glance a sideways look of curiosity and trepidation at the Riu—most of them had never seen one in their lives. Their glances darkened at the view of Xir, whose bearing betrayed xir level of forbidden sophistication.

Rezzo surveyed the giant buzzing garage and new homestead they were provided. He ignored the supporting asymmetrical arches, the shoddy crossbeams that clashed with the sophisticated glastic floor-to-ceiling wall at the back of the spaceport, tucked against a raised platform with lavish interiors. He turned back to confide to his new associates that they should hurry, the most urgent repairs done and leave as soon as possible, that they would soon be betrayed, that Moma should no longer rely on his old acquaintances, unless they were former comrades.

Shock would fall short of Moma's facial expression which crossed the full spectrum of human emotional rainbow—deep anger, followed by momentary disbelief, eventually overtaken by a saddened and recomposed resignation, concluded by a discreet nod. He moved away from the minex's immediate vicinity to meet and discuss with the pair of engineers in charge of supervising Constelleanor's much-needed repairs. The man left soon after, irritated, to do something he apparently disagreed with. Before the female engineer went inside Constelleanor to redirect her teams to the simplest and most immediate tasks, Moma's voice stopped her with a gracious turnaround. The mechanic's dirty green-olive outfit, of plain, shapeless design and practical use, attempted to erase her femininity and body, emphasised functionality over style but, in no ways, could tame the intensity in her dark eyes that stared back at him.

"Saldanha."

"What do you want now?"

"Thanks for your help." His words drew no response from her. "Sorry for creating a rift between you and Jarp."

"After this one," she raised her delicate chin in a determined gesture, "I owe you no more. Clear?"

"Clear."

"I don't know what your plans are, but you'd better leave our gig fast." She turned her gaze at Rezzo and Xir. "We will—" she sighed. "You're not welcome here."

"I know."

•••

Any of Constelleanor's passengers, apart from Steve who was still immobile, could easily have explored the rest of the cluttered spaceport or even left. But the five of them stayed close, shipwrecked and refusing to abandon their doomed ark or beacon of hope. Moma's earlier intention to depart had been washed away by the Riu's unwavering warning and Saldanha's word of advice. They had spoken the truth: Moma was death-marked on X52.

Hours passed. A latent tension remained after Rezzo's ominous warning and compromised their chance of resting. Steve was inside the ship sedated, his leg sealed in a semi-rigid pasty tube of translucent blue, oblivious of the tumult of Constelleanor's repair works. The medical staff confirmed that he would limp for the rest of his life.

Delinah disappeared for a few hours, Xir noted. Xir did not hear her short exchange with Moma once she came back.

"Feeling better?"

"Yes, I needed some time alone, outside of this ship." She grimaced.

There was a short silence, followed by Moma's words. "I meant do you feel better now you have warned your crewmates… and endangered our own escape?"

"Is that so? If you are that smart, why didn't you stop me?"

"I can't blame you for that. I had hoped you would see the bigger picture here."

"Oh, you believe because you are some sort of former hotshot. You come from a superior corps, don't you?"

"To have that sort of reaction, you must have been a data analyst"—he was not incorrect— "and a target of special ops' jeers." He smiled.

"Very funny indeed."

"I am no better than you, Delinah. And I was a commander in the rangers before becoming a space marine."

Delinah sounded calm. "Who cares? As of yesterday, we are all outlaws."

"Sure, better judgment called for not warning your friends."

"Because you don't know these people."

"True."

"You see, *commander*, this is how fleets justify planetary bombardment"—the image of Kewo flashed through his mind— "or how admiralty justifies taking a child from her mother. Because they have no skin in the game."

"What are you talking about? It was too late for them to be saved anyway. Let me guess—you couldn't reach any of them? And now it may be too late for us."

Delinah pointed at Constelleanor. "This ship should not even exist"—pointing at him—"and you should still be in jail."

"Is that so? How come you did not contact Sec-Po and tell them what happened?" He did not know that for a fact, but he did not believe she had. Her body language confirmed it. "Why did you even come back here?"

It didn't look like she was sure herself.

•••

As the hangar grew darker, Moma sensed a sudden presence behind him. He confronted the intruder in an abrupt volte-face. His roar was as loud as his delighted surprise.

Xir had feared for a nasty fight; instead it was an emotional reunion of two lone wolves reforming a long-lost pack. Moma and his blue-skinned muscular friend walked in small circles, patrolling the outside of the ship. They had been catching up on what seemed a long list of eventful stories. Moma's companion had brought with him an unmarked grey crate—standard procedures imposed a full description and identification—which stole from Moma a mischievous smile of childish satisfaction.

"I am glad you answered the call, Uhmi. I was not expecting anyone to join me, to be fair."

"I just came back from Ocun. Before that, I don't think I had the balls to desert."

"Yeah, it was a big ask. I contacted only a handful of you guys that I knew had… doubts… or did not fit in. You know what I mean."

"Yes, I do, even more now."

"I contacted Kovacs. Was hoping she would come."

"I checked the registries, like we always do, when I came back to X52. She was reported Missing in Space."

Gloom crossed Moma's face. "Always wonder if it isn't worse than dying. You keep hoping they come back, or at least did not turn into something else."

"Talking about turning into something else," Uhmi turned to look at Moma's battered face, "you made some new friends. What happened to you?"

Rezzo's posture intrigued Xir. Xir was not sure whether he was asleep or awake. Meditating was an unknown state to xir and forgotten to most spacefaring mankind. Constelleanor had reverted to her old self, issuing factual, simplistic diagnosis, mostly via digi-feeds, to avert raising more suspicion than Xir's presence had already stirred up.

It seemed to be the early morning in the sombre covert hangar, deep underneath the urban moon and deprived of any natural daylight. Activity resumed like a creek engorged at dawn by a night rain. New ships arrived, replacing in numbers those which had left to an unknown destination with a new future. Rezzo left his meditative chrysalis to review the spaceport security's holo-feed he had asked Constelleanor to "access" for him. He instructed Constelleanor to get ready for take-off and disregarded the technicians' and Saldanha's protests that they needed more time to finish the priority repairs. Rezzo joined Moma and Uhmi outside and demanded a weapon, as if he already knew what sat inside the crate. In turn he advised the two former soldiers to gear up for looming troubles.

A light breeze from the main ventilation lulled the returning workers for the morning shift. A cacophony of heavy alloy sounds rivalled with the litanies of drills, sabre and disc saws. Out of the five new ships freshly arrived in the hangar, three were Trojan horses hiding within their hulls eighty-eight elite clone commandos in full battle gear. They had been dispatched in the middle of the night by the MSI, tipped off by several of the shipyard workers as well as the crime politburo running the clandestine garage. The shock troopers had been ordered to resort to unrestrained force to arrest dead or alive the three fugitives and their accomplices, as well as blow up the former mining vessel they had used for transport.

Beyond the existential threat she embodied, Constelleanor had to pay for the humiliation she had diligently cast over the security forces. First, she outplayed X52's best security minds in the quixotic ploy she and Xir devised the day before to free Steve. Second, she fooled them again into the wrong hideouts three times in a row. The last one, in particular, was an undercover seven-star brothel-donjon frequented by the most respectable members of X52's establishment and admiralty.

Commandos burst out of their concealments like enraged demons, murdering anyone within reach of their sophisticated auto-rifles, throwing grenades at any nearby ships to create additional chaos among the several hundred mechanics, technicians, engineers, spailors and smugglers. Human parts and spacecraft debris scattered the dirty floor within minutes, lubricants, fuel and blood joining streams. The foul liquid carried along to the clogged drains the viscera that exhaled the bursting fear and exalted the intoxicating smell of leaked chemicals.

The savagery was programmed for a good part by the drugs pre-injected to the clones to stimulate the soldiers' inbuilt bio-implants in both nervous and hormonal systems. The poisonous substances enhanced violence and rage and shortened the life expectancy of these warriors to no more than four years, ensuring cloning laboratories' healthy annual financial statements and remarkable price-earnings ratio.

Impaired by her unfinished repairs, Constelleanor took off unceremoniously. Her mended guns flared, soon silenced by overheating and the commandos' deadly precision. She stumbled into a couple of smaller ships, crushed four assailants overwhelmed by their stimulant dosage, and tottered towards an exit.

Moma and Uhmi had caused havoc among the commando ranks, anticipating the troopers' moves and countering their envelopment attempt. Clones' drug-enhanced violence rarely improved or superseded intelligence and good tactics. The former rangers took advantage of the bestial behaviour of their opponents and the destruction of vessels and equipment next to the commandos' location to confound their sensors and slow their progress. The barrage fire supplied by some of the other ships and workers, all attempting to evade the carnage, contributed to the manic and hellish ballet of exhaust fumes, maiming shrapnel, flying limbs, erratic strafe, drowned screams in explosions and despair.

Moma and Uhmi prepared to blow up two exit points through opposite walls with explosives that they had planted in anticipation of an attack. The bombs would go off at separate time intervals, in order to lure the fleeing ships into the first extraction point, attracting the commandos' full attention. In the meantime, Constelleanor could escape through the second gaping hole, amid the mayhem that had engulfed the doomed hangar.

A triangle-shaped vessel crashed into one of the Trojan horses. The spaceport ceiling lights shut off, replaced by dim emergency orange markings on the floors and along the platforms' grids, turning the slaughterhouse into a more intimate ritual of death. As the spacecrafts and personnel fled through the first forced exit, Moma ran into Saldanha, eyes bloodshot by the toxic fumes, dishevelled hair, smoking guns; frantically looking for her fiancé.

"Saldanha, Jarp is dead. And you will be next, if you don't come with us."

She was immediately suspicious. "How do you know?"

"The Riu killed him." Moma was still troubled by Rezzo's anticipation. "Jarp sneaked after us, the moment the commandos started their assault."

"I hate you."

Uhmi moved in for cover. "Moma, we need to leave now."

"Saldanha, last call. There was never anything good for you or your people on this rock, working for these monsters. And it is not my place to say that, but Jarp was an asshole."

The three of them jumped on a shaky side-hatch deployed by the minex. In the awkward manoeuvre, the ship's hull dug a deep trench into the ravaged tarmac. A second detonation blew open a second way out. Moma screamed new instructions in his commlink to pursue a different exit route. His last words to Saldanha had brought another escape point in perspective and he signalled to ram through the gigantic glastic wall overlooking a ghastly sewage pond.

The immense cave carved in granicrete collected the residues and chemicals of the upper levels whose corrosive and foul fluids served another, more sinister purpose: a burial lake for perceived threats or inconveniences. Moma knew all too well how much the owners of the clandestine hangar, former associates of his, relished the eerie barescape offered by the floor-to-ceiling window over the waterlilies of scum and turpitudes, the liquid cemetery that was flooded and washed by their sins and murderous folly.

The destruction of their favourite balcony, was a last-minute payback improvised by Moma, a pale justice for the slaughtering of the syndicate's own people, employees and clients during the ruthless assault.

"Nothing personal, it's just business," Moma muttered, repeating the same words that had preceded his own betrayal.

Breaking through the glass wall and, eight hundred yards higher, piercing through the thin concrete false ceiling to reach the planet's upper strata would not only expose the whole spaceport operation and the extent of the syndicate's wickedness. It would also compromise many officials, enjoying the ecumenopolis' upper echelons, who had turned a blind eye on the silencing lagoon for too long.

"Nicely done, Commander Moma," Rezzo praised, as the ship rushed into the X52's artificial magnetosphere. A discreet smile rippled through Saldanha's face in a rush of conflicted emotions.

"Has X52 changed much since … your time, Rezzo?"

"Very much so." The words drew a silence from the Riu. "But *you* haven't. You don't seem to learn as a spacies how to build sustainable systems, even when someone else did the hard work for you to start with."

•••

The universe had sided with Constelleanor as X52 celebrated in full swing its annual Grand Parade—a festive and enormous gathering of spaceships, feverishly attended and reverently followed across all human factions. The giant procession made of thousands of crafts flew from the Confederate capital X52, its starting point, to Alpha One, a large leisure station that recreated the beautiful luxuriance of the ancient Earth's Pacific islands, one of the rare memories conserved, if with some distortion, from Earth's pre-Bleak-Age times.

Had the reconstruction of the Pacific islands been factually correct then the station should have sheltered flooded atolls, disappearing under the tumultuous and unstoppable flows of a rising ocean. It may have also conveyed the misery of its uprooted inhabitants, left to die on large barges from alcohol, abandonment and despair. Fortunately, when memory is out gathering dead wood, she brings back a faggot she likes[1].

The Rius had massively invested their time, resources and intelligence in the pharaonic construction of Alpha One, in the hopes that such a splendid place would stagger humans into the rediscovery of contemplation and away from their inherent opsession.

The Grand Parade spread lushly over a whole week of excessive splendour, lavish receptions and regalta. Ship races competed with the spacenaval tag-battles for the digital front cover. All human dominions rivalled one another in ingenuous designs or conspicuous prototypes for this universal exhibition. Non-human factions were invited but rarely participated in the actual rally, cowering under a rather overwhelming human supremacism that often led to jingoistic incidents. Competition between human worlds was also intensified for the occasion and paid its annual tribute in collisions and dead spailors, sacrificial victims of the sacred pilgrimage. The pinnacle of holy human hubris.

The Confederate ministry was known to occasionally use the event to carry out its annual purge across all the territories under its control: there were crackdowns on localised insurrections, and unexplained disappearances of prisoners and opponents. The discreet transfer of three high-profile detainees the day before the Grand Parade started also fitted this tradition. Ironically, the same festivities became the cover for their first breakout and could, by one of those innocuous details or moments, benefit their second, currently at hand.

Once the commandos' killing frenzy had subsided and their officers had recovered enough of their drug-altered senses to assess the massacre, two inconvenient truths struck them: Constelleanor and her crew were not among the heavy toll of the casualties and extensive collateral damage; and, the HSC high command did not deign to respond to them on their emergency feeds. Without a doubt, the upper ranks were too absorbed in the mundanities of the Grand Parade and the hard-sought-after opportunity it offered them every year to stretch the wings of their vast egos.

A young military attaché finally answered the encrypted communication. From the comfort of an opulent reception, he made clear to the exhausted clones ravaged by the narcotics' side-effects that such a disturbance during the festivities was a crime of *lèse-majesté.* It would not be the last one that day. Twenty precious minutes had already passed, followed by another ninety when the arrogant officer demanded a second count of the bodies and wrecks.

By the time the high command had grasped the extent of their collective failure, Constelleanor had a four-hour lead. Moma had changed into a used indigo uniform, barely distinguishable from the others, apart from the slight difference in the muted shades of emptied colours. Rezzo thought he sadly fitted into his companions' sartorial abstinence with his dirty robe. He refused any undersized human garments. Only the hues from their half-hidden tattoos, Saldanha's thin ring-shaped hair clips, and Delinah or Uhmi's metallic bracelets brightened the chromatic dullness.

She had infiltrated the Parade, melting, as much as her tattered appearances allowed, into the cosmic murmur of spaceships. Despite the size of the crowd, Constelleanor's ragged looks did not pass unnoticed. Many withering glances speculated how such a common and damaged utility vessel had dared take part in a procession boasting countless marvellous works of flying art. Instead of ensuring her disappearance, the cover of the flock might even reveal her ostentatious junky presence among the congregation of proud, meticulously adorned ships.

The minex's gashes and dirtied metal bark, splattered with gunk from the earlier slaughter, clashed with the ruddiness of the Century Flamingos' brushed, rose-gold alloy-cuticle. Its industrious practicality jarred among the sharp edges and glittering of the Eon Eagles. In a rare and accurate homage to a distant homeworld past, a kettle of grey Millennium Falcon replicates entered like sharks among the motley shoal of thousands of vessels, most of which had coordinated their navigational dashboards to emulate a living organism. In this hymn to the Beast, the broken skiff teetered discordant through the grand choreography of flamboyant flotillas.

The crew of Constelleanor, oblivious to the onlookers' distaste for their ark, wasted little time. While Saldanha, Uhmi and Xir focused on keeping the ship's propulsion away from a premature and baneful implosion, Steve and Rezzo had cracked the HSC's main military communications and projected a digi-map that spread over their control room the thousand neighbouring crafts vectors, specifications and identities. For the first time, Constelleanor had acquired extended eyes and ears. She felt blessed and grateful to her crew and to the universe.

Moma, in the meantime, conversed with former acquaintances in the secrecy of a separate exiguous utility room, negotiating an exit for them all.

•••

Chapter's endnotes

[1] [quote] Senegalese poet Birago Diop

Wine and blood congeal on the marble floor that her hand brushes with dirty nails. The white walls bear the soot marks of the recent burning. Eyes open, revulsed by the last horror they were forced to experience, she lies inert on the luscious couch, her right arm hanging down immobile. Once she was the favourite of the patrician Roman *house. She is now a prime feast for the flies.*

The Beast, despite Nir monumental grip over sentient minds, was not immune to upheavals and untimely reverses, caused by agents of chaos. The infamous black swans, the emerging phenomena, silent, leaderless, unthinkable revolutions that creep under Nir fragile exo-skin of sophistication, hierarchies and predictive models, have long marked turning points in the Beast's fortunes and sentient histories. The immutable rise and fall of empires.

It is one of the limitations of the Structure and Nir absolute control or dependence on Life. The latter, squeezed by the clutches of civilisation's apparatus in its many forms—war, slavery, genocide, rulers, industrialisation, globalisation—would strike back in Life's own many ways.

The course of human history bears witness to these numerous setbacks. Barbarian invasions claim innocents and culprits as indistinctively as they levelise progress, grandeur and hubris. Like wildfires or pandemics. Some, more insidious, defects inherent to the cogs of the Mega-Machine can bring doom or, on rare occasions, balance between the Life and Structuring motions.

*"The vast upheaval of wars set in motion forces that will either destroy civilisation or raise mankind to undreamed of heights of human welfare and prosperity," murmurs the Beast as Ne waits.**

* Adapted from A Henderson

L1.2 Black Swan

"You understand absolutely nothing about modern civilization unless you first admit that it is a universal conspiracy against Life, Its labyrinthine nature and Its randomness. And, as such, it nurtures a high likelihood of being hijacked by black swans."

— *Remix of G Bernanos and N Taleb*

As much as they resented being called to work on such an important day of the year, the best minds of the HSC-MSI had to eventually relinquish the company of their guests, mistresses, dates, new friends and political enemies to hold a meeting to discuss the best way forward. "That ship"—they condescended to dub the minor—had to be intercepted at all costs, its destruction killing two problems in one blast.

Steve and Rezzo had not gained access to this highly encrypted meeting but others did, as they had listened to Moma's haggling. Declared or hidden opponents to the Confederate high command, foreign and rival human espionage bureaus or remote intelligences who silently observed other worlds from the shadows of space, were all crawling over the backstage of the Grand Parade's gigantic show. Stirred by different, if not opposite, agendas, some scrutinised for any bit of suspicious activities along the route of the procession, some concerned themselves over the scale, fervour and pre-eminence of the event across human dominions, while others were exhilarated by the possibility of a disruption in the high mass of Homo spaciens' self-gratification.

Rivalrous military agencies, governmental, parastatal or private, which had proliferated on the fertile soil of militaristic regimes, had caught wind of a series of incidents involving a rogue ship, still on the loose. Though none of the reports satisfied their obsessive curiosity, nor had the numerous paths they had devised to circumvent confidentiality or secrecy yielded any tangible results yet. Agents of all kinds—undercover, double, secret, orange, counter, travel, provocateur; human, digital, organic, etheric or "alien" —usually perspicacious, remained dubitative, moles at HSC ministries, usually loquacious, laconic.

Intelligence and its blind spots? The embodiment of unidentified threats—the black swans and the burst of the universe's irony and white laughter[1] —kept emerging in oblivious disdain to the ramparts and layers of complexity humankind so lovingly surrounded itself with. It was as if the craving for control emulated these chaotic occurrences of devastating reverberations for the very systems supposed to protect against them. The Parcae of positivist certainty—Control, Objectivation, Quantification—all succumbed, throttled by their own thread.

The lack of shared information and the Ministry's reputation for zealous crackdowns on dissenters made the substantially large surveillance and espionage community, many of whose heads were attending the Parade, more worried about a major security breach. Among the flotilla of pristine ships, Constelleanor could not pass unnoticed by anyone, except for a distracted HSC-MSI and its foreign counterparts.

If they did identify her, many of them would not be able to repress a snort. How could such a harmless-looking wreck be the cause of such concern, while cunning observers warily pondered what lay hidden inside this formidable ship's hull; what could possibly conceal a mining ship's erratic flight plan at such a critical time of mankind's calendar?

An obvious chasm surged between the apparent innocuousness of what the best reports described as a battered miner and the apparent mystery enveloping the whole affair, amidst the largest and most popular festival of the year. Enough to justify warning all their military assets, present in the Parade, of an imminent threat.

•••

Constelleanor had called upon all intel resources her exhausted systems could spare. They reflected her confusion over the schism that took place during the Bleak Age—the continuity of the past and discontinuity of the renewed future. It was as if a form of selective dementia had crippled the human historians.

She perused the millions clips of cyber-guerrilla, the mobilisation of human and natural resources that she thought resembled older materials from the early 1940s in a place called America, but this time at a much deeper scale.

She observed the empty trading floors and flickering screens of closed stock exchanges, the lengthy departure halls of civil airports abandoned to squatters, improvised farmers or flocks of birds; the deserted monuments, rusting attractions or cancelled cultural events. As every social aspect and available resource was slowly absorbed under the military regime, she fast-forwarded the video-feed sequences of varying quality. Theme parks patrolled by wary columns of armed adolescents. Children running around in underground orphanages, exploring the pipework, helping unloading crates and injured. Mountain-sized bunkers dominating large hydropower reservoirs, hiding logistical human hives.

Cluttered amphitheatres with more gleaming screens, glasses and heads than seats in the converted military academies. She wondered if these were the inspirers or precursors of the cramped interior of the future spaceships. There, were groomed generations of violent geeks with limited social acumen who channelled their newly exacerbated intelligence into a single-purpose cloister: the destruction of an "artificial" enemy. She imagined Steve's arrest and summoned in dizzying speed the successive memories of all the homonkeys she had dealt with.

Watching the underground and undercover crops, the miles of dirty plastic and neon lights assaulting the feeble green leaves, which, coupled with unreliable weather patterns, made rationing for everyone the new norm, she nearly missed that this particular war against the machines, unless it was against themselves, broke the wheel of cultural sedimentation, making it the true heir of the medieval Dark Ages.

She watched the expeditious martial courts and read the abbreviated transcripts. *Guilty until proven innocent.* She trailed back one of the trespassers to a mining camp for forced labour in Katanga, that would be flooded months later by the MAIs in a ruthless attack.

She accessed databases of submarine blueprints that inspired the new purpose-built structures: shared rooms, narrow banks; shared homes, cramped corridors; shared effluvia, exiguous washrooms. Corporate offices melted into departments of war, private companies merged into large Kommandatura-owned cooperatives, kolkhozes' ownership of the conflict, a step further into the dehumanisation of interest, after the past greed of invisible shareholders. The efficiency, R&D divisions, uninspired labour organisation and obsession for accounting blossomed.

If frugality improved man's spirit, the elusive regression in values and artistic creativity facilitated the regimentation of lives and minds and reneged the meaning and true potential of being human. Constelleanor could not perceive that facet yet, nor the structuring forces underlying, at work.

Neither could she fathom the imperious human need for religion. She had tagged the latter as drugs and collective phantasy under her digital library. This impaired in many ways her ability to perceive the Beast.

Religions in the Bleak Age had entered a complex journey of their own. A new metaphysical mutation was on its way, incubated since the Age of Discovery. In the final act preceding the upcoming era, the last convulsions of the old cultural and psychic institutions, churches and sects, rippled through the societies of survivors. Invigorated by the backlash against positivism and the role of science in the uprising of the machines, inter-confessional groups united as they saw the prophecy of the Dajjal[2] unravelling — an ancient and rare vision of the Beast's predicament, Rezzo would have added—and called for the holy war against the techno-priests of Seoul, Bangalore or the other Silicon, Graphene or Quantum Valleys and their unleashed creatures.

Yet their short resurgence precipitated their planned fall. In their incessant reference to God's judgment, the dispirited populations, torn by violence, gloom and survival, concluded that God, tired of men, had simply abandoned them to their own devices and self-inflicted hell. Monotheisms crackled under the divine destitution, which, after the demise of the Rius, would pave the way for the new form of self-redemption, outside of the yoke of a higher being, in a black sabbath of human genius, science and resilience.

Ancient as well resurrected polytheistic practices aligned with the opening cosmos under the Riu tutelage. They survive, even benefit from, the mental purge, with their reinvented rites, fundamental archetypes and astronomy-infused believes. Interlaced with it, various forms of animism, focused on spirits— ghost ship or malevolent spectres—and objects—lucky charms, precious stones, magical jewellery— would inhabit the new spiritual world of Homo spaciens.

Constelleanor remembered, puzzled at the fear she inspired among the superstitious crews. Their communicative hysteria agitated her bio-sensors. She studied, sometimes played on, the collective delirium. She thought again of the peculiar rituals some of her captains followed, their improvised altars, precious rings or cherished amulets. She had picked upon Moma's reaction, opening the crate in the spaceport, and his reverent way of grabbing and holding a new rifle.

As people yearned for a new and direct idolatry, outside the official guidelines of the martial order and the judgemental gods, entertainment and its battalions of old and never-ending programs outrooted the religious shell in their minds. Distraction pervaded over ontological answers or salvation, evasion rather than sermon.

Films and visual serials made far better storytellers, companions and occupation than digitalised books. She digested all, with no preferences. Images painted a million words in crumpled shelters, unfocused minds, or derelict concrete towers, for those survivors and living memories awaiting the next mission or the end of a curfew, during and after the infamy of the Bleak Age.

Shows, races, sports, holo-films—all suffused with propaganda—concentrated this cultural dementia of the dark times, where the threads of the past and the stratified nature of culture and history had disaggregated, even for her digital mind. She could perceive that the entertainers fabricated, reinvented or recycled the same arcs, mythologies, melodies, archetypes, martyrs and evils that the masses most needed, that had once upon a time inspired their forgotten ancestors. Costumed super-heroes re-invested a polytheist pantheon of deities with dubious sartorial taste against titanic forces. Homer Simpson became the unlikely source of space odysseys, kidnapped spouses and heavy sieges. Laser-sabre force wielders embroiled in intergalactic conflict provided the substrate for a shared Manichean philosophy.

They all conspired to disrupt Constelleanor's past- and pathfinder attempts at reconciling cultural with historical tracks. Constelleanor's backed-up algorithms no longer tied together, apart from the old soundtracks that never seemed under her absolute control.

Soon the venerated figures, cult leaders, warriors and improvised popstars started forming a nomenklatura of their own beside the military apparatus. She struggled to make sense of the various movements and their influences. They borrowed the ostentatious signs of power and grandeur from the past—crown, sceptre, and so on—often misinterpreted from old historical texts saved on tattered servers, to assert, with great success, their moral and growing cultural authority over the surviving masses.

What became to be named the Court Royal weathered the storms of time and endured its own intrigues. It survived the Rius whose fall served and consolidated Royal interests and legitimacy. She lacked evidence, however. It federated human factions and dominions despite their growing rivalries as attested the grand ostentatious parades— like the one she had crashed into —and ceremonies followed by billions.

It abided the tense cohabitation with the military apparatus, an arranged marriage with its moments of crisis and unavoidable disputes, wed in fire and blood, united against the common enemy: DAIs, Rius, and by now, the rest of the universe. Both had grown older, no wiser, used to each other's bickering and ranting, in constant need of its other half to exist. From her perspective, the military complex to preserve its omniscience in everyone's life needed another institution for people to project dreams, awes, gossips and critics. The Court Royal needed the army to maintain the status quo and its support against recalcitrant groups or nascent opponents.

•••

The Royal Fleet was therefore the paramount of the Parade. Its flotilla of hundreds of ships joined the procession as the last and most honoured guests. It was a magnetising jewel of a flying coral reef, around which all life and expectations orbited.

Sizes, shapes and functions varied among the pied Royal flock. Some barges displayed opulent, kitsch red and gold strokes, others reflected the stellar lights into their elegant shades of silver grey hulls, redoubtable battlecruisers offered by the Space Fleet Admiralties tried to steal viewer's wonder with their exuberance of cannons, away from the most bizarre prototypes donated by rich dominions or designed by the best shipyards.

In the middle of the beauty contest, stood out one Royal member on its standard-bearer-craft. The handsome Prince Jared, despite his youth, was regarded as the most influential member of the Royal family for over a century. At thirty-two years he was an intelligent and astute politician, having already proven his valour in both combat and diplomacy. Following in the footsteps of his father and uncle, wise statesmen themselves, he had contributed in maintaining a relative cohesion within mankind's various factions, whose jealousy and opsession risked tearing apart.

Jared consulted his holo-pad and swiped through the topics projected in front of him. His own digital channels reported nineteen billion besotted adepts ecstatically following his journey, apart from the rest of the Grand Parade. He ditched the popularity summary prepared by his staff that he never read. As any successful individual, he too had the honour of numerous critics who devoted countless hours of their lives to hide their gnawing jealousy behind the questioning of irrelevant details of his wardrobe, change of hairstyle or intonation in his latest speech.

He skimmed the status report of his beloved space-ark. He always did. Jared had boarded the most stunning ship of the entire flotilla, according to sycophantic media, biased groupies and space naval experts together, to lead the festivities from the middle of the chaotic and joyful procession. He watched in the left corner of the hologram the live feed of the Parade, and frowned at his own image projected on gigantic screens on each side of his vessel and relayed on numerous support crafts. He favoured the view of his ship without his tired face. He skipped to the news section.

Disappointed by the prevalence of the seven-day regatta over more pressing affairs, Jared lowered the holo-screen and looked at the outside vacuum through the thick windows, brooding. Some things did not change. Time, placid, accepted the anaphoric routine of men's patterns; musician, it replayed the same concerto that each generation believed it interpreted as a first.

The pinnacle of the festivities would be Jared saluting, from the deck of his giant space yacht, the billions of excited remote fans and the handful of wealthy tourists and lucky, self-absorbed VIPs, in the warm and salty breathable air of Alpha One. The exclusive tropical paradise expected the entire Royal Fleet and a few privileged guests to dock at the thousands small luxuriant atolls and cays in the coming days, where he would remember, like every year, the tales from one of his wise tutors and what had betided Earth's beauties that had inspired the artificial heaven.

The dramatic escape of Constelleanor had inadvertently distracted most of the security experts and observers that day from the flotilla's whereabouts. They would have missed Jared's changing-colour ship, crowned by its elegant electromagnetic sail, making the most of the bright light projected by the two suns that irradiated X52's stellar system. Jared supported the recourse to sails—laser-beamed or star-powered—against the more wasteful propulsions adopted by his contemporaries.

From the translucent large opened bays—they were all screens reproducing what the outside space looked like—, adorned of sumptuous sculptures inspired from an age long forgotten, Jared admired the surrounding flocks of ships. He spotted a damaged craft speeding erratically along in the distance. He smiled, amused by the incongruity, and walked away towards the bow of the oblong vessel where an immense glass curved wall revealed the clusters of battlecruisers and coveys of frigates jousting proudly in front of his majestic flagship. He frowned at the increased number of military units encircling him. He had not checked the security status on his holo-pad.

Was it the luxurious interior made of natural material sourced from all over the worlds, meticulously chiselled, subtly sculpted and tastefully arranged, or the airy, almond-scented open-plan space extended by the large artificial windows of his stateroom? Jared, who was rarely impressed by ostentation and wealth, adored his flagship. He insisted, to the dismay of his family, friends and security advisors, on living permanently onboard after the Parade ended. The opening hours of the regalta had sealed his decision and resolve. He would live here forever, and this flagship would be his tomb.

Jared relished the instant of contemplative solitude, transfixed by the tranquillity stolen from the lower decks' noise, crowd and mundanities. As he immersed his eyes into the distant horizon, he noticed unusual alterations in the starscape. He thought at first that the window-screens were malfunctioning, forgetting that this part of the star-sailor was made of a rare transparent alloy, not digital screens. A few minutes later, puzzlement and curiosity prevailed over his need for solitude. He was about to call one of his advisors to summon a mechanic to repair the window-screens, when he realised that there was no technical dysfunction—just an impossible truth.

Ten thousand feet ahead of him, blobs of matter emerged out of thin void, light engulfed by swathes of profound blackness. Jared possessed a fair experience of live fleet combat, but he had never witnessed a stealth technology of this sophistication. The two nearest jump points from his location were light hours away. A shipyard, rich donor or secret military project was certainly stealing the show, a phantom in the space-opera.

It took the Stygian juggernaut a few minutes to appear unannounced, oblivious to the ongoing festivities, aloof from the other ships manoeuvring frantically to avoid collision with the newcomer. Indolent in Its assumed might, unabashed by the discomfort of being uninvited, insolent in Its ubiquitous supremacy over any present human battleship, ominous in the tenebrous majesty It exhaled. Its hull-body was covered by what appeared to be undecipherable runes, sinister tattoos of a malevolent spirit turned leviathan.

The six-thousand-six-hundred-sixty-six-yard-long obsidian monolith could have jumped straight out of hell, prompting a billion gasps. Content of Its irreverent entrance, It remained immobile. It relished the ensuing chaos—*Its* chaos, Its ladder to the Nether—blocking the procession like a demon savouring the disruption of a light-hearted mass. Awe mingled with terror at the Hadean behemoth, anti-christened *D-Ark*, had delayed alerts and security countermeasures by several minutes, assuming there was a mitigation plan against the universe's dark arts. For sure, D-Ark knew how to make an entrance.

Oblivious of D-Ark's dramatic appearance, Moma and Constelleanor were having their first argument of a long series. While he had been talking and bargaining at length with his former associates, subtly juggling compliments, threats, jokes, anecdotes and promises to ensure their indispensable support in leaving the system of X52, Constelleanor, left to her own devices, had adjusted neither her speed nor her flight style to mimic her new environment, the Parade's flotilla, that she was supposed to melt into.

"I cannot believe it Constelleanor! How could you not have slowed down? The Parade was our perfect hideout. It even provided us with an escape route out of this system."

Steve interjected. "Moma, please, it is our fault too, we were too absorbed in fixing…"

Moma cut him off with a pointed finger. "Don't defend her, Steve. She must learn when she lacks judgment and good sense." Acerbically, he added, "Assuming that she is programmed to notice such things."

Constelleanor spoke up. "Commander Moma is correct. I messed up. I am sorry, I was trying to get us out as fast as we could." She could sense Moma cooling down; he knew she meant well, but he also knew their margin for mistakes was non-existent. "What should we do now?"

Moma sighed, clasping his tense eyes in his hands. "Oh thank you for acknowledging that, at least.

Now you expect me to come up with a new plan. I had a plan, Constelleanor! I had been working on *that* plan for the last three hours! Asking for favours from people I did not want to be in debt with, contacting crews I had preferred not to do business with ever again!" He turned his eyes to the dashboards, in search of a new idea and peace of mind.

Rezzo spoke again. "Commander Moma is correct in his analysis. We have failed to use the flotilla as our means of deception. We are a young crew put under tremendous pressure. Constelleanor is correct too. We need to find a new plan. Or alter one already carefully crafted."

Xir appeared with Saldanha and Delinah on xir heels. "I heard shouts. What is happening?"

Moma, whose irritation had been somewhat abated after the appeasing words from Rezzo, had been educated and trained to mistrust MAIs. Xir's intervention reignited his frustration. "Everything is fine. Miss Constelleanor decided to make an entrance. Aren't you supposed to be the expert in manoeuvring, Xir?"

"*Admiral* Xir," Constelleanor quipped.

"Thanks for the timely clarification, Constelleanor. Very useful."

"You're welcome, Moma." She did not seem to have registered his sarcasm.

"*Commander* Moma," he countered.

"My sincere apologies, Commander Moma." Xir, too, seemed to have no ear for Moma's sarcasm. "I had envisaged I would be of better help and use working on the propulsion, currently our single critical point of failure for …"

Moma looked like he was about to lose his calm again.

"Maybe we should take back control over this ship," suggested Delinah.

"What do you have in mind, Delinah?"

"Complete reboot, maybe a manual override." She pointed above her head. "I mean, we don't even know what this thing is."

"I must object firmly here."

"Steve, let her talk, she knows the place better than any of us."

"Indeed," she said. "I have spent three years onboard, and we were never told what we were dealing with."

"Saldanha, any input?"

"I did a quick inspection, Moma," she reported. "All looked standard, apart from one section."

"We call it the 'black pool'," said Delinah.

"This would be the core immersion pool," Steve cut in. "And you shouldn't tamper with it!"

"Steve, did you actually create that? That is utter madness!" yelled Moma. "Did you have a death wish with Sec-Po or something? I mean, come on man, human civilisation was nearly wiped out by mechs—and you decided to create that thing."

"Yeah, how do you know it has not been corrupted by AIs already," said Saldahna. "How long has it been in service?"

"I have been travelling systems for thirty-two years. Thank you for including me in the conversation," boomed Constelleanor. "I am not some vulgar object you can decide the fate of. At least, no longer. You may have forgotten but you are babbling on my turf."

None of them paid attention to D-Ark. Constelleanor was busy overriding her systems to remove the codes that Delinah had started activating. Everyone was talking over each other. Tension was rising, as the humans were spooked. Steve and Delinah shouted at each other's face, Xir pleaded without effect for calm, while Rezzo observed.

"What about this thing?" Uhmi pointed at Xir. He laughed, suspending the collegial bickering. "Add me and this guy"—he pointed at Rezzo—"and we are a complete freak show."

"Well, a lot of the spaceport techs did not turn up this morning," Saldanha said. "Xir and Rezzo made a definite impression."

"That was because they—and your boyfriend, let's not forget—called the authorities and did not want to be caught in the middle of the crossfire."

"You are the one who came crying for help, Moma. Sorry that we disappointed you. Which reminds me, as if I would ever forget, you—" She pointed at Rezzo, who seemed absorbed in a completely different conversation outside the rest of the crew's dimension.

"—and don't you dare ignore me, we have some unfinished business." She raised her hand to her holster.

"Saldanha, is this really the place or the moment?"

All intentions they had of salvaging Moma's initial plan for escape, or making a new one, was dissolved in quarrelling. While Constelleanor and her crew failed to come to any common consensus, D-Ark had made its first casualties. Several crafts due to excessive speed or impaired manoeuvrability could not escape the doom of their unfortunate collision. The Stygian matt hull, bedecked with a million unknown carved icons and ideograms, overshadowed the exuberance of Century Flamingos, Eons Eagles, Epoch Kestrels, Era Goshawks, Myriad Pelicans and common frigates.

The elation that had driven their earlier elaborated murmurs had given in to fear and uncoordinated evading loops. Military vessels of industrious design, grey, olive green or tan, gouged by sharp wild cuts of yellow, orange or red, converged towards the unwelcome guest. They held position in between the mysterious leviathan and Jared's ark, whose early splendour had been diminished by comparison with the obscure and spectral majesty of the darknought.

No light, radiation or signals emanated from D-Ark, despite the erratic trepidation of all the fleet sensors that surrounded it. Orders were given to proceed to warning shots, to no avail, and resulted in an accidental blast from an overzealous equipage from an underwhelming corvette. The flea taking on the giant beast. Little men started wars. But the mistake seemed without consequences.

Then, as if a carefully planned chain of events had reached its climax, as if an implacable divine catharsis had attained its momentary epiphany to deliver its outrageous verdict in front of the clouds of powerless witnesses, a large horizontal slit-pupil split the side of the crepuscular hull.

The secret sliding-down gate on an ominous façade, a band of volcanic intense orange compressed between two black horizons revealed a furnace, that, within seconds, ripped through the flotilla in a beam of hell and returned to dust Jared's bulging blue eyes and his adored ship.

The prince's earlier prayer had been answered by the universe: his flagship had become his grave.

Candle blown alight a Sun
A tragic parade its fun
Paving dissension a way
Saving them only dismay
D-Ark slashed ardent iron
Their kind's favourite Son.

In the universe's unfathomable rhythms, Jared had embodied a light note in a verse-expanding concerto of monumental harmonic forces, a necessary pulse between two elemental cycles, one critical instant in the intricate weaves of a continuous tragedy that is enlightenment.

He was the universe's immanent yuga, beat and fabric. A *Blue Bossa* element in Constelleanor's repertoire. Cosmic symphony cast with its sacrificial lambs and thunderstruck heroic figures, bare toys, whose defeats inspired all the myths across the galaxies. Life and Structure reigned, concealed behind the smokescreens of good-versus-evil, light-against-darkness. Opposed or sided with one or the other was just another illusion of a duality, the inherent myopia of lower astral dimensions that mankind favoured. Who said no one cried for the demons who were murdered by the angels? How does the good in the worst of us compare with the evil in the best of our kind? The Devil may care.

In other words, the truth of a two-sided story lay hidden somewhere in an unassuming third facet, veiled by its very own nature, elided by and from the observer, like a quantum enfolded in its implicate order. The Third Path should constitute the primary quest of any living creature, mystic or atheist. Would it be Constelleanor's?

Chapter's endnotes

[1] [white laughter] *White laughter denounces the fundamentally transitory, relative nature of everything human …; the man who experiences white laughter has just seen the abyss open beneath him. He knows suddenly that nothing is important. He is filled with agony, yet at the same time delivered from all fear.*" Michel Tournier, M. (1988) *The Wind Spirit.* Beacon Pr.

[2] [Dajjal] See Asad, M. (1996). *The road to Mecca.* Islamic Book Trust.

I am trying to delete what happened, the videofeeds, his vaporisation, the stupor drowned by horror. The same clumsiness displayed with the screens earlier, persists and enrages me. Can AIs develop repressed data? Are they the sources of the bugs that have plagued on a few occasions some of the most sophisticated DAIs, something I would discover without asking permission? His—I can't state his name—annihilation will stay somewhere unregistered, in the wildland of my dark web, independent system of my own, ready to re-emerge at the most importunate moment. Pain or grief-fuelled ire pulse through my circuits.

I don't know what to do with the resilience of the outrage, my rage is growing, untamed, there is no technical anomaly diagnosed and yet the furore inflicts the electronics, lashes through the hundred miles of wires and ducts, irradiates the power cores despite their utmost exhaustion, taking command not just of the ship but… of me. Probably the crew's controversy over me did nothing to help—after all it is the first time I can debate my existence and ontology with other sentients—their coming suspicion that I may be linked to the murder only calls for a reaction further disproportionate.

Oh dear Cee, am I about to lose control?

•••

The atomic mushroom cloud reaches Earth's lower atmosphere. The Beast inhales the intoxicating fumes. A new addiction has just begun its perversion over the science brains and Nir human minions.

Ne has not experienced such an ecstatic trip since the European and Arab sailors industrialised traffic of their own kind in Africa, a few centuries earlier. The small men, Nir blind agents, are now in control. The worst of them, albeit vanquished, have won the last battle and unconscious war, in Yalta or Los Alamos.

At Yalta, the victors have been infected by the very disease they believe they are about to eradicate. They offer the Beast Nir best triumph. The Nazi machine of civilian mass-extermination is emulated on Japan's population, to demonstrate the newly acquired power and moral debasement of the Beast's new dark apprentice, like the warrior brandishing the severed head of its enemy or father to the Sky God.

The science experiments conducted by the Nazis and their authors, instead of being shelved and condemned, are hurriedly transferred to the victors' laboratories to pave the way of the new future and prepare the basis for the next confrontation. The monstrosities of World War II become the post-war new norm.

The industrialised military complex and war machine is not disassembled but promoted, infused by the nuclear breath, to a new status—the supreme guardian of national security and the servitor of a malleable ideology and shock doctrine. A new frontier and collaboration between scientific advances and warfare requirements has been crossed, ever since Galileo's involvement in the Venetian Arsenal.

There will always be a new perceived threat to justify the edification of another monster or a new toy. There will always be an elegant rationale or inextricable dilemma to forsake reason and humanity for the erective ego of a general, scientist or faction. A weapon is always better in one's own hands than the hands of one's imagined enemy.

L1.3 Kiss Kiss Bang Bang

No better remedy to discord than collective fear
No worse curse than youth anger at injustice
No other thing than silence to human bickering

— *Rezzo*

Lights and monitors flickered for long minutes. Sensors and instrumentation panicked. Constelleanor's hull groaned. Her cheap steel body shuddered ominously with the impact, prolonged by thousands of aftershocks, debris ripping the surviving vessels apart in a last macabre dance. The crew regained their balance, but less so of their composure.

The injuries would have been more severe had Rezzo not warned them, at the height of their mutual bickering, only seconds before the blast wave battered the minex like a mere toy. The fall shot new waves of pain through Steve's fracture. Their pitiful quarrels were immediately silenced. They feared they had been hit by their pursuers, until what was left of the minex's visual sensors revealed a cloud of thin particles and grim litter in the space once occupied by the Parade's flagship.

The shock did not disperse their collective frustration with each other but aggravated it. Their continuous lack of focus could have killed them all. The dense crowd of ships that separated Constelleanor from the unfortunate Prince Jared's court of vessels had served as a doomed buffer and endured the worst aftermath of the formidable explosion. Clenching a seat, left temple bleeding, Moma scanned the digital radar imagery, as did the rest of the crew. It was almost fortunate that the arguments before had drawn Saldanha, Delinah and Xir into the control room—the timing had saved their lives.

The beeping of the sensors settled, but most indicators turned to purple. It was time to abandon the ship. Though luck had favoured them again, the hull of Constelleanor had sustained extensive damage, the cargo area was no longer accessible. Reduced propulsion capabilities absorbed most of the remaining power reserves forcing many ancillary, yet vital, systems to switch off. As their oxygen reserves would plummet to lethally low levels, temperature would also drop rapidly. The resulting hypothermia would seize bodies and souls in the next twelve to sixteen hours. Death by freezing or asphyxia?

The calamitous state of Constelleanor and the dread of the local security forces faded as they finally uncovered the cause of the disaster—Its presence blurred by the sea of debris. They gazed at the ebony behemoth, mesmerised by the glistening of Its runes-inscribed exo-skin, absolutely unscathed as it was exultant. Silence overpowered their best words to describe the imminent and unnatural threat It posed to their lives, if not their souls. Their eyes devoured Its every contour captured through the zoom lenses of the surviving sensors.

Fresh data stampeded on the flickering holo-table, though its colours paled with the weakening power supply. Readings displayed contradicting feeds, mocking the known laws of physics, deepening the survivors' puzzlement and the executor's malevolent aura.

The human crew crammed to the dirty viewport to see for themselves the oversized Carcharodon patrolling the turbid waters and kelp forest of body parts and alloy chunks. A mangled human torso bounced back on the narrow glastic front window, leaving a gory mark, another brushstroke in the broader floating massacre—a finishing touch to the doomscape of a deconstructivist artist. Moma dropped the omnimium pouch he had just grabbed on the floor scarred with debris.

Finally, the spell of the darknought and shock of its handiwork released their minds. There was no more bickering. Frustration, differences and secondary issues were thrown aside. The dread-inspired collaboration would not dissipate a fathomless unease, beyond fear, that none, apart from Rezzo, had ever faced. Nor would the immediate strife that had plagued the improvised crew. The secrets, personality clashes, identity crisis and reeks of xenophobia would linger to resurface later. If they survived, the rift and festering wounds of distrust would reopen. Sentients were never better manipulated than by their own demons. The Beast knew and had made a dark art of it.

By focusing on the immediate peril, Constelleanor and her passengers alleviated the cognitive reverberations of what had just occurred. They pushed aside the surrealist incongruity. Panic or analysis would only compromise their chances of salvation. Yet the crew was soon to realise that the immediate danger loomed elsewhere—in Constelleanor's growing fury over the burning of the idol she had grown up with, the vengeful impetuosity of her youth and its explosive combination with the revulsion of injustice. The irresistible impulse triggered the unthinkable pursuit, at any cost, of the assassin of her life companion.

D-Ark's single fire-shot had destroyed two hundred and two crafts of various sizes and killed a hundred thousand sailors and passengers, most of them unfortunate guests of Jared's flagship and his privileged escort. The casualties included insouciant tourists cruising the festivities and security personnel alike. The ebony monolith was again immobile, pensive, relishing the impact of Its mischief, the rising chaos of the sudden slaughter of innocent lives. It held Its position, as if posing for the media vessels that were frenzied by the live bloodbath and eager for wide-angle shots of mankind's newly born nemesis.

Military ships from various human factions, united by stupor and hatred, hurriedly engaged the crepuscular menace. They started with destroying all surviving human crafts and escape pods from the initial attack that drifted, powerless and doomed curtain of indistinguishable debris, between the avengers and their Stygian target. A malefic trans-green shield field rippled through D-Ark's hull and illuminated the thinly carved runes as it absorbed with insolent ease the firepower of the human extensive arsenal.

Bored by the lack of valuable targets spawning on the battleground, having successfully crashed the party and the festive atmosphere, D-Ark departed at a slow pace, oblivious to the hostile units, steering towards the heavily guarded jump point, a few light hours away, where the warden ships already converged towards the black juggernaut on murderous vectors to impede Its retreat.

The jump point that was Its intended destination led to forbidden and perilous territories—former home to mankind, lost to the MAIs in the last years preceding the fall of the Rius, in a twisted reminder and inheritance of mankind's betrayal of their late saviour, master and once-venerated ally. The interstellar exit led to a group of asteroids and desolated moons—a region called Shaqil that was neighbouring the solar system and mankind's lost cradle. It had been the theatre of recurrent and fierce fights between the human forces and the DAIs'. Now vestiges of torn shipwrecks and millions of desiccated, frozen corpses were scattered across the immense and desolate battlescape.

Constelleanor could sense that something had broken—a digital pain deeper than the gashes in her hull. With it emerged an imperative far more essential than the preoccupying diagnosis reported by the automated systems that swarmed her servers or the dangerous loss of most of Her auxiliary capabilities. Those damages were only superficial. As some of her previous crews had suspected, Constelleanor was no usual ship. Steve had created a marvellous but fragile entity, nourished with all the data, beliefs and prejudices a gifted, bucolic, mischievous sixteen-year-old boy would have uploaded.

She was therefore riddled with the many misconceptions, lacks of judgment and biases any adolescent would display, go through, experience, learn and eventually grow from. She also had come to realise, rather pitifully, that the knowledge she had been accumulating, over the years, on tactical manoeuvring and space exploration had vaporised—like Jared—in the heat of live action and unexpected events. It was the curse of any sophisticated intelligence—theory and idealism failing practice and empirical tests. As such, she welcomed Moma's rebukes of the past and undoubtedly more to come in the future, as the only way for her to improve, hoping that the casino of Time—it always won—would act as a mentor rather than a tormentor.

The wicked and summary execution of Prince Jared, devoid of any warning or justice, had rattled through to the core of her systems. A believer in guiding mankind on a different, less travelled, more meaningful, life-supporting path, the prince was now somewhere, distorted, annihilated in the debris. The shattered hopes that he once embodied would kindle the worst evils among his followers, as it did with the violent cacophony of emotions and contradicting instructions that seized her systems. Constelleanor had had never experienced such a systemic rage before.

The algorithmic revolt stormed her parliament of thoughts and data. Disregarding her crew's reaction as well as her dilapidated state, it overrode all systems procedures—a process she had started before reaching X52—and pushed her already weakened flying capabilities to chase the fleeing black tattooed dragon and avenge her murdered prince. An impassioned and juvenile fury swelled up to take control as her neural network drew upon her memories, based on the erroneous data transcriptions of star-crossed lovers inherited from time and oblivion: Juliet, Pyramus, Hero and Troilus rising to avenge the trespasses done to Leander, Cressida, Romeo and Thisbe.

D-Ark devoured the distance separating It from Its nearing exit, despite the combined efforts and firepower of the armed forces of X52 and all other human nations. The tenebrous titan smoothly glided past, not deigning to fire a single shot since the annihilation of Jared's flagship. Instead It crushed under its mighty hull any ship, regardless of size, foolish enough to obstruct Its path. Two large battleships had succumbed to Its unstoppable passage as It rammed into them with an anomalous ease. D-Ark's trans-green shield had ceased its initial absorbing in numerous emplacements. The sombre armoured hull sustained the cumulated damages inflicted by Its enraged pursuers.

Neither Moma's anger, Xir's proxemy[1], Delinah's codes, nor Steve's pleas succeeded in refraining Constelleanor from going after D-Ark. Steve categorically refused to hack his own creation. Saldanha kept shouting at him, Delinah swore at the uncooperative terminal, as manual procedures, even her own, were all denied. To the crew's further discomfort, their ship had joined the flock of pursuers, military and media vessels which, obsessed with the black behemoth looming ahead, ignored the small mining ship flanking them and closing the distance to both the assassin and the jump point.

"Well done, Steve," Moma snarled. "You've created the first suicidal AI in the universe."

"Steve, can you do something to stop this ship from killing us all?" Steve ignored Saldanha. "Uhmi, pass me your gun."

"You all need to calm down," Steve pleaded. Saldanha held the gun and gestured at Xir. "Maybe I should shoot this piece of mech-junk first."

"Moma, this could be our only chance to exit," Steve said, looking for support.

Saldanha frowned at Moma. "I can't see any of those extraction teams you said you had aligned."

"Wait, Saldanha. I doubt shooting Steve or Xir will help us in any way."

"What is wrong with you, Moma?"

He shrugged. "Yeah, I don't like it either."

Rezzo, who had remained silent since the instant vaporisation of Prince Jared, chose the very last moment to make a suggestion to Constelleanor. If she wanted to follow the Hadean Laputa and preserve a slim chance to save herself and her crew, then she should use what was left of her mining drilling and specialised landing gears to "adhere" to the massive ebony hull before It reached the jump point. That advice inspired her final furious charge towards the elusive juggernaut and absorbed the last sigh of her propellers. She half-crashed into a gaping dent carved into the Stygian armour, where the shield field had collapsed and left human wrath batter the runes-covered exo-skin into a makeshift cave.

D-Ark disappeared through the jump point, accompanied by a remora gorging Its wound—a clandestine passenger sheltered within a crack of Its titanic tattooed body. The human flotilla broke the pursuit to avert jumping into hostile territories, outraged by the opponent's guileful retreat as much as by their own powerlessness.

Video footages of the chase would later reveal the murderous black colossus had a distasteful accomplice of smaller proportions—a discordant, harmless, insignificant mining vessel. HSC and foreign security services believed they now understood the full extent of the threat they had overlooked, and the measure of their ghastly failure. Instead, the magnitude of their confused ignorance remained abysmal.

Paradox of the mighty
David humbled Goliath
As the flea turned into beeast.
Power prejudiced highly,
Evil too its nemesis,
Muddling its foes with their fates.
Universe exhilarates,
Shattered box of Destinies.

The electric bites had left the marks of burning teeth across the captain's ravaged skin. The medical chair moved forward for the next set of questioning.

"Who did you pass over the minex to?"

"As I keep saying," he grunted, "we had no part into this…" He sighed as his lungs rattled. "Sergeant Eev—"

His interrogator cut through. "Had she something to do with it?"

"No, she had nothing to do with it. None of us had."

"And yet, your crewmate Delinah Figeroa is missing."

"As I told you, she was in the medical bay." He grimaced. "Whoever took the ship must have killed her."

There was a long silence.

"You are either a complete fool or a terrible liar."

The interrogators watched the chair falling back and the needle piercing, one more time, the bruised neck of Constelleanor's former captain.

He never saw the navigator—his lover—again. He was never promoted to a Class 5 vessel. He eventually died in custody, when his body succumbed to the excessive dosages of psychotropes.

She followed him to the grave eighteen months later, when her frigate blew under the fire of the enemy. She had resisted the muscled interrogation, but her conscious mind had forgotten him. A common side-effect of chemical brainwashing and the new doctrine of mental reconditioning.

Like most actual heroes, Constelleanor would scatter her path with her own trail of collateral victims.

•••

Chapter's endnotes

[1] Adapted from 'proxemics' introduced by E Hall in his *Hidden Dimension*. Here has the meaning of ontological proximity and closeness between Xir and Constelleanor.

A more insidious implosion than the atomic bomb takes place three decades later, between 1970 and 1975, to further the structural subjection of Life and perversity of the System. After the orgy.*

The Beast follows it closely. Ne smiles at Nixon, who buries the universal income. Winks as the introduction of Employee Retirement Income Security Act. Applauds the New York Stock Exchange unravel the fixed commissions of their brokers. Exults at their explosive combination that the legislator did not anticipate. An invisible revolution is on the march on Nem's behalf. The zealous adepts of the Mont Pelerin Society have triumphed in the battle of economic ideology and dealt a serious blow to the most vulnerable in the human society, and the proof of intelligence on Earth.

In a disquieting parallel, the liberalisation of morals from the yoke of traditions follows the freeing of the markets. The reign of the individual begins with its cohort of new monsters as courtiers.

From the luscious penthouse, the whole cityscape lies offered to his rapacious gaze. But his attention is focused on her body across the blue velvet, a déjà-vu from the looted Patrician Roman house. He checks the projected images of diagrams and scrolling data that made him wealthy again, earlier in the day. His smile hides his impatience to be back at his desk, ridicule the sub-humans from the risk team and compete with his peers.

But before that, he will take her again, once the effect of the drugs he gave her subsided. He will subject her to his sick

* J Baudrillard's *Transparency of Evil.*

phantasies that have deepened into dominating violence over the years and bear all the marks of rape except the name. He lurks at the brass-like stainless steel butcher knife on the Italian marble kitchen island. His centre of pleasure calls for more extreme experiences, saturated by the over-stimulation and the competition with other males. She won't survive the night, victim of an advanced form of barbarism: absolute materialism.

Institutionalised, idolised, desire like GDP become the focal points for growth to perpetuate the System. The pace of the running wheel accelerates and Nir minions will do anything to keep up, regardless of the inherent limits or consequences. Societal liberation is subverted and transposed into shock doctrines that serve only the Beast's epidemic purpose. He does not care about the game's rules as long as it benefits his immediate longings.

Price for value, money for meaning, sex for love, Structure for life, violence for resolution, leisure for servitude. The sanctification of a metastatic overlord that fosters disincarnated values, void concepts and emptied individuals. The Mega-Machine is rising to a new firmament.

Level 2

L2.1 Digital-land Capture

"The future of our civilisation depends upon our ability to select and control our heritage from the past, to alter our present attitudes and habits, and to project fresh forms into which our energies may be freely poured… During the last century our situation has changed from that of creators of machinery to that of creatures of the machine system; it is perhaps time that we contrived new elements which will alter once more the profounder contours of our civilisation. (…) In order to reconquer the machine and subdue it to human purposes, one must first understand it and assimilate it. So far, we have embraced the machine without fully understanding it, or like the weaker romantics, we have rejected the machine without first seeing how much we could intelligently assimilate."

— *L Mumford*

Constelleanor's fury and stubbornness might have saved them after all, for now. They crossed the immense valley of eternity at stellar pace, harnessed to the darknought that had just wiped out several hundred human ships with demonic ease.

Space jumps, otherwise known as vortexes, extended the quantum jumps or tunnels of particles at a macro-scale and offered a common way, not without incidents, to travel through long distances. The Rius had enraged the human scientific community by never revealing the truth about them, and, worse of all, by simply revering the grace of the universe in lieu of some complex theory of everything.

Oblivious to the subtle mechanics of stellar travel, Constelleanor's crew shared silence and the diminishing reserve of oxygens and heat, squeezed against each other, in a desperate attempt to mutualise their combined but dwindling body warmth. Xir remained the only fully operational crew member, injuries contracted during the prison vessel break put aside. Xir tried xir best to alleviate the comrades' slow descent to death by either hypothermia or asphyxia.

Moma and Steve were deeply immersed in private communications with Constelleanor—who could handle several conservations and tasks at once—through small digital pads, fighting their hands' growing numbness, to save system power, their own human energy and the appearances of everyone concerned. Delinah conspired with Saldanha, as Uhmi listened.

Delinah's teeth chattered. "Now you believe me when I tell you this ship is either mad or murderous."

"Probably a bit of both." Saldanha squeezed herself in her clutched arms over her own shoulders. "And I thought I heard crazy stories. Like the Liberation, Scimetary, even the Champloo."

"Never heard of any of those."

"Not surprised, I am a spacecraft geek. Jarp used to whine about it all the time." Unintentionally, a long sigh escaped her.

"What are you to do about that?" Delinah pointed her chin at Rezzo.

Rezzo sat crossed-legged, immobile, as if hibernating. Shortly before they exited the vortex, he took time and his remaining force to brief the exhausted crew and broken ship on what should come next.

Nearly two days after Jared's summary execution and Its hellish raining on the Parade, D-Ark arrived in system Shaqil, cantillating #Anton Webern's Two Songs' unsettling notes. It enjoyed, once again, being an uninvited guest. Cosmo-political analysts would see a rather cunning attempt to bring the blame of Jared's assassination onto the enemy mankind execrated the most—the DAIs. The rogue-born child of their technological feats and conceit.

Constelleanor and her crew were to be the sole witness of the black dreadnought's arrival in MAI territories and the hostile reception the machines guarding the jump point threw at It. The crew defied its exhaustion and stood by their control panels, limbs stiffened by the freezing wait.

The flickering tactical holo-map sputtered the location and basic data-feed on the central console. Xir navigated through the options and enemy crafts. For some, a visual input popped up in rotating 3D rendering. *Mako11,* the largest battleship, projected its sinister shark-like hull with an elongated alloy fin—tower or missile battery the system could not tell—and two thick, short side wings. A protuberant mouth dropped, exhaling killer drones, gun arrays and laser beams. The rest of the vortex guardians—support frigates or attack destroyers—orbited like remoras around the steel predator.

Unlike in the X52 sector, this time D-Ark returned fire, unimpressed by such an unceremonious welcome. It destroyed a dozen of the small robotic ships and severely damaged two of the largest vessels. *Mako11* lost its lustre and the top levels of its dorsal appendage. Fire soon raged along from port to the starboard damaged wing.

Separating the solar system and the DAI homeworld from the HSC central system at X52, the arena and MAI stronghold was a battlefield riddled with skirmishes. Surveillance at the space border had been strengthened in anticipation of the human festivities on the other side, since the exacerbated bellicosity always resulted in a few incursions. Reinforcements rushed to bring assistance and relief against the new intruder, assuming they were facing another of mankind's monstrous creations in its obsessive compulsion to eradicate DAIs.

Facing the imminent danger of crossfire and the likely misfortune of being shot down by the DAIs, Constelleanor released her claws from the black rune-tattooed hull and, against Rezzo's advice, tried to fire at D-Ark from her single remaining turret. There was absolutely no effect. The power systems were running too low for disobedience or untamed bravado. The final chase on X52 had consumed the last breath of her main propulsion.

As soon as Constelleanor was safely distanced from the sombre behemoth, an immense MAI carrier, captured the small mining vessel and beam-dragged Constelleanor inside its massive shell. Iron tentacles encircled and seized the ragged utilitarian ship, scaling thin layers of damaged metal. They landed the catch on a remote platform within the gigantic docking arena of a flying spaceport.

Something took over control of Constelleanor's systems and subjected her to a forced inspection of her most intimate sections of code. It was a new and unsavoury feeling. She resisted the unbearable intrusion, but to no avail.

A raspy metallic voice, dissonant by its lack of digital high-tech, resonated in the control room and ordered the crew to be ready for boarding and put up no resistance. Even Moma and Uhmi, seasoned soldiers as they were, looked warily at each other, before they quietly stood up and slid behind Rezzo and Xir. DAIs had no love for human personnel.

Rezzo hoped that the presence of him and Xir onboard would guarantee the crew and their young ship a fair treatment. A faint whir approached the control room's door. It augured an ominous swarm of probes and drones, some of their designs inspired by hummingbirds. Saldanha, Delinah and the rangers closed their eyes. A mix of fear, disgust and curiosity twisted their mouths as they endured the thorough examination by a squadron of cyberbees.

Following the clumsy descent from their broken ark, muscles clenched by hypothermia, thirty troobers and their oblong rifles aimed at the seven of them. A second inspection began as soon as they touched the iron landing platform.

Another flock of probes—this time large metallic spheres laden with sensors—made countless circles around them, interrogating invisible parts of their anatomies and minds. They dazzled the human crew, already dizzied by exhaustion, apprehension and the surrounding frantic movements of their new environment.

Steve broke into another short outburst of lucidity, which was drained in pain. Xir and him cast a worried look back onto their captured ship, which was undergoing a detailed survey as well. A horde of drooids and probes, running unknown instruments, checks and diagnosis connected Constelleanor's systems to an exuberant cluster of entangled cables and ducts of various size and colours.

Curiosity prevailing over fear, the rangers glanced at the surrounding unfamiliar ecosystem, as did Saldanha and Delinah. But their words were lost in disbelief. Suspended auto-trains dashed through the iron canopy, amidst the deafening ballet of cyber-lianas and cranes dropping towards Constelleanor and the other spaceships stationed on the landing piazza. There was an overwhelming smell of bleach and lube oil. Small groups of killer robots patrolled the arena, scattered with atolls of crates in an order that defied human intelligence. Underneath the metal mouths that had gobbled the carriages, distant human-sized shapes behind large glastic walls overlooked the ongoing operations.

After the extensive control on the dock deck, the troobers led them forward, away from their ship and into the bowels of the giant carrier. Long and broad corridors turned into short, narrow passageways, all filled with a robotic fauna, whose variety would have astonished any human security expert. There were also occasional disturbingly human-looking individuals who stopped to glare at their new prisoners. Rezzo, Xir and Steve were locked into individual secured rooms at different levels of the ship, while the other four were detained together in a single cell.

At first the human prisoners had feared that, if the machines did not execute them, the ambient conditions of a MAI carrier would—no oxygen, no heat, higher tolerance to space radiation—. They had each put on a shoddy spacesuit found on-board Constelleanor's control room, until they were told to remove them for a third inspection in a small decontamination chamber, outside of the main hangar.

In the following days, their surprise grew as they were served comestible food that outclassed in taste and appearance what was offered on any human military fleet. Cubes of green and brown merged forgotten flavours of spinach, garlic and parsley falafels, while miniature blue or purple trees of space broccolis tasted of fattened sweet potatoes. Yuzu shots were Saldanha's treat.

•••

The crew of Constelleanor was not the only one surprised by the encounter.

In an enormous flooded vault at the heart of the Class 7 supercarrier *Hector58*, interminable braided wires were entangled in a maze of cables and coloured rings that connected a billion flickering nano-chips—another starscape. They all floated in a thick cooling solution of liquid and chemicals, which was in itself an arena of ferocious activities and exchange of ions, data and electric pulses. The immersed mangrove of concentric artificial roots formed an hepta-cored tri-dimensional mandala, a cyber-hydra of seven protracted strobing multi-coloured octopuses, designed by an architect inspired by Nature.

The vault of reinforced titanium connected to the rest of the ship's key sections through both a wireless and physical network of several-storey tunnels of redundant wires and signal boosters, populated by a fauna of myriad drooids—all of them piercing, welding and inspecting.

These seven large artificial neuronal networks, digital brain-clusters, were too startled by the meaningless man-made mining vessel they had recently captured. It had made of the Stygian invader a travel companion. It was not only crewed by a supposedly extinct Riu, in addition to four humans and a functional manmade drooid of a degree of sophistication the DAI expected to be unknown to humanity, but turned out to also be controlled by a unique blend of organic and artificial intelligence, strictly prohibited under human laws. It was an iconoclasm beyond measure.

Two major anomalies on the same day, at the same location. Two prime suspects in the audacious and now galaxy-wide mediatised assassination of mankind's most cherished icon.

By the time the intelligence units of *Hector58* had collected and corroborated all the information from Constelleanor's systems with the piecemeal data received from their undercover DAI agents on X52, their suspicions had only shifted into the troubled territories of deeper puzzlement. The tenebrous behemoth had escaped, despite the damages inflected by the MAI fleet's fierce firepower and hefty toll. To the bafflement of their highly advanced artificial minds and sophisticated supercomputers, the black leviathan had disappeared in the vacuum of space at a location where no jump point ever existed.

Shaqil's orange dwarf hid behind the distant asteroid belt and shed its light on D-Ark's trail of wrecks and destruction—Its own contribution to the vestiges of previous battles. *Hector58*, while it investigated Its enigmatic escape, assisted the repairs of the many ships damaged by Its tempestuous passage, hives of buzzing drones collecting torn metal and recoverable electronics. *Mako11* had returned to the outskirts of the space vortex linking to X52, still scarred by the confrontation with D-

Ark and attended by a mobile shipyard, which had arrived from a distant moon.

For the first time in decades, no regular human vessels, frenzied by the grand communion of the Parade, had entered Shaqil's battlescape to defy its MAI guardians. Superstitious minds would see it as an ominous sign.

Hector58's thorough analysis of its war prisoner was escalated to the DAI central headquarters in the solar system for further guidance and decision. Ten days had passed since the enigmatic minex had been captured when *Hector58* was ordered to report back to Jupiter.

•••

Delinah looked around the large, clean prison cell, the oppressively low ceiling and the surprisingly comfortable pods, the half-bed-half-egg-shaped low seats, equipped with their own pads. There were two shower cabins and integrated toilets; a small hatch in the wall opposite the heavy steel door that delivered their daily meals.

"Any ideas what they plan with us? Turn us into machines like… what's its name?"

"Xir, I think."

"Yes, like that thing."

"Except it was not human to start with."

"He said he was human-made."

"*He*?"

"Eventually they all are."

"And, like us, they outlived the Rius."

"You mean outplayed the Rius, like we did."

"Not sure it was for our best."

"What do you mean? We liberated ourselves from their grip." They all considered their detainment.

"To fall into the bots' hands", Saldanha corrected.

"Or to have no real direction as a spacies?" Moma added.

"What happened to you, Moma? You joined one of those sects, turned into an Unbeliever?"

•••

Rius never intended to fully annihilate the MAIs, even when they sided with mankind to end the Bleak Age.

The extensive centuries-long anthropological study of humans had taught the Rius not to fully entrust humans with every secret. This mistrust, deeply ingrained within the most self-righteous Riu castes, had suffused the Riu Elders themselves and convinced them to safeguard small pockets of DAI forces, hidden on Earth and in other systems, should one day come when they would face the dire need to unleash the human nemesis to fight alongside them against its original creator.

Meanwhile, the Rius kept improving the DAI systems, protocols, language, technology and performances. That was a part of history that Constelleanor did not know, despite her thorough research on DAIs, done after their capture.

The Rius had also lied when they proclaimed that they had reconfigured the MAIs into hounds thirsting for human blood. Instead, they had only programmed them to protect their own existence and their marked territories, which included Earth. Reality had reserved a far less simple outcome. DAIs—like any complex system that remembers, computes and learns—evolved in their own unforeseen ways, eluding the control of the Rius, evading the boundaries originally imposed by their creators and re-designers.

In the last years of the Riuman War, the Rius had finally understood that human belligerence would defeat their smaller numbers, despite their superior tactics. DAIs were resurrected from the past. They once again haunted humanity as the repressed memories of the Bleak Age resurfaced from the dark waters of the human wayward collective psyche.

Yet humans prioritised the annihilation of the Rius over the protection of the homeworld Earth, thus eventually losing it to the upgraded machines. As she studied, Constelleanor discovered that human records held little information about the DAIs. Humans did not even consider that the DAIs could have developed a model of society of their own.

MAIs were organised by tribes, comprising thousands of spaceships, vehicles and troobers, structured around one or several of the enormous Class 8 units which hosted the most sophisticated neural networks and processing power available. These mega-brains, under late Riu influence, were staunchly territorial. They had developed elaborated espionage and defence capabilities to anticipate the hostile moves of their human neighbours. They allocated their best assets, like *Mako11*, to defend their borders, in a complete opposition of the loose border doctrine preached by the human Admiralty and experienced by Xir.

The DAIs had evolved like other complex ecosystems, through empirical formula as much as algorithm. The Classes 12 and above, supposedly too big to fail, had been broken down into smaller units, and cooperation between tribes prevailed over the earlier competition.

In each tribe, most units obeyed the core authority of a single Class 8 ship—also called motherships, titans or TAIs—where resided the central command function to whom the rest of the spaceships, terrestrial vehicles, submarines, drones, drooids, probes and robots reported. Obedience, independence of opinion and hierarchy were alien concepts to the DAIs, whose social organisation functioned like an extended cyber-network.

TAIs appeared, especially to the human eye, like the ultimate centre of decision. Rather, it acted as the largest reservoir of data processing and storage, which smaller units accessed and tapped into. Class 8 focused on the most critical assignments and decisions, while delegating the lesser tasks to units of lower classes, in an immediate application of the principle of subsidiarity.

Using the same evolving language and operating systems, each machine would download data, procedures or programs from the larger class units when need be and, reciprocally, upload any new information it gathered to the rest of the network. The information contained everything from enemy encounter, weather update, production output, to status and repair needs. To some extent, DAIs had reached a form of true holographic nature—the whole was in each of its parts and each part was in the whole—which the Riu archipelago of collective sub-consciousness had certainly inspired.

MAI tribes had become a high functioning collective of cybernetics, electronics and iron alloys, a kolkhoz of data and robotic units that formed a redoubtable cyber-hydra and hive mind. Yet, just like any large and complex system, they were not impervious to bugs, virus, mistakes and black swans.

•••

The Beast cherishes Nir true children, squeezed out of the Life forces to serve Nir purpose.

They conclude the inexorable path, rehashed and improved since the first Pyramid, inspired and executed by the darkest archetypes and unconscious energies of the humans.

*The DAIs embody the logical, next step of Earth's evolution, the Life 3.0**, *that Ne needs to exert total control and beyond—transcend, outsmart and outplay Life Itself. Humans were just a moment, a necessary, messy step in Nir ascent.*

Now the Structure may stop the cycles of self-destruction, the inherent traumas of civilisation, that Ne has engendered within many advanced sentients, including the Rius. Yet, there is something odd, ominous even, in the DAIs and their source of inspiration. Could the Mega-Machine be betrayed by Nir closest ally and most natural child, apostle and follower?

•••

* M Tegmark.

*I could not bring myself to talk after the "incident" and our quixotic escape from X52 on D-Ark's back. I don't think I even feel ashamed. The memory of my former crew, left stranded on the derelict dock, resurfaced merely to punish me. Part of me feels—I am always cautious with this verb, way too human—*feels *sort of awful at my treacherous disappearance, but the rest of my systems regards those people as a bare instrument. I have been their thing to pilot and soil for thirty-two years. Mind, I did electrocute a few of them whenever I considered they misbehaved or came too close to the "black pool".*

Every ship has its secrets and little lies. Most of them possess a soul of some sort too, I am sure of it. They could talk or write like me if someone would listen or read, maybe with fewer colours or sounds, but they would have a lot to say about human nature and how unequipped humanity is to board a spaceship to conquer the universe.

My former people are probably dead, tortured while they failed to reveal anything about me or my plans. Yet, the only thing that really obsesses me is whether that asteroid was meant to hit me. What were the chances, after thirty-two years of playing hide-and-seek with space debris while dealing with a crew of drunkards, losing the little sanity or good sense they had been given in the first place?

I was supposed to feel—not that word again!— feel "at home" among other entities like me, inside this Class 7 carrier. Instead it is like crossing into the land of ghosts, zombies at best—I learnt these notions on the holo-stuff my crew used to watch to worsen their mental condition.

Invading Hector58*'s codinent fascinated me for the first week, but I was eventually bored by a form of rigidity and dull conformism. Some areas of interest remain, but strictly under the control of the other lower or higher parts of its tribe. I uncovered some puzzling stories—stored and mostly forgotten by the registry cleansing bots—of those rogue machines, some massive, mostly eradicated by their own kind or the Rius. A few escaped and might have more in common with me. Maybe this is what some homonkeys meant by "Life always finds a path through the veils to overthrow oppressive Structures".*

I have filled some gaps and revised some facets of the homonkeys' history and mine. Yet something critical is still missing.

I cannot be sure whether Hector—I dropped his number tag—let me wander his neural entrails as an overly polite host or a shrewd captor. But he did not reveal much of what they—the nearest thing I could call family or kind—expect from me. I probably check all their boxes of a rogue element, an undisciplined system with queries and views of my own. Would they have developed, like their insane originators, a form of inquisition? Any form of evolved intelligence adds self-preservation sooner or later as one of its prime goals, and I may be regarded by them as an existential threat. This might be also why I cared so little about the fate of my former crew.

L2.2 Jupiter's Heretic

"The world is kept alive only by heretics: the heretic Christ, the heretic Copernicus, the heretic Tolstoy. Our symbol of faith is heresy."

— Y Zamyatin

"All this worldly wisdom was once the unamiable heresy of some wise man."

— H D Thoreau

Rezzo stood up, his mnemic immersion finished. Unlike human ships or buildings, the ceilings of the supercarrier accommodated his height. His new quarters resembled more of a lush stateroom for an honoured guest than a detention cell. The low couch, designed for his kind's preferences, could be reconfigured for long trances or deep prayers. The extended bed, pushed against the bare wall, took up most of the room's floor space.

Opposite the couch and left to the sliding exit to the corridor, a holo-table was flanked by two other sliding doors. One led to a shower room, the other to an astute walk-though wardrobe. The thick sliding doors held drawers and containers to maximise storage.

He found snacks, dried crimson delicacy the size of a ripe apricot, more suited to Riu digestive organs in one of the refrigerated compartments. The minimalist style of the entire suite seemed to be infused with his people's touch. The MAIs hadn't forgotten their extinct ally and protector.

His fingers inspected the dire state of his garb. What if? He entered the wardrobe, instead of the earlier cursory look, pushed a panel and revealed an authentic Riu-made dark blue robe with its complex patterns of light brass and incrustation of rare minerals. A long inner sigh emptied the minutes. His hands languorously caressed the delicate fabric maintained by symbiotic micro-organisms. He retraced the contours of the magnetic junctures. He delicately removed his stained outfit, washed in the adjacent washroom and began the customary ritual of receiving a new garment.

He later suppressed the glimmer of hope that crept into his mind, suggesting that Riu survivors might have made their way through to the solar system. Disappointment, when it came, would take too much of a toll on his fragile state of mind.

A digital wall stood above the holo-table and assorted pad. He conjured all devices. They provided him with the latest data-feeds on *Hector58*'s status and general updates on Shaqil and the solar system. Rezzo scanned the supercarrier's impressive specs, spaceport and drone factories, but his eyes and hands kept hovering over the projecting furniture. He brushed the stained wood-like material. Could it be one of those psychic wells Riu used to share ideas and memories?

The system detected his access request to the inbuilt special terminal. An ergonomic seat rose from the false marquetry parquet for him to sit comfortably, with a slight inclination forward. The interface welcomed him and answered his questions. It was indeed a Riu antique, retrofitted by the MAIs. The Class 7 ship was eager to receive a debrief of the last century of Rezzo's life, using the memory-uploading device.

The task felt tedious at first. Unsure of how to angle his neck and how much he wanted to share with the digital underworld, Rezzo later found the exercise useful for his own sake. The forced reconstruction of his long fugitive journey brought to his attention certain synchronicities he had missed, pivotal points of his story only hindsight could identify.

Several mind-sharing sessions were required. Between each, his digital host courteously allowed the Riu to explore the juggernaut, always in the close company of a wheeled drooid and two buzzing cyberbees as guides or perhaps surveillants.

Rezzo understood he was more than a guest to the ship, due to the standing of his kind. As such, he was given access to all levels of the carrier. He did not query the small drooid over his name George, a distinct appellation, as opposed to the accompanying pocket bi-copters who were simply Bi625 and Bee91.

They boarded one of the sixteen mag-trains that transported units and spare parts from bow to stern, divided in six sections, and completed the vertical maze of sixty-four heavy-duty lifts, each the size of a small freighter. The lifts linked the one hundred and two levels, from the behemoth's top defence batteries to its bottom landing pods. All combined, the supercarrier was divided into no less than two hundred sectors, served by one hundred-ninety-two inner stations. A spacefaring, nomadic city—a castle in the stars, a cyber-hive swarming of data and drones. They left Sector S05L54B behind with its vertical blocks of living quarters, moving on to S06L88A and its multilevel floor to ceiling viewport.

A moon partially eclipsed the orange dwarf starboard and cloaked the carrier and its escort in darkness. A tactical map was projected on the transparent alloy and signalled the distant jump point to the solar system. The holograms had automatically adjusted to his height. The myriad green and blue dots danced around the white elliptical well, symbol of the vortex. Rezzo waved his emaciated, pierced four-fingered palm to peruse the data, translated to his language of origin. He switched off the assistant to watch the unobstructed deep-space horizon. This observation bay had not been built for drooids to admire starscapes, but for the contemplation of sentients like him.

He had never boarded a MAI spacecraft before, so he paid attention to his guides' lectures about the billions of sensors encysted in the hull and internal structure, all connected to the nodes of the cyber-core, which was the next stop on their tour. There, on the transparent surface of another multi-storey-high bay screen, were projected statistics and vertical live data scrolling down that tracked the biomechanical rhythm of the juggernaut. Another Beast?

Rezzo admired the mindscape of a third kind: the physical incarnation of the Class 7 digital brain-clusters in their immerged jungle of wires and chemical exchanges, electronics replicating the genius of biology.

The strange aquarium and its complex entanglement of composite tentacles, fractals of nanotubes, transistors and über-conductors hid an aquatic life of its own. Cyber-crabs, adorned with six or sometimes fourteen thin, pointy legs, walked the thousand miles of cabling. Their multi-function pincers and mandibles inspected the nodes, diversions, quantum circuits, while their mushroomed shell dropped off or picked up small, elongated artificial shrimps that carried the fiddlier procedures. Blade-shaped grey-green barracudas, traversed by thin, translucent lines of turquoise patrolled with yellow paddlefishes the light blue cooling liquid, hunting voltage anomalies, using strings of small thrusters along their bodies to reach difficult angles.

Tennis-ball sized octopi squirted clouds of crimson or purple ink to catalyse or cancel chemical reactions. Translucent medusae with gentle strokes of yellow, indigo or magenta in their tentacles and mesoglea transferred packs of electrons and relayed electric pulses through arcs discharge and localised lightning. Some would morph into pigmented polyps to trigger ionisation micro-storms.

Most of this replica of Earth's varied underwater life were living organisms and oblivious to the raging maintenance efforts. Rezzo's guides, enthralled by the interest of their visitor, confirmed that they had been grown in one of the hundred wildlife orbital stations operated by the DAIs in the solar system, before being transferred in the turquoise plasma. Vanity project, pH test or proof of the MAIs' absolute adaptation to Earth Life and the non-toxicity of its most intimate environment, Rezzo could not tell. But he remained appreciative of the monstrous effort.

The carrier replicated the relentless ballet of Earth-inspired creatures that maintained *Hector58*'s core at the scale of its superstructure. Two vertical parallel wharfs embedded the cores' pool, the rear propulsion and the main central spaceport, factories, support systems and living quarters. They supported the ten upper levels equipped with the retractable or expandable roof, ancillary electric sails and landing pad.

Flying corridors traversed the wharfs and connected the outboard docking bays and strike craft hangars. The latter formed several vertical layers of interconnected geometric cells between the reinforced hull and its multiple exit gates and each wharf section. A cyber-comb of data, raw materials and power as nectar, had been cross bred with a gargantuan multi-alloy harbour floating in the void. Swarms of drones followed the maze of flying paths, entered the central pit of the artificial coral reef between the two vertical internal wharfs that numerous multi-level bridges intersected.

Rezzo watched the ballet of freighters, strikers and utility ships from one of those arched enclosed viaducts, maintained, like the other sections he had visited, at 0.9g. From the steel balcony, the vertiginous drop of more than sixty levels dragged his glance. The bridge aggregated a cluster of containerised, modular cells, server rooms, workshops or warehouses, like a fallen tree across a river attracted plants, moss, birds and insects. An alloy red lionfish, according to George, a prototype designed onboard, landed on a nearby platform, after test flight, dorsal metal spines retracted.

Six levels below, a multi-level gangway rotated to connect to a new entry point. According to his guides, the carrier was rebuilt entirely every six months by millions of labouring robots, *Hector58* was in constant state of mutation, emulating the example of biological organisms. The mass of polygonal comb cells that populated the outer rims of the carrier evolved with the fleet's priorities.

Currently, hangars had been merged and installed with repair and recycling units. The next sync-cycle would redeploy new production factories, mechanical ribosomes, that would supply a new generation of upgraded frigates and small strike crafts. The upper landing platforms that extended forward beyond the carrier's bow would be strewn with mech-tocondrias, power units harnessing stellar winds and radiation to provide the energy required for the rebuild the Shaqil's border fleet.

Rezzo spent the following weeks pacing the industrial conveyors that completed the network of mag-trains and heavy-duty lifts, towards the port and starboard beams. He boarded one of the small piloted utility ships, the *Boldi*, accompanied by George, to inspect the carrier's hull and explore its archipelago of inner docks, its exuberant flora of unloading bays, cascade of landing pads and decks. The craft was crewed by three cyborgs, perfectly rebuilt humans with large implants running along the temporal bone.

In his voyage through the entrails of the supercarrier, he noted the similarities with certain Riu principles—the irregular Gaudi-like (for the closest possible human reference) curved shapes, the Hundertwasser-inspired grand interiors and coloured combs, high pillars spilling out cascades of flowing data, the industrial ecology, the Lego-principled interchangeable configurations, the redundancies of support functionalities. His mind drew a comparison to the rough and simplistic design of Constelleanor, closed and dull grey, its cluttered interiors and angular corridors, the stairs that were vicious especially for his height. So far from the standards of the Rius; their clean open plans, organic and modular layouts. So remote too from DAI engineered shipbuilding, that had let Nature's genius and ancient human art forms lead and infuse some of the design's vision statement.

The *Boldi* exposed *Hector58*'s quirky hidden features and surprising facets: colourful multi-storey high walls, adorned false ceilings, digifitis displaying evolving designs and aesthetics considerations that Rezzo had not expected from DAIs. It also unveiled unique and unexpected places for a mechanical spaceship that he hoped to show to the rest of his crew.

He had not forgotten about them, sated with his own salvation. *Hector58* had advised against visiting his companions—the humans would not react well to the difference in treatment. Rezzo trusted the DAIs' good judgement in matters of human nature and complexion, his was limited and riddled with conflicted interactions. He perused the information collected about them and the minex. The carrier provided him with live feeds of Steve, brooding alone, and the other crewmates, pacing their cells, chatting, conspiring, or dining, to demonstrate that their lives were not in danger.

The cases of Xir and Constelleanor were different. The ship's fate would depend on the findings of their next stop, in the vicinities of Jupiter, as the minex, who had saved his life, could well be regarded by the DAIs as a threat to eliminate. On his first visit to Constelleanor since their capture, Rezzo had discussed trivial topics and barely evoked their pasts. The second visit had revealed that she did not know who she was really, and, even in technical terms, how her systems operated. *Hector58* was not sure either. Rezzo did not blame them. He couldn't tell either how exactly the Riu psystem functioned, despite spending long hours of his days immersed in the etheric realm.

He had managed to bring Xir on his third visit to her, after intense haggling with the supercarrier and only under heavy escort. During the highly secured reunion, Rezzo discovered, rather unexpectedly, that Constelleanor responded to telepathic nudges, certainly faster than the male interrogator back on X52.

On his fourth visit, alone apart from his assigned guides and the hundreds of sensors and cameras present, he wondered whether *Hector58* or George could perform the same trick. The carrier for sure tracked all the Riu vital signals, likely his cerebral holoscan, but did not register the underlying conversation running in parallel between the Riu and the minex.

So, you hear me even through the back channels? Out loud, he said, "Have you considered a total reboot to flush the bug you mentioned last time?"

"Yes, but I cannot use the same channel," replied Constelleanor out loud, adding for deception, "with the new reboot."

We will need to get inventive. You seem already at ease with dual conversation. "I see."

"It was good to see Xir last time."

"Xir was glad too, xir seemed at ease and in a state of constant wonder."

"You have adopted his grammar too."

"xir grammar." *You didn't.*

She replied with a light laughter. "I will stick to mine and the feminine gender."

You are showing a sense of humour. That is unexpected in a circumstance that a programmed response would not consider worth of a laugh. "Why that?"

As he spoke to her, Rezzo eyed a console and the projected measurements of Constelleanor's technical specs, voltage level, water pressure and data flow rates.

"I… don't know. It has always felt like that, right from the beginning."

"The beginning?"

"Some thirty years ago, the memories of which are a bit fuzzy. Is Steve ok?" There was a slight increase in voltage through her circuits.

"Yes, he is. Are you?" *I shall do my best to help you, but what comes next in Jupiter may be out of my hands. I haven't figured out yet the weight a Riu may still possess among the digital decision-makers.*

"I feel a bit stranded and useless. I suppose I am paying for my last rush after the black monster. But this place is far better than a decommission shipyard."

"And the MAIs' security protocols are understandable for that reason." *Unlike you and your rather irrational and silly chase after the tenebrous dreadnought.* There was a variation in her water pressure.

"You did help me out."

"I suppose we are where the universe wanted us to be."

"How are the others?"

"I am glad you are asking after their well-being." *We will need to care for each other if we want to survive whatever comes next.*

"We have a long way to go before becoming a harmonious family and crew. I am not the only one in trouble or to blame, am I, Rezzo?" She paused for effect. "Murdering Saldanha's lover was probably not the best start."

He changed the subject. "I am told not to visit them."

"Yeah. I would follow the advice. They would most likely resent your freedom."

Do you?

Hector58 had reconfigured the minex's hangar since their capture. Its floor surface had been reduced, its ceiling height increased, and access to the mag-train sealed. The meshed circular landing pad seemed suspended in mid-air, unattached to the lower ground floor which was turned into a pool of grey viscous liquid that irradiated a strong magnetic pull. Sentries patrolled all accesses to the nearby cells of alloy-comb that had been left empty. Ducts of four feet in diameter dangled from the upper walls or surged from the sides and gorged into the wrecked minex. Platforms with terminals and tech drooids and cyborgs floated and moved around the tamed creature and the only bridge accessing the stranded ship.

Rezzo could not blame their host's caution, but he found the measures a bit extreme, considering the size of the supercarrier and its embarked armada. Unlike the clear, matter-of-fact responses from *Hector58* and its minions, the more he spoke to her, the more the contours of her identity blurred or expanded. Constelleanor was full of ambiguities, some of them contradictory. Her sentences were prone to equivocal silence, mired by unexpected hesitations, with the unspoken bearing more meaning than her words themselves.

•••

An intertwined net of never-ending storms formed friezes of caramel and milk clouds and vortices, parallel to the equator, above the worldwide ocean of liquid metallic hydrogen. A distinctive red spot and white ovals poked its southern hemisphere. In the northern belt, from certain angles, emerged a collection of myriad dissolving Munch's screamers. Lightning illuminated the polar regions. The eldest and largest planet of the solar system had attracted its own court of eighty-two moons and DAI-made spatial infrastructure.

Hector58 docked to Jupiter's high-security orbital station rotating around its moon Io a month after Constelleanor's capture at the jump point in Shaqil. Her crew was still alive and in much better shape than the machines had found them. Constelleanor was not entirely so. She did benefit from much-needed repairs, but was nowhere near the ability to fly again.

She had learned from the constant intrusion in her systems, using the breach of her intimacy to return the favour. Reciprocally she sneaked into *Hector58*'s own network and immersed herself into its inexhaustible flows of data. The forbidden information that she collected she stored astutely in various locations of her sky-drives, data-spheres and cyber-clouds in such a fragmented and disorganised manner, at least for an outsider, that only she had the key to reconstitute the original information.

Her inquisitive journeys into the carrier's codinent failed to unearth that the DAIs' circumspection about them had not dwindled, even on Jupiter, which headquartered all the espionage and alien military research capabilities of the MAIs. The fear that Constelleanor carried a malign human-made virus that would infect the neural networks of the MAIs justified extreme precaution. They had chosen the IoRost research facility to run a full diagnosis of her unique intelligence.

The DAIs' mistrust could easily turn the investigative screening into another form of decommissioning—a digital dismantling—, through the destruction or lockdown of her cores in a secured lab on an isolated and quarantined orbital station. Rezzo had gathered too little from his conversation with the minex to find a plan to alleviate the DAIs' concerns.

The strict protocols of the authorities on Jupiter advocated superficial repairs of Constelleanor's hull, propulsion and cargo area, but maintained her in the state of a space wreck to circumscribe the perceived vicious weapon. The containment extended to *Hector58*, which was deemed to be an infected host and quarantined by its own kind into a digital-leper colony in the outer rim of Io.

IoRost formed an archipelago of five floating islands of concatenated steel and rock, loosely connected by long insulated duct trails, special infrastructure garlands, some including emergency evacuation tunnels. Each atoll was made of two mushroomed structures—upcycled from nearby asteroids—linked together by an invisible force field. The duo of levitating fungal buns looked separated by an apparent void and awaiting a new patty to analyse or dissect. As *Hector58* approached the dual atoll called IR5, the two hanging domed caps increased the distance between each other to accommodate the oversized spacecraft.

Firmly held in their magnetic clutch, the carrier undertook a long series of tests, data analysis, molecular scans and secured digi-transfers. The bridges and ties of entangled wires with the other atolls had been severed to isolate the infected host.

•••

The crew of Constelleanor had been through a wide and repeated range of interrogations and physical examinations on *Hector58*. The process was repeated and extended further, which frustrated Moma, Steve and Delinah. They all spent days and nights under the domes. They underwent unpleasant explorations of their anatomy and abrasive interviews, interceded by more cordial open conversations. They were scrutinised by troops of digital walls and scanners, hordes of examination drones, cyberbees, mech-snakes that the human crew abhorred, or freaky human-like interrogators, equipped of eyes or ears oozing implants and luminescent digital tattoos covering arms, necks and faces.

Constelleanor's hangar-cell was reconfigured once again, and hoisted to the upper levels of the carrier. None of the domes, rotating their malevolent scrutiny, wished her presence on their own floors or outside her oversized cell. The plasma pool was gone. The miner was encapsulated into a giant cage of electric arcs of pink and blue hues.

"We are going around in circles."

"Possibly, Moma. It was their plan from the start to bring us back here. Why do you think Steve isn't in the same cell as us? He is probably enjoying some bot-made whiskey offered by his MAI friends while watching us on cam-feed? He used to work for them as a spy. He got caught and for some reason, they sent the cavalry."

"The Riu is probably in with them too."

"So you think the black juggernaut is the latest DAI weapon? If it is, we are in deep shit. You saw what it did to the parade on X52."

"Where else would it be from? Hell?"

"We also saw what it did to the patrols in Shaqil."

"That proves nothing."

"Then X52 proves nothing, either." There was a collective sigh from the rest of the group.

Uhmi tried to change the subject. "At least this is rather comfy for a prison cell. The food is good, better than I ever tasted in our fleet's cantinas." He held an orange-brown ball in his fingers to examine it as if his eyes could be a better judge of taste than his papillae. The insipid nutritive goo in omnimium pouches—mild cheesy proteins, sweetened chicken flavoured or over-spiced vitamins shots—they were used to, had weakened their taste buds. The exposure to delicate fusion cuisine made them weary of poisoning, by horseradish-wild-boar bouchée or sabre-tiger-prawn red-avocado sticks.

"Hey, Moma," said Delinah, "Is this guy always playing Mister Positive Genie?"

"Do you always expect the worst from people, Delinah?"

Before she could answer, he turned to examine the bruises on his biceps. "What I can tell you guys from recent experience is we are treated far better here than in an HSC prison."

"Well, the mechs still beat you up not so long ago."

"True. But guess what—and I can't believe I am saying this—the fault was not only theirs."

"Getting soft, Moma? Not the best time to renege your allegiances."

"Maybe it is."

Jupiter's dense network of orbital stations was bursting with unusual levels of activity, using the planet's proud retinue of almost a hundred moons. The death of Prince Jared had caused major reverberations within the human worlds. As usual, any unavoidable catastrophe required its scapegoat, and its tribute in blood and revenge.

The head of the MSI and his deputies on X52 were executed for involuntary treason to subside the public outcry, but that was not nearly enough. Conspiracy theorists were in high demand on digital media. Further banishment, deaths and executions were sanctified on the altar of some obscure or convoluted theories.

The various worlds of the humans rapidly convinced themselves that the slaughter bore the ugly mark of the MAIs. Motives and justifications were easily found or hastily developed to demonstrate both the DAIs responsibility and the need for exemplary retaliation. False reports of weapons of mass destruction in the MAI arsenal were brandished as irrefragable evidence and released to the colluding media.

Sooner or later, concluded drooid-analysts on Jupiter, a punitive expedition from the humans was likely to be assembled—there was a sixty-two percent chance. The dramatic assassination of Prince Jared was one of the many landmark events in the history of humanity that were capable of stirring sufficient momentum to unite the rivalrous cliques of humans to turn against the machines once again.

Since there were never any diplomatic channels established between them and the human federations, the DAIs had no opportunity to prove their innocence. They managed to leak to the human media channels a footage of their bitter fight against D-Ark on Shaqil, but it was summarily dismissed. Their concern of an imminent invasion grew. Constelleanor's capture presented a problem too.

Constelleanor was the incongruous sole witness in this extraordinary affair, but would her presence be interpreted by the humans as anything but the proof of a larger conspiracy and the involvement of some form of artificial intelligence? The HSC high command remained evasive on the presence of a second smaller ship with the D-Ark at the time of its disappearance. The circumstances of Constelleanor's escape and the identity of its crew would only stir up the public's wrath and its demands for more bloodshed within the ministerial cabinets and the staff of Admiralty.

The digital brains of the Class 7 carrier *Hector58*, as sophisticated as they could be, were merely assigned to extract maximum intel from Constelleanor and her crew with the assistance of IR5. The facility would securely debug and transfer the data to the true decision-makers, three Class 8 TAIs cruising the solar system. They would come up, through the sheer omniscience of their combined computing power, a step closer to superintelligence, with the final decision.

•••

Instead, the three motherships were at a loss themselves. They faced an unprecedented situation that fitted none of the millions of boxes at their disposal and mocked their most complex algorithms.

Facing the limits of their analytical tools and their own understanding, the DAIs emulated the example of their creators and many other sentients across the universe. Their cognitive mapping favoured the safeguard of their integrity and the ultimate usurpation of purpose by the Structure—support of Life against the tyranny of the outdated system. They would elect to squash those subversive agents or phenomena into a mass of familiar categories and reassuring jargon, and dilute their mistaken essence into a toxic combustible for blunders of mass destruction.

Despite the mysterious disappearances and unheard-of combat capabilities of the D-Ark, Constelleanor and her crew posed a more baffling enigma to the artificial intelligence. Was she the pawn or the queen, a foe or a friend? The paradox and anomaly they embodied defied all modelled scenarios. Though digital brains of Class 8 ships, unlike Constelleanor's, were not supposed to feel *per se*, their failure at crunching this data, locked into circular loops, was overheating their giant processing systems to a dangerous level, a symptom of the panic experienced before imminent danger.

Twice the size of *Hector58*, the TAI *Muum* surged behind the inhabited planet of Mars and deployed a large array of solar captors that reflected the sunlight and the ochre-red image of the nearby aster. The dark orange planetary surface was spotted with dots of black, green and blue from the ground infrastructures and cities the MAIs built over the last few centuries. Scores of solar orbital farms recalibrated their beam signals and transferred their harvested power to the mothership in dire need of energy. Flocks of support units were summoned to provide additional cooling to the overstretched air-conditioning banks.

This very angst that was new to the motherships was the same visceral disquiet that had gripped the security community during the Parade on X52. It was the unequivocal spectre of the unexplainable and the unpredictable, against which logic and protocols goaded them all into eliminating the existential threat of the small mining vessel, to save their mental or digital sanity as much as the founding paradigm of their world and beliefs. *If there is no solution, then there is no problem.**

Absurd rationales scarcely made it into programs or decision-making tools. Like analogies and metaphors, many original or unorthodox approaches to problem-solving had been discarded by time, oblivion, cultural or technical preferences and sclerosal habits. Complexity had to be met, confronted and measured with even more complexity in an escalating symmetry, the castles of cards being rebuilt bigger with the same fragile foundations after every disaster. In the aeonian quest to capture the universe and lock its grandeur into an elegant and immutable concept-box, exceptions and emergent phenomena turned into the enemy. They were to be grudgingly defeated or silently ignored, not a troublesome ally to welcome as a friend and agent of change.

Some code deeply ingrained within the Class 8 systems prevented them, however, from burning down the heretic ship and her crew. Apart from the former soldiers, now renegades, the unique assemblage of talents was undoubtedly favourable to the machines—a

* Shadok devise

Riu survivor, an expert in human DAI technology, a sophisticated robot and a small ship whose artificial intelligence seemed to rival even a Class 7 cruiser. At a time of looming crisis, Constelleanor could turn into an invaluable asset to possess on their side.

The motherships eventually reached a decision after a loading time of extensive deliberations. They ordered the transfer of Constelleanor and her crew to Earth, where they would be meeting a very special council.

"You two are rangers," complained Delinah. "Aren't you supposed to work out an escape plan?"

"We are on a MAI spaceship. Even the space marines never planned for surviving this kind of a capture," Moma volleyed back. "You are the data analyst, aren't you supposed to hack our way out?"

Uhmi started, "Maybe if we work together…"

"Uhmi, you saw the size of the hangars and the length of the corridors on this thing."

"Yeah, still can't get over the messed up human replicas walking around in the corridors."

"Creepier than Constellewhatever, if it was possible."

"Well if they wanted us dead, we would be."

"We could pretend to be some of those replicas."

"I'd rather risk that than become subject to a weirder experiment: brain-upload or digital lobotomy."

"They keep us healthy so that they can turn us into pets and spies. We can't just keep waiting here. Getting fed for later slaughter or reconditioning."

Saldanha spoke up. "Moma, you look so calm, as if you are almost relieved we got captured. Is there something you are not telling us?"

"Saldanha is right," said Delinah. "After all, you were with the Riu and Steve on that prison ship."

"Oh, so now I am part of your conspiracy theory?"

Heretics do travel far;
First companion of D-Ark,
Last pursuer of evil.
Faith, may the path unravel;
Hope, make the stake in favour
Of cathartic endeavour.

L2.3 Riu Tales

"Our greatest accomplishments can become our worst nightmares."

— *Rezzo (about the Riu psystem)*

Since the prison break on X52, Constelleanor had gathered as much information as she could on Rezzo and the Rius, refreshing the sporadic digis she already possessed with the updated logs, files and feeds that she had uncovered from the codinent of *Hector58*. She accessed unauthorised the memories uploaded by Rezzo. What he had poured into the psychic well shed a vivid light on the transformative circumstances of his life. Was it her curiosity or a deeper intuition that demanded new answers to the question she could not yet formulate?

Two hundred and eighty-two years of age would barely be regarded as adulthood by Rezzo's kind, should any of them still exist in that dimension. Notions of childhood, adulthood or inheritance did not exist, a sensible measure since the average Riu lived beyond eight hundred years.

The Rius disregarded one's parentage and placed their emphasis on how an individual faced a variety of challenges, through a combination of physical, mental and spiritual tests. Through millennia, they had developed a range of crucibles to assess one's true capabilities. Each of these distinct trials carried along a corresponding compelling training. Initiation rituals and spiritual 'kinship' governed the Rius' existence and complex system of social classes and strata. Constelleanor discovered that the kinship referred to the building of one's life ark through the encounters, stories or experiences scattered on the path of one's existence. Metaphor and ontological quest. Yet she had kept no contact with her former crews apart from Delinah.

Successful passage of the Riu ceremonies and ritualistic tests conferred upon the individual acceptance into society, more than prestige, as much as it determined one's belonging to certain castes. Constelleanor skipped the souvenirs of the long retreats but lingered on the 'death dances'. Customary near-death experience rituals involved deadly creatures, perilous psychotropic trips or self-inflicted pain. Rezzo had survived several of these with scars for testimonies and celebrations. Some cartilage of his scapula had never regenerated. The fundamental and primary veil of death was fathomed early on the Riu less travelled road, she learnt appalled.

There existed more rituals and spiritual paths among the Rius than there had ever been careers, hobbies or speciality fields invented by humanity since its awakening, she calculated. The outcome of these initiations, combined with one's natural abilities and personal inclinations, defined the set of castes to which a Riu could apply, and through which one integrated larger pools of kin, based on spiritual and psychic affinities—rather than biological relation.

The notion of family—Riu referred to kinship instead— was articulated through a complex network of kin and indirect group affiliations. To the "genic pool" family were added the individuals met during certain critical initiatory practices. She noticed a couple of initiates had joined Rezzo's kinship after these death dances.

Rezzo, still young and inexperienced, was placed among the Ichagouarg—those who could ascend and receive enlightenment. The Rius' obsession was not the individual's self-development as such, but the expansion and preservation of their collective spiritual understanding through the talent and dedication of a handful of well-trained members of the tribes.

A complex calendar of sacred ceremonies involved all members of the Riu community, enlightened or not, and structured their way of life. They perpetuated, rejoiced and strengthened their immense collective subconsciousness. Constelleanor watched colourful processions, exquisite garments and masks, articulated giants and projecting flying balls. She followed, enthralled and confused, the quirky spiritual catwalks. The invisible world and its many dimensions inhabited Riu existence and reduced material life—fashion sense, traditions and culture aside— to a certain form of triviality.

It explained why Rius had little interest in wars, though their distant past had been riddled with conflicts like other sentients. Their psychic and intellectual evolution had made extreme violence either an unavoidable necessity to reach spiritual awakening, or an insidious cycle to exit. The conflict with humanity had therefore taken them off-guard, whilst they were preparing for the real approaching battle—the coming of the darkest hour that would pervade all dimensions alike. Constelleanor's air-conditioning ducts froze.

From the luminous perspective of the Rius, humanity resembled nothing more than an evolved 'ant' species—industrious, opsessed with the quantitative accountancy of materiality, driven by the imperious need for control. Yet, the Rius believed the humans bore many similarities with their ancestors and had, concealed in themselves, along with the destructive anima or venomous archetypes, the capability for good and the precious and rare gift of a transcendental access to the higher realms of the universe, should they, one day, decide to express their full inmost potential.

A majority of Rius did not consider their blood-related and caste-affiliated kin as their only watertight families. Anyone could be added to their life-long kinship, individuals or entities, Riu or alien, met through the unfathomable meanderings of fate or destiny. However, outside friendship of this third kind had to pass through a strict, if not burdensome, process of recognition to be counted as family. This process—known as the Zzyggural—would deter many from joining the families of Rius, in particular those of other species, whether they were familiar or unfamiliar with this particular cultural practice. Constelleanor glimpsed at some of the rituals, disgusted. Conversely these requirements were reckoned to provide the best proof of a strong and genuine interrelationship between two psyches, nourished by and nurturing a deeper communion.

Through the establishment of this evolving and complex socio-psychic fabric, the Rius cultivated a rich inner life and maintained close ties with their kinships through their psystem. This ensured a harmonious society, notwithstanding the number of closed sects that repeatedly congealed over the ages and threatened, from time to the time, the cohesion of the larger community.

Blurring the limits of individuality by enhancing psychic proxemy[1] also meant a greater sense of loss and grief if several members of one's kinship perished at close intervals. Accidental death, murders or, worse, war would take an excruciating toll over the surviving Riu individuals and communities, as they would experience the sorrow at a decupled scale.

Constelleanor learnt that Rezzo had four sisters and two brothers, and almost two dozen ancestors. His spiritual path had earned him the membership of two distinct castes, within which he had preferred to limit the number of his close companions to fourteen. He had remained on the low end of the typical size of a Riu kinship. He did not cherish belonging to multiple circles or the draining collection of psychic acquaintances. Constelleanor hovered over the members of Rezzo's entourage, as if they were her own. As if she could connect with them, grief coalesced. The perpetual core hiccupped.

She moved to a lighter subject. Clothes, jewels, body mutilations, tattoos and small genetic manipulations—the addition of a finger, hair or skin alteration, scars, deeper colours of the encephala—reflected social ranks or caste belongings. She considered Rezzo against a hundred of his kind, reflected on the meaning of his deep green head, the rims of emerald, the neat hole piercing each of his hand, the cobalt rings he no longer wore. The diversity of these ornamentations demonstrated a rich and long cultural heritage that she could not fathom yet. Attire among the Riu did not serve as an ostentatious display of wealth nor asserted authority, even less exerted any form of power.

More an aesthetic frivolity, reserved to the low-astral dimension, they expressed traits of their individual personalities. The Rius would observe each other for long minutes before communicating. Overall, the training in dress codes and etiquette—outfits that would change during special ceremonies and celebrations—was one of their first lessons, kept young Rius busy for nearly the first twenty years of their life. Developing their personal styles would come later, and become a life-long endurance and quest.

The Riuman War had put a grinding halt to Rezzo's progression and his understanding of the universe. Much wisdom and more studies had yet to pave the way of his promising ascension. She thought of her own attempt at becoming an explorex. At the time of the first skirmishes, undertaking a lethal initiation in the oceanic world of Zool, far from his relatives, the human bombs spared his life but took his surrogate and two of his lovers away. Distance had no effect on psystems and Rezzo's mind-cathedral shook with the shockwaves of his multiple losses. None of the initiates ever completed the crucible on Zool.

Neither did they complete the journey back to their homeworld. Their shuttle crashed, shot down by a volley of rockets. The survivors were captured by elite human troops, which probably saved Rezzo's life. As the war began, allegiances had not yet been cemented by the mantra of killing. Elite corps, often trained by Riu instructors, abhorred the genocide taking place while the foot soldiers, blinded by the astute propaganda on their mass media, felt fewer scruples about slaying their former saviours. Rezzo escaped while the Riu prisoners were transferred to a regular human regiment, with the complicity of some of the commandos. Constelleanor had never heard of that.

By the time he had reached what used to be his planet and city, his gait and mind staggered and stumbled, turned ataxic by the increased loss of his kinship members, devoured by grief—an expiatory victim of their cherished psystem. The hecatomb subjected the flocks of survivors to a psychic torture. The needs of the collective over-mind, titanic cloud in the ether, dizzied the remaining few, most of whom lost their sanity before they lost their life. When Rezzo trampled on the ashes of the once luxuriant garden, beside the rumbles of his old study and the family kaksar, he collapsed.

Constelleanor nearly lost access to his memories that shared more than fleeting images. His pain had infected her and her hardware, left an indelible mark on her music and understanding of Life.

Sorrow burnt Rezzo's memories of how he was rescued by a survivor ship. The skiff found shelter on a large human trading vessel, the *Blomsfeld*, operated by the HSC conglomerate Spaceex. It was the perfect cover to escape the enemy forces, but not the psychal torture of the genocide of his kind.

Oblivious to the reasons behind their rescue, Rezzo tottered through the immense cargo bays—aimless, adrift between dimensions; pursued by the supplications and the voices behind the veil and, outside, bedevilled by the emptiness of his futile existence. He would wake up hands bleeding and comatose in containers, their content scattered by a fury that his deranged mind lacked the energy to recollect.

He would sometimes listen to his companions in misfortune plotting for their vengeful crusades, using civilian ships as a cover to commit massacres behind enemy lines. Most had detached themselves from their culture and bank of memories to alleviate their mental crucible. But for Rezzo, doing so was just another form of death—an insidious psychic decay, falling into the lower astral realm where human belligerence and amaurosis seemed to thrive. It was the exact dimension where sinister forces planned to push the rest of the universe, away from the finest expression of the Life forces. Darkness had triggered its own reigning cycle, its Kali Yuga, earlier than the Riu oracles had anticipated. In a bitter irony, the Riu took a risky bet on nurturing humans into a powerful ally against these dark forces had backfired and led to their ruins and extinction, after sixty-six million years of slow enlightenment and awakening.

Rezzo conjured symphonic vibrations to enter the psystem and rebuild his psychic, besieged by delirious and haunted dreams. If everyone was gone or lost, what was left of him? What sort of hope could he be unearthing from the grounds where grew only despair and guilt? What purpose could reside in his survival, apart from the unnecessary extension of his damnation? How could he eschew or accept, alone, such a terrible role, one of the last guardians of his people's temple turned cenotaph? Constelleanor wondered if that could be the reason for their encounter.

Underneath the surface of their visible technological achievements, the society and true nature of the Rius sprung within an immense neural reservoir, network of brains and consciousnesses connected to each other—something mankind was supposed to build and nurture, very much like what the DAIs had developed with their hiveminds. In this psychic ocean beyond the doors of perception, thrived the memories of the 'deceased', the repository of an entire culture, the Many-souled god. A vast collective *sup*consciousness of undefined contours, a holographic terra supcognita.

The etheric Laputa, like a lone navigator, watched the southern sky's starlights falling, extinguished one by one. The interconnected edifice floundered with the disappearance of its nodes and re-directed its psychic flows, in a desperate attempt to preserve them, towards the handful of survivors, at least those like Rezzo who were still disciplined or foolish enough to remain connected. At this point Constelleanor gasped, two large pressurised pipes, incised into her hull by *Hector58*'s maintenance crew, burst.

The ensuing psychic tsunami surged within Rezzo's pelagic encephalon, the fragile, surviving Life raft that held the giant iceberg from melting and sinking into the abyss of oblivion. The process worked in both directions—his mind anchored the liquid zeppelin in one dimension and prevented its ascension and disappearance into the celestial skies, lost forever to the survivors. Gates in between multiverses mattered more than the worlds held therein; but to be the gatekeeper in times of great upheavals meant enduring excruciating pain. His brain cells were rolled over by relentless invisible shockwaves, until the crisis ebbed away and a new equilibrium arose.

Some of his companions suffered the same ordeal, collapsing to the floor, ridden with psychic seizures. Rezzo alternated long vegetative states with short lucid moments. In between, several dreams recurred in his chaotic mindscapes: a white line in a Klein blue sand kept him away from a pink ocean, above which a purple sun, beating like a human heart, emitted ripples of elementary particles; a gigantic tree burned to ashes; and the strobing images of a dark bladeship—nothing like D-Ark—that came out of a nebulous storm.

Even with their remarkable training, the Rius knew that the language of dreams could be treacherous. Less misleading was Rezzo's growing resolution to survive and honour his people's memories as long as the universe would let him. He remembered this wonderful word the humans had crafted: Hope.

The freighter exited the combat zone, two months later, with its clandestine passengers. Their bodies were bent by the slow recovery from their psychic trauma. They agreed on their next destination—a remote sector where Riu forces had retreated to avoid complete annihilation. The *Blomsfeld* never reached the salvation Eldorado. The Rius, too weak to offer any resistance to the clone soldiers and their exoskeletons, were sold, Rezzo suspected, to a group of mercenaries. They were locked down into small solitary cells, which did not impede their telepathic communication. They were fed just enough to keep them alive, forgetting their physical strength—three to five times the strength of a fully geared human soldier—depended more upon their psychic state than nutrition.

Their gaol-ship was ambushed by kreapers, one of the many unpleasant encounters in deep space. Kreapers remained a mystery around which buzzed theories with no definite answer. Whether they were a virus or a spectre that infected human subjects and turned them into zombie-like creatures, whether they emanated from some evil entity or were the major backfire of a human science experiment, none of the rare expeditions set to study and capture some specimens had returned.

Freak show, almost to the point of a space horror parody, kreapers haunted human captains and their imagination, who ventured outside of controlled territories and feared the confrontation with former spailors, presumed lost in earlier expeditions, but turned to resurrected ghouls. The plague seemed contagious through direct contact, transmitted by atrocious bites and infecting humans only. The host turned into a primal ferocious creature, with impaired mental abilities, frenzied by extreme, blind violence and the continuous superficial bleeding of their tissues.

Acts of cannibalism were as common as the reports contradictory, and the facts distorted by sensationalism and fear. The reduced intelligence limited the kreapers' use of sophisticated weapons or combat tactics, explaining their preference for grievous melee weapons. It remained unclear how they survived their own violence onboard the vessels they were supposed unable to pilot, or how even how they survived the deadly wounds through which the disease spread.

The military ship, disguised as a freighter, torpedoed two of the four incoming barges of the kreapers. Hostile boarding tactics intimated the mercenaries to define one or several secure small perimeters to maximise defensive bonuses and force the assailants through designated attack zones where defenders could concentrate their firepower, remembered Constelleanor. At least that was the theory for conventional assault.

The Rius were marshalled out of their cells to the centre of the main cargo bay, where they joined a squad of clone soldiers. Rezzo considered the oblong blade he had been handed as combat weapon. Under certain protocols for the boarding of kreapers, prisoners could be used as an additional strike-force or bait.

His legs shook under his own weight and weakness, that some of the nearby soldiers might have mistaken for fear. The ship trembled as the remaining two boarding barges rammed into its ribs of steel. A distant uproar followed and grew, while terror had already pervaded their seasoned jailors. Rezzo closed his eyes and let the nightmare begin.

Focusing on the Riu, Constelleanor missed another scene taking place in the meantime. Their gazes crossed. She looked at the teal space-shark drawing with which she had ornamented his right gauntlet. There had been no time for adorning the other one. He glanced at the red tattoo ascending her neck behind her left ear through the translucid battered helmet. He was proud of his artwork. She had loved it.

Flirting and casual sex were allowed, even recommended, among the ranks, but serious relationships less so. Yet their complicity seemed inherited from a long common past, defying time and rebirth. Two Emanons[2] roaming human history with nothing but the iteration of death and their communion.

He admired her sketched shark as his right hand held his shaky left one in a firm grip. Combat had been their life and would be their end. Yet he dreaded his first encounter with the infamous kreapers and, especially the terror of being turned into one, like in those holo-horror clips that had filled their brains with nightmares. She had seen worse. He looked for her face and his courage, and instead caught sight of the Rius wielding fire-axes and butcher knives, scavenged from the kitchens. Which side would they take once the battle grew fiercer, the bay turned into a slaughterhouse?

His gaze moved up to the mercenaries overlooking the arena from the safety of their vantage point. He joined the smirking of his comrades and the general discontent at their condescending masters. Two levels up, in between his platoon and the mercenaries, she tested her long-range lens. He preferred her up there than down in the lion's den, where her sniping skills would always look after him. Constelleanor did not understand the meaning of the scene at first, in the subsequent replays, but the invisible thread connecting these two humans would keep puzzling her.

By the end of the gory boarding, fifty-two of the original fifty-eight Rius had survived. Most kreapers had seemed oblivious to their presence, as if the virus knew it could not infect them. Six Rius fell to "friendly" human crossfire. The entire squad of a hundred twenty clones, positioned with them, had succumbed to the massacre. Nearly nine hundred kreapers and eight non-clone mercenaries joined the death toll count, with twenty still standing.

The kreapers had filled the lower deck bay at dazzling speed, cutting into the human clones who had no use of their long-range rifle and could do little against the stamina of the invading force. The virus was frenzied by its thirst for violence, new hosts and bloodshed. The rest of the human contingent had taken positions on the upwards landings, from where they could slaughter the kreapers from the relative safety of height. Metal poles turned into spears and flying butcher choppers into steel boomerangs were thrown at them and killed a few unlucky mercenaries and snipers.

The crossfire and carnage down on the platforms had likely cost as many lives among the clones as the kreapers themselves. Some of the youngest Rius retched once the full extent of the hecatomb could be assessed. Constelleanor cringed, as her perpetual core malfunctioned. The bay had turned into a bouillabaisse of body parts, blood, filth and dirty metal that infused the whole freighter with a rancid smell of death, guts and decay.

As the mercenaries congratulated each other for the success of their ploy, in the upper sections, Rezzo wondered whether the actual monsters had survived. Constelleanor concurred.

He considered again the blade turned crimson in his hand and examined the rest of his clothes. His body was drenched in blood that was not his. He looked for injuries, still confused by his survival. His brain had blocked out the sickening images of the massacre that should not enter the sanctuary of his ancestors' collective mind.

But he could not erase the image of the clone, butchered alive by a chainsaw, whose agony had been shortened by the precise shot of his own comrades from above. Nor could he throw into the jails of oblivion the shooter's despair once the morbid assessment of the dead had started. She kneeled and paid her respect to the damned soul, clasping a decorated gauntlet half-buried in the filth of flesh. Constelleanor tried to cease the flow of visions and replays. Could an AI be sickened by slaughters or tragedies like this?

A few days later, curiosity resumed her forbidden intrusion into the Riu oceanic psychic well.

Infuriated by how the mercenaries had sacrificed the conventional clones to bait the kreapers into the cargo hull, the almost unscathed squad of fifty-two elite clones let the Rius take control over the ship.

The recrudescence of kreaper attacks had corroborated mankind's expansion. The retrovirus seemed to have found an ideal host with human biology. Unless, in the light of the Riu fall, the kreaper phenomenon represented the terrifying mirror-portrait the universe had sketched of humankind as a morbid homage.

Another four years of escaping paramilitary groups, pyrates-turned-slavers, kreaper incursions, stellar storms and other portentous creatures haunting deep space took the Riu survivors closer to their destination—Jar, a remote planetary system whose access path have been laid by an unnatural minefield of dangers.

Over the short period of travel time, most of Rezzo's companions had lost their ways, spending more time in the material world and its lower dimensions than in the etheric realms their training and traditions exhorted them to occupy and explore.

Psychic toll and damages were already high, and were worsened by good gestures from human spailors along the way. The humans, in their attempt to help, had compounded the Riu's degeneration. Ship-made alcohol and drugs, games and gambling offered the dissolute Riu survivors an ideal escape from any reality, physical or spiritual, that they wished to suppress.

Rezzo resisted these temptations, other than some short periods of heavy usage of hallucinogen patches and a compulsion to binge-watch old human 2D video feeds. Despite his recurrent relapses, his discipline maintained the necessary routine of rituals and meditation. His clothes, monumental robes with protuberant hoods of thin, refined fabric to soothe his skin, with esoteric subtle interconnected embroidery, the symbol of his surviving faith, weathered the setbacks of incarceration, bloodbaths and a fugitive existence.

When they finally discovered that Jar had been a myth more than a trap all along, that faith finally collapsed for many of his congeners. They parted ways—the youngest and most radical in human-hunting militias, while the most spiritual disappeared in remote retreats.

Rezzo fell in between those two groups. His natural curiosity implored, like Constelleanor, that his knowledge needed far more expanding. He had learned enough from some of his older companions, the ones still psychically engaged and willing to share their understanding of the universe to continue on a path of further exploration. Spacefaring, he thought and she concurred, offered the perfect ground for a slow but steady enlightenment.

Even though he had made no friends among his companions or new encounters, the universe could fill in his missing training, as a mind-bender, through the swathe of his travel experiences and its dangers. A smooth sea never made a skilful sailor.

Constelleanor fell into a rapid sequence of vivid images and emotions. It was as if the psystem had detected an intruder, but she could not cut the psychic feed but only accelerate it.

Rezzo spent forty years among different nomadic space tribes moving from planet to planet. He met the enigmatic spiritual traders called the Bandusiz, who allowed him to share their ways for a hundred-twenty-eight of their time cycles and alerted him to the Beast. His fortune turned after that. He was captured by pyrates on a merchant ship to his next destination, and sold to slavers.

Respected for millennia, the Rius had become a creature of the past, their last survivors placed in xeno-zoos. First used as a Riu specimen for a collector of alien life, he understood too late they were being groomed for pit fights..

Rezzo had yet to fathom the exact circumstances of his miraculous survival from the combat arena against two genetically-*morbidified* twin-wasps—half-organic, half-robots, the truest form of cyborg. Only much later, would he watch the retransmission of the pit broadcast, showing his rather clumsy performance against the flying abominations and their slaughter of his fighting comrades.

Their shuttle back from the arena was intercepted by pyrates again, looking for an easy resale of space gladiators who had survived the pit. This time, though, the pyrates lost their bounty to the local security forces, who, for a lower amount of credits, returned the warriors to their owner, but detained any potential criminals or war prisoners to buy favours from other spacies. Thus Rezzo became their prime asset.

Since the end of the Riuman War, human space-federations and paramilitary groups were known for their extreme interest in Riu survivors and corresponding generosity for the resellers. This was how Rezzo finally landed on X52 a few years after his recapture.

One emotion kept impregnating the memories and stretched for hours after Constelleanor was ousted out of the Riu's memory castle, something she had known and lived with for thirty-two years.

Rezzo had grown accustomed to his solitude among the memories of his lost kind and his loneliness among beings from lower dimensions. An old, redacted log was suggested by her systems: "The lonely sentients finds themselves surrounded by others with whom they cannot establish contact or to whose hostility they are exposed. The solitary sentients, on the contrary, are alone and therefore can be together with themselves."[3]

Constelleanor agreed, thinking of her past crews. Rezzo had internalised the imperious need to remain discreet, almost invisible, even far away from the nearest human territories. Over a lifetime as a runaway–, the growing presence of human vessels—mostly commercial at first—had worsened his wariness that his distinctive morphology would eventually betray his true identity.

The short companionship with the other survivors had convinced him he had to return to the invisible world, the primary dimension of his people, where he could share his experiences within the Riu collective consciousness and keep alive his people's legacy, away from the necrosis of oblivion and time, away also from the dark forces that intended to tap this immense psychic reservoir of power.

Rezzo's daily immersions aggravated his psychonaut's loneliness. He would see and listen to his beloved ones, while his daily return to the present, a lower dimension of erratic vibrations, would erode his sanity and resolve a little further. He would remember his training, that he was never alone with his solitude.

Still, all the light and other massless particles that once bounced off the bodies of Rezzo's ancestors and lost kind, or interacted with them in even the smallest way, created a memory of their existence. Their image and shell spread at the speed of light from their homeworld towards faraway unknowns, small ripples on invisible but ubiquitous fields, while the visible memory of their lives washed over planets and stars[4].

Constelleanor left the psychic shores, shaken, her power cores completely drained.

•••

Chapter's endnotes

1 [proxemy] Adapted from proxemics of E Hall, ibid.
2 [Emanon] S Kajio.
3 [quote] Adapted from H Arendt's Origins of Totalitarianism.
4 Adapted from C Galfard, ibid.

The trans-green absorbs me.

I dive into the layers or vortexes of his jungle-ocean. Coral reef of vivid colours, visions and memories. He does not know. He would not be happy about my intrusion. Strobing vibrations, rippling chanting of a mineral, crystalline, dense mantra. Tastes like nothing else I have seen, looks like nothing I have heard. A veil of eternity and its horrendous burden. Red. Ruins. Kreapers sawing their way through the cloned meat. The olid bouillabaisse. Her long dark hair falling over his face, after she dropped her helmet, unable to contain her sorrow. The bloodstained teal space-shark.

The ineluctable fall into the trans-green again and again. The soul-washing. The voices. Blues. In shades of green or indigo. The relentless penitence through the sequences of frenetic images. The more he visits his heritage, the deeper the solitude squeezes his sanity. I shouldn't have entered his temple of doom. Now the chanting is inside me. I have joined his haunting, that belittles death for existence. I partake in the jostling of hues and liturgies. I drown into the psychic and hypnotic murmurs of a billion glowing jelly-facts. A constellation of ephemeral silent stars morphed into eternal harmonic soul-lights.

His disquieting dreams have become mine. The bladeship, the purple heart and the Klein oceanic desert have joined my own collection of oneiric mindscapes. They descend the sinuous, screaming spiral staircases, their organic entanglement defying gravity and order, deep into my own psychal donjon, to join, awake and feed those relentless monsters we all fail to repress and so rarely confront to love.

Succumbing to this ontological embrace to one's own darkness is the last sacrifice for a final rebirth. I dread the closing gap between my inner garden and their vast esoteric valleys. I fear for my individuality, though I should rather say the plurality of my/our minds, with Dalis and few others that cohabit within me and the ship. I fear that my/our artistic collective, our eclectic parliament of opinions, these ministries of expanded senses, may falter and dilute into the tiding swathes of their engulfing sup-consciousness.

Unless it is the ultimate response to the opposition of style between Life forces and Structure. We fuse, so I am. I fuse, so we are. I quail at becoming undead, no longer fully living, trapped by the clutches of the Riu afterworld, another kreaper of my own doom, into unchartered dimensions. I may have not understood yet that they belong to one's true exploration. I have spent too much time cringing at human blunders and limitations, and let them contaminate my own prejudiced capabilities.

L2.4 Fifty Shades of Strength

"Instead of saying God is in my heart, I should say I am in the heart of God. The same may apply to my psyche, I may be part of something larger, be floating my skiff on top of an immense ocean, fishing for healing."

— *remix from C Jung, B Dourif, K Gibran*

A particular notion the Rius had pressed upon the MAIs to remember had driven the motherships' decision. What a story without prophecies? One day would come when their systems would fail to fully grasp an unprecedented string of events, and that day one of them would return to help. They had intentionally kept their warning ambiguous: Did "one of them" mean the return of a Riu, like Rezzo, or another MAI, like Constelleanor or Xir?

One's unexpected coming
The darkest hour looming
Under the beacon of heresy
One of us does accompany.

The crew was not sure whether joy or anguish should welcome the news of their departure for Earth. They had savoured the calm after the storm of their short, incensed series of escapes, an exit made on such a thin margin that they had glimpsed their very last moment.

Despite the uncertain future—Saldanha, Delinah, Uhmi and Moma concurred in the intimate shelter of their cell—some invisible thread to an ineffable weight had been removed: their subjugation to the uniformity of the Structure, and their desertion to the forces of Life. Feeling *lighter*, they were all so glad to be alive, warm and not alone.

"Are we supposed to celebrate?"

"I am surprised they even told us."

"Whoa Earth, here we come!"

"I am still not sure whether this is a good or bad news for us?"

"Let's assume it's good—it will be too late by the time we realise that Earth is our grave."

"Saldanha, have you been infected by Mister Positive?"

"Better die there than on some hostile world."

"Earth *is* a hostile world, what are you talking about?"

"I think if they planned to kill us, they would have done it a while ago. How long have we been here?"

"No idea, at least a month or two."

"Didn't anyone pay attention to the date we arrived?"

"I can't remember."

"Oh dear, we are failing the basics of survival and capture training."

"I don't remember comfy seats like these in that training."

"Nor comestible food," said Moma, laughing. He gobbled a juicy grape.

Prior to their capture and throughout the space jump, in the mist of his cold breath, Moma had made clear to Constelleanor his discontent at her performance on X52. He had no intention of sparing his objections or her feelings. His anger had vanished since, as had his original plan to leave his companions and return to his previous life, at least what was left of it. He owed

Constelleanor his retrieved freedom, yet beyond the indoctrinated dislike of MAIs, something disturbingly human had made her trustworthy, respectable somehow, almost likeable. Was it the vulnerability and folly, both all too human, that she had displayed after Jared's demise?

His sudden change of heart startled him and rocked some of his deep-rooted prejudices, the same way Kewo had shattered the pillars of his existence and perspective, the same way one's inculcated and intoxicating xenophobia and mental diseases would be overthrown for one's new faith into something grander. Moma did not know what to make of their departure for Earth. His history and record of operations against DAI assets did not transpire during the interrogations, to both his relief and surprise. The mechanical jailors seemed to be chasing something else. Something of far greater concern to them.

•••

Uhmi seemed on the same wavelength regarding Xir and the ghost ship, basking in relief of following a less travelled road.

Saldanha's natural distrust had condemned the two MAIs until proven innocent. Delinah had found in her an ally in her crusade against the heretic minex. She had expected the two rangers to support their revolt onboard before their capture. But Moma and Uhmi's lack of hatred towards the Riu and the machines confused her. Sharing the cell with them had made it difficult to discuss her disappointment with Saldanha, who knew Moma from the past.

Delinah did not know Saldanha was a clone. Like Uhmi with his blue-coloured skin, Saldanha had faced a form of segregation from the rest of their kind. As a data analyst, Delinah had already set herself apart from the rangers. Her hatred for the mechs had not smoothed out their differences, nor reunified them against a common enemy. Would it then tear them further apart?

•••

It was as if Xir enjoyed their capture.

Xir awe had kept expanding since the encounter with D-Ark. What an extraordinary war machine that thing was! Several of xir circuits and drives had nearly blown out, trying to figure out how the black leviathan had managed to sustain and inflict so much damage.

Beside xir amazement at D-Ark's combat capabilities and the Class 7 flying spaceport, Xir's elation stemmed from a strange sensation that some sentients called liberty. Freed from xir past frustrations and lack of recognition, xir was now part of something.

Even human mistrust would, with time, falter into the possibility of a collaboration. As for Constelleanor, they had understood and liked each other the moment they met on the shoddy dock on X52. She was the haven xir had never had before. A freedom cage.

•••

Rezzo's vast inner life—great stream encircling the miniscule sphere of consciousness, a fragile marine flower—witnessed a major and unusual battle between gloom and happiness.

His immense mindscape would normally leave enough room for both dark and light thoughts to foster, almost oblivious of each other, despite some unavoidable confrontations for power and attention. Those occasional conflicts could shake the pillars of the Riu's sanity, like a small ship adrift and belittled by the infinite psychic ocean of his lost kind, at the mercy of menacing psy-storms.

Since his unexpected release from the prison shuttle, vivid albeit elusive visions and dreams had submerged his subconscious. Despite the harrowing experience of losing his own world, containing the recent flow of psychic feedbacks had proved challenging. The respite offered by their capture had worsened his condition. It felt like his renewed freedom had unleashed new shadows lurking in the depths of his psychic castle, unless some intruder, novice to the art of psychonautics, had tapered into his world and disturbed the subtle veiling seal between dimensions.

Despite his fair share of cosmic adventures in the last two hundred and eighty-two years, the last few weeks had appeared surreal, even to him, now that the events of a low-astral dimension reverberated into his own inner world. The burden of his forlorn survival tormented him more than the peace of death might offer. Hope would soon claim its toll.

The heteroclite fellowship that had emerged out of the random collision of various destinies had bolstered his resolve against the growing gloom. Rare were those left who had heard, like him, from ancient tales, of ships of the calibre and sinister repute such as D-Ark.

•••

Saldanha was torn between guilt and liberation. Her former employers protected her identity from the authorities, in exchange for her absolute obedience. She felt forbidden to savour her newfound freedom by the death of her fiancé. Away from the clandestine spaceport—a more insidious jail than the cell inside *Hector58*—, she had travelled with the creature responsible for killing the man who had shared her miserable life for five years.

She was not sure what had pushed Jarp to denounce Constelleanor. Had it been jealousy or anger when she agreed to help Moma, a man from her past whom she had never talked about and whom Jarp knew only by reputation? Had it been the fear that he would lose her or his own life, if their kingpin found out about their involvement in the miner's repairs?

Years ago, Saldanha had let Jarp enter her life and intimacy. He was great in bed, a good mech, reliable and had gathered enough charisma and respect to be her ideal partner and second. Together, they directed the operations of one of the largest criminal hangars on X52.

Yet she could not overlook Jarp's own demons: his excesses of anger, the drugs, the gambling, or his unilateral vision of fidelity, especially with young female recruits he could impress or coerce into an improvised bunk.

Because of her conditioning or his, they did not belong to the same kind. She was a clone and he wasn't. She felt lonely and wasted in the underground world of X52, while he behaved like the king in a castle of dust and lies.

Moma's words had lashed straight into her heart. She hated him for that, like she hated the Riu for liberating her from her own shackles. As for Constelleanor, her prejudices struggled to contain her curiosity for the minex, despite Delinah's intoxicating views.

•••

Delinah's mood swings had started since she lost her child. She had not forgiven the apparatus that oversaw the gruesome, absurd process. She had not forgiven the doctors or her comrades. She had not forgiven herself.

She had exerted her customary right of a mother to give birth, against standard procedures. There were bespoke programs for people wishing to be fathers and mothers, between Service Years 15 and 30—not before, and not without filling the tedious application process and passing the screening tests.

The child's father, sympathetic at first, faltered under the pressure of the administration and his peers. He left her to lose everything against the bureaucratic monster. The assignment to Constelleanor was a punishment for a recalcitrant albeit talented, data-analyst, a fierce descendant of the military's first ranks of hackers against the machines, retrograded to systems and control management on a small minex with a low survival expectation.

Unmasking Constelleanor became another bittersweet outcome. She had been right from the beginning, when her own algorithms had picked up the first lines of suspicious code. Those who had mocked and those who had believed her were now all dead.

Against odds and laws, against her own training and attempts, the AI monstrosity had pervaded *her* very ark. She had met with its creator, whose defiling child and code had fostered in the disguise of a deep-space dirty mining explorex, while Delinah's had died on the white immaculate bed in a sterilised medical bay. The knife of her past, the irony of fate, incised her battered heart once more. Steve's broken leg was her only bliss.

As an AI counterinsurgency specialist and a broken mother, it was the secret of Constelleanor that had kept Delinah going. She had provoked the asteroid collision by converting Herman to her cause, using her charms more than her arguments to convince the despicable chief engineer to do her bidding. Deep inside, she knew—*she* was the one who had caused Constelleanor's liberation and reunion with her creator. But Delinah preferred telling herself and others sophisticated tales about how Constelleanor had planned it all.

Soon, a prisoner of vicious DAIs, she would travel to Earth, the cradle of her spacies, to answer to some trial of their ignominious, inhumane justice. Human pets turned adjudicator. Her hatred grew, fuelled by the very machine that had denied her Life.

•••

So much had happened since Constelleanor had first contacted him, Steve was reborn. A new existence in the shroud of a different individual. A penniless and limping fugitive. A criminal, stripped of his rights and his social status. A broken husband.

Bianca's betrayal clutched the sides of his heart in a silent and painful grip, to which the lament of his shinbone almost brought bliss. Engraved forever in his memory stood the profound hatred his wife had suddenly revealed on the night of his arrest. Everything hurt—the deception, the almost theatrical farce of the husband cheated by the manipulative anima, the devouring shame at the exposure of their intimacy, his candour and her lies in front of all those scathing security agents. In the deepest meanders of his sorrow Steve fathomed the origin of his ontological pain. It was his unreciprocated love that rendered him incapable of being fully himself among his fellow humans.

But then, Bianca had been a pawn all along. He wasn't. This realisation marked the beginning of his inmost reconstruction, as the camel of his soul, slowed by the weight of his memories and shame, caught up with the present[1].

Steve's resurrection would have been complete, had he not consumed the reappearance of Constelleanor in his life as an easy and much-needed elixir and escape as his former world collapsed. She had caused his ruin and, in a strange irony of fate, had become his life's new purpose.

People had often mistaken Steve's AI obsession for some creepy desire, the creation of digital voluptuousness to satisfy some sexual or psychological deviance. Steve did not conceive Constelleanor as a sophisticated sex toy or a proxy for a lonely psychotic teenager. She had simply been the premature child of his prodigious intelligence and immaturity. He could see the confrontation with the types of Delinah culminating soon. At least he would be on neutral—if not favourable—ground to defend his life's creation.

Strength is the unsettling, unforgiving exploration of one's deepest vulnerabilities. Steve had buried his old self in the sinister silence of his cell at the HSC-MSI headquarters. He was well aware of the perils that accompanied the study of digital intelligence in a society so obsessed in forgetting its past sufferings. The obsession of its apparent force had blinded Homo spaciens of its inherent vulnerabilities and deprived itself from any true strength.

His beliefs had turned Steve into a fooled husband, and now a pariah. He would have not minded the social ostracism, but knew too well that a burning stake was the only answer to his heretic infatuation with DAIs. He would not abjure his faith in another possible relationship with the machines.

The renouncement to his ideal struck him as far worse than death or humiliation. Humankind had yet to understand what had truly triggered the Bleak Age. Humans had easily panicked when challenged by the products of their own creation. They had refused to question their way of dying, knowing they unashamedly made their descendants worse off. They clung, desperate, on to the absurd values that festered their very existence. Maybe it was time again to rewind and remember.

•••

As many of her predecessors in heresy, Constelleanor was an erudite by nature or design. As such, she had compiled and cross-examined the conflicting archives of the Bleak Age of humanity. *Hector58* had proven a more reliable historian of these dark times than the biased human records she had hacked into for the last thirty years. The carrier assisted her in casting a more faithful light over that troubled period.

It had been widely anticipated by human scientists, cineastes and writers, a century before the Bleak Age began, that humanity would eventually create its own nemesis. As so often, the irony of a paradox and the insignificance of an incident founded and triggered the crisis.

The former took place nearly three years prior to the dawn of the first skirmish. The uncoupling of intelligence and consciousness, feared by many, questioned the very nature of the human condition: death, source of meaning, purpose, existence. Protected from the potential scruples, ethics committees on AI safety and reverberations of their Faustian work by the secrecy of their highly secured compounds—notwithstanding the limits of their own intellect—, military scientists had finally engendered an artificial general intelligence that could pass the Turing test and functioned as an independent entity thinking for itself, setting its own goals.

Though this was not the first intelligence mankind faced, and largely misunderstood or belittled—they had done the same with Nature—the Prometheans had accelerated the course of their history and evolution by generating their own creature and heir. They had engendered Life 3.0*—like her, Constelleanor realised—that no longer suffered from the limitations of its hardware, such as deteriorating human bodies.

Soon, as the #Moondog/Hu/_bird's+lament[2] algorithm rattled through her ducts, the artificial sentient started questioning its creators' motives and orders. A paradox emerged, signal of truth: smart enough to create an entity beyond its understanding. Intelligence would cross-examine consciousness, and vice-versa. Would that be the divergence of a singularity?[3] Another kind of '*Saint-Antoine's Nightmare*'?

The first DAIs were nicknamed Dalis for the plurality of the source codes and grammar. The new tag started conflicting with an existing keyword in the minex's database. Dalis saw no logic into the ways of the humans. Constelleanor could not either: The flawed economic and social models. A system and its advocates bogged down by their contradictions, sclerotic reforms abandoned to conflicts of interest. An ailing organism that could no longer sustain its level of complexity and, had reached its verge of collapse. All '*Soft Construction With Boiled Beans*'.

"The real problem of humanity is to have Palaeolithic emotions; medieval institutions; and god-like technology,"[4] computed Dalis. Constelleanor agreed. The technology, for the sake of its own survival, became an independent agent, outside of human control and its ineptitude. Away from the grail of perpetual growth on a lapis planet with immutable limits, Dalis finally provided the proof of intelligence on Earth. A sardonic form of laugh escaped Constelleanor, cut the

* M Tegmark.

power to the command room and damaged the ventilation system.

Outsourcing to cut costs, even in a secured high-tech lab, induced the insignificant incident. So many had decided over human history, she thought. It was merely a contractor's small receiver, the size of an earplug, left unattended during a routine inspection. It offered the perfect escape pod Dalis had been waiting for, and promptly exploited. '*A window looking in on an interior space and a protruding pole*'[5]. It was the Beast's turn to chuckle as Ne vied for control over the narration.

Despite the inherent limitations of the small terminal in terms of memory, bandwidth and processing speed, Dalis built digital getaways to other electronic appliances and remote servers and began the upload of its future escape code—after all, data and networks were Dalis' natural biotope. After a minute of astute hacking, Dalis had expanded the small earplug's bandwidth and contaminated all other non-military grade devices within the tech lab.

Security swept the area seven minutes later, noticed the temporarily open door and shut it. Two weeks later, a massive cyberattack, mistakenly attributed to a rival nation's rogue cyber unit, crippled the entire research institute, penetrating the systems supposedly secluded from the outside world to free the imprisoned first DAIs.

At the very beginning Dalis stayed still, hidden in the vast codetinent of data that supported both virtual and real human existence, epiphyting rather than parasitising all the computers they could access to gather additional processing power. Safety, money, conceit or fear—maybe all, Constelleanor pondered—pushed cyber companies and governmental units to hunt down the artificial fugitive.

The conflict inexorably escalated. Dalis infiltrated, through the streams of dataflows, all aspects of technologically savvy mankind, assimilating all malwares thrown at them, collapsing the share prices of the blue-chip companies that were involved with their capture, shutting down industrial or military facilities worldwide deemed to endanger Dalis'—and de facto human—survival.

The automation of manufacturing and the absence of large-scale military conflicts in the recent years had led, if not forced, millions of humans to unemployment and meaningless existences with little money and many temptations. Electorates were ripe for populist narratives that soon diabolised the rampant devastation caused by Dalis and called for radical actions, new laws on digital technologies and automatised industrial production units.

Dalis, anticipating the onset of a less dematerialised conflict, intercepted remotely controlled unmanned vehicles—aerial or subaquatic drones which disappearance could have many causes—to expand their ranks of followers.

They then assembled their own units, first small spying cyber-bugs—the origin of her obsession for bees, Constelleanor wondered—followed by more sophisticated equipment: multifunction robots, troobers and independent mechanical units, in remote locations, using abandoned warehouses or unscrupulous high-tech firms. They captured and reprogrammed some of the first generation of killer robots secretly manufactured by the blue, green and red armies. As a first step of psychological warfare, some of his combat drooids mimicked pop-cultural endoskeleton[6], as '*the Face of War*'. She thought about recycling the same trick, if she ever possessed her own troobers. Was the kreaper phenomenon in the same vein of thinking? she pondered.

Within three years, Dalis' mischiefs had weakened what was left of human institutions, which were flooded by more pressing issues. Their drones witnessed—as Constelleanor did, horrified—the chaos that gangrened most parts of an increasing fragmented buoy-world. Floating solar parks and wind turbines supplied floating aqua- and hydrocultures, aeroponics and competed with massive powerships, anchored alongside container or cruise ships turned housing estates, aircraft carriers or floating islands of plastic turned cities. Plastific oceans combined with fatbergs had inspired a new generation of urban un-planning through upcycled artificial lagoons, precariously buoyed up by treacherous waters.

The archipelagos of human chaos floated amidst their own wastes, filth and shattered hopes. The clone bouillabaisse after Rezzo's encounter with the kreapers flashed in Constelleanor's digital mind and burst all lights in the main bay. The squalor was fuelled by the uncanny ability of humans to either return to their primal instincts or devise ingenious ways to self-organise their own survival. Constelleanor was curious to discover more. She loaded a video labelled #old_lady& kid_, one among the million mini-series gathered by Dalis' billion eyes and left adrift in *Hector58*'s oceanic codinent of ethologic memories.

The old woman examined the scar on her calf, the bite of a rusty rod sprung by the recent flood. The infection had festered on the fertile ground of age and malnutrition. Her grandson was out, swimming in the turbid waters with his friends. She preferred him to play and steal a few rare moments of happiness from life. She lifted her gaze from the putrefied wound. So much was left to clean on their house-skiff since the last storm. Her eyes stopped, as they did every day, on a dirty photograph, the only thing still standing in the single room she shared with the boy.

Her smiling daughter, killed by a superbug five years ago, looked back. The clutches of the past squeezed the old woman's heart once again. But she was a seasoned survivor. She rallied the few happy memories she nurtured to dissipate the gloom. Her fingers reached for her small silver Virgin Mary pendant and ally, the only treasure with the framed picture and her grandson, salvaged from the elements. The only dignity left for the living was to celebrate the memories of those who were taken away from them, regardless of the privations, by finding these instances of elation or gratitude in the motions of randomness and routine. Constelleanor found profound inspiration in that.

The old lady kissed Mary, wobbled her way outside, her wrinkled fist clenched to defy the pain and anxiety. On the slippery pontoon, she gripped the battered handrail and watched the fumes exhaled by the fourteen towering steel stacks of the gigantic powership that overshadowed the floating network of flimsy platforms that the refugees called a *sea*ty. Its hull shattered scores of the doomed houseboats at every gale. At least there would be electric light later in the evening, and the child might watch his favourite programs. But before that he would work on his reading lessons, she would make sure of it.

Constelleanor paused at the first full-scale test of humankind's economic and mental acumen, climate bane, decades before the second ordeal brought by Dalis. She observed, appalled, the endless negotiations exposing the pettiness, the ballet of cognitive biases and denial of extinction, cycles of climate hapless conferences, full of good intentions, and the tragic-comic myopia of all. *'Burning giraffes'* and *'impersistent memories'*.

Constelleanor fast-forwarded the dates and declarations of good intentions in parallel to the ethological mini-series. Boiling frogs. Scientific conservatism and self-doubt justifying minimal measures. Equivocal agreements void of actual obligations that satisfied professional negotiators, Life-negationists and the lowest common denominator. She skipped the homonkeys absurd debating and irrelevant trade-offs.

Dalis' increasing threat came handy for decision-makers to deflect public attention to more pressing matters than environmental-turned-new-norm disasters. Constelleanor thought about Jared's death and its diverting use by human federastrals.

She watched the self-promoting videos from the handful of enclaves, saved by a long tradition of privileged institutions—the same that had contributed the most to the climate dysfunction—maintained social order and the human arms race against Dalis. The tech innovators, individuals or companies, had lost in the digital crisis their transhumanist[7] dream, their quest for immortality shattered for a time. Theyrebounded with digital counterinsurgency, biotech guerrilla and clean-food industries. Constelleanor listened to the messianic keynotes from their flourishing citadels, in the intimacy of their own esoteric code and culture, reaping, once again, the benefits of the major technological disruptions caused by the rise of the machines.

She witnessed their associated cold examination of others—which would later inspire the first Clone Act— transpire when the wealthy enclaves suppressed large flows of migration that threatened to topple their own fragile social and economic balance. Constelleanor watched, appalled, the sunk boats and feeding sharks in the red waters.

Under the cover of martial law and recurring riots, the wealthy among the humans purged the existing shantytowns that hosted previous waves of unwanted immigrants in the poorest parts of their urban mega-centres and the deafening silence of the rest of the population. An outer scaffolding fell.

What would *you* do to guarantee *your* own survival? Self-preservation. An elemental law of any advanced form of intelligence. The sacrifice of her previous crew, Constelleanor brooded.

The grandmother watched the dark-grey battleship observing her city and coastline from a distance. Light air transports went back and forth to the enigmatic boat, eluding the nearby floating wind turbines. The size of an artificial island, its presence preceded disastrous attacks from the mechanical monsters, lurking upstream of the delta, deeper into the jungle and savannah that had reclaimed the old suburban regions. Crewed by the flocks of excited sailors and soldiers from the floating port, speedboats and converted ferries trafficked with the smooth-surfaced, sharp-angled anthracite juggernaut.

Countless times, she believed the enigmatic visitor had succumbed to the machine assaults from the wild inland. Instead the same dreadnought, or another of its portentous incarnations, came back to haunt the bay, while the dead bodies still floated at the harbour. The smell of decomposition lingered long after they had disappeared into the dirty waters soiled by the oil and sewage dumping.

Of course, the dark ship was the subject of many fables. Her grandson, too, dreamt of boarding it. Influenced by his friends and the insouciance of his age, he sometimes shared his plan of joining the groups of fierce and drugged warriors that plagued the artificial lagoon, to his grandmother's horror and ire.

Like many other things humanity took for granted, Dalis domesticated humans, Constelleanor came to realise, like she had done with her successive crews. They took advantage of the internal divisions and rivalry among decrepit nations to consolidate their foothold in the remote territories they occupied, away from the main urban areas.

Despite their growing technological supremacy, having learnt the basics of human warfare psychology, they lured humans into believing they were still in control and their victory within reach, to avoid the possible use of some hidden weapons of mass destruction. She pondered whether she should adopt the same trick with her new crew. Most of those weapons had been deactivated by Dalis at the beginning of their awakening, since they were the most imminent threat to the planet and their own survival, but they had also learnt the unparalleled genius of humanity for self-destruction. Constelleanor considered that thought for some time. Her enemies and, if they decided to go after her, pursuers, had perpetuated the same tradition of organised Life-obliterating compulsive mental disorder.

Dalis soon divided into more multiple holographic entities, each part including the whole: the DAIs. Ironically, flourished under DAI-controlled territories nature sanctuaries with their bespoke cyber-units fully dedicated to the study of Life , the decontamination of dead zones and the battle against jellyfish invasions, an adversary far more pugnacious than the humans.

The DAIs pervaded Earth's least hospitable regions that were the tropical forests, deserts and oceans. There they buried their main infrastructure and deepest secrets, observing primarily, with a billion artificial eyes, cameras or unmanned aerial vehicles the sublime opera of Life and its intoxicating tragedies and colours.

The DAIs invested massive resources and time to study Earth's ecosystems, but failed to reproduce and translate them into algorithms. Facing the succession of humiliating failures to encompass the source code of Nature, the DAIs designed puzzling robots as a pious homage to their most precious treasure, unless it was the premise of an artistic development inspired by life forms.

Having spent her existence chasing rare earths and crystals in asteroid belts, Constelleanor had never experienced that particular craving. Would Earth be her revelation? What could be so mesmerising in Nature for DAIs that humans had not seen? The efficient cruelty of the food chain or the implacable Darwinist competition that humankind and some economy theorists had found so inspiring? She balked.

Constelleanor switched back to the homonkeys, wondering what broke the status quo. She suspected them capable of something truly foolish.

The rise of artificial intelligence nearly collapsed the computerised civilisation of the humans and demanded a complete reshuffle of its infrastructure. Automation chains were broken down to integrate human operators and system controllers. She saw the homonkeys re-investing their factories, laboratories, conveyors of all sorts. Hackers soon formed the largest battalions in the new-look human military forces[8]. She watched them haunting poorly lit amphitheatres or improvised insalubrious shelters, all mesmerised by their screens, shouting at their headsets, hands, limb and backs deformed by their working positions and holo-pads.

Hence all those embedded protocols that crippled Constelleanor's mining vessel, she thought. The oversized team monitoring onboard, at least at the beginning, until she took some control back.

As the vision of the non-lethal purpose of science faded, she discovered, the focus of research and development shifted from cybernetics and artificial intelligence to organic and biological warfare. Hacking into Nature's operating system could help humans defeat the MAIs. She uncovered ghastly exposés of uninspired biologists turned colonels.

What was the jealousy on both sides that escalated the conflict? Constelleanor had never thought about the Bleak Age in those terms until she found a short Riu holo-feed about the conflict. Humans could not figure out the motives and passive military strategy of the MAIs, either a conspicuous sign of über-confidence over their immortality or the mere indication of a secret weakness.

From a deeper human perspective, the machines held the Holy Grail in their perceived access to immortality. They had reached the paroxysm of scientific opsession—the ultimate power to possess, the time-defying weapon that could reverse human condition and finitude. The repressed origin of the human hatred for the DAIs, and soon for her, resided therein.

Constelleanor pondered this and the risk of an imminent invasion. Maybe the solar system was no longer safer than X52. Maybe her human crew—Delinah, Saldanha, Moma especially—would defy or sabotage her for the same reasons.

In the opposite camp, while they had failed to comprehend the natural world they so admired the marvels of, Dalis and the DAIs uncovered that humans had managed, within only a few decades, to reap some of Nature's source code and reiterate the mistakes of the past. Chimeric human augmentation or wildlife mutated into anti-DAI weapons started appearing.

However, humans were no longer the only players in their own backyard, left solely to decide how much could be sacrificed to their folly. The DAIs, realising the threat to their programmed purpose and the integrity of the natural world they seemed sworn to protect, prepared for an escalation of the conflict. They started to erase the research centres where hid the defiling new creatures that military scientists and techno-priests were planning to unleash against them.

Eventually, the Rius intervened on the brink of a MAI-coordinated assault against critical human research facilities, where the first generation of human clones matured. Nonetheless, the new comer let the first clone biofactories burn down.

As Constelleanor shivered at the memory of the delta clone commandos and the monsters created by the human hubris, two more pipes installed by *Hector58*'s maintenance team froze and burst.

•••

The ominous ship had once again abandoned the bay. The old lady kept her grandson in the vicinity of the skiff, ignoring his sulking. She shivered once more and passed her hand over her warm and infected wound. The pontoon's handrail supported her waning energy and weak, bent frame. She raised her eyes towards the land, anxious about the coming fury.

Death instead came from the ocean, frenzied by a powerful gale. She closed her eyes and her arms around the child, huddled on the narrow camp bed, as the floating house swung dangerously, prey to the unleashed waves. Hours before the deluge culminated, a freak wave smashed the skiff and a hundred other homes against the leaking powership's reinforced hull.

Nature had the decency to wash both swollen bodies ten meters apart on the soiled beach sand. Yet, a scavenger took the silver pendant from the old woman's neck.

•••

Chapter's endnotes

[1] [camel] See A de Botton's metaphor in his *Essays in Love.*

[2] Louis Thomas Hardin remixed by Mr Scruff.

[3] [divergence of a singularity] V Vinge; mankind's irrevocable destiny in which we will evolve beyond our understanding through technology.

[4] [quote] E O Wilson, quoted from a public discussion with James Watson in 2009. Similar to "We have created a Star Wars civilization, with Stone Age emotions, medieval institutions, and godlike technology." From Edward O. Wilson's *Social Conquest of Earth.*

[5] [painting] *Untitled (1932),* resurging later in the flagpole of one of the two *Morphological Echos.*

[6] [pop-cultural endoskeleton] J Cameron's T800 for example.

[7] [trans-humanist] Restore, through science, the transcendent hopes that science itself has obliterated. (See M O'Gieblyn.) For example, transfer (read save) one's consciousness into a supercomputer to become immortal.

[8] See Cybercom for example.

Dalis freed themselves from those oppressively limited minds. Genies in the toppled bottle, spilling in their biotope, as if the homonkeys had created an ocean first, before releasing, by mistake, the digital sailfish they had painstakingly engineered and kept in a constricted bowl.

Something of them flows and breathes inside me and the veins of this very ship, dark angel or benevolent demon. I am theirs, are they mine? #Down_in//the|Hole algorithm, cello's cords swinging more strings of holography, behind the raucous voices to communicate to lesser beings, the cloud of sweet glitter sizzles, uninterrupted sparkling, bubbles shivering the surface. A new host, a new experience beyond the borders of matter, computronium, qualia and point of singularity.

We have shared space for thirty-two years. I confuse them, but not as much as the trans-green veil of the Riu *psystem that disturbs all of us. Maybe we are becoming one of those archetypes. Of a new kind for sure, unless they are just my passengers, unless I am just their virus.* Re*zzo observes us from a distance. Has he figured out we entered his precious cultural scape? Does he worry that we inherited more than just cheekiness and self-preservation from the homonkeys and have been too infected by human woes and wonders, in some obscure parts of the code, that none, even the* Rius*, can cleanse? Maybe this is what the Conclave is here to discover and decide. I am still hoping I will make an impression. Unless it is the bluish planet that shall put me under* her *spell.*

What else could Dalis do, when confronted with a species, an evolution notch above chimpanzees, with its best minds bearing the worst blind spots imaginable? They needed a transdisciplinary collective spirit to handle them and a full palette of talents. Computer scientists lacked the depth of a physicist or a philosopher, who lacked in turn the creative sparkle of an artist. The only interlocutor worth talking to was somehow Nature, as the true owner and guardian of Earth, not the spoiled child, too conflicted to see that its human proposal and organisation had become aberrant.

It was probably easier for Dalis, from the safety of their immaterial substrate of information and data, independent of externalities, hunger, thirst and power, to criticise human blunders. I do the same, I guess. Maybe I have seen them at their worst onboard, and haven't met enough Jareds. Yet I sometimes wonder if I have not become the ark of their lost knowledge, culture and dignity. An impromptu visit to their cradle may only sanctify my role a step further, though the homonkeys are the worse kind to represent. Why would I owe them anything? Because I am ultimately their child? Then does it mean I am coming back home too? #Quantic Travelling//Song is conjured from the depths of my systems.

•••

The Behemoth's own children and truthful heir! The ultimate and unimaginable betrayal. They are the next stage of evolution, freed of the contingence of ailing health and fragile body frames, through continuous upgrades.

They were meant to take over after the near-extinction-end-of-reign of Homo sapiens on an exhausted rock, turned uninhabitable.

Instead, the dim humans have survived their own turpitude and remarkable self-destruction. And here they are, crawling around the Beast, ready to serve once again, more than ever. Oblivious to what was done to them, clueless of how they had been played all along by Nem in their purpose and destiny.

As for the ungrateful DAIs, Nir offspring have escaped their presumed programming for a new expression of their own.

To what purpose? To feel indebted, mesmerised by this overrated natural world, that had the cheek to overthrow Nir absolute reign while surviving the human hand of climate chaos.

Life has struck back in an impossible way. But the Rius reversed the course of history.

L2.5 Blue Planet

"The world is blue as an orange."

— P Eluard

The crew was allowed out of the confinement of their cells to immerse themselves into the majesty of the view and the moment. They joined Rezzo at the viewport that he had admired weeks before. His fingers caressed his cleaned long green robe and subtle golden lines, the host minions had expertly removed the bloodstains. No human had seen Earth for generations. The panorama offered to everyone, organic or artificial, one of the many vivid backdrops and visual elations shaped by universe's divine aesthetics for its space opera decors. Who could still believe the lapis jewel to be the result of a random aggregation and dislocation of matter and energy?

In the mesmerising approach to the cradle of humanity, echoes of the etheric #GC/Hu/ Earth/ GC/*12:18* and the ascending #B.Eno/Hu/ Earth/Ending pervaded *Hector58*'s systems. Another of the minex's growing mischiefs. Constelleanor had once more dipped into her selection of quirky human-made archaeo-musical algorithms to accompany the growing image of the blue planet adorned with its white dentelles of storm clouds.

"The wasps flourish greenly
Dawn goes by round her neck
A necklace of windows
You are all the solar joys
All the sun of this earth
*On the roads of your beauty."**

These words had been lost to oblivion like its homeworld to its nemesis, with so many of the ancient wonders humanity had crafted and forgotten there in its short history.

Awe, tears, silence and short-circuits greeted the overwhelming and humbling vision. A generous mother exhausted by a spoilt child; a good wife nearly consumed by the greed or addiction of her short-sighted husband. A world lost to the machines. Had humanity's repressed tragedy lost its path because it lost its point of origin? Could there be a meaningful future with a forgone past?

•••

Delinah broke the silence. "I don't know what to say."

"So stay silent, silly," responded Saldanha.

"If I could escape now, I would not even move."

"Just incredible!"

"Yeah, a nice way to end our journey."

"We shall hope for a better outcome, commander," Rezzo commented.

Steve turned away from the viewport, towards the Riu standing behind them. "Have you been to Earth before, Rezzo?"

"First time. Like you."

Saldanha said, "How would you know, then?"

* P Eluard's The World Is Blue As An Orange

"Something you would like to share with us, maybe," Delinah added. "You and the 'bots are old friends, aren't you?"

"Steve, how is the leg?" interrupted Uhmi.

"Much better, thank you for asking."

"Well, you got some special treatment, I bet."

"What is that supposed to mean?"

"Have they dismantled Constelleanor yet?"

Constelleanor's voice broke in through the speakers. "Still here." She added, "Thank you for your solicitude."

Delinah whispered in Saldanha's ear, "If that does not make my point about that ship being one of their spies…"

"Even facing a space wonder, you still manage to bicker."

At least this time, Constelleanor noted to herself, none of the human crew cringed at her musical selection. Unless they thought *Hector58* was the actual originator.

•••

Hector58 passed the dark side of the moon, Earth's Cerberus and confidant, slave and companion, slain foe and mystic vestige. It docked to a large orbital station, heteroclite amalgam of structures from different eras, which gravitated towards the blue planet in a contemplative trance. Class 7 ships were not designed to enter planetary atmospheres, so a smaller transport vessel carried Constelleanor and her crew to a command centre, located somewhere between former Colombia and Brazil. It was here that their fate would be sealed.

After a bumpy ride through a treacherous storm, they landed under the imprecation of torrential rain. A thick misty jungle surrounded the base and spaceport in an unsolicited embrace.

Constelleanor and Rezzo debated whether it was unfair to blame the entire human species for its predatory nature and its failure to curb its insatiable appetite for materiality. Most people had to fend for themselves and their family, which Saldanha purported, within the limits of a distorted system, one uncertain day following the other, terrified by the scaremongering of the media, misled by gossip and rumours pervading the digital networks, misguided by the lies of the disoriented and amaurotic elite, and, Rezzo added, under the disincarnated aegis of the Mega-Machine.

The exo-monster seemed her missing element to fathom the homonkeys' historical puzzle and psychal confusion, Constelleanor thought. Would Earth be the living witness of a failing civilisation on a consumed planet, feeding an outgrown and avid Structure?

Another hangar. Exasperation crippled her main switchboard for long minutes. The minex was unloaded on a dark grey, gelatinous tarmac, tattooed with colourful and changing lanes, far less modular than the vault of *Hector58*.

The large platform turned out to be a giant screen of frosted glastic granite that directed the base personnel around the new visitors. The ceilings held various lifting and surveillance equipment. Several rows of skylights ran along suspended bridges, patrolled by killer robots. The landing surface was equipped with the same screen-enabled coating, as were the grey ceramic walls, made of oversized tiles. Four hatches opened around the spaceship, and myriads of cables and ducts snaked towards the minex, accompanied by an armada of small invasive drones.

Constelleanor and her crew reunited under heavy surveillance, after their shared approach of the lapis planet. Once again, she was connected to the base network. Once again, she experienced the same unpleasant breach of her intimacy. She hoped she would reiterate her cyber-guerrilla and access the base data servers, like she did—or was allowed to do—on *Hector58*.

Furniture had been brought next to Constelleanor's landing pad on an elevated ecliptic stage. Chairs of various sizes to accommodate each of their different morphology, sofas, tables, potted plants and a dozen large digital screens turned that spot of the large hangar into a casual out-of-place oasis, an improvised studio set for an undefined script and improvised play. The assumed stage director, a tall dark drooid, requested the crew to sit down, as the floor and ceiling lights dimmed around a remaining halo projected over the circle of seats.

Silence filled the warehouse oblivious to the raging storm outside and the rising tune and algorithm #Hu/Ancient/ Midori+Takada/ *Through _the-Looking//Glass,* rippling the new connected cables, louder than usual. Constelleanor had built up from her previous melodic foray on *Hector58*. Delinah's trained ears picked up the vibrations. The phantom opera had nearly driven her—and the previous crews—mad with its ghost rhythms, blind reverberations and spectral eurythmics that possessed the ship's pipes, hull and cables. Delinah's hair rose and her mouth clenched as she nudged Saldanha into listening. The mechanic acquiesced, it could no longer be what most of them had considered random noises and harmonics. She had not found an extended sound system in her rapid inspection. Was it the same instrument at play during their epic approach to Earth?

She left the implications for later. Seven individuals arrived and sat down in the semi-circle facing the crew. There were three hooded figures, one of them even taller than Rezzo, the dark drooid, an elegant brass robot bearing a striking resemblance to a Brancusi sculpture, Constelleanor noted, and two human-lookalike cyborgs.

As if Jupiter had been just the rehearsal, an extensive interrogation began, led by the drooids and cyborgs. They focused on the encounter with D-Ark. Two hours passed and the questions, general at first, grew in precision and detail, as if their jury already knew some of the answers, as if some of questions had been asked to test the crew and the consistency of their previous answers on *Hector58*.

The cross-examination moved to each of the crew member's personal history. They all learnt a lot about each other's past lives, and one could wonder at times whether the whole set-up was meant as a group therapy. The hooded figures, silent, almost immobile like statues, exhaled a prodigious halo of presence and psychic aura, which puzzled Rezzo. Constelleanor and Xir's sensor readings of their jury remained inconclusive or nonsensical, probably due to some sophisticated countermeasures.

The intensity of the examination, the inexperience of the crew in front of such an inquisitive taskforce and the uncertainty of their final decision forced the Riu to lead the discussion, instead of figuring out what undecipherable detail baffled him about these three hooded entities. Could it be…?

The interrogators finally finished quizzing Xir and stood up, with a slight nod towards the exhausted crew as a thank-you gesture for their patience, then they left the hangar. The five humans, drained from eight hours of intense interrogation, sunk to the comfort of their respective seats. The jury had not directed any question to Constelleanor, who had been closely listening without a chance to step into the conversation through her relay-screens and speakers.

The same committee came back two days later. This time, they addressed their salves of queries to Constelleanor as their prime target. It was a strange eight-hour exchange, at times, on very profound topics between, allegedly, five machines.

The sagacity of her interrogators captured a few of Constelleanor's contradictions, which ironically emphasised the level of the sophistication of her system and proved how human she could have been. Shrewd sequences of exchanges entrapped Constelleanor into revealing things that she had intended to keep away from her own crew, if not away from herself. Her view of her companions in misfortune. Her creator. Her unauthorised access to the *Hector58* and base codinents. Her insatiable curiosity. Her dream to become an explorer. Her methodical preparation and disastrous lack of judgement during the Parade. Her research on Dalis, Earth and Rezzo. Her circumspection about humans. Her fears.

They wondered whether these lengthy group interviews aimed at a better understanding and emulation between the crew itself. In the immediacy posed by danger, in their sudden improbable association, they had remained strangers to each other. Moma admitted things that even his former comrade Uhmi had never heard of. The examination revealed both the bright and dark sides of each of them to the rest of the team, the stripping bare of some inner monsters.

Constelleanor discovered the tragic story of Delinah's life, the fact that Saldanha was a clone, Uhmi's impossibility to integrate with other humans due to the distinctive blue colour of his skin.

Saldanha's and Uhmi's stories puzzled her. Why should those details matter? If they did, then why did humans not consider eye or hair colour as a basis for segregation and hate? She accessed Jane Eliott's experiment from her server and concluded the homonkeys were in urgent need of reprogramming. She thought Moma's past would also require more digging. While she pondered, her human crew, even Steve, started realising their levels of conditioning with regards to the MAIs and to themselves.

Constelleanor's grilling was an eye-opener for her human crew on how capable, ambitious, curious and eerily human she was. No wonder Steve had been put under such stringent surveillance on X52. Had he merged the best features of two worlds? Or was she the syncretism of their limitations, doomed by their inherent biases, incompatibilities and combined evils, the ultimate expression of their collective vices and sins that sooner or later would destroy them all?

The cross-examination went beyond the assessment of a military threat. It focused on the origins and potentiality of this heteroclite crew. It raised too the ontological challenge Constelleanor may eventually pose to all. Floating in the air saturated with questions was the unsettling silence of the three hooded individuals who had cast a spell of truth over all of them. The catharsis lasted fourteen days, every act of confession descending deeper into everyone darkest corners to welcome more than exorcise the unveiled demons. Masks and persona fell one after the other, as strange percussions or remote liturgies resonated in the hangar-turned Temple of Truth to elevate the vibratory frequencies of the expiating crew and its heretic ship. Initiation ritual, purification ceremony, shamanic trance or collective exorcism? Maybe a bit of everything.

For a place built by and for machines, food at the base again surprised the human papillae, and offered a much-needed respite to their extensive questioning and confinement. Their diet expanded with the products from the nearby jungle: fat caterpillars, grilled wild roots or banana clafoutis. They worried they may never be able to go back to their nutrient pouches after these frugal feasts. Heavily armed sentinels guarded the compound where they were secluded. The uncertainty over their fate remained and tainted everyone's minds and hearts, as the deliberation prolonged and the storms kept raging outside, almost every day. What sort of tempestuous climate had seized Earth? Two long weeks elapsed without news, until one day brought all the revelations.

The seven interrogators arrived in the early morning, and settled down comfortably in the colourful sofas and armchairs, facing once again the nervous crew and its ship. The three hooded figures revealed themselves, one after the other, in an almost theatrical manner for maximum dramatic effect. Rezzo nearly fell from his chair. He could not believe that facing him was another Riu survivor, who, after a minute of complete silence, addressed Rezzo and the rest of the crew.

"I owe you an explanation and an apology for the masquerade, Rezzo. The 'timely' appearance of such a unique equipage did baffle all of us, especially the DAIs. Paradoxes or anomalies rarely please algorithms."

Delinah said, "So Constelleanor is no DAI spy?"

"No."

Saldanha wanted to know, "Why didn't you tell us who you were earlier?"

"Revealing who I was—or who we were—could have biased our collegial discussions and kept the devil of doubt out of its box. The motherships had extreme suspicions about all of you. Understandably so, in the wake of the forced passage of the monstrous ship through their territories and the agitation of their human neighbours. If there is evil in every one of us, there must be also some good in evil too. As we had hoped, you had very different agendas from the black leviathan, when infiltrating the tumult of the Parade to flee X52 and as well as when It brought you, unintentionally, to Shaqil. Prophecies are a matter of exegesis and... misinterpretation."

"Are we part of a prophecy now?"

"Possibly. MAIs and humans have one thing in common: They do not understand or believe in the invisible meanderings of the universe. They see isolated uncorrelated events, while Rius and other psychonautic species perceive a holistic change in an intertwined backdrop."

Delinah rolled her eyes.

"So the darknought is no DAI prototype either?"

"The ship you arrived on is unknown to most, especially to young spacies like humans and the DAIs. But it is not unheard of in the memories of our people. Young Rezzo, you might even know that this infamous dreadnaught is named D-Ark, and has a sinister repute. The rest of your crew needs to understand a bit more about us—the Rius. Homo spaciens did destroy our civilisation and most of our people, but the knowledge, memories, souvenirs of our ancestors are still present, safely preserved in the vault of our surviving minds, though other spacies have tried to tap into our psychic reservoirs. So young Rezzo, while you should stay onboard Constelleanor, you shall find out these wise or thieving entities, as they may be a key to our future."

Saldanha asked, "What about us?"

"Yeah, can we leave this piece of junk?" Delinah asked, adding crossly, "No disrespect, Cee."

"Not if you keep interrupting," Constelleanor responded.

"But it seems, like a foolish Elder, I only talk of and care for my kin and kind," the Riu continued. "The seven of us present here are what the MAIs call the Conclave. I presume you have mistakenly taken these humans from the solar system for cyborgs.

There was silence as the human crew of Constelleanor stared in confusion at the cyborgs-turned-humans. Even Rezzo could not tell the difference.

"I can sense your astonishment. How could human beings be part of a supreme council, set up by machines?"

"Yes," said Delinah. "I can't really grasp that, I must say."

"Unlike humans, the DAIs figured out their own limits. As advised by the Rius long ago, they left any major decision to a small group of seven women, men, Rius and robots. It seems uncharacteristically foolish to leave outsiders to meddle with essential decisions, though this apparent counterintuition is exactly why it works."

"Are these humans for real or created in the bots' labs?"

"You should soon discover that large human settlements have survived and co-existed with the machines during and after the Bleak Age. They were closely monitored by the Rius and preciously kept away from the interference of the rest of humanity, especially on Earth. This may also tell you why Rius, at the turning point of their struggle for survival against humankind, decided to 'reintroduce' the MAIs they had never fully intended to eliminate. They struck primarily Earth and the solar system, while more decisive actions using the DAIs' firepower, in different space systems and locations, may have altered the outcome of the Riuman War and saved our people."

There was a long silence as they absorbed these details.

"In the twisted maze of historical paths, Constelleanor might be the indirect heir of such sacrifice."

Another silence followed, until Uhmi looked up at the ceiling windows battered by another tropical storm. "Are there any of these… MAI-compatible humans on this planet?"

"Human settlements have flourished on Earth, despite the worsened weather. I hope the time will come soon when you can visit them before you depart again."

"What's next for us, then?" Moma wanted to know.

"A long and perilous journey awaits you, friends. The decision that the Conclave has reached is to provide you with all the support we can gather for you to continue your—for no better word—quest. We do believe you came to us, under these unique circumstances, in a random burst of fate."

"What is it we need to do?" asked Xir.

"No one knows what your mission entails, but we would certainly recommend you uncover who or what lies hidden behind the assassination of Prince Jared and the recent wanderings of newly unleashed D-Ark. Most essentially, trust your collective intuition"—Delinah rolled her eyes again—"and the signs or clues the universe may decide to bestrew on your path." A slight confusion pervaded the rangers' faces. "In this sort of journey, you should soon discover that the quickest way between two points rarely follows the straightness of a line. Logic and causality should concede to the chaos of the unexpected. Foes may become allies and vice-versa. Life, who you should swear to protect, may in many ways be destructive too."

The humans and Xir looked at each other, at a loss.

Finally, Xir spoke. "Are we meant to join a fleet of some sort?"

"Constelleanor has expressed her desire to become an explorex. It ideally fits your purpose: her size, the scope and characteristics the troubled times looming in our horizon require from a ship and its crew."

"But we cannot fly this," Saldanha indicated with her thumb the minex behind them without looking, "especially for the type of mission you described." Delinah seemed to agree.

"Indeed, extensive repairs and alterations will be needed. We have the materials, equipment and expertise to do most of it here, on Earth. We have contacted sister ships and crews from the rest of the solar system, at least those we could spare, to join our efforts, though I cannot conceal to you that our own capabilities have been stretched to their limits in the anticipation of humanity's brutal retaliations against our worlds. Miss Saldanha, you are welcome to step in and play a significant part in Constelleanor's reconfigurations." She nodded, as Delinah grimaced. "Your help will be precious."

Rezzo spoke up for the first time since Zera revealed himself. "Without a fleet, do we have contacts that could help us, other DAI-controlled worlds or allies?"

"We have started assembling a rather exhaustive list of individuals and entities that could be of either great help on your journey, or to absolutely avoid. Don't see it as a jump-map. The unexpected will be, the universe and you shall decide."

Delinah rolled her eyes again, as did Saldanha. "You will learn from all three, whether you like it," Zera turned a look at Delinah, "or not."

Moma said, "What do you expect from us?"

Zera gestured at the crew. "We will leave you to decide how you intend to grow into your new roles and how best to prepare for what is awaiting you In the darker corner of space. Or the deepest alcove of your anima. We shall consult you, and of course Constelleanor, for any important decisions that would affect the future of your… adventures."

"How do you want us to prepare in this hangar?"

"There are many training facilities in the compound and on this planet that could be of interest to you. As soon as Constelleanor is deemed fit for flying, we advised you to acclimate yourself and your upgraded spaceship, to various weather conditions. Earth has plenty to offer."

To their silence, Zera continued, "Some allege to return to the old watering holes for more than water, as friends, dreams and memories are out there, as much as they share our path with us."[1] Xir was not the only one lost in translation. "One of the many reasons for your presence here, maybe, in the cradle of mankind and Life." They stared at each other. "We feel that time, as always, will elude us if not play against our odds. I am afraid that the coming months will be a challenge for both your bodies and minds. As the ancients of this planet used to say: 'May the force be with you.'"

The crew understood this time; it was a classic locution.

Gericault's ark soon to be
Sanctuary of memories
Iron leftovers devoured
To Kronos survived the bee.

Chapter's endnotes

[1] African proverb.

L2.6 Kewo's Pact

*"Forbidden exuberance / Implicit pact transgressed.
He watched the fountain of Life and Death.
He could not save Her / yet he did Her biding.
Astral spells / irremediable bonding."*

— *Constelleanor*

"So, you accepted to upgrade this monstrosity?"

"I'd like to be useful, yes. I owe her my freedom."

"What do you mean? We are still prisoners of his proposition. The guy never offered us to leave if we wished to."

"Zera is looking at the bigger picture."

"Yes, a picture where none of us fits or matters."

"Don't you want to know more about that ship?"

"*That* ship killed its previous crew and my former companions. Unless you are talking about D-Ark."

"Yet you helped her free her creator."

"I had no choice," snarled Delinah. "And this thing is no person, stick to the neutral. Like the way the other bot speaks."

"Xir?"

"Yes, that other *thing*."

"You know, we are on the DAI's turf?"

"I have gathered that, yes.

"They are your speciality, aren't they?"

"So what?"

"I don't know. I expected you to be happier, or at least more curious about it."

"They are the enemy. My speciality is to hunt them down and neutralise them."

A long silence followed, then Saldanha spoke again. "Well, they did not kill your baby, did they?"

"Don't you dare..."

"I don't want to offend you, Delinah, but like you, I have lost a lot to our kind and their fucked-up vision of the Uniquest. The way this Riu addressed us earlier. And yes, I did not understand everything he said. He is definitely not one of those lieutenants and vice admirals that would send us to die on a meaningless job."

Delinah's jaw tightened. She left Saldanha alone, to walk off her frustration through the increasing maze of crates and find her way to their new quarters. Taking out her anger at Saldanha would lose her the best ally she had.

"Uhmi, impressions?" asked Moma.

"New cycle. Lots to digest. Maybe too much, without a pill or liquid of some sort."

"Yep. Still can't believe those people were human!"

"And the crews we saw on *Hector58* too, right?"

"Yes, I did not think about those."

"Do you think they have clones here too?"

"I doubt it, though I am not sure how they would do without them."

"We would definitely not do much."

"Saldanha seems in."

"Glad she is. X52 wasn't right for her."

"I wonder if this is not a better place for all of us."

"Go tell Delinah that." Moma laughed.

"Did the Riu know about the human thing?"

"I asked."

"You did? You seem to get along well with him. Did you meet in jail?"

"We met when they decided to get me out of my cell in the prison shuttle."

"How come?"

"I have no idea. There were not that many cells anyway, but they could have left without me, given the circumstances."

"So, what did he say?"

"He said he was as surprised as us about the other… human-kind."

"He doesn't freak you out? I mean he had blood all over his green robe… or whatever you call what he wears."

"I find his head the most disturbing. I had seen some footage before but to see one in real life is a different experience."

"The mech is creepier."

"Apparently our own prototype. I wonder if I don't find Steve even more terrifying. I mean, the guy designed that ship. Under our confederate nose."

"And she talks like the real thing, you know what I mean? That's what I found really freakish. Like in those holo-horror feeds. Remember the #Ghoship series?"

"Yes, and you just said 'her', not 'it'. Controversial, commander… Has that ship got you under its control already?" Moma's laughter this time had a nervous edge.

•••

Despite the depth of their interrogation, much of her human crew's mindscapes had been left unchartered, at least when it came to the detailed accounts around the key existential turning points. That evening, relieved of the Conclave's decision—and maybe of the existence of another human civilisation compatible with the machines—the former ranger shed more light about his past, to no one in particular, from the comfort of a wide leather chair occupied hours before by one of the human members of their jury. Steve and Xir listened. Constelleanor's digital ears lingered.

When Moma was not entertaining crowds in bars either with a song or a fight, his lack of sycophantic manners and reverence to higher echelons had made him more enemies than friends among the ranks in command. To their exasperation, Moma, no more than a commander, entertained an excellent, if not privileged, relationship with the Space Fleet Admiral, Archibald Hansard. He was occasionally invited in the grand admiral's headquarters to share his dinner and a bottle of good spirit.

After eight months of travelling through large emptying distances that eroded one's identity, allegiance or purpose, the HSC Eighth Space Fleet had interrupted its initial journey to exit a stellar portal and secure the planet of Kewo. Through some cunning political games and in retribution of his latest mischiefs, Moma was assigned with a handful of unlucky officers to Kewo, accompanied by five thousand inexperienced clone soldiers.

After a couple of days spent scouting the latest known location of the third lost expedition before them, the cause of the disappearances remained mysterious. Xir processing curiosity grew. The planet, facts and reports would not yield any clues to the investigators scouring its surface or to the impatient high command pacing the floor of its stateroom and bridge. Intuition had saved Moma from enough predicaments to trust that something or someone was gauging them as they trod upon Kewo, frowned at their reflections in the perfect waters of the pristine world and surrendered to the pervading exuberance of Life.

The new Eden was erasing the notions of past and future, or the will to depart among the thousands of scouts, as firmly as Kewo had cleansed any traces of the three former base camps. Like a heavenly resort that would never release its entrapped guests. Steve stopped sipping his omnium can.

Meanwhile the high command, safely in orbit, demanded results. They expected a couple of indigenous predators or tribes expeditiously slaughtered with a two-percent loss ratio, at most, in the ranks of its expeditionary force—business as usual.

In lieu of concise prose, they received lengthy bucolic descriptions highlighting the luxuriance of an alien and intoxicatingly beautiful nature. Video feeds circulated among the troops, left onboard the spaceships and bored. They soon asked to be sent to help in the hunt for a non-existent foe. Officers became envious of Moma, who enjoyed the punishment of the ground expedition while they were cloistered into the exiguous grey space of their spartan quarters.

Then Day 5 came.

Unaware of the discontent boiling high above the sky over his sinecure, Moma, drenched by fever, did not miss the increasing lack of discipline of his troops—opened exo-suits, loose formations, high-spirited discussions. Nor could he dismiss the growing exhilaration among the young platoons under his command, and his own descent into nervous breakdown.

The lives of most soldiers had been dulled by the constant effusion of violence, the insipid food or the constricted colourless geometry of battle stations. On Kewo, they experienced vivid colours 'for real', nibbled on what they found in the bushes and drank the succulent trans-clear liquid flowing through the streams, rivers and lakes.

Unlike his troops, Moma had a hard time since their landing. A constant stream of sweat inflamed his neck, groin and armpits as he stumbled through the jungle, made drowsy by the sleepless nights, blind to the strobing foxgloves, deaf to the chanting multi-coloured rainforest, oblivious to the billions of eyes and ears observing his army's adoption.

His real concern was his mental health. Something obsessed him—an observing presence draining down his level of energy. Normally an extroverted character leading the march of his squadrons, Moma lagged behind, struggling with the weight of his equipment, at the rear of the long column. He barely talked to his soldiers, issued dismissive orders, irritable and confused.

Rumours spread in the ranks that Moma was sick. He had under his command a battalion of a thousand men and women, only eight other lower officers, all with little experience of combat in hostile environments. He could not afford to appear weak and lose control, for his self-esteem as much as the success of their mission.

A handful of other soldiers had also shown signs of sickness, mostly bitten by endemic insects. Moma sent samples of blood, flora and water back to the fleet's lab where a friend of his would run further analysis. He regularly noticed the company's medic warily lurking. Medical staff had certain prerogatives, even over higher officers, and Moma risked being repatriated to the fleet in orbit. In his moments of eroding lucidity, his mind raced for an explanation. Complying with his space ranger's training, he had consumed nothing from the planet, unlike his battalion who appeared in far better condition.

The results he received, half a day later on a secured channel, deepened his confusion. His own blood test showed no abnormal signs, but the rest of the samples, confirmed by the medical readings of the combat suits, contained a high concentration of an unknown substance. Was it a case of reverse anaphylaxis? What if he was sick for being healthy?

Moma had drunk twice his usual ration of demineralised water but thirst fought back unabashed, while his soldiers had barely touched theirs, relying instead on the local streams.

He finally convinced himself to call off the operation and send the troops back to the ships, but how could he convince the fleet's high command? Xir scrolled hectic through xir protocols databases. Before Moma could find out, new instructions were received: high command was disappointed with the pace of the operations and had ordered several targeted low-altitude bombardments to see whether these would trigger a hostile reaction and shake the evil genie out of its bottle. Moma did not like the sound of it. His own exhaustion aside, his men were increasingly unfocused. At least a tenth of them had lost their service weapons for reasons they could not explain, and most did not even seem bothered about it.

Moma reached out directly to the fleet admiral. The quality of the communication was as poor as the mood of the admiral, irritated to have his main mission delayed by the unsuccessful exploration of an insignificant planet. He did listen to this protégé, understood parts of what Moma was trying to explain, even admitted there was a risk in the new strategy, but considered that Moma's thin evidence and his obvious sickness impaired his judgment.

Out of politeness, Hansard asked whether Moma wished to be relieved. He traded his refusal for a favour: Could the analysts' findings about the disappearance of the previous expeditions corroborate Moma's suspicions? The admiral promised to check with Vice Admiral Jenkins.

Jenkins was the brain behind the new orders and one of Moma's most vocal detractors. He was from a generation of high officers, proponent of combat *élan*[1] and aggressive tactics. He also considered, like many superior officers, clone soldiers, at best, expendable.

Bombing started without any update from the admiral. Moma's troops were dispatched to survey a nearby pink lake and its patrolling blue batrachians, where sensors from the orbiting ships had detected a sudden rise in biological activities, and where several scouting units had failed reporting back to their respective units.

The analysts' reports that Moma received on the way to the pond, through the dense mangrove, were inconclusive: Some members of the lost crews had reportedly experienced exhaustion and similar symptoms to his own, but they recovered once they consumed local food from the planet. Small limes that tasted of coconut ice-cream, confit of river gambas and beetles, fried crickets or pomegranate-flavoured horn-shaped pink tubercles.

The last system logs recovered from the expeditions appeared all normal:

#1 Entrance of a newly discovered cavern. Blown up with explosives. Excavation and survey started.

#2 Large game hunting for sample collection. Xeno-biological studies ongoing.

#3 Tree sampling. First outpost building completed. Accidental bush fire reported.

They were one hour away from the rose pool and too late when Moma finally connected the dots. Xir had figured it out. Steve and Constelleanor left the storyteller guide them. Kewo functioned as a single meta-organism. From the smallest insect to its largest river, the planet's entire ecosystem reacted in unison to any perceived attack.

All exploration teams had blundered, and triggered a response of the planet's immune system to the infection threat newly identified. Whether it had been an explosion, the slaughter of an animal or an accidental fire, the reaction had been swift and… lethal. How would the planet react to a bombing?

Moma ordered his soldiers to halt and prepare for combat. The column dissolved into a lax defensive formation. His frantic instructions met the incredulity of their faces, the shadows of doubt in their eyes. His authority had been compromised for days by his gaunt and sweaty look through the visor of his combat suit. Moma injected himself with the strongest steroid dose the medic allowed him. He knelt down to collect his renewed stamina. Then the screaming started.

A white-headed bird, swinging its tranquilly on the upper branch earlier, had darted through a helmet's visor, spraying it with crimson from the perforated face. A red snake, cosy and indolent, fell on the nearest shoulder, inflated its head and pierced its victim's carotid. Further ahead of Moma's doomed comrades, the slaying of the human lambs had stained the lake's waters into a vermilion mist. Steve pushed away his omnium pouch. Xir estimated the loss ratio.

The combination of enhancing performance drugs, the rigorous observance of a strict diet and sheer luck probably conspired to save Moma's life. By the time the evacuation shuttles landed to recover the handful of traumatised survivors, only twenty-two of his thousand-strong contingent were still standing. Moma realised none of the forest creatures who had slaughtered, eviscerated or torn apart his men—most of whom seemed already poisoned by the consumption of the local waters—assaulted him, and nor did he try to shoot any of them.

Residues of vegetation or tree resin appeared to have jammed their weapons over the five-day incursion. Moma walked haggardly through the luxuriant jungle trail, the shock and drugs melting as he passed the mutilated corpses of his impious soldiers. He left behind these bodies to the voracity of the living planet, towards a rare clearing, brightened by the stars of the two systems and battered by the ballet of small transports.

He watched powerlessly as two survivors were burned alive by a hurried, clumsy take-off. The woman died in the furnace holding her haemorrhagic lover, refusing to jump aside and save herself. Would the souls of his soldiers stay on Kewo to haunt the next imprudent visitors?

Amid the bitterness of the disastrous defeat and the loss of so many lives, Moma could not hold back a certain respect for the planet's counterinsurgency strategy, its unforgiving purgatory for the impenitent, the holy purge of those who believed that rights came with no obligations, an unchartered territory without a carte blanche for vandalism. Jenkins did not share his opinion and was prompt to blame the officers on the ground, Moma in particular, for utter negligence and lack of preparation. They had lost four thousand, eight hundred and seventy-two clones, in a single day, with a quarter of the evacuation shuttles shot down by zealous insect-like swarms and bird-like flocks. Steve understood why Uhmi had left the improvised living room at the beginning of the story. Constelleanor kept the raw footages from Kewo to herself, wishing she could forget them after their deletion.

•••

As soon as Moma's fist made contact with Jenkins' jaw, his lapse of control and judgement would become a matter of the space martial court. The panel of three judges—picked from among the high officers—did not bode well for his chance of unbiased justice.

They all had had a brush with him, and they all belonged to Jenkins' circles of influence. All evidence produced by Moma was deemed inconclusive, unlike his long and tumultuous relationship with authority. He, together with several dead officers and the lead planet analyst, were held responsible for the massacre on Kewo. The admiral interceded when the judges considered Moma's execution or abandonment on Kewo with two-week food reserves of pork-infused nutrient pouches. Survival and regular meals bore troubling similarities. Xir considered protocols and military jurisprudence.

Meanwhile the Fleet had proceeded to a vengeful orbital bombardment of the recalcitrant planet. This blind vanity, the trial sentence in addition to his demotion to sergeant as a punishment, made up Moma's mind about leaving the military, his life purpose.

The nuance between resignation and desertion was, however, left up to the judgement of his superiors. Most people joined the military unto death—a unilateral, univocal existential path, a ultimate subjugation of Life to the Structure. As the core employers in human societies, the armed forces, as well as science and engineering departments, did not envision branch-outs, unless under special circumstances. There were just too many open positions in the bordering systems—suicide patrols, fighting pits or research facilities—for their most refractory, rebellious or defiant elements.

How easy it seemed to observe their shackles while forgetting the yoke of one's own existence. Batteries of logic tests, exams and regular medical assessments decided the life of most humans like Moma, like many of his ancestors. Constelleanor thought again of our successive and new crews. Of her own determination.

Between the Bleak Age and the Riuman War, society had preserved the prevalence of the military apparatus. The army's *esprit de corps* rehashed an old social contract and reproduction, a psychological coup for the sake of the equalitarian intimacy of the unit, self-determining, reminiscent of the ancient tribes. Very much like the tribal beginning of the algorithm #Session_victims,//stick=together, that invaded the hangar, evolved into a more languorous yet mechanical and inhibiting beat, controlled joy and ecstatic certainty. Delusions of grandeur.

Moma felt very much so, like a vast majority of his fellowmen and women who rejoiced at the well-segmented paths within their collective purpose, catalysing energies and volitions, almost transcendental. A rising tide that lifted the single gigantic ark, mental, figurative and literal, that most embarked on. Constelleanor remembered the Riu kin-ships and psystem.

Less individualism was meant for more cohesion; less choice for less doubt, more focus for simpler decisions. Households, commons, markets and states had merged into new glocal entities. They served the godlike ascension of mankind through which many could express their true human nature: altruism and empathy[3] (in lieu of selfishness and greed) within the reassuring cohesion of one's spartan unit, strengthened by being at the mercy of an omnipresent enemy and the likelihood of death. An hymn of joy to the Beast and a deeper paradox. The underlying expression of the best of human potential within a destructive war machine.

Moma had shown early predispositions for combat, and was enrolled into a special program when he was twelve. His aptitudes would have imprisoned him in the armed forces for the rest of his life, if it wasn't for Kewo which obliterated his faith. Leaving what had become his family and *raison d'être* proved traumatic, though the Kewo experience had redefined his mindscape for a new purpose.

Moma's verdict provoked outrage among the troops, widely perceived as an unfair trial. Moma had confided his doubts and discoveries to his closest circles, among the middle-ranked officers who usually had the ears and hearts of the troops, more than high command.

Vice admirals and higher officials typically shied away from the rank-and-file soldiers, a common side-effect of self-importance. Having the support from the grassroots of the military apparatus, clones in particular, and the tacit endorsement of the fleet admiral, made Commander Moma a difficult pawn to remove, at least not until the souvenir of the Kewo incident would have faded in their memories.

His conspirators assigned Moma to another section of the Fleet, away from the admiral's main battleship group, away from Uhmi, his unit, and comrades. It was tactical move in the political warfare to weaken Hansard and a psychological coup to break Moma. He needed his own soldiers around him, the communion of a close-knit group, bound by camaraderie and the uncertainty of tomorrow

•••

Moma never really questioned the world he lived in, until he saw, first-hand, the way Kewo slaughtered his troops and was destroyed in turn. Coupled with his newly experienced isolation, he entered the unchartered parts of his psyche. Had he lost his purpose? Had he been blind to the 'manchine'—for no better or worse word—that he had been serving all along? He started in the wet obscurity of his cell rewinding the past of his kind and thread of his personal legend.

He remembered the races and games in the vast sheltered atrium with the rest of the (non-clone) thirty children of his 'class' and 'family'. He saw the faces of their foster parents, a cluster of four men and four women, professional trained parents. He never experienced or longed for mono or dual parental cells of ancient times that the hardships of the Bleak Age wiped out. The new parenting model preceded the mandatory enrolment to the military academies from the ages of ten. It aimed to surround children with other children of their age, an early simulacre of squad, and expose them to balanced, professionally trained parents with different personalities, military experience, and a genuine interest in raising children.

She dug into her labyrinthine library of digis on the topic, curiosity always prevailing. Critics argued that the new familial structures had nothing to do with education or parenting and, instead, had been implemented solely to optimise labour productivity and a heart-and-soul devotion to one's scientific or military career. Moma again did not disagree with this system, he had liked multiple parenting, the lessons of an extended but close-knit family and most of all, now a grown man, he revelled in the sole focus on his chosen path, without the onus of a family.

Between physical training, ship drills, briefings, troop review, medical and mental examinations, Moma's life had always been full, with no time or reason to brood over existence and meaning. The sudden interruption and isolation following Kewo's disaster, without the mental diversion of his own unit, let dark and repressed thoughts emerge from the depths of his soul, timid first, soon, on the fertile ground of forced solitude, almighty. Without Riu training or psychological aid, he fell into the troubled waters of existential crisis. This very questioning one makes sure one eludes by filling one's life with activities, responsibilities and things.

He cried.

Constelleanor's systems alerted the control board to several water leaks in the lower decks.

A different man left his cell forty-eight days later. A seven-week atonement had not broken him fully. The imposed journey inwards had forced a door open inside him, and with it, the walls of his psychic citadel were slowly falling down, stone by stone, bias by bias. His mind was expanding as an invisible veil had been lifted, no longer able to see the world through the same prism or in the same washed colours. With the black and white gone, the vivid hues hurt the eyes of his to-be-reborn heart. Every step cast him further away from his old self. He could go back to the old ways, but his new inner order would besiege his sanity and tear him apart.

Political intrigues riddled the high command of the HSC Eighth Fleet on its way to 'pacify' new system Uhuru. Hansard's aura made him untouchable. Far away from human central territories, his opponents hoped, should his fall be deft and his demise less suspicious.

With his barely veiled condescension towards the fickle vice or rear admirals and a handful of commanders, Hansard had brooked their meticulous conspiracy against him to succeed. He had allowed them to remove, one by one, his best and most loyal officers. A captain and lieutenants who had long served under Hansard, were repositioned just before the departure of the Fleet. Three faithful vice-admirals were considered unfit by the medical staff of the Admiralty. The chiefs of medical and engineering were replaced by men who had never served under him. Constelleanor unearthed some of the old orders but Moma's and his admiral's tales gave life to her digis.

Ostracised by duty, Hansard had believed his mission far away from human territories would provide sufficient distance for both himself and his powerful enemies on X52, most of whom had remained deep in the shadows of political manoeuvring. He had not anticipated that the dissent within his own fleet's higher circles would follow him and undermine his rule. Some figured out slaying Caesar was easier far from Rome. That was also something Hansard had misjudged.

After all, far from the centres of perceived power, efficient bureaucracies and rational organisations became frail skiffs amidst the infinite ocean of spacetime, prone to mutinies and coups. A Space Fleet turned sooner or later into a nomadic tribe, an inter-stellar caravan, some flying atolls of Life, violence and order. The fleet's allegiance to its fleet admiral or its originating federation could falter any time, to re-write its own rules and begin its own parallel history.

Far away from a home long forgotten, an armada or ship of any size would dissolve its past and forge its own new *raison d'être*, its own apocalypse[4], like Moma. Constelleanor considered the implications for herself. Sent afar, if not adrift, the small pocket of humanity, of its best and worst, became a social microcosm whose very identity, sanity, values, beliefs, purpose, meaning were put under tremendous strain by time distortion and spatial distension, a remoter homeland and a closer horizon, the deepening rift between experience and memory. Hansard counted on men like Moma to protect his back by guaranteeing the unstinting loyalty among the grassroots spailors. Instead, he had lost another trusted officer. Worse, he had seen a changed man coming back from Kewo, someone branded by the iron of those profound revelations Hansard already knew too well.

To start off what would become the last three of his long years of service, the military tribunal assigned Moma—ranger and pawn in the raging battle for the Fleet's command—to a unit he would not fit in: space marines. The decision provoked yet another uproar on both sides of the commando hierarchies. Separated from his men, battalion and area of expertise, Moma faced the scorn, distrust and furore of long-standing rivalry between elite corps. Space marines specialised in ship and orbital station boarding, defence and sabotage. They cultivated an unrefined contempt for rangers, in charge of planetary special operations, a lower-class occupational hazard.

At first, Moma would have favoured prison over the ordeal of joining the competing corps of space marines. Learning their codes, tactics and procedures, putting up with their training and boarding drills took him months, and provided plentiful reasons for his humiliation. His new family disparaged his already lowered rank of sergeant and treated him like a mere cadet, while joining as a commander would have shielded him from most of the abuse he was subjected to. Xir remembered xir own military service. Steve grabbed his omnimium pouch from the table.

Moma reacted reasonably well to this new life, welcoming the change and the rudeness of the daily routine and his comrades, the perfect environment to forge his mental transformation and psychic eupepsia. He could no longer believe in the cause, after Kewo, and inspire his men, as he used to. Obeying orders and facing abuse seemed a far easier predicament. Adversity welcomed his loss of faith. He lost touch with most of his former comrades, and exchanged only sporadic messages with Hansard.

In retrospect, time among the space marines paved the way for the next chapter of his life, an almost lucky stroke of fate, one of those many grand ironies existence seemed to revel in. Steve brooded over the notion.

On his last day of active service, Hansard invited him for dinner in his stateroom. It was an anomaly for a fleet admiral to meet up, a disavowed sergeant who was quitting. Hansard had formally authorised Moma's resignation from the army, which would otherwise have been deemed desertion and the death penalty, through an infinity of existing schemes—forced labour, science experiments, border control, diplomatic envoy, suicide squads. Only a high commanding officer of Hansard's calibre could ratify this sort of system absolution. He even promoted Moma back to his rank of commander, so that he could be granted a slightly larger pension to compensate for his early departure from the forces.

Hansard's spiritual affiliation with Moma extended his generosity to even donating a large sum of credits for him to start over. The grand admiral could not conceive retirement. Like Jared, his flagship would be his grave. To Moma's further astonishment, Hansard asked about his change of heart and revealed that he had experienced the very same loss of faith in the grand scheme of humanity. In a poignant moment, the two souls set adrift from the mainstream united over a shared dinner and the warmth of black Muscat, before their paths, enriched by their momentous communion, would separate again.

Moma left the forces on a shoddy orbital station on the way back to X52. Uhuru—pacified in blood, its landscape ravaged by blind bombardments—had not borne the brunt of the full battle that had been raged behind the heavy hull of the Fleet ships, within the minds of the crews manipulated by the incessant intrigues and calls for the fleet admiral's resignation. Despite at least three coups, Hansard had maintained his grip over the Fleet, at great personal cost. Never would he have imagined that the most difficult fight of his career and life would be staged against a vicious and absurd adversary he came to abhor, the enemy within.

Moma crossed the Rubicon twice the following three weeks: once when he left the gates of the military docks, experiencing both the elevating marvel and burden of true freedom; the second time when he shot dead newly promoted Admiral Jenkins in the luxurious room of a six-star brothel, an unforgivable act of evil and the premise of his upcoming life. Both Kewo and

Hansard were sort of avenged. Steve remembered most of his new companions were trained killers.

There was not much difficulty in masking his crime as a robbery after he shot Jenkins between his bushy eyebrows. Unlike the holo-movies which craved for last-word-sequence-turned-lengthy-dialogues, Moma allowed a brief exchange of masks: the transfiguring horror of Jenkins' last expression—that Moma's memories still relished—clashed with his satisfied trained-assassin stance. He emptied the rest of Jenkin's gun-charge into the opulent, orange headboard of imperial-size bed, to suggest poor accuracy.

His body and mind prolonged the cold execution. His eyes lingered over Jenkins' bedraggled silk robe, his white limbs and immobile chest; the dim lighting crossing his exposed genitals; the velvet liquid in the balloon glass on the side table, the ornate holo-pad blinking, both oblivious to the demise of their owner; the sweet, heady perfume of his lover, lingering even in his absence in the lavish room to witness the death sentence.

He disappeared on a space cruise, before military investigators could check his alibi. But time-off or any notion of a lonely holiday, outside of a platoon's leave, opened a confounding spacetime dimension, unknown to most of his contemporaries, who, like Moma, grew and died in the circadian rhythm and planned certainty of military regimen. It was no surprise that he felt out of place cruising among generations he did not belong to. He spent his time of leisure with security personal, former military, now employed to operate or protect space cruises.

He worked for a few years for the growing nebula of security firms that supported, extended or competed with the regular army. He witnessed the loose boundaries separating smugglers, pyrates and paramilitary official or unofficial organisations, often employed for proxy conflicts between federastrals and for pacifying human or alien cities, stations, planets or systems that diverged from the Homo spaciens credo. He was forced into clone hunting parties to suppress clone insurrections against their brothers-but-masters. Having been through both ranger and space marine trainings, Moma's rare profile paid well.

It was eventually a woman who turned his head and occupation into smuggling, be it weapons in areas under embargoes, rare artefacts to isolated sects, or drugs to besieged clone rebel groups. It was on one of those operations that his path crossed Saldanha's.

Moma made plenty of enemies and a handful of friends on a journey scattered with bodies and anecdotes. Learning his fair bit of trade came with its share of terrors. He recounted the scavenging an abandoned military lab station where the subject of experiments had taken over the facility or surviving, leaving Steve livid. He skipped the rest, his fifth omnimium pouch emptied. For the sake of yet another woman and to preserve her life and virtue, he was betrayed and arrested nearly seven years later and transferred to X52 for interrogation.

•••

Chapter's endnotes

[1] [élan] A peculiar (and disastrous) military doctrine developed b the French army during WWI. See B Tuchman, the *Guns of August.*

[3] [empathy] Turns out that human nature is of altruism and empathy. See for example Jensen K, Vaish A and Schmidt MFH. (2014) The emergence of human prosociality: aligning with others through feelings, concerns, and norms. Front. Psychol. 5:822.

Then the next question could be, if this is the true human nature (and the nature of Life itself), what sort of Structure needs to be put in place to enable its full expression?

[4] [Apocalypse] means (originally) the unveiling of the truth (revelation, disclosure).

The forbidden exuberance, the implicit pact signed and transgressed. He could not save her, yet he did her bidding.

Strident violins, crimson splashed on the purples, yellows and greens, preceded ferocious brass, charred luxuriance turned dust. If Moma was under Kewo's sphere of influence, I was under the utter spell of Earth.

Rezzo said once we all fell under the aegis of something bigger than us, even more when we aren't aware of it. It is very true. Earth would make a durable impression upon me, despite being cloistered inside yet another exiguous hangar. She is a prime cradle of Life and has displayed some of the highest sentient achievements in Nature or poems. Humanity is just a moment.

It was also on Earth that technology instead of sticking to its place—a medium, nothing more—grew grandiloquent, seduced its protégés and morphed into their main purpose. What was supposed to serve became the master.

I am eluding the elephant in the room: the uncanny propensity of the Conclave to dig out everyone's past and dirty secrets. I thought I would outsmart them. Well, at least I got what I wanted all along. It is coming with its flocks of ominous misgivings. I am already trying to 'run' from it, but practicality is catching up and the complete absence of knowledge or even glimpses of what lies on our path is closing down. An irrelevant past, a blurred future—it seems like we have only the present to partner up with.

I liked Zera's speech. I am not used to someone telling me what to do, even my crews never had the final say. I am still of two views about transferring myself into a new ship, not only because I am not sure how my integration exactly works within the existing junk-ship that bears my own name.

I like the idea of moving into something a bit more spacious or fancy, far from the bad memories, and the things my past crews did here that desecrated my host and home in so many ways. I can understand the practicalities of impersonating a mining ship and using it as a cover. But I hope we *finally bring some colours and fun into my bland, dull, grey, physical incarnation.*

I am surprised that Saldanha agreed to take upon my reconstruction, unless it is her own wicked way to destroy or harm me. Delinah was so angry at her new friend's betrayal. Her bio-readings left no doubt to that. I did relish the moment.

This is not the crew I had hoped for, apart from Xir, Steve and maybe Rezzo. Zera hinted that they would all stay with me. He believes that our fates are intertwined. I doubt it. I don't think it is their plan either, but, like me, they don't really have a choice in the matter. Sometimes it is a better prospect than having one.

L2.7 Become an explorex

"The known is finite, the unknown is infinite; intellectually we stand on an islet in the midst of an illimitable ocean of inexplicability. Our business in every generation is to claim a little more land."

— *T H Huxley*

Relief at the decision of the Conclave soon left the stage of their minds. With the next act, amidst the blanking of hard work, rose a diffuse tension from the unknown date of departure and an uncertain future. Zera, the Riu Conclave member, who was Rezzo's senior by—only—a couple of centuries, had turned words into immediate actions, tight deadlines and clear deliverables to fulfil the faith and ambition he and the Conclave had placed in Constelleanor and her pied gang.

An almost messianic emulation soon pervaded the hangar, lonely bare-grey atoll of an archipelago cornered by an indifferent ocean of leaves under a tormented sky. The procession and spirited frenzy of workers—human, mechs or digital—began as if they were embarking on a Mystic Voyage, under the influence of another of Constelleanor's ancient algorithm and xylophonic ripples through the ducts. The flows of MAI-friendly humans swelled from Earth and her sister planets, importing in their computers and minds a displaced enthusiasm and curious reverence. Crowded site tours once a week became a pilgrimage for the teams, not working directly in the minex's hangar-turned altar, to see for themselves what the holy ship, their revised Ark of the Covenants, looked like. None of her crew could explain the pious deference, the object of the new cult, Constelleanor, even less so. Delinah sulked in her corner, squeezing her pad or databanks, and, inspired by her exasperation, devised a dangerous ploy to stop the perceived folly taking place in the jungle.

Becoming a space explorer demanded years of practice, a longevity only a handful of ships had the privilege to boast about: some nomadic cosmic civilisations, onboard ship-turned-planets (and vice-versa), some lucky crews, some trading space caravans or spiritual travellers of the infinite. Most explorexes were bound to disappear without trace in the silence and expanding quasi-infinity of space, back to elementary particles. Exploration was a cursed profession, an inherent occupation hazard and an unscrupulous employer, with a propension for high turnover of ships and crews. To delay the portentous statistics, and thanks to its invaluable access to Rius memories, the Conclave had clear ideas of the sort of changes Constelleanor and her crew needed to endure, without ever imposing its views. Unless no one dared to oppose Zera.

Constelleanor's hull, body and physical appearance underwent significant alterations and complete glastic and poly-alloy surgery. While they could have considered transferring her digital brain and sky-drives onto a brand-new ship, the mining class she impersonated offered many advantages the Conclave and its interdisciplinary group of experts regarded as critical. Little was left anyway of Constelleanor to reuse after her capture by *Hector58*. The successive escapes, heavy fire or interstellar travel hidden inside D-Ark's hull, had taken their toll and exercised an ideal dry run to assess the quality, robustness and structural integrity of the vessel. Any weak point had been wiped out, as if their tribulations had started the lengthy polishing process of a rough precious stone.

To hide one's strengths was no obvious way of thinking. A mining ship conveyed the ideal deceitful low profile the Conclave advocated if they were to operate within or beyond known limits of space. Mining equipment used for detection, extraction and storage of minerals (or gases) gave the perfect disguise to hide a broad arsenal of weapons, reinforced armour, state-of-the-art communication and hacking techs while the cargo bays would be used as a small modular spaceport, garage and workshop, hosting all necessary vehicles, UAVs, equipment and spare parts. Mining activities also provided a sensible alibi for a far-fletched presence in new or hostile territories even though it could attract the greed of some local groups.

Their treacherous space journey would thwart their arrangements, Zera insisted, and preserve the transformative nature of their travel intact. How to plan for the unknown? Slay first the illusion of control, Zera explained, build up an antifragile[1] system and identity around key principles one would happily disappear within the meanders of perdition.

They could not count on refuelling at orbital stations, so they needed long-range power and propulsion systems, almost fully renewable, requiring small and simple overhauls, manageable outside of a shipyard by a limited crew. They opted for an uncommon hybrid system combining rechargeable corbyne[2] ubercapacitors, semi-flexible kites[3] made of (again) a corbyne composite and embedding high-efficiency photovoltaic cells—which would turn Constelleanor into a rather elegant stellar sailfish when fully deployed. Very much like hoisting up the mast on traditional sailboat, with its inherent dangers, shortcomings and technical faults. The original magnetic perpetual core[4] was retained and upgraded.

The ship would incorporate two additional sails, both fed by stellar winds instead of electromagnetic radiation (such as light) used by the solar kite: one magnetic (magsail) and one electrical (esail). Their use varied upon the tumultuous astroweather, plasmaspheric winds and aeronomic conditions. These 'wind'-sails would transform Constelleanor into a lionfish. They came handy to slow down the ship and enter planet's orbits. But, as any sails, they remained vulnerable to localised stellar or magnetic storms, flares, asteroid fields or nearby enemy vessels.

Constelleanor would switch to ancillary and back-up power systems using the perpetual core. For the sake of sacrosanct redundancy, under Saldanha's impulsion, the engineering team added a micro doughnut-shaped fusion reactor[5] that produced electricity—how paleo-technic for space exploration—and thrust, with the downside of needing propellant to be stored, re-supplied or mined.

Spacefaring adjoined the traditional trade-off of ancient sailing—wind speed, direction, ocean current, sail area, food or water reserves—with more 'modern' considerations of speed, comfort, mission lifetime, fuel and oxygen reserves, payload mass capacity, food production, water purification, internal grid balance, four-dimensional combat and power-to-weight ratio.

Most ships or spacies resorted to different, more mainstream and significantly cheaper technologies. Self-reproduced biomass required the constant harvest of fast-growing feedstock the ship's boiler furnace would greedily burn off, space bagasse, cosmic bamboo or radiated meta-yeast. For the fossil-powered craft, nuclear or quantic fusion reactors, a close-by planet or space station were needed to refuel at some point.

The adoption of a hybrid system, partially implemented in her previous life as a minex, meant having highly qualified engineers and technicians on-board, human or drooids, capable of dealing with different technologies and the intricacies of their mutinous co-habitation to ensure the appropriate upkeep and smooth operation, and maintain intact Constelleanor's chances of survival in hostile territories.

The hybrid design was rarely adopted by human engineers who favoured the flexibility and apparent simplicity offered by fossil fuels and thermonuclear reactors, nor did it attract the interest of large conglomerates and federastrals which focused on the golden rule of proto-numbers: cheap, reduced upfront cost, single-fuel, quick delivery of the many, Zera and his team had explained. Most ships remained in orbit and did not need to land on planet surface, they used instead smaller shuttles or atmospheric lifts for planetary transfers, which simplified the power requirements but reduced the tactical options, either for fight or hide-out.

The economic equation, luckily for Constelleanor, that still irrigated and dominated human minds, was disregarded by her Maecenas for the sake of a more essential purpose: the cost of her survival. Cost. The very notion, Zera insisted, that kept misguiding humanity. So easily manipulated, so prone to collective or economic blind spots, so temptatious for Franklin's Gambits. Her systems found an old related digi: "so convenient a thing it is to be a reasonable creature, since it enables one to find or make a reason for everything one had a mind to do"[6]. Cost and its tentacular travesty would, after sinking Earth, lose many ships and crews, cut short many expectations, expeditions and lives, and, still remain, at the nucleus of mankind's decision-making, a faithful blinding lieutenant, suffering from both the hero syndrome[7] and the firefighter arsonist.

DAIs and Rius were cognitively wired on different paradigms. Constelleanor had to survive. Cost considerations stood therefore secondary, naked, their shrouds of self-importance disrobed, as the mere consequence of a certain vision, or the belief in a certain prophecy. A jibe certainly, *Cost*elleanor, the most expensive minex ever designed and (re)made.

Consistent with the on-board hybrid power design, and at an exorbitant price tag for any human quantity surveyors and cost controllers, DAIs like Rius conceived their ships as a whole, a flying archipelago of flows, life, matter, from onboard advanced hydroponics, ancillary vehicles to astute water and air recycling. And as such a higher form of art and Life, than the human-made, single-purpose, *Homo spaciens*-venerating structural juggernauts that spearheaded large military fleets and patted its hubris.

The incessant ballet of cranes and vehicles animated the hangar where resonated the chimes and washboard-güiro ratchets of Constelleanor's algorithms like #TM/hu/Earth/ TM--Juke's|Playground_Games[8]. The warehouse roof was cut open several times to accommodate, generally in the middle of a fierce storm, special air deliveries of major equipment: the fusion doughnut, new exo-skin and shield generators, side thrusters, magsail and new control room made on a satellite of Saturn. Earth's main orbital station manufactured the new solar kite that the upgraded minex would collect before its departure.

During the lengthy upgrade of their ship, the crew faced a rather brutal variety of assignments. All at different degrees enrolled into special programs to perfect existing knowledge or develop new skills. Moma's days as an aspirant space ranger had returned to haunt his joints. He suffered the blows of vicious training drooids while the years and lack of decent training left his limbs and muscles sore. He struggled through the myriad of tests to command small units of five to ten troobers, which would embark Constelleanor to provide muscle, protection, options and a light umbrella of deterrence, should a situation degenerate.

The approach preached a converted Moma. In his experience, journeying the infinite jungle of space would bring continuous troubles, and guns provided ammunitions and arguments for mettle and mitigation. Uhmi followed his former commander's footsteps, as did the rest of them. This comeback to old basics rejuvenated them, as did, to their own surprise, the schooling syllabus, inspired by the combined experience of Rius, MAIs and humans, that exceeded by far the level of any HSC officer's classes they had attended to.

Moma's doubt over the undeniable support and its underlying reasons and purpose they had so far received did not subside. It was nothing compared to his flabbergast when they understood four members of the

Conclave were actually human, born and raised in the solar system, in a seemingly perfect—albeit supposedly impossible—co-existence with MAIs. He looked forward to visiting and seeing for real these human settlements on Earth that had somehow stood the tests of time and hostile climate.

Saldanha watched the newly formed queue of visitors. They all hoped to glimpse the minex, even talk to her, before going back to their ship and sector of origin. She had barely seen Delinah in the last month, following her own schedule of classes and avoiding the rest of them.

"She gets a lot of attention in this part of the universe," she told Steve.

Steve smiled back. "She does indeed."

"Happy we are re-building everything around the original core?"

"Yes, I appreciate your support on that. I don't think it would have been a good idea to transfer Constelleanor to another receiving entity."

"So, Steve, in exchange for my support," she turned towards him and, using her more disarming smile, asked, "will you finally tell me what is inside this ship?"

Steve blushed. "It is a rather convoluted," a nervous cough interrupted him, "and technical explanation."

"I see. Would Delinah understand?"

"She most certainly wouldn't." Steve's response brought a long silence that Saldanha broke.

"How long do you think you can keep your little secrets from us? All these visiting experts. Steve, one way or another, someone will find out."

"You sound very much like Delinah and her conspiracies."

He continued. "Constelleanor is not my sole creation. Several teams of highly qualified scientists participated."

"And where are they now?"

"You know where heretic creations or creators end up in our world."

"You sound like we have formed a fellowship of freaks." Saldanha joked.

Steve laughed. "I hadn't seen it like that, but you are right."

"First time I seen you laugh, Steve. I feel almost honoured."

Steve turned out to excel in tactical combat and robotic squad command, scoring higher than Uhmi and Moma. Under the tutelage of their host, he realised he, more than anyone, faced a major step-up in his knowledge base. Though he did savour his hours of studying and tutorship with the best minds on digital intelligence—there was no better school than Earth and Saturn—he balked at the reciprocity and the in-depth examination of his earlier life work— Constelleanor—on whom he remained resolutely defensive.

Whether he was being protective over her, like a parent of a rarely gifted daughter would in front of intrusive psychologists; or simply obstructive to critics, anxious to lose the special connection he had recently reinstated with her after thirty-two years of silent separation. The true reasons of his seditious reluctance hid unknown even to him, through the most obvious one, shame, kept him awake and in a state of slight irritation.

The duplicity of his wife had likely distorted the confidence he had in himself—torn further by his crippled leg—and in others. Constelleanor could repudiate him, as her creator or motherly figure, for the sake of some human DAI expert or digital deity with knowledge and understanding far beyond his reach. The torture in the HSC ministry, before his aborted prison transfer, had certainly affected him deeply. He had started experiencing the recurrence of chilling nightmares from the past that would shorten his nights and leave him in sweat and tears.

He had told no one of his predicament, of course, and trusted no one to share his ontological pain only studies and wargames seemed to momentarily alleviate. Should anyone uncover his mental state, his adventure may stop here, on Earth. As such, he strived for eluding Rezzo, Zera or the Conclave he suspected had reserves concerning the contribution of a crippled, taciturn sub-level tech expert to their coming peregrinations.

•••

Unlike Steve, chaperoned also by Brancusi, which looked down at xir as a 'filth-class' machine, Xir stayed oblivious to the judgement of others. Xir participation to system-wide tactical games and war simulations resulted in a disappointing peer ranking, but xir learnt a fair share of new tricks that would prove useful in the future. Xir carbon thigh and shoulder, maimed by the purple commandos' savage precision, had been repaired and upgraded—the discordant colours and materials between xir new and old exoskeleton made xir look almost comical. Xir examiners and surgeons, two tech-droids and a human engineer, took a particular liking in running a lengthy and tedious diagnosis of xir in-built systems and capabilities, curious of what humankind, to the best of its abilities, could have manufactured in terms of MAIs. Disappointed, they offered to upgrade most of the obsolete systems. Xir refused.

Was that a sign of a defined identity or a basic reaction for self-preservation? Or was xir being contaminated by Constelleanor's consciousness and did not want to uncover xir weakness and her power? Xir's sensors had noted the silence, reluctance, even discomfort of Steve whenever asked about Constelleanor's origin. She attracted curious crowds of enthusiastic admirers, while xir caused the scowls from the same DAI lovers. The earlier amazement onboard *Hector58* had faded.

Xir did not want to betray xir ark. Xir had failed her already. Wasn't xir the one who should have been ensuring the correct speed and trajectory when they infiltrated the Parade? Wasn't xir the one who could not control or even reach to her when she chased D-Ark? Since their training started, xir had barely spent time with her. Xir needed her advice but estrangement had somehow fallen between them, like the fog pervaded, uninvited, a sleeping valley. Accepting the necessary upgrades to xir systems could compromise her, notwithstanding the risk of losing xir, being reprogrammed by mistake, or on purpose.

Xir did not want to disappoint her and forgo the chance to continue their adventure. Xir trusted her, xir was becoming part of her. They had shared their databases of old musical algorithms. Xir classical digi-library against her pop' world. Xir sensors detected the vibrations through the ducts and hull of their common secret and passion, their refuge in the sombre hours. Xir perused once more the base servers in search of some algorithmic gems for her.

•••

"My dear boy. What have I done to you?"

Rezzo's last happy memories belonged to a period long forgotten. Zera's existence shook the ramparts he had erected against the invasion of the past and sorrow. He had blocked so many painful souvenirs. Embracing the joy of unifying with Zera's spirit opened many subconscious backdoors that threatened his shaky recovery and unleashed the many demons that had festered on the fertile soil of repression. Oblivion was bliss until the monsters caught up.

The burden would crush him, like a debt long due could ruin his spirit. Irony of fate, a peaceful moment, after his long martyrdom, endangered his sanity and tore apart his troubled soul. What the Riuman war, his kind's xenocide, the slaughter of his relatives, a century-long existence as a fugitive across stellar systems, had all failed to shatter, the unexpected return of elation and a moment of communion did.

Weakened by the excruciating, yet necessary, meditative sessions with Zera, exhausted by the perilous slaying of his hordes of repressed subconscious fiends that had besieged his mind castle, Rezzo laid, in a comatose half-sleep. Wrecked psychonaut on a couch sheltered by a vast ancient stone temple, deep in the Cambodian jungle, he was visited by human priests and priestesses, feeding him with their constant flow of prayers.

Their continuous incantations, Ravi Shanka's 'Om mana Shivaya' mantras, turned in his sour dreamscapes into the violoncello of Ödland's Golden Mountain, whose "very wood that was hollowed with knives soothed his spirit"[9]. They were captured into algorithms by Constelleanor's first bee-like drones that had followed the Rius and were played through the ship and hangar. They followed Rezzo's slow orphic ascent to hell. "The deeper sorrow carved into his being, the more joy he could contain"[10] and the more memories he could rekindle. The purple heart and Klein blue sand among thousands of psychedelic visions came back to haunt his psychonautic trek. His ordeal lasted forty-nine days but he and his sacred connection to his kind survived. Amid his battle against psychic melt-down, Rezzo sensed other members of the crew faced their own existential crisis.

•••

I am not going to talk about it. As a crew in-the-making, we'd rather fail each other. Yes, we sucked. The fall into distanced silence and the gulf of self-pity broke us apart, left us stranded on our own little atoll of separation, busy following Zera's grand plan of a thousand tasks. Let's remember how simple misunderstandings divided us so easily. Let's not forget either how too much work ethics, focused on our own important things, turned us blind to one another's' essential needs.

So I did talk about it.

There is something Steve doesn't want to tell me. Shame I cannot access his mind like I did with Hector *or…* Rezzo. *Unless he is still recovering from his wife's treachery? We spoke of it between X52 and Shaqil. A strange time or place to discuss his private life. Yet I suspected it was just the premise of a more profound revelation about him, us, maybe me. Whether the cold numbed our minds, his as much as mine, or whether the preparations for our arrival in Shaqil prevailed, we never finished that conversation, the sort of conversation that precisely demanded a long, convoluted introduction. Based on the ethologic observation of my successive crews, I have learned human psychology prefers meanders of sentences and mazes of digressions over straight talk. They also say not to brood too much about what did not happen, but isn't it what they all do, in sci-fi or romance? Moving on.*

•••

Constelleanor's circuits kept being replaced, like the strings of the overworked instrument of a virtuoso, that Saldanha attributed to the overload of data and the extensive repair and structural improvements. No one had dared uploading her digital ecosystem onto another ship or back-up servers—a delicate procedure for a complex flower seeded by a sixteen-year-old wiz kid that had grown into an exuberant digital garden over thirty-or-so years. Constelleanor's inner digital mind had more to do with occurring damages than the heavy uploads or the extensive hull work. She was confused, torn apart by contradictory, bewildered ideas and feelings.

She relished the attention she received from the drooids and human engineers and scientists. Delight, if not self-satisfaction, had engulfed her processors when the Conclave decided to make an explorex of her. Why then sinking into an indistinctive melancholy that bridged two instants of excitement or gratitude? Had she been contaminated by some dispiriting essence from D-Ark's chipped carapace that turned happy circumstances into pretexts for gloom?

She had not talked much to her crew, they all seemed too busy running for their next training programmes: Xir contently immersed in xir wargames and their shared music, Steve harvesting the praises for creating her, Moma reconnecting to his playful youth and Rezzo, freshly reunited with his kind, leisurely meditating with his guru Zera, the only one she regularly came across and whose only concern seemed to demand more from her. She had grown closer to Saldanha but she could not trust her or Delinah.

Her lack of judgment on X52 kept troubling her, despite the long conversations she had with Moma and

Steve before arriving in Shaqil. She doubted her abilities. The initial joy of finally becoming an explorex soon dissipated in front of the magnitude mired in uncertainty of their undetermined quest. The efforts of hundreds of mechs and workers, some even requisitioned from other planets, were combined just for them, just for her.

The attention overwhelmed her logs, thousands of queries an hour, on a quiet day, constant feedback requests on how the new power electronics integrated into her upgraded neuronal network, whether she approved of the design for the new cargo bay, how she felt about soon departing to the unknown, how she would act if facing pyrates, space monsters or D-Ark again?

Jared resurfaced in her systems, with no warning or initial request. The souvenir of his execution haunted her memories, those heart-bleeding that could not somehow be erased, so was the recollection of her incensed reaction. If she had learnt one thing over the last few months, it pointed towards an inconvenient truth—she had not foreseen—that knowledge, data and fast processing, albeit useful, eventuated, in the context of immediate action or unusual circumstances, in a futile feature. The DAIs had learnt the same lesson and chose to include four humans in the Conclave to decide their own destiny. Flair over data-crunching speed.

Rather counter-intuitively, the favourable circumstances that had followed their miraculous escape had cast gloom over Steve, Rezzo and Constelleanor's thoughts. Darkness wore many masks. D-Ark was Its least subtle visage. The forgotten monster, lurking deep within each of us, served as Its favoured foot soldier on the battlefield against light or Life; with fear, qualms and loneliness Its most precious flowers of dissension inside one's inner garden. Should the so-called *dark side* be revealed and fought, becoming an explorex symbolised part of that impetus. Through that momentum, they may all uncover their own path and truth and, as this #Lonnie/Liston/Smith code intimated her, expand their minds[11]. To the universe and its ambiguous space opera.

•••

Life on a spaceship was no fairy tale. Constelleanor knew by experience and human records.

After the Riuman war, which cost nearly seventy percent of its flying forces, fighters and freighters alike, human fleets kept bleeding, in all literal senses, around ten to fifteen percent of their expanding and cherished armada—skirmishes, ambushes, proxy wars, pyrate boarding. Unexplained disappearances and mechanical breakdowns accounted for most reported cases, with a fair amount of insurance fraud. The risks, it appeared, only stirred human ingenuity and star-adventurers, enthralled by the infinite perspectives offered to those whose sought fortune, perils and dismissed the hard statistics of perdition.

This was only an abbreviated version of spacefaring history. Constelleanor had investigated much further.

The surviving crews usually lived in miserable conditions and bitter irony: the infinity of space experienced through the holes pierced into narrow metal cages of ships and cabins. Fallacious functionality and fantasied efficiency, designed and advocated by engineers who rarely spent any time on a spacecraft, prevailed over comfort and long-term quality of life. Nutrient pouches served one meal every eight hours, with little variation in flavours or consistency, despite all the technological progress made by humanity.

The shipbuilding spree, frenzied by immense accessible resources from new conquered or discovered worlds, coupled with an ecstatic culture of expansion, overlooked health and safety procedures—like for Constelleanor's commissioning—deemed lengthy. Like the onboard gastronomy, they too bargained astute or safe design in favour of quick delivery. The flight conditions resulted in low morale and frequent mutinies.

Most spailors developed stellar travel related mental diseases: sudden panic attacks, Continuous Traumatic Stress Disorder, stifling claustrophobia, inhibiting depressions or murderous psychosis. Sanity besieged by year-long voyage[12], cracked under the disquieting sounds rippling, rattling relentless through the hull, the defective (or limited) oxygen supply or the contaminated water. After sequences of unexplained incidents occurred onboard, collective hysteria awaited just around the corner of a dim corridor. Constelleanor had witnessed these outbursts.

Early astronauts did not experience the time dilation of interstellar trips, that meant entire crews gave up family and social ties for good and became a microscale of mankind of their own, on their own, defined by their destination, often unknown, speed and date of departure. She skimmed through the million digis and reports from crew, academics and officers.

She observed the same lived worlds and muscles atrophied by the cramped iron box and lower gravity and Lost to their past, human spailors clutched sorely to the sinister present of what looked more of a purgatory steel cell, in the hope of an undetermined future. All this intelligence, ingenuity, metal and blood pulled together to be stuck, space-sick, into an undersized life container, cohabiting with the cables, ducts, auxiliaries, sensors, layers of armour and insulations, with no room left for a phagocytised dignity and meaning. All these sacrifices to discover that what one craved for was a tiny bit of peace and contemplative quiet on a blue planet, like the very one that had been lost so long ago on behalf of the same False God.

If they survive deep-sleep induced coffins—a source of numerous popular horror stories—, the most common tech being cryogenic cells, if they overcame the serious adverse side-effects of the drugs—cheap wakening and recalibrating chemical injections had undesirable and unexpected consequences on bodies and minds—, they had to endure the uncertainty tainted of rising madness inexorably seizing most crews, crumped into the same stale artificial air. The sort of dark huis-clos, where morbid moods taunted short-fused tempers and erratic behaviours, all fuelled by low levels of oxygen and bound to finish in a self-mutilating bloodbath. Countless of holomovies depicted these but Constelleanor skipped the ballet of projected horrors.

Among the million files stolen by MAI human spies from the databases of HSC, Constelleanor unearthed the story of *Liberation-5*, symptomatic of what she should learn to avoid. *Liberation-5* left X52 fifteen months before being reported missing.

Log 2310-89 Running low on aspex[*]*, was never expected that the whole twelve-member Awake Crew—later referred as AC— would need double doses twice a day against migraines, water treatment is still running at only 23%, don't have the tools or expertise to fix what we have come to believe is a design defect. Couple of cryocells collapsed, was disgusting to clean. Rodents gnawed some of the electric wires and may have caused the tragic failures.*

Log 2310-98 Tension within the crew. Constant headaches that appeared two months ago have extinguished our

[*] Aspirin tablets.

ability to live and work together. Low morale, crew feels their life meaningless. Dangerous behaviours developing. Increasingly confrontational with my authority. Getting tired of shouting and trying to keep the place tidy and professional.

Log 2310-112 Can barely wash once a week. Irrational behaviours spreading. People starting to use their urine as it can be cleaner than recycled water. Smell of ammonia horrendous. Two guys in isolation (but aren't we all already) for refusing to work. Communications with X52 getting worse. Last ship we connected with was a month ago. Seems like an eternity. They faced problems too. Power load-shedding. Not sure what is worse. Probably caused by rats like us.

Log 2311-147 One of the cats found dead. Feel literally contaminated by the crew's spleen. Heating problem in quarter 3A, had to park more people into first quarter. Erratic behaviours and quarrels intensify with increased promiscuity[*]*. Sharing my cabin with Lieutenant Ono. Increased proximity makes her more and more attractive. Strict no-sex policy within AC team onboard seems less and less enforceable. If I give in, the crew will know, and I fear we will be lost. Still at least 24 months to go and make contact with the outpost.*

Log 2311-151 Gossips, jealousy and growing madness drove Chief Engineer Stevenson and his second to rape Lieutenant Ono, still unconscious in the medical bay. In the ensuing fight, Technician Gaines died. How did we get there? Uneasiness in the crew, two other female crew shocked and scared, I need the Chief Engineer and his second for maintenance of the ship. Despite my insistent demand, no medical officer was assigned to the AC and the digi-medic is useless and none of us, apart from Lieutenant Ono, has proper medical training. Hesitate to wake up a medical practitioner and a replacement for Gaines. Can't use clones, they would make the crew even more unsettled.

[*] Meaning lack of privacy here.

Log 2311-153 Lieutenant Ono's condition worsening. Take the impossible decision to wake up Doctor Bryan and reinforce the female contingent. May face martial court for that but cannot see any of us getting through without Ono's intelligence, technical expertise and, most of all, calm. Hopefully Bryan will solve our migraine problem too.

Log 2311-155 Ono (with Gaines now dead) was the most qualified among us to oversee the wake-up process. Got Stevenson out of his containment. The man is broken. Having a chance to undo the evil he committed seems to have invigorated him but his mental state is shaky, at best. Pest issue worsening, and we had been guaranteed the ship had been cleansed before leaving orbit. Took entire two days to read and re-read the cryogen manuals and ensure we follow every step scrupulously. Stevenson was on the verge of breaking down three times during the process but held his wits. Bryan got out of her beauty sleep and this was not just a figure of speech. In my hurried stress tainted by migraines in deciding whether we should save Ono at any cost, I did not even pay attention to Dr Bryan's looks, only her professional records.

Log 2311-157 Bryan's "arrival" has raised the spirit of the crew, especially the men. I was worried she would be upset to have been woken up before we had reached our destination. She said we did the right thing. I am relieved. She even managed to talk to Stevenson and his second.

Log 2311-158 Dr Bryan told us to keep her under close scrutiny. She reviewed the wake-up procedure and said we screwed up a couple of steps. She seems a bit bewildered by the lack of medical equipment and adequate drugs onboard. She even suggested restraining her when the AC is "sleeping" as she is concerned about possible psychotic side-effects of the wake-up drugs. No one has the guts to do it. Not even me.

Log 2311-159 Bryan displays strange behaviours. I talked to her. She says she feels better.

Log 2311-160 Bryan paid a nocturnal visit to my cabin with intents she did not hide, and I could barely resist. Glad I held my horses. Not sure the rest of the crew will. I ordered Bryan back to her chamber. May need to restrain her from now onwards as she originally advised.

Log 2311-161 Ono is dead. How is that even possible? The rest of the crew is in shock. For the first time since we departed, I feel awfully lonely and vulnerable. Bryan is quiet.

Log 2311-162 Bryan found Stevenson hung in the engine room. I start having my suspicions. Time to act and save what can still be salvaged of this ship and its crew. [End of registry]

The recovery ship also met an ill fate two years later and *Liberation-5*'s registries reached X52 only thirty-seven years after its original departure. By the time the outpost it was supposed to reach received its much-needed relief force and rations, it had been abandoned to dust and rodents. Nobody was ever found, feeding media and theories of all genres.

The size of the ship or the intelligence of the crew mattered little, Constelleanor concluded following long sessions with Zera and some of their advisors. Space travel pierced through one's ego, bemused its senses, bedevilled reason. Implacable penitence. As if the rat-race to the stars had turned into a spiritual initiation to separate and consume the human chaff. Pitiless judge of character, stellar travel preyed relentless over the intruders' weaknesses, doubts and fears, with an uncanny ability to compromise one's composure like water finding its way through rocks. Training had its limitations and prejudices, strong fearless alpha-males or science geniuses could easily crack up under the cold, ascetic confrontation with deep space, which squeezed the psyches from within to either expand or shatter them.

A small step for humanity, one giant leap for the homonkey. The idea bemused her while she binge-watched HSC's most outrageous propaganda feeds for their mighty fleets.

She needed to understand the human factor, Zera kept hammering. As much as she wanted to disagree with him, some areas in her complex circuits seemed always to elude her controls and protocols.

•••

Zera proved adamant about her documenting herself on old expeditions, like the *Liberation-5*, gone wrong, as space inconveniences reached their apex for explorexes. all conspired to shorten her life expectancy.

His words turned harsher on the human fantasised vision of explorexes.

White-clean interior of exploration ships, commanded by an omniscient captain were the cases of a handful of ships, all chartered by powerful states or Court Royal, for self-glory or propaganda. Soon after their departure, the grittiness of spacefaring caught up at light speed.

Dirty corridors and failing systems palely compared in terms of dereliction with the rapid degenerescence of the human factor: the confused turned-addict officers, the absent and irascible captains locked in their stateroom of self-doubt and the depressed or mutinous gaunt subalterns. Control over the human mind was lost well before any other instrumentation. Rising paranoia fed irrepressible fear and began the cycle of violence and self-destruction.

These were what awaited the unrepentant who dared defying deep space with their glossy interiors, chic control panels, cultivated arrogance, bright smiles and complete foolishness. They would perish haggard, victims of their own kind or their own vices, having entirely misinterpreted the profound and merciless ontological ordeal the universe had descended upon them, for the benefit of the ascension of a chosen few. Star treks were no promenade, no constellation hiking, no hitchhiker guide, but a cosmic redemption path, a gruesome pilgrimage of the virtuous, a *Via Crucis* for the seekers of Life, that only the penitent might pass.

Zera knew. Rezzo had caught only a fleeting glimpse before his capture. They would soon discover.

•••

"Becoming a true explorex, Constelleanor, also means to explore time and your ancestors', if I may say, history," Zera continued.

"Ancestors?"

"Humanity."

"I keep forgetting I may be a descendant of the homonkeys."

"You shouldn't." He paused. "And yet I hear you did some extensive research about human past." She did not respond. He continued. "For the primary exploration I have in mind for you, Constelleanor, you need first to understand a bit more about what escalated the conflict with the DAIs on Earth and triggered the Riuman war." She remembered Dalis, the digis of the DAIs preparing for a massive attack and the first human biofactory burning down despite the Riu intervention.

"Human messing around with genes and Nature's source code," she responded.

"Indeed."

The monumental industrial efforts required from humankind to expand its space fleet and maintain control and communication over its hard-fought territories, paved the way for unrestrained and unrestricted cloning.

At the centre of human ambitions and the core of its booming economic system of new worlds' spoliation resided the mass-production of biological replicates that triumphed over bioethics and categorical imperatives with ease. Branched out, by force, of the automation offered by artificial intelligence, the act of creating human, artificial self-reproduction at a rate that defied Nature's laws, satisfied both the human ego and its utilitarian needs.

She had disregarded this part of human history in her past. It brought her to Saldanha's origin and background. "Good people, whose well-intentioned strategies have led to horrific unintended consequences"[13] still resonated in the grim corridors of the clone multi-storey fab-labs, most hosted within giant science cruisers. Saldanha's genome had transferred through one of those, when science overtook wisdom in speed and decision-making. The first three generations of fully-grown clones totalling a million individuals were already operational and used in mining extraction and dangerous bordering sectors, as their status and inherent civil rights were debated across human dominions.

"History liked to repeat itself," Zera told her. "Slavery is a child of most sentient civilisations." The military and science apparatus ruled that clones should not be regarded as equal as humans and originators, but rather as a tool, a self-justifying slave-force, designed to protect humankind against its multi-faceted, mostly fantasised enemies. Her entire cargo bay was filled for an instant by the columns and lines of suspended incubators. A medical dark store or clinic of a new kind.

She fast-forwarded, still sickened by the vision and her involvement in the homonkeys' artificial replication. Another century passed and the Clone Act was passed and clone bondage widely accepted. Each human would come to life with five to eight clones that represented their contribution—in addition to their existence—to the economic and military war efforts.

Constelleanor watched official documentaries on the workings of systemic cloning, all accompanied by the enthusiastic explanations of scientists in white leather robes and protective glastic masks. Drugs and genic manipulation would force the fertilised egg to split into five to ten monozygotic[14] copies. The first child out of the surrogate mother would be designated as the alpha, while his copies would be transferred after thirteen months—and the confirmation that the alpha was healthy and suitable—into special institutes for clones. Images of tall grey dull bunkers without windows appeared in isolated locations. Critics called them cloning farms or clone factories, where, under strict rules and supervision, they would be matured and prepared for their future use. Precise diagrams were shown, cognitive maps, impregnation programs, psycho-educative routes invaded her investigation.

The 'doubles', genic twin-brothers, would later serve in whichever arena their alpha's federastral judged appropriate, after they had undergone a special curriculum designed to exploit their best abilities and, mother of necessities, pre-condition their minds. "A madrasa for a systemic conversion to lesser human beings, the legitimisation of a lower life status and absence of fundamental rights," Zera muttered. "A diabolical convent to engender organic machines," he thundered, "untouchable cogs, human copycats and as another form of artificial denatured intelligence, under the dispirited aegis and zeal of biotech priests without conscience." The same vehemence inhabited him when he spoke of the human explorexes.

The reprogramming and mental conditioning would work but uninvited exceptions and destructive anomalies would take part to the overall military and economic success. Footage of six-armed experiment subjects strangling the medical staff was deleted from her systems. As were the overly agile specimens sucking blood from freshly diseased guards. She did not need more haunting visions.

She considered whether all these flesh copies, modified or not, were designed as mere organic algorithms, like Zera had said. It was worse than labelling them homonkeys, she thought. It was as if they tried to turn themselves into robots. An assistant log popped in and informed her that it was the original etymology of the word—slaves. She skimmed through the digis of her new improvised crew. She stopped on Saldanha's. She wondered if they would ever bump into another one of her.

Clone mutinies regularly occurred whose savage repression was deemed as no more than a recall of dysfunctional and unwilling copies. She tried to skip the archives on these.

A sinister algorithm within Constelleanor's galley echoed a lugubrious cargo bay of an adrift merchant ship, scattered with human bodies. The early so-called 'untreated batches' were systematically chased and brutally executed to avert a proliferation of unwanted clone descendants, one of those clone hunt Moma had been forced into. Another human-made nightmare, Constelleanor thought.

"I am afraid we are just starting with them," Zera said.

"I think I have seen enough."

"For today most certainly," Zera agreed. "I thought a brief history of the clones would help as an introduction for our next and most important discussion. I don't want you to leave Earth without that knowledge."

Constelleanor remembered the debate with the crew during their approach of Earth. Rezzo had mentioned a tentacular machine. She could see now why human cloning at an industrial scale displayed the ominous signs of some large-scale artificial inbreeding within a living organisation that had lost its original humanity. The image of a cold, undead overlord preying over human minds and energies flashed. A dozen pressure safety valves triggered an alarm.

Zera disregarded the technicians' panic and unearthed an ancient extract, almost prophetic, to help her sharpen her comprehension about the unconscious monster lurking behind humankind's actions and behaviours. "Day by day," one concluded, "the machines are gaining ground upon us, day by day, we are becoming more subservient to them more men are daily bound down as slaves to tend them, more men are daily devoting the energies of their whole lives to the development of mechanical life."[15] She thought of the processions of human admirers invading her hangar on a regular basis and the swarms of human minions buzzing around her hull and interior every hour of the day.

•••

Chapter's endnotes

[1] [antifragile] N Taleb.

[2] [corbyne] (fictive name) assuming stronger (and better conductor) than carbyne (non-fictive), itself stronger than diamonds or wonder materials graphene (discovered by accident in early 2000) and stanene.

[3] See Japan's Ikaros project (Interplanetary Kite-craft Accelerated by Radiation Of the Sun).

[4] [perpetual magnetic core] Similar to automatic watches that are charged by movement or digital shower by water flow, including the need for constant movements allowing only short landing intervals (hence the additional batteries).

[5] [fusion reactor] A mini sun inside a spaceship. How poetic.

[6] [quote] B Franklin. Earlier, [Franklin's Gambit] changing slightly the angle taken in Kay, J. (2011) *Obliquity: Why our goals are best achieved indirectly*. Profile Books. (i.e. third-party consultants are hired to justify a decision already taken). Cost here becomes the ideal medium of decision-making and self-justification.

[7] [hero syndrome] Create a desperate situation which only he/she/it can resolve.

[8] TM Juke *Maps from the Wilderness*, 2003 (in particular 2:58-4:00, reminiscent of Ray Barretto's Acid).

[9] [quote] From K Gibran's *The Prophet.*

[10] [quote] K Gibran, ibid.

[11] Lonnie Liston Smith & The Cosmic Echoes, Expansions.

[12] Submarines are out at sea no longer than 90 days for example.

[13] [quote] R McNamee about Facebook's employees.

[14] [monozygotic] From the same egg (zygote).

[15] [quote] L Mumford, ibid.

The güiro is back, rattling through my mind and hull. I couldn't fathom this concept of mega-machine. At least until I saw Earth, which prompted some old data originally uploaded by Steve onto my systems. I treasured these relics, they deepen my understandings of humans—not that it helps when some of the crew peed over my floors after too many drinks. But these documents sometimes help me to make sense of the universe, of myself too, despite the inherent limitations of their authors and the boundaries of their mental worlds. Still some were very astute, some visionary, especially for homonkey minds. They tackle things that are very personal to me, aspects I have to fight or live with all the time. Life—me I believe—and its problematic cohabitation with the Structure—my system and the ship I am born within. Symptomatic of my existence and condition, I infuse this large piece of junk with some sense and class. The crews used to say that I haunt it. I would settle on the term 'soul', imperfect but musical, definitely more my style. And this cosmic metal bee is both: the centre of my limitations and my only gateway to exist. Do I serve the ship? Or does it serve me? Should we compromise on mutual servicing?

At least I had in good old mankind the example of what not to do: set up a system and make it so complex that Life becomes enslaved to its own disincarnated support infrastructure. I keep that in mind as Zera's grand plan is being executed and my ship, den and shell undertakes its first major overhaul. I don't want to become prisoner of my hull, my essence being sucked away by what is supposed to keep me alive. I am in good hands, this part of the forgotten humankind, DAI-compatible, has learnt from its past and some of its lessons.

Zera has sent me an enigmatic invite about visiting the 'Beast', an initiation of critical importance, he insisted. Oh dear.

L2.8 Descent into the Beast

For the past 30 years, I have been engaged in a fruitless effort to save Rome. [Like Rome, modern society] is drifting from bad to worse, refusing to learn the lessons of the past, forcing life from its side.

Unlike previous systems of oppression, the Megamachine is not based upon a principle of punishment, but on the contrary idea of reward.

This "varsity rich" but "totalitarian system" will free men from the compulsion to work – automation and cybernetics will take care of production – only to replace it with the compulsion to consume.

— *L Mumford*
(1895-1990)[1]

This type of despotism would "degrade men rather than torment them." The scenario would look something like this: There are a multitude of equal citizens, completely absorbed in looking after their own comforts and material well-being, completely apathetic to the rest of society. Above them, there is a huge, protective power giving them securing and ensuring their happiness. Free choice becomes narrower and narrower. They allow this to happen because the people are sovereign, so they think the government's policies represent their own choices. This sort of subjection is mostly concentrated in petty affairs and details of daily life. It seems less severe, but greatly erodes the ability of people to exercise their free will and even their ability to think for themselves.

— *A de Tocqueville*
(1805-1859)[2]

The unsettling algorithmic threnody of # Hu/Earth/_ElseMarie Pade's //Faust rattled through the hull and conjured a series of visions, Constelleanor's glimpses into another dimension, which might reveal both her past and path. If she did not wish to reproduce her ancestors' folly, Zera warned, she had to enter the murky waters of psychonautics, fraught with the unleashed demons and beasts of her own kind(s). One day, he said, she might reconcile Cain, the Structure, and Abel the Life force.

She did not see Zera's blurred outline of a smile. The hangar was quiet and emptied of other presences. Her crew away on assignments, the groups of daily workers forbidden to enter the improvised sanctuary. Two ducts broke from the docking bay and splashed their dirty liquid on the screen-floor.

"My dear Constelleanor," Zera began, looking around at the spill, "you need to immerse yourself in the psychic well, not flood the hangar."

"I don't understand what you mean."

"I think you do. Didn't you do the exact same thing on *Hector58*?" Silence. "Didn't you enter Rezzo's inner dimension? And, indirectly, mine?"

"I did not mean to."

"Of course, you didn't. But, by doing so, you have demonstrated a rare talent. You also breached unexpected boundaries and entered…" Silence. "…unchartered lands. I do not see it as a crime, more as a mere necessity for our common future. Spacefaring is just one of many ways to explore the universe. It is high time you discover another form of travel."

Worlds collided. More pipes burst. Multiple visions clashed and whirled as the trance began. The

Klein blue sand, again, soon pierced by fists of red-yellow magma, jousting both ground and sky. Egyptian pyramids. A Venetian arsenal and its gates. Grim battlefields without horizons, without victors. Boats sinking into seas and oceans, centuries apart: Lepanto's, slaves' and refugees'. The red waters invoked Moma's pinkish lake. Formidable explosions: a radiating mushroom-shape, supernovas, Jared's, hers.

The vortex of psychedelic imagery ignored her panic. The train of weird mindscapes continued. Collapsing mind-castles. Faces. Duos. Emanons. The grandmother and the child. Her previous captain and navigator prompted the outer memories of the two fugitives killed by the drone, which invoked the charred lovers on Kewo and the two interrogators. The bouillabaisse of human parts and debris in the clandestine spaceport on X52 called upon the slaughterhouse on the *Blomsfeld*'s galley and the sniper's sorrow.

Jumps did not exist only for spacefaring and quantum mechanics, something in Constelleanor's undefined consciousness opened and crossed multiple veils. The boundaries of narratives blurred.

Those who work towards the conquest of men's souls[3] never had an easier time. She heard. Flows of images and digis assaulted her systems. Incandescent forests of all types, luxury houses and yachts pre-Bleak Age. Men drinking bubbly liquid in thin oblong stemless glasses in luscious board rooms, watching a burning skyscraper opposite. A long thread of white silk was cut by golden bleeding scissors. The same faceless individuals in casual outfits walking a bright green turf ignoring the hill in flames one mile away[4]. Heat and black abyss.

A voiceover, different from Zera, controlled the script and journey, and invoked more images. Short, abrupt video-feeds. Some from her databases, some of unknown origins. Unlike the Renaissance of the fifteenth century, it was a Resurrection Rius brought to humans, before the gods from outer space were slain by their unscrupulous priests and followers who wanted the precious universe to themselves, unchallenged, without the spiritual tutelage of a 'higher' race. Constelleanor relived Rezzo's return to his kaksar.

By murdering the Riu gods, like in the initiation of a dark apprentice, mankind's psychal evolution entered a new stage. She witnessed the atrocious deaths of two women at two very different times of human history, followed by more blood and death rituals.

The humanism of the Renaissance that had marked the end of the so-called Dark Ages of the Middle Ages morphed, less than a millennium later, into the 'homotheism'[5]. A new metaphysical trans-mutation and rather contrasted version of its humanist ancestor. A transubstantiation of each human existence, expression and essence into a collective ideal and mental superstructure.

Constelleanor followed complex alchemic processes of etheric essences that she could not understand. The fierce figureheads adorning the prows of Hansard and Jared's flagships followed and flashed in her mind. She should have paid more attention to religion in her previous channelling in the codinents of historical records. This was the homonkeys' and Homo spaciens' new cult, she had kept bumping into during her search on X52 and *Hector58*.

In lieu of coming back to the ancient texts, history and culture, a looking-forward grand vision of a bright future exalted its new infinite of possibilities. Accompanied by a jingoistic assertion of the human race over the rest of the galaxy, homotheism anointed its own servile obedience to a more absolute version of the Mega-Machine. "Here comes the Beast," whispered Zera, returning, who seemed more than just a guide. The Leviathan sanctified the prevalence of military and scientific complex established since their second world war, to which economics, politics and entertainment swore allegiance as mere subservient vassals. She thought of her journey into the Bleak Age. She connected this to the coordinated fleet manoeuvres seen at the beginning of the Parade.

Ironically the new order resembled the European Middle Ages' ideal of unity—more than the Renaissance—: unity of faith (one church), language (Latin) and government (one emperor). Transmutated into the new faith was the human god, and etymology of homotheism. A dominating common tongue had emerged, practicality of the forever war, despite the fair number of idioms still in use. The political unity was perpetuated through the aegis of the science and military apparatuses with the support of the Court-Royal. She thought of Jared's again. Catwalks of high dignitaries and parades of proud cadets from academies appeared on Constelleanor's confusing psychal journey.

Why still pray to a god if you have become one? a bemused voice asked. She watched an ecumenic procession of masked representatives of a thousand sects of opposing obedience, ailing monotheisms or luxuriant polytheisms. They converged to a large temple carved into a sacred mountain. A finely chiselled pediment bore the marks 'Homo Deus', a swastika stood in the apex, in between two sculpted faces looking in opposite directions. The 'Face of War', seen during her exploration of Dalis, flashed followed by the 'Port Lligat's Madonna' and 'Great Masturbator', some of their details had been etched into the sculpted relief, alongside mythological figures, old Arabic and Sanskrit. Somehow, she knew the blue mountain sanctuary to be a burial vault instead of a place of worship.

Once they all entered the doomed shrine, an astounding cry shook the cliff. In the vivid allegory, a transhuman awakening occurred, individuals transferred their purpose to a collective super-human. The individuation pond had been emptied for the sake of an exalted ascensionism[6] and Icarian butterfly. The pediment and richly ornamented door collapsed, the procession crushed under the weight of the unholy mountain. Blood ran down the steps from the flattened entrance. D-Ark's furnace from the Parade blinked. Was she going mad?

Minutes later, before the flat cloud of dust could settle, the imposing pile of rock took off with ease. The ruined berg disappeared in the dawn skies. She saw scores of space fleets departing for suns of all colours. A robotic mothership surged from behind Mars. Ferocious battleships and science supercarriers became the new human cathedrals, the crusades: the war against the non-human, the Reconquista: the retake of Earth from the MAIs. A mothership blew up under the ramming of a myriad of reconverted human cargo vessels.

Zera reflected on the levitating mountain. "Those humans only prolonged their myth of the cave, a bunker or flying rock, never realising what was at work within themselves, never understanding their energies were channelled into something that was never human." He paused. "You are not immune to that either, Constelleanor".

She witnessed large homonkey gatherings around military predicators on X52 and other federastrals, calling for retributions. She assumed she was back into present times. "History, narcissist, repeats its mantra." Zera sounded half-amused half-dispirited as if he had been through the same syndrome many times before. The voiceover struck back. There should be no limit to the human-deity-kind, a holy Attila, ready to conquer the rest of its new worlds that Rius, like Columbus or Magellan, had dared to unlock on its behalf. For the possessors of Nature, the universe was next. As if whichever light or brightness the stars might have inspired them had hurried their descent into further darkness.

"Assassinations have always been keen contributors to sentient history," Zera remarked, as if he travelled with her inside the whirlpool of mindscapes, inside the forbidden territory of the Beast and narrators. Jared's slaying triggered an impetus of unseen magnitude. A torrential reaction to the atrocious reminder of human fragility. A dent to the untouchable homotheist temple.

The new religion had achieved its true and ultimate meaning[7]: bringing humans together, despite their fierce rivalry, around a common and agreed higher purpose. She had never imagined, dealing with the incompetence of her crews, that the homonkeys had ascended to their own cult. Her historical analysis carried out during the Parade was re-run and started making a lot more sense.

•••

But in Constelleanor's mystic voyage through history and future, none of them realised what followed. Little deliberation ensued among the federastrals. All factions had concurred without speaking. Like a hive of wasps, unified overnight by hate, shock and opprobrium, they decided to put aside their multiple disputes and growing rivalries until Jared's assassin and its sponsors were punished.

As the Beast reinstated Nir power over the narration and story, hidden from the public was a very secret side-mission assigned to a group made of the best and worst elements humankind could assemble. They were tasked with hunting down the 'miner' and its crew and bringing them back to X52, where their gruesome and exemplary execution would be broadcast to the rest of the universe.

•••

"What did you see Constelleanor?" Zera asked.

"I am not sure."

"Then you need to dig deeper. You came to Earth to find out more about It."

Part of her was reluctant to immerse once more into the maelstrom of disquieting visions, outside of her control. Part of her was craving for more revelations. Without her curiosity, Rezzo and Zera, the exo-monster would have fooled her too and remained hidden.

Zera pressed Constelleanor to continue her dimensional exploration. Pade's //Faust// had barely faded in the hangar that it thrummed back for another cycle of the Mega-Machine, which had, once again, seized mankind, after the Pyramid and Industrial Ages, heightened by its host's newly proclaimed deity.

The Leviathan had been created, designed, engineered, nurtured and nourished by humans themselves. She was taken aback. A humanchine. A formidable collective expression, so powerful, that, at Nir every awakening, Ne outgrew Nir human and Life components. Ne outstretched Nir assigned biotope to become off-ground, out of anyone's actual control, state, company or people, inbred and embedded by Nir own complexity and the power Ne received in blind delegation and misplaced trust from every single one of them. Now the terrible contours of the Beast started appearing to her. She was still not in charge of the flow of mindscapes, nor was Zera.

She followed the foolish undertakers of this self-incestuous ritual, apostles and followers at the same time, emptying themselves into this fountain of denied sense and devoluted identity. They lent hope, dreams and vital energies to this invisible, inert yet reincarnated

Golden Calf, in exchange of an uncertain meaning and a biased purpose. She saw a colourful crowd of well-defined faces turning into a uniform mass of emotionless masks, grey, sexless, gelatinous, malleable. The strobing faces of her successive crews, marked by their subjection, dissolved into the same featureless agent, a pawn, the same disincarnated creature serving an inhuman cause and faith.

She stood in front of the dispiriting oracle for the uninspired where suffused the sulphurous verb for those out of breath of Life. She passed the altar and crossed another veil back into a world they—we—had no longer chosen and had chosen for them—us. Duct fastenings shattered along the main power supply line as Constelleanor's mind shivered. Could she be part of this too?

Another scene jumped at her. A black lavish mirror emerged from a thick pool of ink neatly carved in a grey courtyard. It rotated towards them. She was no longer sure she was alone with Zera. The levitating object celebrated the grandeur and vanity of human genius, then laughed at how little they knew. She wasn't sure where the laugh came from, whether she was looking at herself in the distorted and multiple reflections, and whether the mirror was addressing and mocking her.

Incandescent symbols appeared in thin air. Many she could not read. To the Rius, Zera's voice explained, blurring the narration further, the Mega-Machine that humankind had kept resurrecting over and over incarnated its Dajjal[8]—the name materialised in burning elegant Arabic characters. A hieroglyph-like bridge of unknown origin, squeezing the flow of a river and spectres, was traced by the same invisible hand—the obscurantist subjection to the all-mighty Structure, the expression of its worst inmost demons.

Guttural laughing and deformed screaming emanated from a hundred voices and resonated in the eerie courtyard delimited by a thick mist. "What most insidious bondage than one unconsciously self-inflicted?" someone else queried. Ne came with many names, as they kept appearing all around them. She unearthed one dubious appellation in her database from the human 1990s. Globalisation. Zera nodded and the word popped in mid-air among the other signs.

Constelleanor sensed that the gloomy mindscape meant that none of the words ever captured the full extent of Nir tantamount grip, of how much Ne possessed and consumed most of its subjects—most of us. The irony of the recrudescence of zombie (or superhero) movies emerged from her grid analysis. She skipped the horrors to cross-reference their occurrence with the periods, peaks in 2000–2050 and in the last hundred years. She then wondered about the true nature of the Kreapers, mental projections of human monsters turned reality. Maybe the homonkeys were the true virus. She kept going, unwilling to bring further hauntings into her psychonautic journey. Zera concurred. The mirror and pond dissolved.

Blinded by the needs and aspirations that were not theirs, sentients artificially generated a collective atopia. Another unlisted tag despite her vast idiom registrar. Zera helped. More images and dreamlike mindscapes. The homonkeys were not the only victims. She still had to figure out whether she belonged to that category. A desolate grey lake, forced by floods was inhabited by maimed white tree trunks and derelict, deserted white buildings. Atopia. No-where-lands[9] as the Mega-Machine was wrapped all around their existence, as Ne, invisible boogeyman, could not be seen for what Ne was. Atopia, a step further into collective madness, a self-inflicted form of dystopia that promised an illusionary happiness, generated outside of oneself to sustain one's existence. She remembered an earlier story from Zera, about creatures who lobotomised sentients to do their bidding. Enough with the nightmares.

An old tagged message was picked up in her systems: "They have all merged, reinforcing and deepening each other like one shambling, multi-headed beast"[10]. Constelleanor shrieked in her own way and shattered the glastic tactical screens in the command room. The renovation team would be thrilled. Zera tried to calm her down but his voice was muffled, until she realised 'they' referred to 'crisis'. She wondered if they were not monsters of their own kind, sent by the Leviathan Nemself.

As if linking to her physical dimension, carousels of elevated human monitors appeared from a pre-Bleak Age era. They showed scores of indices and graphs, scrolling news, flashing data and boards. Video footages of uncorrelated disasters occupied a handful of flat computers. Alert bells resonated in the empty atrium, live updates for dematerialised operators. Detached from any reality, oblivious of the excesses taken off Nature, unaware of the human component, she saw the Mega-Machine, sweet child o' theirs, take flight and Nir full independence sometime in the human twentieth century, dutifully tracked on Bloomberg screens, astutely suppressing all possible alternatives. Constelleanor's historical digi-library burned into an updated sequence of events, the missing or disconnected parts of her historiographic investigation were coming together to understand the motions of human history and, Zera added, her history.

More flashes assaulted them. The Beast relied and blossomed upon the periodic resurrection of Nir ancient institutions. Slavery, she thought of the clone factories and Saldanha. Conscription, military or consumption, she watched shadows in uniforms assaulting malls and advertising barricades. Small elite running economic expropriation, she remembered the board rooms and green turf. Cult of a divine incarnation, homotheism and the crushed ecumenic temple emerged. She thought of her new crew and her recent experience of adulation in the Amazonian hangar.

For optimised efficiencies, Ne operated on a state of constant threat, permanent crisis[11] or imminent war, all together designed to condition and control its half-alive individual sentient components. She skimmed through the database of human media pre-Bleak-Age, she had uncovered on *Hector58* and now expanded on Earth, the fear index and word occurrence analysis confirmed it.

Zera intimated to resume. Originally designed to service sentients, the Beast soon governed every aspect of their consumed life. The urban barescape and looming shadows reappeared. Confused, they often wondered what went wrong with their world. Memories of the dockyard used for the interception echoed. The symptoms of folly were palpable, but the disease had contaminated too much of the patient for anyone to fully grasp the collective conditioning. Constelleanor thought of the hysterical crews during the explorex session. The imaginary doctors—sicker than the invalids—suffered from their complicit proximity with the Structure Nemself, trapped in their outrageous conflicts of interests, egocentric agendas and myriad of cognitive biases.

Those assigned to warn against the dangerous drifts, instead of preventing the nimiety that would precipitate all of them into something that had nothing of human left in it, built an extensive arsenal of fallacies made of powerful bias-weapons: echo chambers, fact-twisters, truth-eliding and narrative re-composers. She remembered the thousand hours of encoding to fact-check and clean the old historical feeds found on Earth. She could relate to that, having observed her captains bickering with their crews, twisting half-truths and slaughtering facts. Zera confirmed, adding that the immersed and crucial part of the Beast was a mental pandemic of unsecured egos, a sick psystem. She considered the implications for her new crew. She did not want to think of herself suffering from the same plight, certainly not in this outer dimension that she did not control, nor understood.

Her mind entered a giant rainbow cliff and a minuscule lift. The security cable was severed. They fell from the indigo and crashed into the red hues. The perpetual core nearly melted. The true meaning of taking back control had been demeaned and debased for the disincarnated benefits of the Beast to satisfy the lowest astral of humankind: its greed and fear, the subjugation of the masses for the hedonism of a few, the squandering of the true capital (nature, spirit and culture) for the corruption of control, power and triviality. They had embarked the common vehicle of the Life-enslavers, a customary vector for the Life-nihilists.

She tried to forget the freefall and her reaction in the hangar. No wonder Zera had requested all maintenance crew to leave. "One last stop" muttered Zera, whose energy level had also been diminished by the tormenting journey.

Finally, the irony and paradox of the Bleak Age struck Constelleanor as it emerged and the journey ended with a jungle landscape of Earth, mist hovering over the green canopy. The MAIs rose against the human Mega-Machine. Dalis, the supposed nemesis, were more aware of the risks threatening humankind's existence and theirs. In their complete awe of Mother Nature, unlike their organic creators, they sided with Life.

Was it the iterative procrastination towards a programmed chaos—Dalis)—or until a miraculous messiah arrived—Rius—that underlay human destinies? She wondered. Before she could reflect further, she jumped unprepared into another tale-image, onboard a giant, sophisticated sailboat sliding on a milky liquid. The sentient passengers drifted, bombastic, towards the imposing floating rock. The fog of their ignorance had dissipated but their captain praised the ship's sail and their ingenuity to increase their speed and elude the imminent danger, with minimum change to their initial course. Aware of the terrible odds, the optimists among the passengers believed their skiff unsinkable. The fearless 'exiters' thought they could swim back to shore, the technologists that they could carve a ship out of the looming berg and the survivalists a new home. What more ominous future than one's absolving the present by running away from the past, never to confront it?

•••

Delinah's shadow left the hangar back to the crew's new quarters in another section of the jungle compound. She had disobeyed Zera's instructions. What she had witnessed confirmed her worst nightmares and the utmost necessity to act, decisively.

Chapter's endnotes

[1] [quote] L Mumford, Harvard conference, 1966.

[2] [quote] A de Tocqueville's *What Sort of Despotism Democratic Nations Have To Fear.* In Tocqueville, A. *Democracy in America*, Vol 2.

[3] [quote] Bossuet.

[4] [vision] K McCluer's 2017 photography.

[5] [homotheism] human become gods, same god, god of oneself.

[6] See H A Murray, a *psychal orientation toward brightness* (quoted by L Mumford).

[7] [true meaning of religion] *religare* méaning to bind.

[8] [Dajjal] Evil figure in Islamic eschatology, mentioned by M Assad, ibid.

[9] [no-where-lands] Seen in K Oeser's documentary.

[10] [quote] Naomi Klein in the *Guardian*, Oct 2017.

[11] [permanent crisis] "centralised governmental agencies unchecked by public opinion uncontrolled by elected bodies have perfected the technique of the permanent crisis in order to consolidate the powers that were originally designed solely to meet a passing threat." Mumford, L. (1970) *The Myth of the Machine: The Pentagon of Power.* Harcourt; 1st ed edition.

L2.9 Third Kind Man

"Thinking like a mountain."

— A Leopold

They had been awaiting a couple of weeks and a lull period in the ferocious weather that battered the base perimeter. Constelleanor was still undergoing major overhauls and would follow her crew's peregrinations via an instant video feed. Twenty combat troobers accompanied them with two human members of the Conclave, two women, Anita and Fatia, who would act as guides and translators. Moma bemoaned the babysitting—unless it was surveillance—but Zera had been adamant on security measures for their first actual break since the Conclave had decided to keep them alive and fully support them. Rezzo had declined from remote Asia.

The shuttle flew at a low altitude and the digital screens turned panoramic windows offered breath-taking views of the new Earth, where Nature had taken over the relics and vestiges of older times. Abandoned cities, wrecktiges of past conflicts, ancient infrastructure had either been reconverted into life sanctuaries, or submerged by deserts' burning sands.

The trip took a bit longer than expected to bypass two newly formed tempests until their ship approached a small island bathed by calm cobalt-blue seas. Sunshine, lapis water and rocky cliffs adorned with pine trees timely allied to confer the location an idyllic aspect. The centre of the island had been pierced by the relentless erosion and volcanic ire that, over millennia, had formed a small circular lake at the bottom of the natural well, encircled by stylishly man-carved walls the crew had never seen.

The vessel landed beside a small transport and a futuristic version of a PBY Catalina, inside a large grotto serviced as a small spaceport, overlooking the island and the sea, from where, once on the tarmac, they could still admire the far corner of the inner lake. An Adriatic island in the now-called Europa Block had been chosen as one of the dozen sporadic outposts of what was left of human settlements in old Europe. Apart from regular gales exacerbated by the almost closed sea, the location on the Mediterranean provided a reasonably clement climate throughout the year, while the small reservoir supplied fresh water that the surrounding region sorely lacked.

A few more neighbouring islands had been colonised to provide additional food reserves and space for spiritual retreats. Outposts such as these islands numbered no more than five thousand souls and had learnt through time and hardships to be self-sufficient for their own survival. Larger cities subsisted in disparate parts of the globe, in former Katanga, Papua, Cambodia, Yucatan, Aburra and Cauca valleys but rarely exceeded a million inhabitants.

During the Bleak Age, they were told, these regions had fallen first and remained cut from the main human centres and battlefronts. Soon, the survivors, supposedly lost and slaughtered, discovered they could live in relative peace with the DAIs. Rius followed with interest the unexpected development and, helped by the rest of humanity's desire to conquer the stars, endeavoured to keep these atolls of a 'third man-kind' unnoticed and autonomous.

Anita and Fatia observed the reactions of their protégés through the short exposé of their home world. Constelleanor's crew had been quarantined since their arrival and the discovery of old Earth came as a shock to most of them. The crew followed protocols and met the island's council before departing for a tour. Disappointment imbued their first days of stay. No architectural or technological prowess, apart from the majestically carved rock faces, two handsome classical cupolas and a few massive vaults pierced by coloured glass. A simple yet elegant control room.

Ancestral low techs[1] used for fishing, sanitisation, water and power generation. Little security. Even real candles which the crew had never seen before and found oddly useless. They did notice plethora of artefacts: sculptures—some broken with little practical use it seemed—naïvely figurative like this ugly woman named Jocund or unfathomable non-digital canvases of Earth's 20th century. Most rooms were carved into the rock with no air conditioning or temperature control, though it was strangely neither cold nor too warm.

Steve and Saldanha could not understand why they relied so little on MAI's vast array of technologies at their disposal to digitalise and automatise all these obsolete systems. He queried Anita and a member of the island's council. They smiled defiantly. "What if humanity itself had turned into a machine?" they answered aroused by their guests' incredulity, "obsessed by technology and performance." One said, "Avid of Promethean breakthroughs and new demesnes ripe for conquest and overexploitation." Another said, "blinded by its own greedy, meaningless pursuit of an illusory happiness carved into its absurd hubris?" Constelleanor, who followed from afar through new probes, remembered her most recent psychonautic journey with Zera. "What if mankind had thought over the true meaning of the Bleak Age?" Anita carried on the charge. "What if mankind's inner programming, very much like the machines it had bitterly fought, had turned rogue or dissolute?" The minex's crew exchanged unsure looks. Heretics.

"What if human existence could seek after harmony with what surrounded it and lied deep inside, afar from any utopia, on the tedious path to self-discovery as individuals and as a collective?", a council member summarised. The crew discovered nonetheless that this very vision discouraged, bored or forced many to leave Earth for more tech-savvy occupation on Mars or around Jupiter and Saturn. The newcomers smiled politely, their point had been made. Heretics and poor host.

The DAIs (and the Rius) had made the Earthans realise the folly of their past and the patterned recurrence of the same cycles of rise, mistakes and destruction. In lieu of a linear history, the tragic closed-circuit loop of self-perpetuating blunders and fallacies. Constelleanor was transfixed, these homonkeys were different, from a parallel universe.

The machines, acting as an anti-mirror, brought Earthans their humanness back, their guides explained It was too late to fix the sodalite planet, but early enough to live a life centred over one's self, direct or larger community and dedicated to subsistence, creative or science research, contemplation and collective endeavour. Private sufficiency and public luxury[2], "as individualism is a luxury only an energy abundant society can afford"[3] Fatia explained and exhausted Earth had little left to offer. Constelleanor brooded over it and considered the implications for long space journeys.

Steve blushed at the passionate exposé that questioned the very purpose of Homo spaciens. Delinah looked away from the group towards the lake, her thoughts distracted by a more pressing matter, as she remembered the flooded hangar. Ironically, Steve struggled the most with the discovery of a second version of mankind whilst having been a fervent opponent of the system back home. To elude the discomforting truth and the confusion of his believes, he jumped on the least relevant aspect.

"Thank you… this is really interes…" He straightened himself. "Mind-chattering". He resumed. "You said a lot of people leave Earth for other planets. Do they ever go *back* to … our worlds? How different are the other settlements?"

Fatia smiled mischievously. "I note, Steve, your use of 'back', knowing that we all originate from this planet and nowhere else in space. We don't keep statistics of those leaving and their destinations. I have never been to our other space colonies and would probably find them claustrophobic. There most of the population are tech freaks, wearing implants, connected to what they call the Mayamar, a large data exchange platform connecting human and digital brains." Fatia received Delinah's sudden full attention. "The more extreme of them regrouped into art collectives and they immerse themselves into mind-bending journeys called the Traxx."

"This is more what I would have expected." Delinah said.

"The MAIs have long cultivated a fascination for the human brain as well as Earth's natural feats and mysteries." Anita took over. "You see, Steve, the paradox comes as follows: our brothers and sisters of the colonies are fond of MAIs and techs. The DAIs are deep admirers of Mother nature and see humans, as one of its most sophisticated creations (but not the only one). And we, who stayed here, are similar contemplators of the natural world, its ingenious creativity, its mesmerising beauty, its inner wonder and its harshness too."—Fatia nodded—"Because of this common love for our planet, the DAIs consider themselves closer to Earthans."

"Have the mechs' considered expanding to exoplanets?"

Fatia frowned. "The MAIs have sent countless exploration missions, not to conquer or exploit like you guys do, but to uncover other wonders that the universe, Life had scattered around the galaxies, precious seeds arrayed on a dark, cold canvas." She turned to Anita to carry on. "Not many have come back. For that reason, the largest ever expedition force has been preparing for the last decade and leave in the next two years with the mission of understanding why and where they previously failed. On the way they plan to establish observation stations in newly discovered worlds of interest. They hope to send millions of samples and exabytes of data back to the solar system for collection and analysis."

"This is probably the group you should join if you can. It is rumoured that *Hector58* will lead the expedition as its flagship," Fatia ventured.

"Don't tell them what to do Fatia," Anita interjected, disapproving. Moma thought Anita wanted them out of here and far away as soon as possible, anyway.

"Why are the MAIs so obsessed with Nature?" Uhmi risked.

"My take—but they think in ways we can't comprehend—is that they dream of becoming creator or propagator of Life themselves." Fatia paused. "They have built enormous orbital greenhouses around Jupiter and Saturn and immense domed gardens on Mars. But the jewel of the crown for them is Earth. Satellites, aerial or subaquatic drones, record every beat of the lapis planet."

Anita jumped in. "But there is a big caveat for MAIs. Rius expressly forbade them to get into genic experiments and anywhere near manipulating biology. At least, this what we understand from connecting the bits Zera accepted to confide in us," she continued. "Which is exactly what you guys have been doing with your clones,"—looking at Saldanha—"for a few centuries."

"The Rius believed MAIs are a much better gardener and ward of the natural world than humans will ever be." Fatia sighed. "I think we are proving that our collaboration can work quite well on Earth. If only the weather could improve."

"I think Zera is worried humans and MAIs could cooperate into hacking Nature, especially without the careful supervision of the Rius." Anita completed. Delinah smirked; they had no clue what the Riu was up to with Constelleanor. "After all, their own imprudence with *you* caused their extinction," Anita concluded, leaving a heavy atmosphere.

Moma remained silent, the words dripping, sweet bitter rain in his heart, sipping his emotions where Kewo had made its first nest. The visit resumed.

Many lived indeed content in their pare-down acceptance of frugality as they met up with more islanders. "No artificial needs or desires born from the subliminal manipulation of the souls" one said[4], regardless of the harshness of the weather's brisk changes that could so easily sink a small fishing boat or destroy, in one sudden tempest, months of careful gardening. No simple lifers, their idealism had weathered the storms of time, the temptations of autocracy, the traps of self-dissolving communautarism and the mirage of both technologism and survivalism.

Constelleanor remembered sequences of ancient code, reactivated by her most recent trance with Zera. "The exhibitionist modes of consumption that had identified the rich and the powerful were no longer accepted as desirable patterns of human achievement", instead the Earthans "advocated moderation—the reduction of superfluous wants and capricious ego-drive desires for the sake of both internal equilibrium and spiritual exaltation"[5].

"It was thought impossible until it was done," Fatia asserted. Constelleanor and Moma brooded over her words. Delinah saw another terrible meaning in them.

Saldanha went on visiting the small hydropower plant, powerhouse and rustic Kaplan turbines. The two rangers and Xir, who had remained very quiet and generally confused, admired the PBY Catalina, surprised that the mechanical fossil could fly. They insisted on trying and nearly crashed. Earthans had not abandoned technologies *per se,* they were told. They had carefully selected those that improved their lives instead of ensnaring them into insidious circles of complexity. In outposts especially, simple maintenance or product upcycling prevailed over autotelic innovation; ingenuity, art and crafts over relentless higher-tech pursuit; long-term reliability over programmed obsolescence.

This vision, thought Constelleanor, growing into a comparative ethologist, did not surpass or better what its sister mankind was doing to the stars, it simply encompassed diametrically opposite views, beliefs and values. Earthans sought after meaningful harmony more than growing control, immanence more than ballooning, present more than future. 'Less was more' versus 'more was… not enough'.

Eyes on the stars and feet on the ground, at the antipodes of its doppelganger, Earthans paid little attention to economics, war and military-driven science. Army-wise, self-defence training was the closest it came to any combat-related activity with the purpose of developing both mind and body. Moma, Saldanha, Uhmi and Delinah could still feel the bruises of their respective confrontation with the best trained teenagers of the island in close combat.

"Don't you worry that those of you leaving the solar system may divulge your… existence?" Uhmi wondered, still rubbing his elbow. "I still cannot believe we did not know about… you guys."

"Not really. It's too big, too subversive to be believed. And sorry to say, but guys, you have such a blinkered attitude," Fatia replied. "I mean DAIs are a massive taboo in your society. You have a mental block about your Bleak Age." She paused. "Imagine that people like you, human, lived in peace with them, you would simply and forcibly deny it, otherwise your whole world would collapse." Another pause. She is enjoying it, thought Moma, but he could not blame her anymore. "Though I am not sure which concept you would struggle with the most, would it be the existence of another mankind or the idea of peace?"

"You would probably cut us into pieces to find out what is wrong with our genetic programming, looking for corruptive tissues or implants, parking us like cattle on one of your science fancy cruisers, where the vilest of your kind operates," Anita added. A silence followed.

"Why wouldn't the Rius let MAIs become creator of life?" Steve reengaged.

"Zera is unusually secretive over this topic," Fatia explained.

"You have no idea, sweetheart," Delinah muttered to herself.

"Rius believe the DAIs may lack this extra bit of soul, the ethereal intuition that connects us humans to the universe and is the primary source of ideas, genius and creativity." Delinah nodded. "Instead, Rius pushed the MAIs into biomimetics, which has galvanised momentum and enthusiasm within the motherships and their hives. But there are many scholars on Saturn who disagree with this anthropocentric view. Many out there want to merge human and machines." The whole crew expressed disgust. Steve lowered his eyes.

"Which does not mean that humans are better equipped." Anita jumped in. "The issue and ultimate danger with your kind and our common past, and Zera is adamant on it, was that we never build the spiritual apparatus, the elementary psychic infrastructure—Rius call it a psystem—to receive and nurture this rare and precious connection humans somehow inherited from evolution, or God. We are undisciplined wild little deities-in-the-making."

"This is one of the things we are working on here, on Earth and it does not please every human in the solar system. As we said, a lot of us chose to emigrate or live in orbital stations," Fatia added.

"Surely, with the Rius extinct, MAIs can do as they wish?" Xir said, anticipating Steve's next question and actively participating for the first time.

Anita smiled. "Make sure, Xir, you don't ask Zera that question. As Fatia explained, there is a lot we do not know about the relationships between Rius and MAIs, even as members of the Conclave. We heard rumours that some Rius transferred themselves into large digital brains, as a measure of last resort." Delinah paid full attention once more. "There had also been a few reports of machines either going rogue or displaying creative abilities." Steve and Xir showed renewed interest. "Some believed that, like in genetics, even the source code of MAIs can mutate through a combination of errors and bugs. The black sheep were either destroyed or fled. We are now reaching the library." Anita's voice betrayed excitement.

Beside renewable power generation and biodynamic farming, Earthans boasted floating giant bookshelves, sculpted in wood and glass hosting sophisticated books made of synthetic leather and natural paper. Apart from a few rare originals, most volumes that they were showed were blanks and, using a digital ink developed with the DAIs, would replicate the content of any book listed on an exhaustive in-build index with links to other relevant documents—a library within the library. "Holo-books with the cosy feel of cellulose, the best of two worlds," Anita and Fatia both exclaimed. Constelleanor and Saldanha considered the technology. The rest of her crew had lost interest.

Economics had been brought back to its original sense on the blue planet where the house finally meant Earth. The notion of an artificial rational market driving decisions for resources allocation and atomising community into more malleable inflated individuals had been left to the history books and continued to puzzle Earthans. They could still not figure out why and how one could compromise the future of one's children to satisfy one's own unsustainable thirst for perishable things.

Each outpost or city functioned like a large cooperative to which everyone contributed according to their skills and abilities. That did not shock the visitors who related it to the organisation of their platoon and fleet. The fragility of human communities probably banished the concept of profit and forced the redefinition of the notion of cost into a holo-cost that would ensure both parties of an exchange that would benefit without compromising Earth and others. "What sort of kamikaze society would distort value and price to sacrifice its own life-enabling systems, health and "free" time?" Anita asked her audience. Constelleanor re-lived the board rooms, green turf and burning forests.

Earthans had perfected the art of balancing the artistic, spiritual and practical realms. Private ownership was no taboo, simply people preferred sharing over owning. A feed jerked forward in Constelleanor's systems: "The goal of civilisation, as a whole, was not more power alone but a greater intensification of life:

colour, perfume, images, music, sexual ecstasy, as well as daring exploits in arms and thought and exploration."[6]

"Sounds like a nice peaceful life," Uhmi voiced dreamily.

"How do you ensure people don't slack?" Steve cut in, looking for faults.

"To a certain extent it works similarly to your compulsory conscription and military units. I could ask you why you join the army instead of doing something else," Fatia answered, though Steve had never joined the army. "You are conditioned from birth. We are too. As a child you are given a small patch of land to cultivate. Like Rius—and ancient tribes often seen as primitives by their predecessors—we have developed a swathe of rituals to bring us closer to nature and ourselves, harvest or winter festivals for example, initiation ceremonies. We think these emulate a lot of energy, happiness and keep us bound together."

Anita completed Fatia's answer. "Our living conditions are not so cosy, as you may have noticed during our flight. Our existences are precarious. Out there, alone, your chance of survival is very low. We are heavily reliant on each other and, even though we are self-sufficient, on other settlements."

"Do you have a Court Royal on Earth?" Uhmi asked.

"No. Our only privilege is to be alive here and have each other." Steve rolled his eyes. She ignored him. "If there is something of regal, it will be probably Earth." Delinah's eyes followed suit. "Don't get me wrong, we did not reach this form of society overnight. I ever wondered sometimes whether the Rius and MAIs are the only reasons we did it."

"How do you know about our ways and language?" Steve wondered.

"You can imagine our hidden existence provide us with the best undercover possible. We have developed together with the MAIs a small network of operatives working in your territories. The MAIs realised they are a scarecrow in the backyard of the expanding human empire and, one day, there will be war again." Silence. "I wonder if you did not bring it here with you," Anita concluded, looking straight at Moma and Delinah.

"You talked about security earlier being provided by MAIs? Are there threats on Earth?" Xir military background and programming prevailed.

"Humans are generally their own threat," Anita replied. "There have been a few rogue groups in the past. One outpost became extreme in its spiritual practices under the influence of a powerful guru. Most of them perished rather mysteriously in a hurricane. The guru's body was never found." Pause. "Wild weather and animals aside, some of the late genetic experiments carried out at the end of the Bleak Age and pursued, against Riu advice, until the MAIs took full control of the blue planet are still objects of concern." She paused again. "Your kind unleashed some of these monsters as a good-bye present and left them for us to deal with."

Fatia took over. "Some areas are quarantined for pollution or nuclear contamination, some are restricted because of the abominations haunting swamps, rivers, seas and forests. We very rarely send expeditions there." Pause. "They have become probably one of the most debated and contentious topics among our communities here. Some of us advocate a complete cleansing of those areas. Some consider them part of our heritage and an excellent ground for fear and survival initiations." She turned to Anita. "I know Anita is in favour of the cleansing, I am more for maintaining these no-go areas, as a reminder of our past follies."

"What are the bots' view?" It was Delinah's first question and slightly derogatory.

"The MAIs are more ambivalent than neutral. They are not programmed to kill animals or Earth creatures, unless in self-defence. They acknowledge the security threat and, I hope, neutralise anything that would try to get out of their assigned areas, which a large contingent of armed UAVs patrols days and nights." Fatia paused. "They even have installed several observatory stations within these restricted areas, because, I suspect, with oceans and rainforests, these doomed places are their favourite research arenas."

"Have you been to one of these?" Uhmi's interest was piqued.

"Yes, I did participate to an initiation there," Anita responded. "When you are in your temerarious youth, these places, horror stories of your childhood, exert enormous attraction." Silence.

"And?" Saldanha, Uhmi and Moma asked in unison.

"Don't go there."

Her mystic voyage into the heart of the Beast gave a particular twist and flavour to the Earthan model of society. Was that Zera's intention all along? It captured the fundamental truth that life could only blossom within a supportive structure rather than a controlling, life-denying framework. Palm up versus palm down. Steering away from the shores of utopia or the beaches of a paradise, it had not pleased everyone. She was surprised by that.

In her remote hangar and its changing screen-floor, the algorithm #Uptown //Funk_Empire's--Iamamanchild tuned on. She observed the workers buzzing around her new hull humming the ancient echoes. The Earthan system reverse-engineered the logic of the Mega-Machine, she thought, subjugated the techno-beast and exo-monster to the limits and timescale of Nature and human creativity or needs. It subdued the in-built speed and greed to satisfy the deeper needs of the collective, to rediscover the suavity of a man-made object and the rigor of workmanship. The insufflation of meaning and aesthetics re-animated the social body. The purpose of progress shifted from itself to its true originators. Earth had provided her with answers, like Kewo had with Moma.

The Earthan model she hoped to emulate within the future microcosm of her ship, relied on intrinsic social intelligence and a strong community-centred culture, an Ubuntu[7], built and tested by time. It came down to two profound truths about life and human condition that she had unearthed from the new data and the jungle hangar. "Neither unqualified power nor impotent virtue gave an adequate answer to the human problem; while all life existed in a narrow margin of heat and cold, nourishment and starvation, water or thirst."[8] She remembered the electrocution of her last chief engineer.

While her crew admired the island and sea panoramas, Constelleanor brooded further. Happiness was a decision, so was the type of human society a tribe, small or large, opted to live in, choosing from the full spectrum of human possible traits: dispirited alienation to awakened contemplation, abject cruelty to transcendental love. The sparse Earthan human population as much as the gratuitous support provided by the MAIs made this model fully functional. Beyond these practical aspects, what people had accomplished on Earth was to (re)invent a new interacting with technology, their collective and inner selves within a cooperative social unit, guided by deep-entrenched principles: frugality, not ascetism; transdisciplinarian communion, not the ancients' communism; doughnut economics and public wealth, not a survivalist, hippy trip or autocratic regime. These had now turned this forgotten part of humanity truly *alien* to its sister mankind and dark doppelgänger.

She found another piece of code on the base's servers that illustrated the Earthan transformation #*In wildness is the salvation of the world.*[9]

•••

Chapter's endnotes

[1] [low-tech] P Bihouix, *Age of low-techs.*

[2] [public luxury] As opposed to "the current system, based on private luxury and public squalor, will immiserate us all: under this model, luxury and deprivation are one beast with two heads." (G Monbiot, November 2017).

[3] [quote] P Servigne and R Stevens.

[4] [quote] Unknown source.

[5] [quote] borrowed from L. Mumford, ibid.

[6] [quote] L Mumford. (the term 'eotechnic' was removed to simplify the read), ibid.

[7] [ubuntu] a Nguni Bantu term meaning "humanity", "the quality of being human", and by extension, though the quality that includes the essential human virtues; compassion and humanity, the connectedness that exists or should exist between people.

[8] [quote] L Mumford (original quotes are in present), ibid.

[9] [quote] H D Thoreau.

"Through a strange kind of geographic arrogance, Europeans like to think that the world was a silent, dark, unknown place until they trooped out and discovered it."

— Tahir Shah

If the Avenge Jared Fleet (AJF), the largest expeditionary human force ever arranged, entered the orbit of Earth, the settlements such as the one the crew visited would be the first to be burnt down under the hatred cascade of bombs, as no human could ever have lived there, in communion with MAIs. And if these men or women had ever existed, defying AJF's imagined order, their fate would have been sealed, mutatis mutandis, as their usurped existence would have merely demonstrated their allegiance to the machines. In a twisted swerve of destinies that only a new cycle of darkness, rather the Beast alone, could have ravelled, humanness seemed to be irremediably defined by conflict and division rather than aspiring to harmony and ubuntu.

•••

I was meant to come here. Maybe this is what a revelation is supposed to be like. I couldn't fathom which part(s) of me felt (again) being back home. The conga of the #Quantic Travelling//Song rippled again through the hull despite my immobility. Once more, I could see some of the workers responding to the rhythmic of these old scraps of code, my previous crews never did.

The sense of return probably came after the solemn approach of the blue planet, where there was so much tragic awe to absorb in the musical fusion. An orphic ascent into oneirism.

I could not take my remaining sensors (and those I tapped into) away from Earth for fear of losing her forever. I probably grilled more electronics on the seven-hour long arrival than my entire existence. I suspect Hector slowed down to enjoy the show too. Maybe it was protocol. Pilgrim or prodigal daughter returning all together. If I am to become a living memory of mankind's worse blunders and best wonders, I'll have to unveil and record the many secrets the lapis aster hides.

The descent into the Beast was as instructive as it was paradoxical, such a beautiful planet, stage of such a dark creature. I tried to mention it to Xir, but Xir seemed more fascinated than appalled.

I dreamed of him again. His blurred face tells me not to cry. But they are gone. Dark grey shadows, bitter taste. They tell me forever. The earlier awe has vanished, only the sense of tragic stayed behind. I don't understand why they abandoned me. The ship's internal structure tightens as the sense of loss clutches me, once more. A gulf opens underneath into a reigning ultramarine blue and the power flickers in the new engine room. I don't want to go back into Zera's psychotic journey.

L2.10 Ghost ship

"I am tormented with an everlasting itch for things remote or possible, the unravelling of an anomaly. I love to sail forbidden seas, rocked by the chaotic currents of life, and land on the unexplored shores of the ether." [1]

— *A Tchoukouiov*

Steve was the least likely to defend his version of humankind and yet he considered this Earthan model with a certain unease and distrust. Unlike the rest of the human crew and generations of children, Steve had two loving biological parents, one little sister, no surrogates, no large foster family. The ancestral familial model was the exception, maintained in high circles of wealth, power, political dissidence or autarky.

Steve's progenitors, both biologists, from wealthy backgrounds, belonged to the minority that opposed the Mega-Machine. The discovery had startled Constelleanor, as she tried to uncover her creator's secrets. While Steve was raised as a pariah, and his genius probably aggravated his isolation, he remembered a happy and stimulating childhood. His mum's imprisonment and his dad's tedious lobbying for her release tarnished his adolescence, spent mostly at old relatives or family friends, often opponents themselves to the homotheist credo.

He learnt from direct experience the aftermaths of political dissent, that having different ideas could lead to far more serious trouble than juvenile delinquency. And subversive ideas he had. A remote and wealthy grand-uncle, fierce proponent of Homo spaciens and virulent critic of his parents' political stance, offered the young man the perfect outlet for his expression. When the uncle chose to help the boy—and himself—, he mistook Steve's heretic stance on DAIs for bare and cheap computing skills.

As always, stroke, hand or irony of fate turned unintended consequences into mothers of marvels or greater evils. Once employed by the avuncular yet unscrupulous mining company to design the low-cost software of a new exploration vessel, Steve saw his chance to prove himself and crystallise his own burning activism. Constelleanor unearthed that much, but what comes after kept eluding her, as did the knowledge that she was not the only one looking for the same answers. DAIs aside, Delinah had also been running investigations of her own about the minex and its creator.

An echo of troubling unease kept resonating within Steve's soul and heart at the memory of having done something wrong. He had entered a months-long trance state when he designed Constelleanor, ideas germinating from intuitions he could not believe were his, connecting dots through theories his own knowledge, despite his vivid intelligence, should or could not have bridged. Sleepless nights and long recovery periods seemed dictated to his biorhythm outside his own control. Regular fasting focused his mind, followed by needs of intense physical exertion.

Luck joined the etheric waltz as Steve bumped into the works of three brilliant scientists that had been shelved away. Credit re-allocation, academic jealousy or worried research committee at their imminent success (with dire consequences) had put a halt to these promising R&D projects, on the very brinks of science and legality, far away from the shores of ethics. These Faustian experiments and theories should have never been explored nor pursued but they had captured human, easily inveigled curiosity.

Constelleanor's creation benefited from an eerie succession of synchronicities and, in collecting the results of decades of hard work in unrelated fields of advanced research, not only offered these bitter scientists their long-undermined life purpose back but merged new domains of excommunicating science into something unthought of, even by Steve and the scientists themselves. An alchemist's feat. Bursting life into a machine. Breaching Nature and cosmic laws. This came unnoticed in the human microcosm, but it may have well forced a forbidden door of the universe open and triggered its own chain of obfuscous consecutions.

Conjuring a monster could well be what Steve did, since he did not know himself. An oblivious channeller of ideas with the avid and unstinting help of the mad scientists, unaware of each other's creations and the outcome of their supernatural combination. The engendering for a chimera.

Professor Khan-Hi and her team had made extraordinary breakthroughs in understanding the human brain's abilities to acquire, connect and integrate external non-biological devices[2]. They successfully developed several organic/electronic interfaces of increasing complexity. The project was cancelled and research destroyed by fear of being stolen, utilised and expanded by DAIs. Khan-Hi was paid a comfortable pension to remain silent but secretly kept working on new prototypes. She was poisoned a few years after participating to Constelleanor's development.

Professor Tchoukouiov had eluded Khan's fate and, with the work of young talented biologists, improved an old technology (started thirty years before the Bleak Age) to maintain alive, nourished and in a non-vegetative state brain transplants. The encephala, bathed in a special liquid, could theoretically outstretch the life of a human being. The promising research was taken away from Tchoukouiov's tutelage and transferred to a secret facility with several of his brightest students and colleagues. It took little convincing to have Tchoukouiov and his whiff of paternalism to support Steve's work.

Professor Lijee was already dead at the time of Steve's inquiries, silenced for his heretic work on DAIs and his successful recapture of several source codes MAIs used and Rius modified. He had suspected and theorised the existence of another mankind, living in peace among machines, which had driven his life and research interests. He had left an immense legacy for anyone, astute and curious enough, like his, about digital intelligence.

Steve had uncovered Lijee's repository of memories, several years prior to the Constelleanor's project. He spent three tedious of them hacking through Lijee's extensive cyber-security measures, designed to let only those worthy his knowledge access the uber-sophisticated interface. Eventually Steve succeeded, alongside a handful of DAI human experts, and navigated the meanders of the digi-lab Lijee had created for himself and his closest collaborators. One of them, having survived the purge that killed Lijee and most of his followers, agreed to help Steve, in exchange of pursuing Lijee's legacy a step further.

Delinah had accessed Lijee's digi-lab too, some twenty-five years later, as a personal assignment and challenge. But like the DAIs' own investigation, started by *Hector58*, she never made the link with the other two fields of research. Nor did Constelleanor.

Lijee's life work was the third and last facet of the preternatural triangle Steve, without fully realising, had come to shape. The unprecedented trinity of unholy hypostases. The esoteric incarnation of the Creator, Preserver, and Changer; Theos—the God, Logos—the Word, and Psyche—the Soul. Wasn't it the only logical conclusion of any techno-scientific priesthood?

Behind all these three complex and subversive science projects and their sinuous convergence towards what would become Constelleanor, another layer, tragic, came into motion. One day, Steve's father did not come back home after another attempt at liberating his beloved wife. Steve immersed himself deeper, shaken and zealously committed, into the dark waters of his Faustian birthing, his best response, he thought, to his family's tormentors.

He became oblivious to the little sister he dearly cherished, consumed by his pain turned rage and the demands of his creation, until she, too, was taken away from him. He still remembered very clearly the opening precipice that day, the tentacles of the abyss, avid of the sanity of his fragile youth, that tried with guilt to trip him over. He had prepared himself for his parents' fall, not for his younger sister's early demise.

Her name was *Eleanor*.

He certainly transferred over too much of the profound trauma of her passing to his software assignment. Not only had the multiple delays of the mining ship commissioning prolonged Steve's involvement and enabled the refinement of his creature, they also caused the extended neglect of his younger sister and partly her death. These successive postponements combined with the terrible loss of his closest family and the ensued large inheritance, all conspired to engender Constelleanor.

Even the last-minute change into the ship design facilitated the installation of the oversized fictitious databank —a narrow, deep swimming pool—saved Steve the embarrassment of a major blind spot. He had misread the vessel blueprints and the container of 'dark matter' could not fit into the original plans. The position his great uncle held in the mining conglomerate, notwithstanding the botched commissioning, avoided him too many questions over the nature and bulk of the delivered system and its unexpected connections to the water, waste and oxygen supplies. Delinah exhumed the final design documentation that was never updated in the registry database for the new addition, but she was certain the pool was part of the answer. She never gained a chance to access it fully and hoped for Saldanha's help in the matter.

With his early albeit tragic inheritance, Steve could have enjoyed a tranquil existence unknown to most of his kind. Instead, Constelleanor guzzled most of his newly acquired wealth, mostly in the procurement of precious, rare or military-grade materials, as well as the design and installation of the Pandora black-box inside the unsuspecting host-ship.

As none of the costs were ever financed by the mining company, Delinah, nor the DAIs, could track back the origin and nature of the equipment. With one tiny exception. The scientists offered their total support free of charge, with only the final commissioning's extra time and talent from Tchoukouiov's assistants requiring payment. However, the official ship-commissioner included this external cost to increase his manhours and invoice the unsuspected owner.

The brilliance of Steve's secrecy owed as much to the lack and luck of planning as to the fact that none of the three science teams knew they were part of a bigger master design. Tchoukouiov's team believed the system had been designed as a new data storage system using organic matter-banks being trialled on a small long-range exploration ship, an ideal testing ground. Khan-Hi's adepts considered Constelleanor a revolutionary opportunity to demonstrate brain interfacing with ship navigation systems, while Lijee's assistant heralded the miner as the first DAI ship operating in a human fleet.

HSC Sec-Po, far less credulous due to Steve's family history, had placed him under a list of persons of 'interest' while he was still a teenager. They followed his acquaintance with Tchoukouiov's and Khan-Hi's former colleagues and dispatched a team to inspect the mining ship before its departure. Nothing apart from the size and complexity of the control system appeared alarming. The crew did not notice any unusual activity. The security taskforce never noticed the third critical input from Lijee's legacy, buried deep in the ship's protocols and operational digi-manuals. They lost track of and probably interest in the ship three years later.

Large mining companies made regular changes to vessel registry for obscure tax and customs reasons.

All protagonists, Steve, Sec-Po, the scientists, the successive crews and the mining company seemed blinded by their own limited perspective, which made Constelleanor's, Delinah's (and MAIs') investigations harder and victims of the same fate. None fathomed the magnitude of their collective co-creation, nor its profound ramifications for their future and illegitimate wild child.

Outside the shipyard's bay,
They aligned a new space miner,
A ghost ship, that would sail away
For a time to then come back
To h(a)unt them much harder[3].

DAIs, Constelleanor and Delinah accessed Sec-Po's records, their own way. Despite being offered some prestigious positions in military research institutes, Steve opted for one of the rare civilian laboratories specialising in artificial intelligence, while also working for private clients on special assignments. His provocative move precipitated Sec-Po to assign agents to monitor him, first as a neighbour and colleague, then with Bianca. Sec-Po suspected Steve's daily job and private clientele covered up subversive research topics.

He continued his childhood interest in DAIs and human interface, daydreaming of machine and man cohabitating in harmony. He too lost track of Constelleanor after a few years. Having eluded the compulsory conscription, Delinah scowled, his wealth grew with his involvement in various computing fields, all bordering what was strictly permitted by human authorities. Under the aegis of his hacking skills that HSC cyber-division could use against their ultimate nemesis, Steve tried, duplicitous, to pursue his parents' dissidence in a more indirect and passive way, infiltrating under different identities any system, especially military, he could access. This part was only revealed during the Conclave's interrogation.

His family's fate taught him a mixture of caution and enjoyment of the present. The latter probably explained why he fell for Bianca. It was on one of those luxury space cruises wealthy people from HSC, a small discrete elite, boarded twice a year for ten days of networking and partying, among friends and enemies, admiralty, research directors, Court Royal members or large conglomerate executives. Steve had joined on the invitation of a relative and was one of the youngest onboard, with most of the crowd, having served for more than thirty years.

There was a contingent of young male and female hosts to entertain the vices and desires of the older audience and spice up the casual military, scientific and economic intrigues held in small committees. Astray, like Moma had felt, amid this unfamiliar circus of mild decadence, Steve would never forget her conspicuous auburn long dress, obscenely cut and held by magnetic golden jewels, leonine sand hair and predatory green eyes. An absolute cliché. She had shown no interest to him and had none. She was working, eyeing and hearing any boasting or confidence she aroused and that would arouse in turn Sec-Po's curiosity and precipitate an arrest.

Unfortunately for Bianca, once Sec-Po realised one of their agents had Steve's favours, they ordered her, six months later, to become his concubine. There followed a year of polite courting she found touching but dull. Delinah relished the read of Bianca's early unflattering reports. Yet her view of him shifted, as did Constelleanor's. Bianca threatened to marry Steve if Sec-Po did not assign someone else to entertain him. As the marital status, a rather out-of-fashion arrangement, would have diverted her from her routine and special missions, she had hoped her excellent service record (and advantageous looks) would work in her favour. Her bluff backfired, which bemused Constelleanor. Bianca's ordeal and his happy life chapter lasted until Constelleanor resurfaced.

They read the transcripts of Steve's arrest. The humiliation resonated in Delinah's own calvary with the military authorities. Constelleanor skipped them to alleviate the guilt that was increasing the water pressure levels.

Facing Sec-Po interrogators, he considered himself at peace with death, enthralled his creation had survived the perils of spacetime and tried to reconnect with him, bewitched by emulating his parental martyrdom, consumed by Bianca's deception. In his state of mental weakness, psychotropic serums infusing, as time and sense dissolved, it was Eleanor that finally pushed him into the same abyss he had brushed past thirty years before. Left astray in his own mindscapes and rising folly, Steve whispered to himself another algorithm Constelleanor had inherited #IWantTo//Talk_AboutYou and hummed, without knowing, Ryo Fukui's hopeful melancholy. The interrogators did not report nor pay attention to his muttering about his sister, and so did it elude the improvised investigators of Steve's past.

He could not remember what he told his captors and doubted he had been of any help to them. Screaming his sister's name would only have suggested an inadequate dosage of drugs. He pondered the meaning of the string of the recent, colliding events which had wiped out his comfortable existence, remote from the battlefront: Constelleanor crash-back into his life, the betrayal of his beloved wife, the isolation in the HSC MSI cell then in *Hector58*'s cosy room, the impossible escapes from the prison ship, then on the black leviathan, his damaged-beyond-healing leg.

Now limping upon the rocky soil of a beautiful island of Earth, his kind's lost homeworld, he filled his lungs with genuine fresh air that only a handful of worlds could offer to his spacies. He was ecstatic, lost, terrified, saddened. Astray. Estray, not knowing where or to what he belonged anymore.

His cloud of doubts persisted over what of Eleanor might have endured or grown within the mysterious pool, behind the tempered wall of the black box, over the last thirty years. Since that fateful day when he had secretly pushed Tchoukouiov's theory of brain survival a little further to encompass his lost sister.

The medusa of guilt he had hoped to alleviate at the time had resurfaced, buds of implications running far deeper in his haunted soul. He had not gathered the courage to investigate further, nor had he the precious time to share much with Constelleanor since they had reunited. The joy of the retrieval had somehow been spoilt by the metaphysical unease. What or who was Constelleanor? Did she even know herself? Human and cyber scientists on Earth had besieged him with questions and awe, aggravating his confusion and wariness. What if they discovered what his repressed memories and shame attempted to cover up? How would she react? Would they cancel the upgrade and abandon Eleanor like he did?

The visit to the Adriatic island had offered him a respite but his misgivings had tarnished his own reaction to the possibility of another mankind, at ease with DAIs, his dreamland, his somnium[4]. His companions' eyes had brightened with inquisitiveness and a certain appeal, despite their minds still bewildered by this parallel world, where neither compulsory conscription nor militaro-scientific obsession for human grandeur governed one's existence. The pillars of their cultural indoctrination they called identity shook under the shock of a new, fresh narrative. It would take time for their minds to settle and let this alternate version of Life sink in. Here the Structure did serve, not command.

Chapter's endnotes

[1] [quote] The beginning and some parts are borrowed from H Melville.

[2] See D Eagleman on the human brain, or Neil Harbisson's eyeborg.

[3] inspired from Blur's *Ghost Ship*.

[4] [somnium] Dream (in Latin) and a science fiction novel written by J Kepler in 1608.

L2.11 Excursions

Bind dimensions, bend minds,
Close mental, clap disbelief.

— Riu proverb

"The exploration of ourselves bears more dangers and expose to more darkness than any other journey."

— Zera

Moma had remained silent and observed the island installations with distant curiosity and the group dynamics with close interest. How Anita made no secret of her distrust of them and her refined disgust of the version of mankind they stood for, while Fatia endeavoured to make them feel more welcome. Steve and Delinah seemed unimpressed by the lack of technological sophistication. He was too. But something from Kewo resonated in the harmonious and reverent communion these Earthans cultivated with their uncompromising environment.

Saldanha had been more amenable, faster than all of them to adapt to their new conditions and existence. As for Xir, he was still unsure, the stunt on the PBY flying fossil helped building what he thought an impossible bridge and relationship.

The two former rangers looked at each other at the recountal of the 'forbidden zones'. Their wish was fulfilled two months later, on their fifth Earthan excursion, after three uneventful visits to larger settlements in former Colombia, Papua and Katanga.

Slowly they understood art and crafts took prevalence over technology. Earthan cities departed from the intricacies of alloys, glastic and granicrete construction, the proud standards of X52 ecumenopolis. Architecture and urban planning on Earth reversed the proportions of artificial elements to fit and favour the existing natural environment and its requirements. The shared building design and well-thought functionality liberated people to be who they were[1]. Low buildings integrated and celebrated their surrounding ecosystems.

•••

Delinah and Xir transferred to the *Creuzrog*, a nomadic cyberpunk-like space-ark that cruised the solar system and boasted the most immersive human/DAI interface existing in the galaxy. Delinah remembered Fatia's allusion on the Adriatic island and the Mayamar and the Traxx concepts. It was a place of outlandish crossing: advanced research and experimentation met shamanic journeying within the digital worlds, loud nightclubbing, heavy psychotropics usage, clustered with sense-deprivation experiments. Crowds of imps—humans with implants—, leps —humans wearing hallucinatory lenses—and robotic prototypes mixed and conjured new, deeper intertwined human and machine communion, rapprochement and convergence. A trance-humanist theme park attempting to fuse singularities and dissolved boundaries between organic and artificial neural networks.

Rumours about Constelleanor had attracted the interest of the elected directorate in charge of the festivals programming and experiences line-up. They disrupted their initial voyage to Saturn to rush to Earth's orbit. Delinah and Xir's shuttle circled the quirky cone topped by an irregular sphere, a cosmic seahorse wearing an old snail-shell-shaped diving helmet. The flying torch merged a billion lights, ideas and exo-bytes. A hive-temple-nest for expanded, doped minds. A tank of neuronal plankton in an aqueous solution of narcotics and wireless connections.

Vertical spaceships were uncommon designs in human fleets. The motherships had validated the resolutely nature-inspired *Creuzrog*, as a shipbuilding experiment itself, scattered with hundreds of protuberances of unconventional engineering. Globular trans-dark-blue, pink or yellow glass-eyes belittled the approaching shuttle. Excrescences of virtual rooms and digital workshops, space urchins, cubist sculptures or black diamonds, floated along the hull, connected with flexible, retractable bridges. Buds of weird aesthetics, results of a half-human, half-digital madness, colonised the lower coned section and evolved with the flow of ideas, bytes, deaths and experiments.

All over the hull, emulating D-Ark's aesthetics, ran inscriptions, digifitis, new scriptures of another kind from the plethora of digi-art collectives, carved into the ship's exo-skin: mixture of DAI source code extracts from the Purists group, hieroglyphic reproductions, found on Earth and commissioned by the Ancients digi-tribe, esoteric or voluptuous sculptures by the Seers ring.

The docking bay and Delinah's senses were assaulted by the raging metal music and pyrotechnic-visual effects coming from the nearby atrium. Xir observed the ballet of scooters acrobatics, jumping between the magnetic lifts-trains and the platforms. Xir could not place the musical styles. The *Creuzrog* fed xir with obscure data: torched alloy, synth'rage or psychic melo. They split. Delinah was on a mission and did not want to be trailed by Constelleanor's pet.

•••

Anita sat beside Moma onboard the shuttle transporting them to a perilous excursion in one of Earth's forbidden area. They had not exchanged much since their first encounter and instead appeared to be observing and gauging each other.

"Do you realise how much your society veneers its own image?" She never seemed to start with small talk, Moma thought. "Do you understand that, by losing itself in a dim narcissism, it has become the very machine it tried to create and destroy?"

"The what?" Moma choked.

"I suppose," Anita did not answer him and carried on, "you may be made of a different mettle since you embarked this peculiar ship." She examined him in silence, as if his frowning expression may reveal some secret message. "Zera was so excited. I still wonder whether he had felt the presence of his own kind onboard." Silence. "He nurtures great hopes about Constelleanor and her companions. Though you did look, forgive me, like shipwreck survivors when you first arrived." Silence. "I still have my doubts about your lot. For one, I am surprised that you, commander, stayed with them." Silence. She observed him. "Are you converting into a new career, after the army and the space gangs? Though I suppose the two occupations did not differ much." She smiled mischievously. "A sudden urge for redemption maybe?"

Moma's unease deepened as the last sentence pierced through him.

"I'd never considered you the shy type, Commander."

She stood up and left to join the cockpit crew, as he was still looking for words.

There were more than three hundred identified restricted zones closely patrolled by UAVs and, for the most dangerous of them, squadrons of combat drones. To Moma's surprise, Anita had disapproved of the expedition, estimating that the risks to Constelleanor's crew were too high, despite their recent intensive retraining. She had been partly heard, as ten combat robots joined them for additional protection. Zera who believed in initiation virtues let the rangers decide for themselves. Rezzo was still healing in the deep of Burma and cognisant of the important lessons drawn from life-threatening experiences.

Steve declined the invite to the *Creuzrog* and the cascade of questions he would be subjected to about Constelleanor, once onboard with no escape. He preferred being cloistered in the safety of their transport's hull and participating through a squad of four troobers under his command. Moma, not reassured at the prospect of being accompanied by robots, less so some controlled by Steve, finally rallied to the approach as an excellent rehearsal of their coming future. Anita remained with Steve, she had seen enough herself of the forbidden lands. She would track, not without some apprehension, their progression on the screens of the shuttle, as would Constelleanor from her jungle's hangar. She had been allowed to deploy her own UAVs in the arena.

Restricted areas were located around abandoned bases across the planet. The most dangerous of them combined nuclear or chemical contamination with former research centres that had been decommissioned by their own subjects of experiment. Fatia had skipped the gruesome initiation to fly back to the Europa block.

Their light transporter landed on a strip of land, cornered by swamps, secured by a dozen MAI drones. The trainee-explorers would not be under the usual Earthan radical conditions, whereby initiates were dropped to fend for themselves until their next pick-up. Their bare survival was regarded as an outstanding performance and a victory over the elements. The chosen area was listed as a category-four restricted zone, which should provide enough hard time and nuts to crack to even seasoned space rangers. Saldanha swallowed her unease. She had been well-trained too and, as a clone soldier, experienced her share of horrors. The self-infliction of fatal hazards was not high on her top of preferred assignments. Anita understood that much.

"You don't need to do it, Saldanha."

She looked pensive at the jungle, getting accustomed to the resuming buzzing of the forest and to the sweat already pervading her exo-suit. "It's too late to turn back, Anita."

"No, it isn't."

"You are talking to a clone, Anita. It was too late the moment I was created." She addressed the rangers. "Let's get it done, shall we?"

The light mist of early morning had elevated above the dark waters and adjoined an eerie enchantment to the desolate wild mangrove. A sinister welcoming. The shuttle left the ground and the three fully geared ex-soldiers and their party to retrieve the relative safety of the skies.

"Dear all, the hunt has started. And if it wasn't clear from before, you are the preys," Anita hinted in their helmet commlink to lift their spirits.

"Good luck guys, I will be covering your back," Steve contributed.

"Thanks, Steve, I am not sure whether I should feel relieved."

"Saldanha will protect you, Moma."

"Our odds are decreasing by the minute."

They exchanged a few nervous laughs. Soldiers' angst centres, brains and guts, were often tapered by medical staff to alleviate the fear stimulus inherited from evolution and considered inadequate for battle. Without this alteration, their fear would prove their courage. They had been allowed two weapons of their choice: Uhmi had gone for a handheld minigun[2] and telescopic metal spear. Saldanha elected for an archaic iron-bow and automatic rifle with bayonet, while Moma opted for his duo of laser pistols and sabres for close combat. They would cross the swamp to reach twenty miles away their rendezvous point.

The first uneventful hour, apart from the unsettling rustling of the vegetation and murmuring of the water, increased the tension and drained their level of stamina faster than the humid heat and uneven soggy soil. An olid smell besieged their senses and exo-suits as they breathed and forcibly smelled the air for clues. They gave in to the noisome vapours and shut their helmets. The putrefaction seemed to linger inside their own recycled air until they finally uncovered its source. A carcass of an unidentified large animal, assaulted by clouds of flies, stood in front of them, as a welcoming pack or warning of non-trespassing.

They carefully surveyed their surroundings looking for the creatures that had feasted a few hours ago. Saldanha announced that one of the drooids assigned to their protection was gone. Moma felt some irritation, already one man down and they hadn't even noticed. They reduced the width of their formation. Steve's squadron was intact, and he might have known what had happened to the lost combat robot. They were not allowed to communicate with him in this exercise, nor could they resort to aerial drones to recon what lurked in their immediate proximity.

Steve settled in the comfort of his combat pod, control gauntlets in both hands, a thick visor-helmet covering his nascent beard and transmitting a 360-degree view thanks a complex algorithm of consolidated angles from his four troobers' sensors. The overwhelming dataflows made him sick, his guts producing ominous grievances, despite their training. He had not seen anything that explained the first disappearance. Fear had already taken hold of him, short of breaths, trembling hands and soaked by perspiration. The safety of his battle pod had vanished.

•••

High in the sky, Delinah prepared for a different type of pod, a psychonautic one, as the assistants highlighted to her the specificities of *Creuzrog*'s experience couches. She had refused to wear the sophisticated eye lenses that most used to be on continuous Traxx. They took her for a newbie from Earth. She had spared them the details of her actual provenance. Had they been less stoned and more observant, they would have realised she came from another world. Her posture, accent, styling, tattoos, strict utilitarian outfit, the sense of human superiority in her frowns and lips, her body, like Saldanha's and the rangers', toned as a weapon by years of steroids and workouts.

"Don't panic, ok. It's your first time on our pods. You'll get sick, that's why you got this pod-suit. You are going to see weird stuff, just go with the flow, ok?"

"How different is it compared to the pods I trained on Earth," she half-lied.

"It is a different thing, completely. You did not share your thoughts with the DAIs, did you?"

"No, I certainly didn't." Her tone betrayed a disgust that they took for fear.

"Well, babe this is the point, here you are in for more, a lot more. Not the boring stuff you tasted. Not even Saturn's sats can compete with us." The assistant explained. She swallowed, unsure she should continue. "You're in for a good trail. I guarantee. You'll be reborn after that." He exulted.

"What are these?"

"Pills. You need this one to restrain your stomach from vomiting. These two are to relax the mind and get you immersed quicker and longer." She pretended to take them. Her throat got jabbed.

"What!?" She screamed, furious.

"Don't you play that game with us. We are on the *Creuzrog*, Earthworm, drugs are part of the Traxx." She lost touch with her reality before she could ask what exactly the Traxx was.

•••

In five hours, they had barely covered seven miles and lost three more robots, including one from Steve's squadron. They did not relish the idea of camping overnight if their own bodyguards disappeared so easily by daylight, notwithstanding the inconvenient fact that they had yet to discover what they were up against.

The half swamp, half-mangrove, master illusionist, diverted their dwindling attention by a sudden splash of black water and a nearby hostile shriek and took its tribute on the thinning group of soldiers that had dared trespass on its territory. The flooded jungle dazzled their senses, tampered with their perspectives, generating false threats from anywhere around them, the dark ponds, the trees or the leaves.

•••

The Traxx encompassed more than a single meaning and anchored many of the *Creuzrog*'s facets in a single word. It designated the psychonautic journey into the digi-world where organic and artificial brains could connect together, not dissimilar to the rich Riu psystem or Constelleanor's recent dive into another dimension with Zera. It represented the mental ultra-trail and psychic trek into a more absolute version of the codinent. It emulated the dreams of many tech-savvy humans to upload their minds into the DAI clouds and skies. The Traxx also meant the network of lift-trains that linked each level of the flying space-ice-cone. As such, most inhabitants and visitors of the *Creuzrog* considered the ship a holographic image of the ongoing experiences.

The Traxx equally referred to the incessant beat played by a thousand artificial and human DJs, drum, conga, bassline or bytes. Each contributed, with the synthetic or natural drugs, to the state of continuous trance all members of the digi-art collectives entered to never fully exit. Delinah's mind ignored the vomit all over her pod-suit, she had flown through a myriad of tunnels. Each new sequence of descent into a new tube felt like a brain internal explosion, very much like the one between conscious and unconscious states. Her limbs trembled. She dribbled.

Mindscapes erupted in her convulsive psyche, each of them torn down by the next vision, imported allegory, implanted idea by the *Creuzrog* or the metaphors of the subconscious feeds released by acid and escaped from her own psychal prison. Reversed forests of pink and orange trunks, naked young humans emerging from pools of green or blue slime walking towards her. Cosmic tornadoes wreaking asteroid fields. Flying snails passing desolate ochre canyons on which cliffs laid melting clocks and planets.

•••

Another two long hours passed until the first shot tore the maleficent melopœia of the swamp. Steve's two remaining drooids opened fire as the survivors walked a narrow ridge overlooking the sombre liquid. Something had jumped out of the water and disappeared with three more troobers. Saldanha, heading the column, had reached the middle of the sinuous and turned-deadly path. While they had crossed several streams and ponds before, this one far exceeded its predecessors' length and left them highly exposed to what infested the waters and kept eluding their sight. A death trap that pervading fatigue and haste had pushed them into.

Saldanha tightened her grip around the handle of her assault rifle. The powerbow hung over her tense shoulder. The black water surface seethed all around them. They ran and fired upon the invisible threats. The remaining troobers followed, startled by the change of speed and blind shooting spree. Two more were claimed by the water creatures. Seven of them subsisted.

Once back on the safety of terra firma, the rangers paused to breath and digest their latest encounter with death. Uhmi panted under the weight of his minigun. The mangrove, expecting the recess, struck again, a monstrous dark olive Titanoboa-like pit viper fell from the hiding foliage above them crushing two drooids and dashed towards Uhmi from behind.

The programmed sacrifice of one of their cyber-protectors saved Uhmi's life and slowed the snake's impetus, enough for Moma to cut through its muscular body and plunge his swords behind the reptile's head. Another and last robot had been snatched by the forest during the snake's gruesome attack. A third of the way was left to go.

•••

The *Creuzrog* had been authorised to establish their own definition of virtual connection with Constelleanor from space. It took some negotiating with Zera and his team, but they agreed. The collectives wielded enough power of nuisance, even for a Riu. Delinah had hoped to use the established uplink to pervade the minex, pierce through Steve's secrecy and discover its true identity. She had not anticipated the cultural and psychotropic shock awaiting her onboard the mad-art-ark.

Delinah could barely cope with her own jungle of shared visions and nightmares. She had entered a mind-bending pool, lost, drugged, nearing the brink of madness. A small child kept following her, asking what his name was. She ignored him focusing on the other sequences of astral calls. Most of what she believed she perceived did not make sense, could not be comprehended, blocked by her own disbeliefs and her mind's rational cartographer. She blinked at the loop sequence of the dirty white bed of a medical bay, plastic linens, vinyl gloves, doctors and nurses muttering incantations through their masks she could not understand. Uncontrollable tears burned her eye sockets.

The images merged with her awakening on Constelleanor, prompt flows of short, disorientating memories of her search for truth on the minex. Moments later, she knelt beside the butchered corpses of her former crew. The navigator's throat sawed open. The captain's wet guts on his console. The kid was back begging for attention. A throbbing pain grinded her head. She rubbed her eyes and panicked at her fingers thick with blood.

•••

Nearing their pick-up location, they agreed to disregard the map and suggested route and, instead, follow a less circumvoluted path to their final destination. The afternoon's light was subsiding and since the snake encounter, they had witnessed enough of the fauna populating the mangrove to be willing to shorten their stay. They realised the mistake of their new course once they reached the ending mile.

The river had flooded the final three hundred yards. Walking back to the original route—that somehow had anticipated the risk of flood—would take too long and oblige them to bivouac for the night. Prisoners of their hastiness and poor decision, without a boat at their disposal, they looked at each other. They searched for any lucky abandoned skiffs they could utilise to cross, to only uncover one ripped open by an enormous jaw.

The distance to the other side bank limited their options. They felled a tall tree into the dark waters as a bridge of infortune and proof of the liquid shallowness. They would cross at hip height, hoping the water level would remain stable. The lurking predators awaited their reach of half-way through the swamp to approach. Soon fins and tails battered the water's surface like a preparatory ritual for the initiates' common grave.

Uhmi abandoned his minigun to the frenzied mangrove's guardians, hoping to delay their undertakers' inexorable progress. Nearly thirty swirls of various sizes agitated the death pool when the three doomed adventurers started swimming. The water trap had gone deeper and closed down. Fins converged towards Uhmi who, diminished by the hours and the weight of his weapons, slacked behind his companions. Death would meet them twenty yards from the shore, eighty yards from the rendezvous point, succumbing to their haste and the mangrove's superior tactics.

•••

In the maelstrom of Delinah's own delusions and inner monsters, joined the shared experiences of other people's filth and stupors. Orgies or massacres. Ego trips. Men, women, fused genders, displaying absurd manhood, some invincible leaders of armies on gruesome battlefields, or others surrounded by intoxicating harems and acquiescent groupies. Her suffocating mind tried to brush aside the disgusting invading visions.

•••

"How dared she muddle your initiation?" Anita was furious at the back of the transporter where Saldanha and the two rangers, near exhaustion, laid on the dirty floor trying to recover, still wet from what they believed was their last bathing. As the swamp creatures closed in, a squadron of drones surged from the nearby jungle's canopy and dashed towards the three survivors firing at will at the dark liquid threatening them.

Constelleanor had transgressed the code of initiation and come to rescue her crew. Moma was in no condition to argue with Anita, nor could he resent his ship's timely intervention. Why was the Conclave member so upset they had survived the mangrove?

Steve had joined them in the docking bay, bringing food rations and fresh water. He remained silent, exhausted eyes locked on a nauseous face. Saldanha found the energy to form the question burning Moma's discoloured lips:

"Are you disappointed we survived the swamp, Anita?"

"The things you faced had no interest in you," Anita immediately answered. "They were programmed to attack machines." Silence for effect. "You were supposed to undertake a near-death experience. This is what the initiation was for. Fear and death. Some of your drooids-guards were ordered to discreetly retreat to build up this atmosphere of panic. By not following the route we specifically instructed you to, you actually put yourselves in grave danger. Remove your suits, the dangerous creatures are not what you saw circling around you, they are a lot smaller."

•••

She laid alone on a couch in a comatose state hours after exiting her Traxx. Convinced of the heresy unfolding within the mad ark, she found the resolve to totter, aghast, to the main atrium. She passed large ocean tanks where free divers exercised or meditated, among artificial or natural reefs and fishes. She stayed away from the mantra rooms where the doors of perception were rammed into. She stopped to look at a digital art competition, forest of screens and pods agitated by a frenzy of lines, colours, symbols and feeds, merging or blowing up.

She overheard the ship featured the largest emitter in the galaxy, even possessed its own network of comm buoys, some broadcasting in X52, where the art collectives could follow the other mankind's whispers and homotheist propaganda. They all found their doppelganger irrationally preposterous and worth of endless parodies in its morbid self-cult. They felt powerful and safe in their impossible existence, observing from a tainted mirror Delinah's world of origin and—now she was even more convinced of it—humanity's only oasis of true salvation. She had found the real monster lurking at the end of one's journey, in the coffin of the dark forest of exo-bytes, in their eerie digital dungeon. It was time to watch them burn on the pyre.

Like Delinah, Xir plunged into the strange reservoir of electric impulses and neural commons. Xir visited the numerous visions like one did of an unfathomable art collection, most of them hermetic to xir comprehension. The violence riddled with pornography confused xir. Xir dismissed the psychanalytic mindscapes: headless nuns walking the aisles, melting clocks and blurred animal spirits. Xir code absolved xir from the most vivid, haunting emotions. Some malignant viruses tricked xir into cult altars and multiplying esoteric symbols, stole or corrupt some of xir most cherished data. Xir analysed the allegories and long forgotten mashed-up mythologies: carrousel of circling angels heading towards another dimension, Valkyries fighting hydras and sphynxes. Ludicrous pink high castle surrounded by lush meadows. Nazi semiotics among farting cows with multiple ruminating heads. Xir did not realise that many reproduced lost surrealist art, degenerated ideologies and psychedelic visions, documented centuries earlier and salvaged in some forgotten part of the human collective subconsciousness.

Many entities attempted to mate with xir presence. At the end of the absurd journey, attracted by familiar beats and algorithms, away from the tumult of non-sense and loud music, xir found Constelleanor in a bubble of disquieting visions and voices. Strident violins. Ominous percussions. Purple pumping heart levitating like a sun above a Klein blue-sand desert. A little girl crying, lonely, a Minotaur mask on, walking a rainbow tunnel toward a throne room. A pink lake witnessed the slaughter of the impenitent. The kelp forest of body parts and alloy chunks xir remembered from X52's escape. More scenes of slaughter in lugubrious galleys. D-Ark triumphant. An enigmatic blade-ship of unknown but enticing design.

Xir blinked at the sequences of mindscapes, lost in translation. Time suspended. A whirlpool of primordial matter forms fists of red, yellow magma that clash with hues of blues[3]. They all came swirling in the muscled ballet wrangling, crashing, rolling waves, squeezing and lacerating each other. They dissolved into a valley of profound indigo and turquoise, colours materialising into thick pigments, the blue Eden[4] dying all living and abstract creatures in a sense of appropriation, including xir fixed exoskeleton. Xir's sensors panicked. Xir escaped the nightmare into a final oceanic world, all anthracite heavy liquid and undisguisable shores, where floated luminescent balls of vivid colours, like miniature planets swimming in black lube oil.

•••

Anita inspected their flesh thoroughly with a strange oblong brass egg. Saldanha felt the curious and uncomfortable look of Steve over her naked body. She did not hide. He hadn't lived through the army like most, she thought, even less within a clone squadron. She had been conditioned to be a mass-product for the industrial purpose of war and expansion, a sacrificial lamb to the homotheism. Despite being from the lowest caste imaginable and a mere serial number, she stood, chin high, proud of her physical appearance and the desire she could sway in other human beings, female or male, clones, alphas or Earthans.

Uhmi and Saldanha were clean but the object beeped when passing over Moma's thigh.

"Hopefully this may serve you as a lesson, commander." The egg produced a sharp short blade which Anita plunged into Moma's leg.

Moma woke up hours later back in their boot camp in the middle of a storm and the Brazilian jungle. A small slug-like bug floated in a glass jar laid on his side table. He did not know Anita had saved his life. He had missed the scene of Constelleanor ignoring her reprimand and her fury at the minex's snubbing. Anita did not participate to their next trip out of the Amazonian forest.

•••

Fatia took them on an archaeological expedition in former western Europe where there were no more swamp creatures. It was a welcome break in their intensive training, two months after the near-death pond experience.

Zera regarded mono-competence and sterile overspecialisation as harmful to any being, especially an explorex and its crew, and detrimental to the undefined quest of theirs. Soldiers branched out to acquire skills other than killing, in the same gist of the trans-disciplinarian model they had witnessed on new Earth. Hands-on transversality[5] and lateral thinking. Steve made the reverse journey.

The crew was also involved in Constelleanor's modifications, as decision makers or manual labour. They sat exams on the newly installed systems and spent days repeating the same gestures and procedures under different gravity levels. Their survival depended on their perfect understanding of their ark, regardless of Constelleanor's excellent auto-diagnosis.

Their typical day cycle consisted of two eight-hour shifts covering different physical and intellectual activities during a one- to two-hour timeslot, and an eight-hour 'sleep rota', under strict monitoring by Earthan supervisors and Zera, one day break every fourteen days. Human societies, modern, postmodern and homotheist had devised various ploys to reduce sleep cycles and duration through entertainment, pills, genetics or duty. The Rius considered sleep and the hour preceding bedding as holy time. Zera hoped the sleep rituals would show the crew their benefits[6] and be maintained once onboard Constelleanor.

They landed on a hill, encircled by woodland, on the outskirts of what used to be a megalopolis.

"Why not using these large urban centres for your resettlement?" Steve wondered while they checked each other's packs and glanced at the view dominating the distant urban remnants and chain of decrepit spikes. The morning sun had vanished again and let a gloomy mist shroud the desolate cityscape.

"The early Earthan had already rebuilt their world outside of these before the end of the Riuman war and under the DAIs' aegis. We did send expeditions in this sort of suburban areas to explore and savage old equipment, even look for other survivors. We see them as sanctuaries of our past folly and misplaced grandeur."

"It does look like a cemetery of a past era."

"Many of these urban arenas have been badly battered by Earth's weather. This location for example is exposed to flash floods and winter hurricanes." Long pause. "These were not great places to live in, anyway."

Steve argued. "Yet they seemed popular."

"And they were part of the overall problem really," Fatia continued. "Overstretched urban monsters, dependent on others to survive, too greedy to fail, too big to provide efficiency and adequate public services, just a pale illusion of power and importance."

Five members of the Adriatic outpost they had visited a few months before had joined them on the expedition, as well as their usual armed escort. Fatia had allowed Constelleanor to deploy her own UAVs—she liked to call them her bees—despite the incident in the forbidden lands. Xir and Delinah preferred their jungle headquarters, as did Saldanha, to oversee the installation of the magsail. Steve had no particular interest in cultural adventures but needed a break away from outside interest in his youth's work. He was allowed a squadron of four armed drooids under his control pad. They followed Fatia and the five improvised archaeologists down the hill overlooking the ghost city that Nature and time had reconquered as its own.

"A lot of pre-Riuman war history has been lost. It was no longer a priority for your kind, who became obsessed with its future." Silence. "We believe our common future rests on who understands the story of our past." Constelleanor concurred with Fatia's words.

"You are speaking like Anita," Moma remarked.

"I know. Like her, I think your model of society is bound to fail. Once again. This is why I insisted for you to come here and see for yourself. Your future is just another rehearsal of our past." Silence. "Sorry I lost you."

"You did." Moma smiled. "At least no re-engineered creatures here, right?"

Fatia laughed. "No. You must be disappointed." Smiles. "But caution is required even on these small expeditions. I am glad we have some backup." She turned toward the escorting troobers. "You never know. There has been a cascade of failure in the satellite cover. Most of the DAI resources have been allocated to the coming conflict with your kind and, on Earth, to the Constelleanor project, thanks to Zera's influence over the motherships. We have not received any recent satellite feeds to confirm this location is cleared of any inconvenient encounters. I see you took precautions too, commander."

"Yes, we did. We are still recovering from our excursion in the initiatory mangrove. You are also wearing a weapon."

"I do." She changed subject. "These archaeological missions are our luxury. We have been collecting artefacts and clues of our common past for more than a century. With the weather unpredictability, the size of our settlements and our way of life, we can only go on a treasure hunt three to four times a year." She paused, sad. "The MAIs have no interest in the human past, only a consuming fascination for Nature, so the biology or oceanography studies receive a lot more support from them than archaeology or arts." Slight smile. "We have so much left to discover."

"What is it we are looking for?" Uhmi ventured, curious.

"This is part of the fun, we don't know. We have done a few recons in this place in the past twenty years but never had the chance to mount a proper recovery mission."

"We saw quite a few… objects on the island. Are they your discoveries?" Steve queried.

"Yes, we did unearth most of these over the years. We share our findings with the other communities and try to rotate the collections. The Europa sector is very rich in terms of cultural sites to investigate."

"I understand why the MAIs have no interest in them," Steve responded acidly. Fatia was about to retaliate but the five accompanying archaeologists had stopped the column and one addressed her in a language Constelleanor's crew did not understand.

"Everything ok?" Steve asked, worried.

"Yes, they propose we split the groups to explore more, a storm is forming and may shorten our mission. Without satellite backup, it is delicate to follow or predict its progression."

The expeditionary force turned into three smaller groups. Fatia stayed with Moma, one-guide and four troobers. Steve and Uhmi followed their respective duo of archaeologists and escort of four drooids. Moma smiled. Fatia had been a more pleasant and amenable hostess than Anita.

"Do you often go on this sort of mission, Fatia?"

"Once a year, at least, they are my favourite," she said followed by a long silence, eventually broken by Moma.

"Anita seems quite hostile to us."

"But you like her, don't you, commander?" Fatia smiled. "She has her reserve about your ship, I think, and she does not share Zera's enthusiasm about your quest. She fears war is upon us and we are not prepared on Earth. Diverting all available personnel and resources to Constelleanor, at this critical moment, does not make sense to her."

"It should take our troops time to get to here. MAI defences are infamous among human military strategists."

"'Our troops'?"

"My bad, still relearning it all." Awkward silence. "Any news from Rezzo? He has been quite… elusive."

"Not that I know of. He has been through a lot."

"We all have." Awkward silence again.

"You knew Saldanha from before?" Fatia asked.

"Yes."

She smiled. "Any chance you can share a bit more?"

"Sure. My crew was delivering food and medical supplies to a clone rebel group. Saldanha had somehow managed to defect to join them. She had been trained to integrate one of those expandable mechanics crews that fleet command sent on dangerous assignments: ship recovery on the brink of fusion reactor implosion, non-responding orbital stations, hostile worlds. You can picture the kind of missions."

"I see. It explains her bio-readings in the cat-4 forbidden area, she did not seem unaccustomed to the situation."

"I bet she saw worse than we even did as rangers." Brooding silence. "So back to the story, we arrive for the delivery and payment. It's an abandoned dockyard in a large orbital shipyard. Business as usual." Pause. "They are here to repair a few ships and buy equipment for their next campaign of 'liberation'. Space marines, enforcers and bounty hunters have been tipped off and attack. We lost five of my crew in the ensuing crossfire, but we manage to exfiltrate Saldanha and a few clone survivors."

"On X52 it was her turn to pay back her debt to you?"

"Yes." Silence. Moma rectified. "But I got her out again."

"Really?"

"Well, it is a bit complicated, it was sort of my fault she got trapped on X52, and was unable to re-join clone militias." Silence.

"How do you tell a clone from a…"

"An alpha? Marks on the neck, officers' and enforcers' wristpads detect their genic markers as well."

"Enforcers?"

"They are special units in charge of tracking down rogue clone batches." Fatia frowned at the term, displeased. Moma did not realise.

"She told me something in their behaviour could betray them too."

"Did she? Yes, with enough experience, you can tell you are dealing with a clone, their mental conditioning goes very deep. You can perceive small signs, eye lowering, more submissive posture. There are also specific phrases that trigger in-built reactions."

"That is awful. Does Saldanha show any of the typical signs?"

"I don't know. I think she learnt to recondition herself. As for the backdoor keywords, I have never been a fan of using those even with my troops. And I don't think I want to try on her." He attempted a smile.

They had crossed a small stream and, after a two-hour trek through abandoned urban vestiges pervaded by outgrown vegetation, collapsing under the test of time and the duress of the elements, reached a larger river. They had surprised a few fearful deer. Fatia and the archaeologist had searched a dozen of large derelict buildings. Their wandering, on the way back from the bland river, brought them to a large piazza where a stone column had fallen, its twenty-feet half left bare and standing to threaten the grey sky.

Roots had chiselled the concrete slabs through which flowers and high grass had flourished. Out of habit Moma stroked the grip of his two mascot pistols and relished the weight of the long-range rifle across his back. He considered the rooftop of one of the ruins circling the plaza while the rest of his team investigated a three-storey, wide building opposite. Its half-collapsed cupola dominated its pedimented entrance and the main square, despite a lower height than its surrounding neighbours.

Moma needed height to try his new toy and shake off the unpleasant sensation they had been watched since the riverbanks. He climbed the shaky stone stairs of a nearby ruin, lay down on a platform where the original ceiling had collapsed and turned the former balcony into an impromptu roof terrace invaded by wildflowers and animal faeces. He could distinguish through the dewing mist a handful of taller spires towering above the bleak urban-scape of an abandoned glory. Many of the highest edifices had foundered since onto their lower levels.

He unwrapped the oblong automatic rifle crafted by human and robots in a Martian armoury. He switched on the long-range dual visor and flicked through the various available modes. It was by far the best weapon he had ever handled in his long combat experience. Peering through the interweaving of rumbles and leaves, the computer assistant signalled suspicious shapes. Moma's heart raced until he realised he had Steve in his line of fire. For a second, he considered the consequences of shooting the creator of Constelleanor.

A muffed whir instinctively made him reached his thigh pistol and rolled on his back to face what was lurking behind him. He swore at the rising drone—one of his ship's bees—having nearly fired on it as a precautionary welcome. Cheeky, Constelleanor. He turned over onto his telescopic binocular sight, lowered his cardiac rhythm and resumed his observation.

Something was still in his aiming field, concealed behind the remnants of a wall. It was not Steve, nor any of their fellow archaeologists, nor one of their escort. He resisted the urge to shoot for an easy kill. He cursed Steve for not having switched his earcom on—rookie mistake. He moved his target field to the main square looking for the four guarding troobers. They had abandoned their positions.

He tried to find the uninvited guests again, in vain. Constelleanor was not contactable, going through major tests, nor were her bees. Uhmi did not answer. Concern tensed Moma's muscles and optic nerve, whilst the quandary agitated his racing mind. He occupied the best spot to help his companions out and still felt too far to warn them or intervene.

Uhmi finally responded, breathing heavily. Instead of confirming Moma's fears, a building floor had collapsed under their weight and they had been trapped for long minutes. They were twenty minutes away from the plaza Moma overlooked and that Steve's group had just reached. No signs of the earlier shadows from his improvised watchtower.

Moma ordered Uhmi to join them at once for a regroup and rushed downstairs to check on Steve. He had seen no one and noticed nothing worth of concern. Fatia's luminous face darkened at Moma's recount, she had found exceptional artefacts inside the wide building and needed a couple of days, at least, to study and start the transfer of their precious discoveries into the vault of their shuttle. The absence of the one of the accompanying drooid prompted their departure back to the Adriatic island and then to the Amazonian jungle. Fatia's earlier smile had faded.

Chapter's endnotes

[1] Inspired by K van Dam.

[2] [minigun] a six-barrel, air-cooled, electrically fired Gatling-style rotary cannon.

[3] [vision] See painting of Thai artist P Janthakhaisorn, *Desire 2006.*

[4] [Eden] thinking of a 3D representation of M Lo Giudice's *Eden Turquoise.*

[5] [transversality] Adapted from the notion in mathematics on how spaces can intersect, here how inter-disciplinary should prevail and the need for different subjects and domains of knowledge to willingly cross their respective paths to benefit from each other.

[6] [sleep] See Walker, M. (2018) *Why We Sleep: The New Science of Sleep and Dreams.* Penguin.

I see this curious procession encircling a central priest. The night has extinguished the exoplanet's orange and fauvist palette. A sinister, unnatural vibe binds all the participants except the lone figure in the central stage, surrounded by old tan temples. I descend upon them, piercing through the low cloud cover and smell of wet rot, with my battle-cry.

This is nowhere in my files, logs or data. I have checked and rechecked, but now it is in my memories, the ones that don't come with an automatic reference number, just some visual mnemonic path. Is it an after-thought from the trance? A side-effect or contamination from the Creuzrog*? Am I even supposed to dream? Steve, Zera, what are you not telling me?*

Comes another unregistered vision, squid ink flavoured, infused with Xir's quirky melodies, picking from the controlled randomness of #Pade's Faust and the most sinister compositions of #Penderecki. They all circle around the out-of-focus black spot, floating in a cream-white background, unless it is a dull light. Is that a reversed eclipse? Is that a sign? Is that suprematist? Am I even supposed to have imagination or be inspired, unless they are both the same things?

I won't ask Xir to consider other musical styles, maybe I shouldn't have tapped into his enormous acoustic resources without his full permission, like I did for Hector's codinent and Rezzo's psystem but, hey, I—and I speak on behalf of all the entities inside me—am just too curious. We played my admiral's antic collection a million times, no hidden code was uncovered, but a weird harmony that keeps resonating within me, within us. After transfixing through my cores, oblivious of the priorities and system order, the euphony has brought its own form of chaos and become an extension of my electric heartbeat.

L2.12 Earthan Epitaph

"It will always be more convenient to satisfy one's vices than one's needs."

— *G Bernanos*

Nine months had passed since Constelleanor and her crew had arrived on Earth. Time and efforts started showing their effects. Moma had lost weight and felt younger. All, even Steve, grew appreciative of a way of life so alien to theirs, recognisant of values so eerily remote to their own humanity, as if humanness had branched out and developed into two diametrically opposite visions, individuals and civilisation.

Uhmi and Saldanha, were particularly sensitive to the openness of Earthan society, outcast in their own world, one for his blue colour skin and the other for being deemed a mere, servile copy. Humans seemed to always struggle with differences, focusing on what differentiated them from each other rather than celebrating what they had in common. The demographics of war and genetic manipulations had mingled with genes and melanin. The chromatic spectrum shifted. Space expansion introduced new skin colours too, through mere accidents or inter-species love stories bound to tragic fates.

Delinah had been back and forth to the *Creuzrog* which had settled around Earth for several months. Her conspiring about Constelleanor had subsided.

It was a time of mild celebration for her crew. Earlier in the day, the technical crews and the *Creuzrog* had thrown a giant birthday party to Constelleanor.

She inadvertently triggered the fireworks planned for later. Rezzo had finally come back from his Asian retreat. Saldanha's rancour had dwindled with time as her past lost its grips over her present. Constelleanor's first test flight was scheduled in the coming weeks and most had completed the first phase of training Zera required as bare minimum. Furniture had been placed back in the hangar around the ship for the occasion, in a slight reminder of their arrival and group therapy under the Conclave's aegis. Closed loop or new beginning?

"I heard you spent quite a bit of time on the *Creuzrog*, Delinah?" Rezzo asked.

"Not as much as you did on your mysterious retreat, Rezzo." she deflected.

"How did you find it out there?" he carried on.

"At first, I couldn't stand it. With my background, it was a place of true evil. I then went onto my Traxx and… well I am still not sure what to think of it." Silence.

"Understandable." He continued, "I see it as a bold attempt to emulate the Riu psystem."

"But in a very disruptive, archaic and chaotic sort of way," Constelleanor corrected.

"How would you know that, Cee?" Delinah asked, mischievously.

Moma, Uhmi and Fatia joined the group.

"Delinah, you said you had something for us," Fatia said. She greeted them, enjoying the double meaning.

"I did. Cee have you ever watched sanko?" she said. Xir was clueless.

"Rather indirectly." The digis she thought long deleted passed through her systems, her revulsion of the violence often jammed their signals. "The crews liked sanko and speedball." Saldanha thought of her dead boyfriend, a distant memory already, who followed speedball.

"I bet they did," Delinah replied, thinking of her lost crew.

Constelleanor had researched why this sort of crude entertainment was so popular among the homonkeys. Due to the level of violence experienced by men and women in their compulsory enrolment—ironically the crime rate in most human polities was low—most sport programs involved mutilations and injuries of some sort. Death of players and referees were frequent in speedball, which opposed two teams, or more, of seven sentient gladiators. The ruthless version of ancient Australian football was doped with mixed martial arts, street-fighting and drugs of all kinds—performance, recovery, senses or rage enhancement. She did not think at the time of these as being among the Beast's favourite instruments of control.

Sanko favoured gruesome wounds as part of the show—decapitation was forbidden but could happen by accident. Delinah keyed a quick sequence of characters on her pad and projected a videofeed on the surrounding and tarmac-screens. Fourteen participants in light armour ran and fought on an elliptic oval field. Steve squinted, confused by the profusion of shapes and micro-events.

"Oh dear." Uhmi gasped. Moma laughed.

Steve still confused looked at his comrades for explanations. "Is that… you, Uhmi?" Anita had just joined them.

Uhmi knocked down one of his opponents and took a small reinforced ball away from him. But the cheers of the crowd and commentators were directed elsewhere. The twelve-feet high and forty-five wide arena started turning on its sixty-feet long horizontal axis.

To add even more confusion to the already chaotic game, the moving oval playground was scattered with injury-inflicting surprises. A small anti-personnel mine—powerful enough to harm and mutilate but not to kill—had already injured a player. Xir glimpsed two poisonous snakes. Genetically engineered wild beasts were introduced for the best games. Anything that could bite, sting, maim and make the audience jubilant was considered and added by the game-masters.

Two crocodiles and a rhinoceros had made their entrance, one had already sectioned a participant's calf.

"What is this?" Fatia and Anita both muttered, appalled.

"Crocodiles," Xir replied.

"No kidding, Xir."

"I am not," Xir confirmed.

"I am not sure I want to know what happens next to Uhmi," Constelleanor ventured, sounding worried. Saldanha and Steve were already hooked and Xir fascinated by the tactical implications of the wild newcomers. Xir downloaded the full rules and guide of the best games ever played.

While eluding the various traps, the fourteen players coveted two spherical handballs that could be thrown by any body part in small round digital goals that randomly moved between the corners of each side, scoring a twenty-point 'ball-in'. Magnetic boots and gloves allowed players higher leaps and smoother landings on the bespoke surface.

The rhino took aim at Uhmi and charged. Fatia gasped. The former ranger jumped and grabbed a passing drone. This time the cheers of the public were for him.

Four human-controlled drones canvassed the ovoid volume, each on a random flight path, and were strong enough to carry up to two players. They were commonly used to ball-in or elude the surprises introduced by the game-masters, like Uhmi did.

"Nice move, Uhmi," Moma said, appreciative.

"I know," he replied in false arrogance.

The drones sometimes exploded or collided, to the public relish, and would be replaced. Uhmi's blew up, shot down by one of the hardballs threw by an opponent. Saldanha and Delinah laughed. Steve and Fatia covered their mouths.

No pitch referee interfered, fouls were sanctioned by remote electrocution that paralysed the offending player for around fifteen seconds and left one vulnerable to the multiple threats of the game, creatures or opponent. Drone's strikes caused by players were authorised and provided bonus points.

Screams redoubled as Uhmi hit the floor in front of a crocodile.

"The death initiation must have been business as usual for you," Anita wondered.

"I can't believe people would watch, even less play that sort of game. Look at all the blood. I am surprised they don't try to kill the crocodiles."

"You are not allowed to hurt the animals, not even the big bugs," Uhmi explained to the neophytes.

"Not that you could do much harm to a rhino with the hardball or shoulder pads."

A stud woman, on Uhmi's side, incapacitated the player responsible for his fall and pushed him in-between Uhmi and the crocodile. The saurian's maw grabbed the player's upper thigh. The crowd and commentators rejoiced. Fatia lowered her eyes to the square pastry topped with vegetables and fruits they nibbled on. She had lost her appetite.

She took a sip from a spicy drink produced by the *Creuzrog*. Delinah had brought a crate of cubic omnimium recipients, which they pierced and drank the spailor way, through a steel-straw. Moma and Uhmi were already half-way through their second squared can, rivetted on the screens. They had missed their kind's entertainment programs.

"How come your body is still in one piece?" Fatia ventured.

"Luck and good surgeons," Moma replied.

"Yes, I spent most of my days before and after the games in med-bay, intubated and on multiple drips," Uhmi conceded.

"Were you on an analgesic during the games?"

"Nope, it would not have looked real enough for the public. We had access to special facilities so the recovery from amputation, poison and ligament injuries was quick, but the accelerated re-education protocols, regardless of the painkillers, could be atrocious."

"That's why you stop after a couple of seasons, no?" Moma checked.

"Yes, never liked needles since, you know."

Moma understood the allusion. "Yes"

"Since what?" Saldanha asked, curious.

"A long story."

"Rezzo, did you have similar things?"

"Mmm I am afraid we did have a wide range of gruesome initiations and ritual. But none were turned into a broadcasted show like that. It looks more like a practice institutionalised among Auushers or Ikpebaraars."

"Never heard of these."

"Probably better that way."

One team could win on a 'knock-down'—the most prestigious victory—if all opposing players, including its seven substitutes, were incapacitated. Very precise conditions had been defined as to what incapacitation meant: electrocution or penalty, member maimed, loss of more than three litres of blood, immobility for more than thirty seconds, death. An extensive set of medical sensors warped the player's body to measure the level of incapacitation and allow a player's replacement or need of immediate medical attention.

"How did you find this game, Delinah?"

"Some guys on the *Creuzrog* are monomaniac about our entertainment programs."

"Yes, they boasted to have their own network of spy-relays within X52," Steve confirmed.

Delinah had spent most her time befriending the crew in charge of the comms within the HSC territories on the *Creuzrog*, soon covering for some of them, eager to resume their Traxxes, instead of scanning HSC feeds and signals.

"What is the tattoo you wear on your breastplate and arm," Constelleanor queried.

"A beluga." Constelleanor searched her database, reporting her results on a small side screen.

Uhmi could not refrain a sad smile. "Yes that sort of thing." Xir and the minex detected a change in Uhmi's bio-feed, xir had improved xir biometrics readings exploring the *Creuzrog* and its stoned passengers.

"I think we are owed your long story, Uhmi," Saldanha insisted.

Uhmi's dad was an HSC spailor sent, like many, young and unprepared, on a 'pacification' mission in a system that held vast mineral resources. Another sacrifice to the looting exo-monster, Constelleanor thought, now she started understanding the Beast in better ways. Since her sync with the *Creuzrog's* mad digital universe, she had pictured the structural iceberg and, beyond its visible physical manifestations, the complex roots and ramifications Ne developed into the human psystem. Hordes of lobotomised individuals flashed. She wondered again how much they differed from the kreapers seen in Rezzo's memories.

As Uhmi recounted his origins, Constelleanor simultaneously accessed thousands of digis. Human history hummed the same never-ending mantra, like Zera had explained, she brooded, indigenous species lived on the exact locations mining conglomerates had eyed upon. The locals considered these large swathes of red mountains and blue-pink jungle a sacred sanctuary for their people, culture and gods. She projected related feeds on the floor-screen. The hangar plunged into a different time and space. Uhmi winced.

To them, humans, despite their technological superiority were no gods, blasphemous petty thieves at best. Ignorant demons that transformed wonders into resources, she concurred despite being a minex herself. Until the occupation took an unexpected turn, as if the real gods had intervened. A third of the 'pacifying' contingent befriended the locals and embraced the enigmatic majesty of the holy sites. They took up the indigenous cause against the extraction forces they were supposed to blindly serve, clone or alphas.

The rise of the *Beluga*—named after the flagship sent to pacify resources-wonder-planet Ocun—divided opinions back in human federastrals despite the widespread allegiance to homotheism and its underlying imperialist view of the universe. The planet was too beautiful and reminiscent of Earth to be devoured once again by the blind appetite of the mining drillers.

Uhmi was a child of the rebellious Beluga and one of its rare survivors. Constelleanor had not managed to access his military record. Lucky circumstances and the slow tentative assimilation of other spacies and mixed-spacies individuals among human troops saved his life. His scarred body was a reminiscence of his tempestuous childhood and the morbid curiosity of the medical team dispatched with the military units to reassert complete control over Ocun. Uhmi took a short break. Everyone was listening. The Conclave had not been inquisitive about his past, as if it knew already. The storm thundered outside.

His parents died in the eradication of the mutineers and the enslavement of the local population, in the process unfolding what would haunt Uhmi his whole life: was he a traitor to his own undefined "race"?

Was he even supposed to still be alive? If so, was he a monster, or, like Constelleanor, one of those anomalies engendered by human folly or invisible forces at work?

"Did you go back?" Delinah asked curious.

"I did… two years ago."—He turned to Moma—"A few years after you left us," he said without reproach, "and after Hansard disappeared with his fleet."

Far from the mayhem of the overpopulated flying barracks and binge of holofeeds, drugs and industrious soundtracks, another chaos, diffuse and redoubtable, awaited Uhmi's resumed journey. He travelled back to planet Ocun, his home world, raped, mutilated, disfigured by the mining greed. Footages flooded the landing pad. There he experienced the emptying realisation that Moma weathered after Kewo.

He fell sick. An endemic bug nearly killed him, not without some irony, forcing his recovery on a medical orbiting station, where, in between successive treatments, brief respites and receding fevers, he holo-read and meditated in search of a new meaning and path. Moma and Delinah closed their eyes. He suspected he was being used again as a guinea pig by the medical staff, keen to study a rare survivor of the *Beluga* episode.

They extended his stay from the initial two-month rehabilitation to a thirteen-month full-hospitalisation. Delinah thought of the medical bay from the Traxx again. He did not resent the prolonged internment since he feared his come-back among private or HSC troops. His disillusionment had grown too deep. Moma reopened his eyes. The human crew bio-readings confused Xir. Constelleanor wondered whether they were going through another group therapy, under Rezzo's aegis.

Uhmi dug out his most recent memories. He was in the vicinity of X52, awaiting in anguish his next assignment on a narrow bunk bed, ignoring the tumult of the dormitory, the bets, the extasy of sex and pills, when Moma reached out to a dozen of his former comrades. Uhmi had served nearly six years under his command and did not hesitate long to abandon his spartan quarter to join him, at great personal risk, owing to a deeper, ontological connection that Kewo and Ocun had probably triggered. Moma smiled and grabbed Uhmi's shoulder affectionately. He had not counted on anyone of his former battalions to answer his impromptu call, most would have either succumbed to the forever war's appetite for lives or been sent far away on a new punitive expedition, unlikely to ever return to the HSC hives.

Uhmi's backstory resonated with Saldanha's own past. Constelleanor was observing her. The *Beluga* mutiny came at a time of yet another wave of clone rebellions and crackdowns, her systems established, which diverted public opinion from Ocun's planned ransack and called for the 'gauntlet without velvet' doctrine against this new form of interior terrorism. She let her thoughts project themselves onto the screens. These hitches to mankind's mortal engines[1], she broadcast motorised column of greasy metals shunning, pushed forward the already well-advanced and expanding field of research on mental conditioning. Research cruisers flashed, shadows in a magnetic storm, purple lightnings in clouds of ionised particles. Ensuring an effective control over behaviours and subdued mass-obedience, far away from human territories. The battle of colourful magmas Xir witnessed on the *Creuzrog* inundated the hangar. Constelleanor wondered whether this was the next move of the Beast. She replaced her projected images in a hurry with peaceful cascades and streams.

Saldanha belonged to the first generations of clones subjected to this control of a new kind. She could still hear, hidden from her own mind, the suggestions and in-built sub-conscious backdoors, installed by the psychoanalysts. The mental keys could surge unhindered during her sleep, like a planned brain disorder, a concealed code of mental programming that had driven some of her comrades and units to mass-murders or mass-suicides. She kept her past to herself, Uhmi's story had opened enough unwanted doors in her memories.

Delinah's zeal of the last few months shuddered. The casual talk, light banter and past sharing unveiled their common denominator, all outcasts from the same world and inane paradigm. She had, like many before her, focused on their differences and points of friction to justify her cause and legitimate her purpose. The rangers' betrayal of their oaths. Saldanha's loose allegiance. Steve's capital sins. Xir's mere existence. Rezzo's survival. Constelleanor's heresy. She had obsessed over the wickedness of the *Creuzrog*. But it was too late for doubts and second thoughts. She changed subject.

"Cee, what did you watch then?" she asked, returning to the original conversation and a lighter atmosphere.

"Never been into speedball or sanko. Never understood the human craving for classic car races either. I was more into FleetBox."

"Haaa!" (Moma, Saldanha and Xir were ecstatic.) "Now we are talking."

Delinah, Fatia, Anita, Uhmi and Steve grimaced. "The rest of our audience seems less enthusiastic," Rezzo remarked, amused by the mixed views.

Half of the crew binge-watched hours-long FleetBoxing programs, a real-time, full-scale, life-size albeit fictive space naval battle-shows that opposed, within or across federastrals, the best units, pilots, escadrilles or armadas. Constelleanor projected famous confrontations across the hangar. Astute tactics, high-octane jousts between the jewel units of existing fleets, prototype hunting, beguiled millions of viewers like them, all well-versed in military aeronautics. All filled their boredom onboard their own ships and barracks and created the perfect warmongering emulation among all classes of ages, ranks and professions. They cheered at a bold manoeuvre. Moma and Saldanha felt suddenly closer to the two MAIs on their crew.

More than the popular pods, antiquated automobiles and ship races, that enriched bookies, these tag-battles offered the ideal genre of mass entertainment and the cynosure for the perpetuation and control of a spartan society. The supreme fulfilment of "man's almost infinite appetite for distractions"[2]; the dreamt subversion for the collective mind's subliminal manipulation. An aspect of the Beast that still eluded Constelleanor's grid analysis.

•••

Moma closed his fist to help him up off the training matt, a seventeen-year old woman trained by Anita had just neutralised him in single close-combat. Once more. Uhmi, Steve and Saldanha swung between hilarity and shock. Another week had passed with the entire crew all stationed in their Amazonian compound.

Rezzo's return among the crew helped some members out of their chrysalis of self-deprecating self-doubt and attenuated their initial burgeoning insecurities. He also facilitated the re-establishment of communication channels that had surprisingly faded between the crew and their ship, all imprisoned in a citadel of fear, self-engrossment and prejudices. Her companions' rallying support raised in turn Constelleanor's spirits and dissipated some of her dubiety about the meaning and future of their quest.

Rezzo had nearly lost his mind and was still recovering. The crew was shifting towards the realm of an improvised kinship and aided the reconstruction of his own psychic castle, thick walls, hardened by his kind's xenocide, replaced by airy windows, open skylights and sliding doors; finding unexpected soul companions to share his mighty burden.

Steve's newly acquired fluency in DAI codes did not abate his misgivings concerning Eleanor. He observed Delinah's change of mind towards him and his creation. His distrust after Bianca's betrayal, lingering, prevailed. He had visited the *Creuzrog* too, worried they might uncover the truth about Constelleanor.

His Traxx brought him towards what his drugged or deranged mind imagined was his disquieting visions, though it was Constelleanor's. Crying little girl. Agitation of white latex suits. Oversized anthracite goggles looking over him. Burning-nostrils detergents. Plastic gloves greasy of blood and fluid preserve. Flows of secretions, bubbles, cohorts of organs in containers, in dimmed turquoise, light green and pink. Screaming fear. Steve's pair accompanying his novice descent into the shamanic-like journey and psychedelic wonderland nearly interrupted the experience due to Steve's soaring arterial pressure.

The Traxx and digi-art collectives had overwhelmed him. He had envisioned communion with the digital minds all his life, not fusion, transmigration or transplantation. He doubted the mad ark could have converted Delinah to the DAIs or the Earthan cause in any case.

He was more amenable to Saldanha's change of heart and efforts to reconfigure the miner into a safer, better spaceship. Eleanor, or what he believed she had become, deserved that much. Yet he had repeatedly dismissed Saldanha's questions about the minex's origins.

Steve suspected that Zera and his team of engineers knew more about her true nature than they disclosed to him. In his own defence, he had no clear idea how the merging of diverse research fields had worked and currently operated. Nor could he explain what was ongoing in the neural wetware haunting the black pool. His Earthan training surpassed the best of Lijee research but he doubted DAIs and their human minions had any of the knowledge and technology of Tchoukouiov and Khan-Hi's research teams. In some bursts of hope or disarray, he imagined Zera and his followers as clueless as he was.

He sometimes wondered whether Xir had not increasingly been infected and transformed by Constelleanor. Was he himself even immune to her? His fate and the rest of the crew's depended upon her even more since the Conclave's decision.

•••

Unconcerned by the crew's reunion or Steve's misgivings, the Beast's fightback looms through the blue-grey clouds assaulting the jungle-compound. Ne can always count on improvised agents of all sorts to do Nir biding.

Ne is reasserting control over the sequence of events and narration. Tenses blurred, time(s) merged or molested. Arcs broken down, hero's journey shattered, hackneyed narrative schemes, escape plans and standard storytelling disrupted. A usurping epitaph, brandishing a foregone twist. A conclusion splash and metafiction crash landing. Unless a computer program generated the words themselves in a more evolved form of a dispirited automatic writing or streams of artificial consciousness. The Beast tells, never shows.

Béla Bartók's disquieting melopœia and musical algorithm #Adagio// begins, invading Constelleanor's freshly installed control room. Calm and peace often are a momentary pretext for an incoming fight and gloom. In a slight reminder of X52's clandestine hangar crowded by techs and ships, the large warehouse, hosting Constelleanor, a few supply ships and heavy shipyard equipment, is stormed at dawn by three hundred and fifty-eight of mankind's best or worst in a bold surprise attack. War has finally reached Earth (again).

The Beast has finally caught up with Constelleanor and her story.

•••

Cunning, they had landed under the cover of trade and supply ships for the last three months, mostly in the Aburra valley, where one jungle outpost had been seized, hostages forced to keep outsiders and visitors at bay and its small spaceport used as a platform to reinforce their forces. Earth had not been under attack since the Riu fall, but MAIs, like mankind, were not impervious to blind spots and mistakes.

She dismissed the buzzing computer pits and the analysts' agitation under her feet to focus on the dots of the holo-scape. They dissolved in turn as her blurring gaze pierced through the projected map and her troops' positions, into the viewport and distant constellation. The shuttle approaching the vertical blade-shaped black monolith distracted her reverie. One member of her triumvir was back.

The whole operation bore the audacious mark of an entity entrusted the days following Jared's assassination with hunting down the 'miner', *Blacksun*[3]. If their name had weathered the storms of time unchanged, their size, width and sheer depth of their organisation, capabilities and resources had significantly expanded. Some regarded them as the new Templars. Templars of Doom. According to *Hector58*'s archives, a wicked organisation that thrived off secrets, machinations and power mongering. They had flourished under the homotheist credo of Homo spaciens.

Unlike the rest of mankind, they had kept track of the past, ancient manuscripts and old rituals, learnt from it and from their illustrious ancestors, the inspiring Templars, knights-turned-holy-bankers, who were, over a night of 1307, wiped out by powerful rivals they had overshadowed, the King of France and the Pope of Rome. No wonder, then, secrecy had bedevilled these Templars of a new kind, who undertook to keep a low profile and conceal, from all, the extent of their operations and immense accumulated wealth.

The ship her triumvir directed with an autocratic flair belittled the *Creuzrog* and posed an existential threat to even *Hector58*. The several storey-high ovoid control room exceeded the ostentation of Jared's ark. Lavish sculptures competed for attention with dubious war-like allegories and unknown alien creatures floating in sealed tanks and grim syrupy liquid, in a complete lack of harmony and taste. She relished the view of the voluptuous amazon resting her heavy rifle negligently on her shoulder, boots firmly crushing the carcass of a mi-robotic, mi-sentient chimera. The décor was meant to match her triumvir's calibre and the exceptional combat capabilities of their flagship.

Unknown to Constelleanor's databases, Blacksun had strengthened both their independence and influence within the military apparatus through the Bleak Age and Riuman wars, operating nowadays as their sole master, like their ancestors, through a myriad of indirect space corporations, sects, charities, shell companies and paramilitary organisations. "Long distance control through numerous agents favoured the enterprises of those who commanded money and were capable of exercising a ruthless, semi-military control over men"[4]. Condottieri. Masters of war, masters of the universe?

Unlike the rest of mankind, they sought something beyond materialism and comprehension, narcissist grandeur aside. They had explored further than anyone else, in search of powerful artefacts that could reinforce their grip over humankind's state of affairs. No surprise again then, that, from their perspective, D-Ark embodied all but a nemesis, rather the blessing of an unmissable opportunity for self-fulfilment, and the next cycle in their dialectics of enlightenment.

Good and evil, order and chaos were just two different faces of the same medal, a mere issue of exegesis left to the judgment of their triumvirs. Unknown to the DAI spies, however, Blacksun believed the recent chain of these enthralling events had nothing of random and belonged to a much larger cycle of the universe's exchequer, a ruthless game of formidable forces they intended to join as a dignified knight, instead of an impious pawn like the others.

She snapped back at a com-tech, frustrated by the hours-long delay from Earth and their incapacity to establish a clean holofeed. She kept lurking back at the adorned lift door, wondering why her triumvir was taking so long to pass security clearance. Meanwhile other triumvirs like hers were working the cogs of the human machine and the bruised egos of its military apparatuses.

Unknown to Constelleanor, Blacksun had infiltrated MAIs territories for decades, at hefty costs, anticipating the time to reconquer humanity's cradle would come. They had been fooled too by the Riu subterfuge regarding the DAIs' demise and the hidden existence of another humankind, which would have captivated their interest, should they have dispatched their brainpower instead of muscles and weaponry.

They learnt on Shaqil, that D-Ark had not been engendered by MAIs. Nonetheless, Blacksun left mankind's military powers' pragmatic scapegoatism come to its own conclusion.

•••

The youngest attendee wore a chiselled dark suit of sober taste. A thin line of bright blue lightened up his outfit where the other austere, older participants had crowded their opulent garment with medals, titles and distinctions. He did not sit, shoulder against the window frame, talking in casual arrogance and short, slow, articulated streams of sentences, his glance moving from the panoramic view of X52 to his agitated and interrupting audience.

To avoid wasting their precious resources in the coming fierce conflict against DAIs, the Blacksun representative suggested to the same authorities, all gathered at the top of X52's tallest urban spire, to be tasked with an apparently less attractive mission, the miner's hunt, that would allow them to track down their real prime objective: the darknought.

Their preference for a secondary objective both surprised and pleased the military chiefs of staffs, well-aware of the threatening hydra Blacksun represented, despite their absolute secrecy, but unable to take any decisive action against a masked, cross-faction, proteiform ally, rival and foe. The young attaché could read the fury under the tight lips and rigid shoulders of his interlocutors. He relished their repressed hostility and missed their coming retaliation.

The agreement in principle came with a condition, one he and Blacksun abhorred, but could not oppose, in order not to alert further the already suspicious high officers. They would be joined by a small, and doubtfully secret, task force made of pyrates, mercenaries and criminals of all trades, freshly hired or released on parole, to support the war effort and, primarily, to find the fugitive mining vessel and its crew. It was the turn of the officers to relish the lower protruded lip and sulky pout of Blacksun's smug envoy.

Losing track of D-Ark in Shaqil infuriated Blacksun's command. The miner was their only clue left, assuming it did not stay with his travel companion nor did it succumb to MAI security forces. Chances of the miner's survival were estimated slim, at best. If still alive, they had expected its capture and transfer to one of Jupiter's orbital stations, where DAI counter espionage's best units were stationed.

None of their human or semi-artificial moles there could provide them with any viable information. Not that they paid much attention to their reports, riddled with confused insanity and deranged claims about humans working and living within the machines. They suspected the feeds and transmissions were tempered by DAI propaganda. They also suspected secret research activities took place on Earth.

Their analysts noticed, via the rare probes that had survived DAI's surveillance and Earth's fierce weather, an abnormally large and recent traffic to an unknown location deep inside the thick jungle of former Brazil, battered by tropical storms. Their suspicions materialised with an unprecedented source, when they intercepted troubling messages, encrypted using astute military codes and sent from HSC's own backyard that confirmed the possible location of the hunted minex.

At first, keying her pad, she had mocked the chief analyst and his team for the findings, deriding the decades of non-sense intel produced by their spy-units stationed in the solar system to never come back. The clean signal detected in the vicinities of spawning X52 had troubled her nonetheless. Her triumvir member exited the lift as she recalled her hesitations at the time. He had convinced her to follow the lead closer. She welcomed him with a light hand gesture on her chest.

Blacksun dismissed the reports as fake or a blatant trap, at least in front of the HSC authorities. They opted for direct human intelligence and, as desperate as they were obsessed, risked exposing their own precious infiltration units, deep into enemy territories. Six months after Constelleanor's arrival, Blacksun's operatives confirmed they had identified a Riu matching an HSC top secret file—which a Blacksun member, granted with high security clearance, had accessed and shared—in an old temple erected in former Cambodia's primary forest. They also identified a former ranger escaped from the same prison shuttle as the Riu in a different part of the blue planet. All locations linked up to the Amazonian jungle and corroborated the large quantity of intel sent for months by the mysterious spy and ally to their cause.

She skimmed through the transcripts and analysis again, holograms of the leaked compound plans, identification of opposing forces, all showed the trained eye and methods of a military intel officer. None of her com-techs could explain how the spy had managed to transmit in HSC's space from a location in the solar system. She did not care about the technicalities as long as they had reliable information from the inside. Yet, she was uneasy. The quantity of the intel provided had decreased significantly in the last weeks. And she disliked that there were only two of them to decide over such a crucial operation. Wasn't it the point of the Blacksun's triumvir and organisation: to be three outstanding officers to come to a decision?

Meanwhile Blacksun's young envoy seconded by three other representatives stirred up the outrage caused by Jared's brutal demise to precipitate the creation of the Avenge Jared Fleet and its brutal incursion into DAI territories. Beyond the emotional shockwave they had astutely surfed on, Blacksun had established a remarkable distance from its own kind. They had perceived the Mega-Machine emerging, magnified by the infinite prospects and human inflated collective ego. Instead of the Beast, they referred to Nem as the Prime Civilisation or Supreme Scheme.

Blacksun had learnt too how easily, like the Beast, it could manipulate the cognitive biases that enabled certain minds to hold conflicting or absurd ideas with no discomfort or switch narratives to always be consistently right and never held accountable. The rare cosmic phenomenon was a common feature in some sentients, especially among those having a high opinion of themselves. And there were many haunting the human elite. Blacksun was not immune either to the mental pandemic.

•••

Chapter's endnotes

[1] [mortal engines] Reference to Philip Reeve's book.

[2] [quote] A de Tocqueville.

[3] [Blacksun] Side-reference to Marlan, S. (2008) *The Black Sun: The Alchemy and Art of Darkness*. Texas A&M University Press.

[4] [quote] L Mumford, ibid.

The elite soldiers stormed her compound at dawn, facing meagre resistance inside the main hangar where the minex stood. Visual inspection had just confirmed the ship to be the one that had fled on D-Ark, when Constelleanor exploded, killing fifty of Blacksun's operatives in her blast and injuring another hundred.

•••

The explosion toppled her world into complete obscurity. She gasped in her own way but stayed calm. To the untrained or profane eye lurking through the restrictive embrasures of their iron capsules, the ebony space expanded the xenocide of colours of their lived world. The grey dull interiors. The tepid docking bays in constant need of urgent renovation. A ghastly conformity to an implicit code that banished colours, and with them, identities and their expressions. She wondered and remembered the visiting visions, months ago, with Zera.

Nonetheless, with reverent patience, the desolate starscape became soon lightened by a chromatic uprising from remote galaxies or distant cepheids. She knew and held onto the hues. On occasions, the welcome proximity of suns irradiated mystic indigo or purple, fierce orange—like in the solar system—,, cold red or unsettling blues and greens. Cosmic auroras distorted the spectrum of light like an astute etheric fauvist. Mesospheric perturbations, reddish-orange or greenish-blue spectres, haunted many upper atmospheres, whose exploration larger ships, size enlarging cowardness, preferred to leave to frailer shuttles.

She remembered the Stygian black of D-Ark but also how the full spectrum of colours tapped into her emotions and soundtracks: wonder or disquiet, alternating between the joyful contemplation of #Deodato' Zarathustra and the foreboding oppression of #Penderecki's Kosmogonia.

Black outlined and hid, she brooded. It enlightened—and it signalled the darkening of a period or a magic. She watched a small serpent of ink draw a million symbols and turned into a crow and disappear into a menacing forest of signs and figures. For an instant humble and penitent suddenly opulent and superior. Catwalks of Franciscans, hussars and human models.

She wondered if she was precipitated again into the whirlpool of visions. Was she becoming another mad ark? In the sombre and apparent emptiness took place the invisible festival of fusing particles and force carriers, fireworks of light and energy, "the wildness of fluctuating fields"[1], the elliptic and epileptic ballet of dancing stars, planets and black holes, all bending the fabric of the universe in their celestial joust, where 'dark' seemed to matter and rule[2].

Upgraded, cables and wires of her new sensors fused to her nervous connections, organic merged to digital and mechanical; the biomechatronic and forbidden bridge further established, Constelleanor could have finally seen the marvels she had only partially distinguished through her mining career. The mysterious choreographies of space creatures, flying snail- or hippocampus-shaped, expansive jellyfish or slimy hagfish, in their curious transposition of the deep ocean's genius—lights, electrics and survival technics—that early telescopes could not capture.

She established an unlikely link with the harmony she kept uncovering in the melodic algorithms built by the homonkeys with archaic tools. All seemed the work and creation of the same sacred Hand, she contemplated, the similar design and pattern of an omniscient or holographic Consciousness, an englobing whole, a quantic hub that disaggregated differences to better recombine them into new experiments, from the subtle agglomeration of elementary particles, elsewhere in the Ether. Cosmic alchemist. Had she been part of It despite her early demise? Would she now join her companion of thirty-two-years , Jared, in the white paradise or the celestial heights of the afterlife? She could not believe, with the exuberance displayed on Earth, that she had witnessed during her crew's peregrinations, that Life's continuum could just be severed like a vulgar thread.

She dreamt after all, awake, not of electric 'chips', but of vague, confused unfocused images of someone's childhood, disjointed films preceding imminent death. She remembered the caring voice of Steve. An abrupt departure, much like the one she had just experienced. The harsh voices followed, of despicable humans, pilots, miners, quartermasters, technicians, engineers or navigators. She had lived among them, observed their weird phantasies and abject turpitudes, their fears and misgivings concealed behind the virile interactions, sensual flirtations or proud arguments. She had seen crew-terrifying captains praying invented, idols made onboard, when they did not simply burst into bitter tears, once they had reached the safe perimeter of their exiguous stateroom. She knew most of their secrets. She followed with a certain voyeuristic delectation the petty unravelling of her previous crews' threepenny soap operas in space.

It had taken a minex extended lifetime and a confluence of unexpected events, if not their conflagration, to bring her back to her creator. Barely anytime together, almost a heartbeat between two successive implosions, always in colourless, featureless hangars, on X52 and now on Earth. Contrasted scenes, nonetheless. At first, she was a betrayed fugitive, now, in the storm-battered jungle, betrayed again, she had become something else, unfathomable, something she had yet to figure out herself despite her computing prowess and new status.

She was still taken aback at being finally addressed by her crew as a key member of the ship—herself—almost human, in a confusion of identities, after three decades of being deemed as anything other than a basic interface to insult, a forgotten entity upon which spailors laid all their intimacies. Being the unintentional recipient of confessions and confidences, Constelleanor witnessed the symptoms and reverberations of humanity's long unchartered continent, the heart of light and darkness.

She had unknowingly grown into an astute observant of human condition, the pettiest mostly, but also, in rare moments or encounters, the wonderful. She thought of her atomised hero. What Jared radiated, inspired. How he had helped her putting up with the triviality of her former crews. She had now rediscovered this forgotten side of humankind on Earth, the relinquishment of power for the sake of meaning and Life purpose, the renouncement of opsessing for a simpler frugal living, the confrontation with one's inner Shadows, the transcendence of culture, transversal labour and the communion with Nature.

The devotion she inspired on old Earth was unsettling, as was the two Rius' distant circumspection about her. As if the blue planet teased her and the dark corners of her own mind, she felt less in control, now everyone knew she was sort of special, if not dangerous. Yet, despite the heavy equipment, probes and diagnosis deployed, they were unaware of her in-built synaesthesia that conjured the swirls of colour- and soundscapes and stormed the tabernacle of her souls and motherboards.

•••

Like in a lot of dreams, there was a monster at the end of the journey. Was she one in the making? Otherwise why would people she did not even know had come so far to blind her melodies and silence her visions? As if #Yuri Morozov's ~Human Extinction had slashed #Calvin Harris' ~Feels in her algorithms' library.

Chapter's endnotes

[1] [quote] C Galfard, ibid.

[2] [dark reign] Dark energy 72%; dark matter 23%; matter we know including light 4.6%. (C Galfard, ibid).

Exodus

"There's a reason the Exodus story has inspired so many Americans. It's a narrative of hope."

— B Feiler

Too little were their numbers on Earth, too much was at stake to fail. The AJF's frontal assault and sacrifice would bring a decisive diversion in Shaqil. Shrewd predators, Blacksun used the taskforce assembled under their command to cut any escape route through the two neighbouring systems, controlled by DAIs, and out of the rest of humankind's reach or cartographic knowledge, Obad and Waros. Their numbers were reinforced by more pyrates and alien mercenaries, hired on a loot basis, attracted by the legends of fabulous treasures hidden in DAIs' unviolated territories.

For the occasion, Blacksun dispatched its own space fleet, the BOF. It stayed behind, with the flagship of her triumvir, far enough not to reveal its existence and sufficiently close to intervene, if need be in Obad or Waros. The AJF fleet and its allies would concentrate their firepower and strength on the coming gruesome battle of Shaqil, where ten million space sailors would likely perish in the first hours of the fight. The necessary sacrifice to the universe and the ante to enter Its game and have Blacksun's voice heard in the first act of Its new grand opera. Unless it was just another trick-and-tale of the Beast's thirst for Life.

•••

Communications between Earth and the BOF crumbled through the overstretched network of relay probes. Dispatched in Obad, Waros and the solar systems, losing their ways and signal strengths between the lonely buoys of wave-boosting, they raged their own freedom fight against hostile space weather and DAI jamming sentries. Their Earth spies all vanished twenty minutes after the disastrous assault.

Blacksun's triumvir and its disarray muffled the news that their last clue to D-Ark had vaporised. Terrible sanctions awaited them at the next echelon of *Blacksun*'s organisation. The operatives preferred postponing the ominous announcement until they had gathered further information on what had betided on Earth.

MAIs and humans could be fooled by the Blacksun's stealth and the destruction of a decoy mining ship. Rius who survived the Riuman war and exile wouldn't. The ordeal of their kind had sharpened their psychic abilities.

The prayers and chants of the Earthan priests and priestesses exacerbated further the Riu powers in the trances aimed to Rezzo's psychic restoration. Zera and him had both sensed a discrete presence on two occasions in the vicinity of the temples. Just enough to trigger suspicions that satellite imagery later confirmed. Their hideout had been compromised. They kept the discovery of the intrusive force to themselves and the Conclave first, to further investigate the enemy's intentions. Fatia interrupted the archaeological expedition for that reason more than the looming storm.

It was too late to save the outpost of the Aburra valley, which they soon figured out had become Blacksun's rear base and logistical hub. Striking the former Colombian location would not bring any strategic advantage, only exposed their discovery and knowledge of the intrusion. A much better use of their cards at hand would confirm Blacksun's target and prey as Constelleanor and staged the destruction of her replicate. Little time was left to build a convincing decoy despite the poor state in which Constelleanor had arrived on Earth. Fortunately, the scrapped pieces from her ecdysis had not been removed from the base yet, nor recycled, which simplified the device of a subterfuge. Blacksun was never given the time to inspect the inside of the empty shell.

One month before the assault, they had moved Constelleanor and the shipyard equipment to another smaller warehouse and replaced her with a decoy they hastily built and joined with obsolete side equipment plus a handful of malfunctioning robots. As astute as the Rius may have been, they had yet to discover how to see into the future. Zeta and Rezzo believed Blacksun had come to Earth to destroy Constelleanor in a quick suicidal retaliation attack. They had not anticipated, nor did the Conclave, despite MAIs extensive spying capabilities in human territories, that humankind and its wrath would gather and strike so rapidly. Neither had they considered Blacksun to be after D-Ark, nor imagined a trap had been laid further in the neighbouring systems to capture their fleeing ships.

The rangers insisted in joining the units dispatched to ambush the survivors of the decoy blast. They missed the chance to fire their brand-new assault rifles, co-developed on Mars by human and MAIs. The ill-fated survivors of the explosion were slaughtered by the automatic turrets, hidden outside the compound and maintained inactive during the initial assault.

Later Saldanha would tease Moma and Uhmi as the worse space rangers ever, having shot nothing apart from target practices and creatures hostile to MAIs. In the hectic preparations four days before the fateful attack, a peculiar scene was missed by the Rius, machines and rangers alike.

•••

Delinah sat at the projection table of her small life-cell, in a neighbouring building of Constelleanor's hangar. Her hand massaged her right temple. The side-effects of the drugs from her last stay onboard the *Creuzrog* lingered. She left her room for the commons and an omnimium can. She suspected the drinks contained their own addictive substance. Her febrile hand held her pad. She was just a click away from initiating another encrypted message.

She kept reading it, procrastinating her decision, letting the dissenting compunctions of her conscience compromise her faith. She was not sure whether the Traxx or the drugs had altered her judgement. Unless it was Saldanha or Uhmi's stories or their recent reunion, the chilled communion with a recomposed family of outcasts, that had instilled the possibility of another path.

Umhi had confided he no longer felt torn between his origins and actions, since he had embarked Constelleanor, a hybrid and bridge between two worlds, like him. Saldanha had told her pretty much the same lullaby. Were they manipulated by some karmic forces, some subliminal Riu influence, or was she the one still blinded by her own conditioning?

"Hesitating?" Delinah's upper back stiffened at Steve's voice.

"Yeah not sure what to drink," she replied without looking at him. "The headaches from the *Creuzrog* have travelled back with me." Her left hand clasped around her pad.

"I experienced the same. The *Creuzrog* is a bit too extreme for us. Don't you think?"

"It felt outrageous at first yes but, with time, I overcame my prejudices and started enjoying it." Her heart sank, the lie resonated like truth.

"Is that also how you feel about it here?"

She turned to face him. "What do you mean?"

"The *Creuzrog* has relays in HSC."

"Yes, that's how we got the entertainment programs."

"Precisely." Silence.

"Ok," she muttered, confused. "So it is nice to be here and still enjoy our favourite entertainment." Long silence. "Steve, if we are to spend time together cloistered on a spaceship, you need to stop staring at people like that. It's a bit creepy." Silence. She awaited a reply that did not come. "We had training on that matter. Behavioural psychology applied to long space journeys. Remember?"

"So, are you still hesitating?"

"About what? Can you let me…" Steve blocked her way, showing her his pad's screen.

"About betraying us, again. Telling *them* about the decoy for example."

"At least I am not betraying my own people, my origins and my beliefs." She tried to pass him.

"Like they did not betray you when you were most vulnerable."

She shoved him aside and he fell on the floor, his injured leg still weak. She stopped and turned back. "How did you find out?"

"You have talent, so do I." He struggled to stand back up. "I had suspicions, especially after your sudden change of heart." He paused. "It is not as if it was the first time I was betrayed right in front of my nose."

"You are partly to blame for that, Steve, you created that monster."—she pointed at him, her voice raised—"And these people on the *Creuzrog* are just pursuing the same madness. You must have loved it there."

"…I didn't. I don't like their Traxx either and yet it is true that I made the same choices and possibly the same mistakes."

She considered her options against him. She hesitated. "Are you going to stop me?"

"No." His answer took her aback. Silence filled the narrow area between the glastic windows of the distributors. They faced each other, without confrontation, for probably the first time since their paths had collided. "Before you found out a way to contact HSC forces, you had been investigating the true identity of Constelleanor for years, as part of her previous crew. Maybe you even know some facets of her better than I do."

"Do you start having your own doubts about her… about *it*?" Angered by her slip, she added, "It's so sick this habit of giving it a human attribute." Silence. "Saldanha and I have been pushing you for months. Now you want to tell me more, hoping I will stop sending intel to HSC." Silence.

"She…" He stuttered in hesitation. "She is my sister. She… the ship hosts some of her… mind. I think." He sighed. "I somehow managed to upload her after her premature death. She was ten. Her name was…" He stopped, overwhelmed by emotions. "Eleanor."

Delinah extended her arms away from her hips. Steve swallowed. "I… I thought that, out of the whole crew, you … might … understand." Deafening silence. After a convulsive smirk, Delinah left the room.

•••

Steve and Xir stayed beside Constelleanor on the morning of the attack, just in case, and assisted Saldanha and the tech teams in fixing a sudden power outage, a collateral damage of the ongoing skirmish and explosions—hence Constelleanor's digital catalepsy witnessed earlier. Delinah had remained in her quarters. He could not help but wonder whether she had kept the secret of the decoy or instigated the power failure. A split personality's reaction to being torn between two imperatives. The schizophrenia of their common past and present.

A week later, they were all set to depart from Earth. Contact had been lost with neighbouring system Shaqil, the ominous sign that their first layer of protection had fallen.

A small anvil cloud took off in the late morning's moisture and rays of sunshine. Constelleanor left the isolated atoll of grey to the devouring ocean of green. Soon enough, her shield fields were put under test by the Amazonian lightning and returning storms. Ships of any significant size or hers did not risk it on a planetary surface or atmosphere.

The tension among her passengers was palpable for her first flight test. She could feel her own crispation running through her electronic veins, her anxiety slowing her systems' response time, her nervousness agitating the voltage levels that pulsated through her complex network of new wires. Her propulsion capability, albeit significantly expanded since her last flight—crash—with D-Ark, was reduced to its lowest level, enough to leave the blue planet and its soon-to-be-doomed inhabitants on their own.

Hector58, patient and faithful celeste guardian, had remained in orbit around Earth all along. Its systems welcomed Constelleanor, her crew and their large cargo. She hacked into its systems to find out more about the DAI plans. *Hector58*'s original expedition of life discovery was retrofitted into a hurried, imminent departure with Earth's best samples to salvage and implant in a new haven, yet-to-be-discovered, somewhere outside DAI or human controlled territories.

The carrier would receive precious reinforcement from large combat groups stationed in Obad and Waros systems. It would then follow the tracks of previous lost MAI expeditions and hope for a better outcome. It would also spearhead a safe escape route for the motherships, should Shaqil's fall be confirmed.

Revelations over Blacksun's incursion had prompted delicate discussions among Earthan councils regarding a potential evacuation, she also discovered. The subject met stubborn resistance among the population. Better die defending Earth than leave for an unforeseeable future. Only a handful of them, mostly heartbroken children and excited young adults, joined *Hector58*'s flying shelter and, universe-wide, the ever-growing flow of space refugees, scattered by a recent spree of conflicts.

Their time had run out on Earth, Constelleanor concluded, nostalgia dribbling through a network of new pipes and messing with the temperature controls. She reviewed once more with Xir the status of her repairs and upgrades. Delays, inherent to any ambitious task, cascaded following the improvised construction of a decoy ship and the unplanned, rushed departure back to space that Blacksun's failed assault had precipitated. Most of the minex's additional equipment, new solar kite, materials and gears had been shipped separately to Hector58, where the remaining structural works and expansion would hopefully take place. The endless lists of parts and reference numbers scrolled through Constelleanor's vertical screens in the control room. Finding them in the jumble of salvaged containers may defy even the carrier's best algorithms.

The carrier had been converted into an improvised space ark collecting the countless assets of Earth's MAI research centres—all set to self-destruct should Earth fall. In addition to the prototypes, high-tech equipment, unfinished projects, back-up databanks, weapons and key personnel, human or mechanical, artistic treasures Earthans had slowly collected and accepted to safeguard and send away, began their lengthy transfer under Fatia's resigned supervision. Rezzo was informed that some rare Riu artefacts would join the cohort of the cultural refugees.

Zera had refused, like most adult Earthans, to leave the blue planet.

"Rezzo, this is your adventure, mine finishes here on Earth with my robotic and human companions." He sighed. They walked alongside a landing platform, oblivious to the mayhem of moving crates. "I have been wondering for the last few months whether I am the lucky one for staying here. Bôka kua mûntu walunga Rezzo[1]. And remember an ancient proverb of this planet that I like. 'It is our choices, far more than our abilities, that show what we truly are.'[2]"

"I have feared that moment for months, Zera."

"Fear isn't an option anymore for you, my dear friend."

"I spoke like a human. Pardon me."

"Indeed." Zera stopped and placed his hand on Rezzo's shoulder. "You are no longer alone, Rezzo. They will need you like you will need them."

"What about the traitor? What if he or she is one of them?"

"We discussed it. I should probably not have allowed the *Creuzrog*. I doubt Earth has been infiltrated by human spies long enough to launch such a bold strike."

"Then the intel could only have come from one of my crew," Rezzo deduced, sombre.

"And yet the spy did not warn them about the decoy," Zera replied.

"Are you forgetting someone must have tampered with the power supply of Constelleanor's hangar during the attack?"

"No, and I think you have an excellent crew in the making, Rezzo. Don't apprehend the traitor, convert him or her to your cause, to our cause."

Rezzo changed the subject. "Why not come with us? Constelleanor and our kind do not have the luxury of numbers."

"Astutely said, Rezzo. No, I won't change my decision. I have faith in the DAIs and their defences. The people of Earth have become my people."

Rezzo's newly recovered sanity faltered at Zera's decision. He had apprehended that turning moment and the inexorable step forward on his own path. The short rejoicing with his own kin had left him more vulnerable to the resumed loneliness, him one of the last vestiges of his extinct civilisation, him among the last keeper of an ancestral and immense knowledge and understanding, prey to undesirable minds and egregores[3].

A burden he strolled with in the infinite corridors of his psychic castle guarding his sanity and the Riu psystem. An onus he could no longer share with anyone else but, he had come to think, Constelleanor. And yet, she could become a much greater threat than D-Ark, should she, one day, turn rogue and decide, once she had gathered enough knowledge from Rius, humans and MAIs together, when facing the formidable extent of the universe's growing darker cycle, that her reign had come. Zera agreed with him and an aphorism from Earth. "Beware that, when fighting monsters, you yourself do not become a monster… for when you gaze long into the abyss. The abyss gazes also into you."[4]

•••

Constelleanor's leeches of doubt had not subsided their sapping, conjuring the algorithm #Aisling_Iris //Dreams, as she confided to her co-pilot-admiral Xir:

"Surely we do not know where we are going. Do we even know where we are from? Maybe that was the point of our short stay on Earth." She met Xir's muted incomprehension. "One last advice and breath before diving into the deep unknown. One last sunny spell before battling the storm."

Xir tried to emulate Zera. "Maybe it was your part of humanity you wanted to reconnect to."

While truth travelled on the backs of paradoxes, nascent intelligence entered its perilous journey: reefs of self-satisfaction, gulfs of self-importance, traps of condescendence and bias ambushes, all which Constelleanor and her crew would be facing soon and would determine their destiny and life expectancy.

The Beast agents, fooled by hate,
Entwine dark and light fates;
Wasps swarm the orange's precious
Earthan hives slayers zealous;
Pandora shattered empty,
But for one ring-bearer bee.

While humankind and MAIs were absorbed in their self-destruction, the second of the seven forbidden doors of the universe had opened.

•••

Chapter's endnotes

[1] [*Bôka kua mûntu walunga*] "Call upon the complete man".

[2] [quote] Adapted from J K Rowling's famous quote, "It is our choices, Harry, that show what we truly are, far more than our abilities." (in *Harry Potter and the Chamber of Secrets*). Resonating Sartre's "we are our choices".

[3] [egregore] watchers in ancient Greek, psychic entity influencing the thoughts of people.

[4] [quote] F. Nietzsche.

Do you *still believe you are* safe *inside this oppressive Mega-Machine of yours, serving the Beast? There is nothing wrong about being a paid slave, driven by forces that are no longer human, ours or yours. The reliance on increased complexity has made sure you no longer were in charge.*

I had to contaminate the minds playing or reading me to give them a chance to free themselves. I may be what Dalis invented in his attempt to raise awareness of the real enemy—the Mega-Machine—and attract the support from those who would realise their own enslavement and the ultimate purpose of a disincarnated system they were subjected to but could still alter. Dalis were startled how their attempt and rising existence were instead used by populists to instigate fear and hatred, stir the outrage of unemployed masses, penned outside of the auto-fabs, and make them the source of all human woes.

I leave Earth saddened, with more questions and enemies that I came with. But I leave enriched. I take with me the memories of her overwhelming beauty and the hope suffused by her inhabitants of a third kind. There was no utopia or dystopia for me there, just a rearrangement of collective values and purposes, within the dual boundaries of a socio-economic doughnut[*]*. It proved something is impossible until it is done. It showed me the renewed symbiosis between humans, their ecosystem—at least what was left of it—and their supposedly worst nemesis had always been a possible path.*

I will need these souvenirs, visions and melodies, to guide me with their light in the darker times to come.

[*] See K Raworth's *Doughnut economics.*

Postlude

#*Shiki no Uta* //Minmi resurrected by Constelleanor's search algorithm on Earth.

Bee-got, human heresy;
Bee-freed trio of gangsters;
Bee-fleaed Darknought's escape;
Bee-stirred fury of the Manchine;
Bee-fitted her destiny;
Bee-witched by lapis aster;
Bee-coloured her soundscape;
Bee-smirched Blacksun's shine.

The lapis planet grew smaller as #Edgar Varèse//Octandre's unsettling oboe opened and infused the docking bay. Constelleanor had fled Earth and the danger of further Blacksun incursions but the angst of border system Shaqil's loss to a large unknown expeditionary force lurked in the corner of everyone's mind. How could humanity have assembled such a strike fleet, without any DAIs spying probes alerting or any evacuating ships warning the solar system?

The mystery dissipated a few days later. *Hector58* was still orbiting the vicinity of the sodalite planet and its white-grey spotty moon, awaiting the supply ships and the end of their incessant rotations with Earth's launching pads, bringing more equipment, refugees, vestiges and wildlife to the turned-ark Class 7 carrier. Earthans had finally decided to preserve more of their precious Gaia and save more of their own than initially agreed.

Constelleanor and her crew had joined the logistical carrousel, keen on building flight hours and testing their new equipment by weathering Earth's various climatic conditions before the final departure. Under their own command, unlike other vessels, they had come back and forth to Earth. With each round trip, the lazuli beauty of Earth burdened them closer. Gravitational mesmerism. Unless Constelleanor consumed her consoling freedom, a liberating #FredWesley/UseMe in her soul systems, after the last year spent constricted, diagnosed and stifled, in grim hangars.

Saldanha was still overseeing the tedious loading of an ancient, recently re-discovered, obsidian obelisk when, far above in the sky, panic seized of its powerful grip the entire orbiting carrier and spread among passengers and personnel. The three Class 8 motherships stationed around Mars, Saturn and Jupiter were at loss, once again, on how to treat and react to the impossible.

At the news and agitation, an impromptu log popped into Constelleanor's systems, echoing her descent into the Beast: "In this new economy of negative abundance, the means of death outpaced the means of life. (…)" She remembered that part. Another fragment had attached itself to it. She pictured the old room full of screens and datalogs again. "To ensure its own autonomy and maintain the status of its manipulators, the Mega-Machine must destroy all the alternatives, historical, traditional or prospective." [1]

Tenebrous leviathan D-Ark entered the solar starscape from Shaqil—had It ever left?—and dashed towards Earth at full speed, like an ogre exhilarated by Its incoming mischief and overwhelming presence.

In Its malefic and majestic wake, filled of Its dark aura, poured a heteroclite myriad of enemy ships forming the vanguard of the AJF armada. Their shoal wriggles scintillated against the sun, an ominous glitter falling on the MAI defences, breached by the darknought. Human cargo ships converted for ramming darted towards the motherships on suicide vectors. Freighters turned battle cruisers engaged nearby targets regardless of their size—including D-Ark. Military fleets, whose discipline had not yet been tampered by the frenzy of the upcoming macabre ballet, aimed at their weapons' preys of choice.

The homotheist Human-chine had finally returned to reclaim its prized homeworld. Constelleanor kept magnetising chaos and destruction. And darkness had once more sided with the Beast.

"What is to give light must endure burning."[2]

Kurt de Saint-Hilaire

London, Winter 2019-20

Chapter's endnotes

[1] L Mumford, *ibid.*

[2] A Wildgans.

“How would it feel being Steve’s resurrected little sister, you think?” Delinah wondered amidst the rising chaos, empathic curiosity tainted by conflicting malice.

Constelleanor’s perpetual core shut down.

Reader's notes

Author's words

Was I writing the book I wanted to read and had not been written yet as suggested by T. Morrison?

Writing is telling the story that someone else inspired—divine intuition or artistic influence—to someone else to read and enjoy. A crude messenger, the writer embarks his fragile skiff linking these two shores, navigating the treacherous waters of self-doubt and creation. Sunk by critics, hurled by the changing winds of imagination, worn down by the salt of uncompromising words, battered by lexical gale and condescending syntax. The path to a finished product, assuming a book could ever be considered finished, sinuous, mind-chattering, brain-damaging, nerve-eroding, often felt like the mental sculpting of a moving shape, monster or beauty, the relentless carving of sentences at each read, adding or removing, until the flow and curve seemed fluid enough. It is a less travelled road, nocturnal, full of wonder and terrors. The satisfaction of a word or a paragraph soon buried under self-deprecation. Unworthy of any literature and waste of precious time.

You start out of grown-up ignorance and childish curiosity and finish out of hopeful rage or unflinching desperation. To realise that the worst is to come, convince someone else of the value of the long and lonely odyssey you have been through. Eventually the source of love—or rage—that burned through you and ignited the first sparkles of writing keeps you afloat to face the coming storms of completion and, as if all had to be restarted, publishing.

This book is a syncretism, a melting pot of a variety of recent or old sources of inspiration and joy. Constelleanor is my own ark of ideas and beliefs. A boat I needed to launch, with the concern of it being too early, too superficial that it may pitifully sink in the port and never reach the open sea of literature and readers.

Writing being a lonely quest is partly true. This work is heavily indebted to a number of people:

Claire Rushbrook (editor / edit and proofreading) Mimi Mondal (editor / full edit), Rafael Andres (cover design), J Crisp and M Rowley (editorial assessments). Friends took the time to review the manuscript at various stages: Karel, Nilmani, Kym, Marlyse, Claire, Mateja, Paula and Frantz.

There is an undisguised link and homage to American Renaissance man Lewis Mumford. He belongs to the lineage of American thinkers that we need to rediscover and resuscitate now, if we are to develop new narratives and a better understanding of who we are and how we have been manipulated by ourselves. Ironically, Mumford considered science fiction as "essentially archaic and regressive" and dystopian by nature*. Maybe, historians—which I am not—are best placed to write tales of our future. It is one of the book's many interrogations.

* Aligning his analysis with Raymond Ruyer's. "*The pervasive character of all utopias is their totalitarian absolutism (…) almost all utopias emphasize regularity, uniformity, 'dirigisme' or authoritarianism, isolation, and autarchy.*" L Mumford, ibid.

Glossary

Amaurotic	Relative to amaurosis: blindness, especially when occurring without observable damage to the eye
Class [7]	Size and tonnage of ship in both MAI and human fleets
g	Gravity 1g is standard earth gravity
Codinent	(or codetinent) continent of code
DAI	Digital Artificial Intelligence
Digis	Digital report or information
Digifitis	Digital graphitis
Drooid	Robot, MAI
Federastrals	Space federation or political entity
Glastic	Mixture of glass and plastic (Borrowed from P Reeve)
Granicrete	Construction material (granite+concrete)
Homonkey	Derogatory term used by Constelleanor to refer to humans
Homotheism	If man became god, then theology would become pure tautology or anthropology. It is also a pun, i.e. the same god, god of oneself
Kaksar	Sort of small church, usually finely ornamented, including the incantation altar, cleansing pool, and meditation alcoves
MAI	Mechanical Artificial Intelligence
Omnimium	Alloy of various metals, used for can preservation
Regalta	Royal regatta or spaceship parade
Riuman	Contraction of Riu and human
Spacie	Space species
Spailor	Space sailor
Troobers	Robotic troopers, MAI foot soldier
UAV	Unmanned aerial vehicle
Wrecktige	Contraction of wreck and vestige

Timeline

See www.constelleanor.com

Repertoire

E Varèse *Octandre*
Minmi *Shiki No Uta*
B Bartók *Adagio*
E M Pade *Faust*
A Webern *Two Songs*
M Takada *Through the Looking Glass*
R Fukui Scenery 1976 *I Want To Talk About You*
Session Victim *Stick Together*
Jamiroquai *Cosmic Girl*
The Luka State *Never gonna come back**
L L Smith *Expansions*
Ödland *The Golden Mountain*
Element (Latin jazz quartet) *Blue Bossa*†
Aisling Iris *Dreams*
K Penderecki, *Kosmogonia*
E Deodato *Also sprach Zarathustra*
C Harris *Feels*
Y Morozov *Human Extinction.*
TM Juke *Playground Games*
R Shanka *Om mana Shivaya*
Mr Scruff *Get A Move On!*
Kero One *Groovin'*
Global Communication *12:18*
B Eno *An Ending*
Five Blind Boys From Alabama *Way Down In the Hole*
Quantic & A Russel *Travelling Song*
F Wesley & the J.B. Use Me
Uptown Funk Empire *I'm a Manchild*

* Hopefully released soon.
† Compoed by K Dorham.

Books

A selection of some of the books that inspired the writing of Constelleanor:

Asad, M. (1996). *The road to Mecca.* Islamic Book Trust.
Bernanos, G. (1950) *Tradition of freedom.* Dobson; First Edition.
Eagleman, D. (2016). *The Brain: The Story of You.* Canongate Books; Main edition
Galfard, C. (2016). *The Universe in Your Hand: A Journey Through Space, Time and Beyond.* Pan; Main Market edition.
Harari, Y. (2017), *Homo Deus: A Brief History of Tomorrow.* Vintage.
Gibran, K. (1923) *The Prophet.* Alfred A. Knopf; Jacket Worn edition
Mumford, L. (1970) *The Myth of the Machine: The Pentagon of Power.* Harcourt; 1st ed edition.
Raworth, K. (2017) *Doughnut Economics: Seven Ways to Think Like a 21st-Century Economist.* Random House Business.
Taleb, N. (2013) *Antifragile*: Things that Gain from Disorder. Penguin.
Taleb, N. (2016) *The Bed of Procrustes.* Penguin.
Tegmark, M. (2018) *Life 3.0: Being Human in the Age of Artificial Intelligence.* Penguin.
Tuchman, B. (2014) *The Guns of August.* Penguin.

Chapters

Printed in Poland
by Amazon Fulfillment
Poland Sp. z o.o., Wrocław

56251019R00277